A Different kind of love story

By

Felicia Lewis
Prince T. Patterson
Riiva Williams
Seven Steps
Marie A. Norfleet
Darnisha King
Briana Cole
Elijah Forman
Deryl Ali
Tiffany Turner
Ashley Jackson
Lauren Horner
and
Darryl J. Johnson

ACKNOWLEDGEMENTS

Thank you to Dottie Designz for the awesome work that you did for the cover of this book.

Thank you to our editor Tanya Cole. Thanks for your great work and I look forward to working with you again in the future.

Thanks to the twelve awesome authors that took part in this Anthology.

We would also like to thank you the public for taking time out to read our work and helping us towards our cause.

A Different Kind of Love Story

-An Anthology Written by-

Felicia Weeden Lewis
Prince T. Patterson
Riiva Williams
Seven Steps
Darnisha King
Briana Cole
Marie A. Norfleet
Elijah Forman
Deryl Ali
Tiffany Turner
Ashley Jackson
Lauren Horner
Darryl J. Johnson

The REAL Housewife

By

Darnisha King

If only there was true love to discuss- then this would be a love story, but it's not. So listen up!

"I'm Angel; some things that I am going to tell you will make me sound like a whore. And maybe I am, but I have been through some real stuff in my life- with my husband, with his mistress, with his father, with my sisters, and my parents. So, excuse me for wanting to fuck a couple of niggas to relieve this stupid ass idea of love. I'm going to also rid you of the fake ass love story that's in your head. Hear me and hear me clearly – THE SHIT DOESN"T EXIST.

Sure we all love people, but we have all been hurt by the ones that should love us most. So, I'm going to give you the story in a nutshell. Don't be a hater though. I don't need your advice on the way that I should have done it nor do I need your judgment on where I went wrong. I just want to get it off my chest. K? Cool!

Chapter 1

This ignorant dog didn't come home again. He is always yelling about how he loves me and will never leave me. He got me barefoot, pregnant, and barely takes the time out of his busy schedule to give me a slap on the ass- let along a conversation. After being married for 3 years, this shit ain't what they tell you in the movies about love.

When we were in high school, I dreamed of being with Jordan Harold II forever. We were going to live in this beautiful house with a white picket fence, 2 children, and one on the way. My kids would go to private school, my husband would be in the NBA, and after his retirement he would be the Chief Executive Officer of his law firm. And as for me, I would be a house wife, doing laundry, caring for the puppies during the day, tending to my kids in the afternoon and evening, and being a complete freak for my man at night.

Baby please! This Bullshit is a nightmare. We have been together for over 10 years. It's been 8 years since our high school graduation; which was the night that he proposed. But like I told you earlier, we've only been married for 3 years. I don't have the 2.5 children that I wanted; although I am about 5 months pregnant with my first. My "Husband" and I use the term loosely wanted to wait until he was financially secure. All that NBA and CEO shit was a crock of bull. Shit – his ass didn't even finish college. We moved into our little 2-bedroom apartment on the 2nd floor when my sister died; which is far from the white picket fence that I envisioned. And our apartment complex won't even let us have a damn dog.

My husband works as an office paralegal at the public defender's office and he also works as an overnight tank fuel person at the airport. I work as a patient care tech at the county hospital up the street. We are not broke and struggling by most standards – but we cohabitate up in this bitch like friends who usually hate each other.

I'm going to divorce his ass. I know it sounds like it's not that bad, but listen to all of the stuff that I found out last week. He thinks I don't know – but I'm from the streets. He looking at me like I'm going to always be there, but we all have skeletons.

One Week Ago:

"Hello Angel!" My girl MoMo said through the phone sounding extremely panicked.

"What's up Mo? What's wrong?" I was already fearing the worst.

"Are you sitting down?" She said trying to calm herself down.

"I can be!" I sat down on my couch, getting more and more nervous.

"Jordan is a snake. He has been dating this woman named Jana for 5 years. I didn't hear it through the grapevine either. My mother gets her hair done by her. She came over our house last week to get money that my mother owed her. While she was there my mom started talking about how she wanted to help her with the wedding.

To prove her point, she wanted to show her pictures of the different weddings she had designed. She pulled out your wedding pictures and Jana immediately jumped up, held her head, and started to scream. I thought she was having a brain aneurism or something, but she said that Jordan was actually her fiancée." MoMo explained the whole situation.

"What Mo?" I interjected. "How could he propose to someone when he is married to me?"

"Angel, why would I tell you something that is completely fabricated?

"Well what are the facts then Mo, since you are all Inspector Gadget in my marriage?" I asked sarcastically.

"Well one thing for sure, Jana's ring is almost identical to yours. She has 3 young kids and they are practically raised by your husband. She is driving a car that is in his name and she has done your hair before."

"Does she know about me, Mo?" I softened up. MoMo had been my friend for 20 years and she wouldn't lie to me about any of this.

"No. She thought that he was her man. Although he has cheated on her before, she never thought in a million years that he was married. She even asked for permission to call you and she gave me her number for you to call her. You know just in case."

"I'll call her, but I can't figure this out just yet. Jordan is no saint, but he is not a magician either." I wanted all of this to be false, but I knew it wasn't.

"True that!" Mo said after thinking quietly for a few seconds.

"And you said she has done my hair before?"

"Yeah. She said she recognized you from the pictures." Mo answered me.

"Jana? Oh shit, she has done my hair a few times before. And this bitchbeen sleeping with my husband?" I had to gas myself up, because the shit was about to hit the fan.

"Ok Angel, now how was she supposed to know?" Mo legit was trying to take up for the bitch.

"Because I told her who he was and that I wanted her to do my hair for the wedding. She did her 2 trials on me and the day before the wedding she cancelled. She said that she and her boyfriend had been in a huge fight and he stole her car, so she couldn't make it." Shit started to become a little clearer for me the more that I thought and spoke about it.

"Quite the coincidence that he fought her the day before your wedding. Then, he took her car so that she couldn't make it."

After me and Mo hung up, I had to call Jana. When I called she answered the phone and immediately knew who I was. She said that the first 3 digits of all of our numbers were the same because apparently we were all on the same plan. She gave me her address and said that he was in her washroom right now. She told me to hurry up and get there before he tried to leave or before she killed him.

Just as I pulled up, Jordan pulled off. Jana started to yell to me from her balcony as she threw all of his t-shirts and shit over the banister. I looked down and picked up the black and white t-shirt that I bought him a few months ago when I found out that I was pregnant. It said "You are the best". He told me that he lost it playing basketball when in actuality it was over here at his mistresses' house. But the way she was throwing shit over the balcony --- maybe she really felt like a fiancée.

After she stopped having her bitch fit, she invited me up. I stood in her living room and looked at all of the head manikins with beautifully designed wigs on them. There was a picture of her and Jordan with them 3 ugly ass kids on the wall. And the little boy looked like my husband a little, if I didn't know any better, I would swear that he went and had a damn baby on me. There was also a pile of laundry in the corner basket that looked like bleach had become their new best friend. And then there was Jana. She had gained about 50lbs over the last 3 years, but she was beautiful none the less. She was dark skinned with long black hair. She sat on the love seat with tears in her eyes.

"So that's the Jordan that you got married to?" She asked me as she cleared her throat.

"Yep that's him. The same Jordan that you are engaged to huh?"

"Look Angel. I never put 2 and 2 together. I would have never intentionally wrecked someone's home. Plus, I was cordial with you. I was well prepared to do the hair for your wedding too. But Jordan bitch ass played me. I had a black eye and a sprained ankle from chasing his ass. And then he took my car because he didn't want me to leave the house."

"You think he knew that you were doing my hair?" I asked her, but at this point I really didn't give a fuck. He had been lying, which was nothing new for Jordan. He is obviously living a double life and he could care less, who gets hurt in the process. I'm out here - big and pregnant and he out here playing house with another bitch and her family.

"I was pregnant by him 2xs. The most recent time was 4 months ago. He asked me to abort. He said he wanted us to be married before we had another baby." Jana explained they lil situation to me.

This shit was really starting to click. That lil ugly ass boy on their family picture is my husband's son. I still have no idea on how he thought he was getting married though. He obviously didn't think this shit all the way through.

"Look, I have been with Jordan for 10+ years. And I hear you saying that you didn't know, you didn't know. I even see the big ass ring that is identical to my ring on your finger. I feel your pain, probably 5xs worst since I am his "wife". But I can't be cordial or cool with you. That's my husband. He eats, sleeps, and shits at my house. For all I know you can just be some fan trying to get me to leave my hand, hoping that he will run into your arms. Conclusion is -- -- A hurt dog will holler. SO when it's all said and done, I'll know the truth."

Needless to say, that bitch put me out of her house. She was crying and all that bullshit. It wasn't even worth it. She better go get her some side dick and keep it moving.

It had now been about 6 days since that situation and I still hadn't heard from my husband. We were distant, yeah. But not that damn distant. I don't know if he was avoiding me or simply didn't care if I knew. Either way, I couldn't care any less. That double life shit that he had going on was poop next to all of the stuff that I had going on.

Chapter 2

First things first ---- women we do it better! Everything that we do- it's better. Now don't get me wrong, I was a good wife to my husband, but do I sound like the barefoot and pregnant type? If I do, yo ass is just as dumb as Jordan. All that freaky shit that we used to do had to be learned from somewhere and tested in a few other places. He better ask his best friend, his daddy, our neighbor, and his cousin LaLa. Yeah, I said LaLa. She can do some really good thangs with her tongue.

Matter of fact – this ain't his baby! It's either his dad's or the neighbors'. While he was over their playing daddy to his "step kids,"- his pops was over here playing daddy to me. It's crazy as hell how Jana was over there crying and shit acting like somebody had just died because she found out about me. I wanted to tell that bitch to man up. Over there crying and bleaching shit. Take it like a woman and get even. Shit, that same night after the altercation I was in the hotel room with LaLa, where we had been going for the past year.

I honestly am not into women, but LaLa was a stress reliever. She would suck my clit like she was trying to make me fall in love with her. I've told her time and time again, that the shit wasn't going to happen; but it made her try even harder. So you are probably thinking, "Angel if you don't swing that way, why are you in the hotel room with a bitch, right? It started when I was drunk and there was no dick around me.

We went to the hotel and she LaLa'd all over my cat. Since then she has been my bitch. She buys me candy, flowers, and shit. I try not to laugh at her, but she be on that sucker shit. I'm going to get what I can get, but 2 pussies will never stick.

Now, my father in law; Jordan Harold Sr. is a straight maniac in the bedroom, in the washroom, on the kitchen floor, in the car, on his desk at work, over the cell phone; just everywhere. At the age of 45, he is either going through a mid-life crisis or I should have gotten with pops from the beginning.

Me and Sr. started fucking on my wedding day. No NOT during the honey moon! Who do you guys take me for? We started the morning before me and Jordan said I do. I guess while Jordan was over there tending to Jana and them damn kids, his father was checking me out. He had actually made a couple of passes at me the day before while I sat around making last minute arrangements. He was saying shit like, "My son don't know what he's missing. It's the night before your wedding day and he out running them damn streets; leaving yo fine self in here to do the work." But I guess he didn't try anything that night because he knew Jordan was coming home. Jordan did eventually come home, we had sex, he left with his best man, and I didn't see him again until we were at the altar.

But the next morning, Sr. was still there; although his wife, Jordan's step-mom had already left to get stuff prepared at the church. He came in my bedroom while I was asshole naked. Do you hear me, I ain't have on shit. I had to act shocked when I seen him. "Sr. what are you still doing here?" It was fight or flight time now, you know sink or swim!

"To be honest Angel, I want to fuck you. I heard you and my son in here last night and ya'll didn't make enough noise to scare a mouse. I want to make you feel good before your wedding. I want to slide my raw dick in your pretty kitty and make it purr like it's supposed to."

"Sr. what are you talking about?" I asked the question, but I was legit already touching on myself. It was something about that old ass man that just did something to me.

"Bitch you know you a freak and my son not doing it right. I want to show you what right feels like. I want you to come all over my face, my hand, and this dick." He said as he pulled down his pants, boxers, and exposed the most beautiful penis that I had ever seen. It was a shock to me. It was way bigger and thicker then Jordan's. I guess that like father like son shit was a myth.

"If I'm a bitch, come show me whose bitch I am?" I opened my legs to expose my kitty to him. I was soaking wet. And I couldn't remember ever being like that for my husband. Sr. walked over to the bed, grabbed my neck, and started to bite me on my breast and my ears. This nigga was biting like he was hungry.

"Sr. I'm getting married in a few hours, and hickeys from my husband's father is bad." I really didn't give a fuck, but I didn't want my wedding photos jacked up because Sr. couldn't keep his mouth to his self.

"Angel, shut up!" He said as he started to take longer, harder bites.

I couldn't help, but to enjoy myself while I was doing what should have been forbidden. Like seriously, who fucks their father in law. "Oh Sr." I moaned as I felt the pleasure that came from the pain. "Oh Sr. stick that dick in me, now." I started begging ya'll!!! Sr. was really doing something to me.

"Hold on, I want to taste you first and you definitely about to taste me" He said before he laid down and basically forced me into a 69. At that point, I was barely sucking Jordan's dick and Sr. had me swallowing his shit. Sounds crazy, but the moment I tasted the dick of Jordan Harold Sr. I was in love. I mean, I love my husband with something different. I would give him my last. I would probably kill for him, but he was so fucking stupid. He could barely take care of our household, but he around there playing daddy and hubby to another bitch's household.

That's why I grew that love for his daddy. His daddy was strong. He was powerful. He had money. He gave me money and the best dick of my life. He stayed at our house at least 2 to 3 times per week, when Jordan was at work, at Jana's house, or wherever the fuck he was at. Sr. tended to me. He didn't give a fuck about nobody when I was around. If I was horny, rather his son was in the same house or not, he was going to fuck me. Sr. was spontaneous. Unlike LaLa, who was my bitch, I was Sr.'s bitch and I was in love with him.

Don't get me wrong though, Sr. had a few issues. Sometime his authority had him power tripping; so he didn't mind putting his hands on a bitch. I remember one night he came over while his son was gone and I wasn't in the apartment. He called my cell, but I had left it on the kitchen counter. He checked my inbox and realized that I had been texting my neighbor. When I came back upstairs after about 3 hours, he clocked me in the face with the muthafuckin cell phone. He was screaming shit like, "The only other man I will share you with is my son and even that won't last long."

My nose started bleeding, so I rushed into the washroom to clean myself up. He followed me, stood behind me in the mirror, pissed himself off some more by thinking about me and the neighbor, and started to choke me.

"Did you fuck that nigga, bitch?" He screamed as he ripped off my dress.

"No, I did not. I love you Sr." I was gasping for air and shit, bleeding from my nose, and I was still talking about I love his ass.

"You better love me Angel." He said as he loosened the grip on my neck and stuck his big beautiful manhood in my ass.

I was scared to make him stop, but I liked the authority that he possessed. I was lying about fucking my neighbor though. But that wasn't any of his business.

Chapter 3

So we all know I was lying when I told Sr. that I hadn't messed with my neighbor right? We had been messing around off and on since I was like 14 years old, and he was like 25. Actually the apartment that me and Jordan live in now used to be my sisters before she died 5.5 years ago from brain cancer that actually began in her toe. Rare and weird, I know! It's actually the same thing that Bob Marley died from and just like him, my sister smoked weed from sun up to sun down. But I digress---- back to my neighbor LC.

I used to visit my sister often because she was kind of the young, cool sister with no kids, lots of hot boyfriends— who I had my choice of and she would let me drink coolers and hit the blunt every now and then. But anyway, LC was her neighbor that lived downstairs. He complained constantly about how much noise we made upstairs. He was young, a professional and didn't like the ratchet shit. Plus, I'm pretty damn sure that he hated my sister. He said that she was a whore and all type of hating ass shit; but she still admired him from a far. And so did I!

When he would leave the building with his basketball shorts on, I would study him. I didn't know much about sex at the time, but I knew that his penis was swinging too freely for him to have on draws. So anyway, one day when he was coming back in the building, I rushed downstairs pretending to be receiving mail out of the mail box. As soon as he was in close enough range, I dropped the mail and bent down so that I could show him my lil ass. I was a mess back then. Not to be confused with the way that I am now, these days I'm more like a scientist.

"Whoa lil bit! Yo sister is going to be mad that you dropped her mail in the mud." LC laughed.

"Yeah I know. I'm down here trying to show you my ass and I'm being real clumsy." I spoke bluntly.

"How old are you? You don't look old enough to be showing anyone yo ass; let along to me." He chuckled, but his face looked serious.

"I'm 14, but I like you and I want you to see me naked." I cringe when I think about how young I sounded.

"Lil bit – you trying to send me to jail?" He asked as he began to walk up the stairs to his apartment.

I stuck the mail back in the box and ran up behind him. As he began to fidget trying to get his keys out of his pocket and into the door, I ran my hands up his back, down his chest and then I slipped in between the door and his chest and began kissing him.

"Whoa, whoa, whoa! What are you doing sweetheart? I'm over 10 years older than you. You are a minor lil bit. And as sexy and pretty as you are, I can't get myself in trouble like this."

After he said that, I was ready to bow out gracefully. He opened his door and I began to walk away. But he came back out and said "I won't tell if you won't!"

It was on from there, do you hear me? His fine grown ass and my fine want- to- be grown ass ---- I was ready to pop this pussy tonight.

We didn't have sex though. Well, he didn't penetrate me. He sucked my pussy and ass delightfully and he taught me how to suck a mean dick. It would be another 2 years before he actually would have sex with me. It was 2 weeks after Jordan and I began to date, that LC wanted to confess his love for me and how he felt I was slipping away He wanted to make love to me and make love to me he did.

I had only been sexual with two people before and those were my sister's friends, so they were older guys as well. It's obvious that I have always been hot in the tail.... Don't judge me though. Anyway, LC was sensual. He wanted to make sure that he licked every single part of me. He wanted to show me that he was no longer afraid to be with me. He wanted to show me what I could be missing if I chose Jordan over him. LC was very good in bed, if you like that romance novel kind of sex. He licks fingers and toes. He nibbles on ears and sucks on inner thighs. He sticks fingers in yo ass, while his tongue is down your throat. He is thorough to say the least.

But after two years of wanting him, that time had inevitably passed. Once he was done showing me his love making skills and pleading to be my man even if he could get in trouble for statutory rape. I declined. I told him it was fun while it lasted ---- but I didn't want to fall for him and he go off and get married and stuff like that. I was trying to soften the blow. But he had to make this shit dramatic. Here is how the convo went.

"I love you lil bit." He was super teary eyed.

"Aww baby, don't make this more difficult than it has to be." As ya'll can see, I was on my G-Shit.

"So you are going to just say fuck me after I took a chance on yo young ass? He was pissed off.

"LC – you should be an adult about the situation, you knew we wouldn't last forever." I smirked as I put my clothes back on. I couldn't be serious for shit back then.

"Be an adult? An adult like you want to be? You aint shit but a fucked up ass child, wishing that you were an adult." He was about to start with the low blows, but I got his ass together real quick.

"Well I was adult enough to seduce you and have you sucking on my pussy 20 minutes after you declined. I'm adult enough to have you willing to go to jail over some avoidable shit. I'm adult enough to have yo adult ass in here pleading to be with me. So how is that for a want to be adult?" I was tired of being patient with him at this point. I liked Jordan and I wanted to move on and be with him.

"Man fuck you! I can't believe you got me this open, like I'm one of them lil high school niggas that you fuck with. I was willing to be yo man, but you right – this shit will never work. You are a cold hearted muthafucka and I actually give a fuck about the next person's feelings. And furthermore – I picked yo ass up, but I'm not dropping you off. Here is $1.80 for bus fare with yo dumb ass." He was pissed off. He went to the washroom. I left and I didn't speak with him again for two years.

My sister had slammed her toe in one of her drunken rages. She kicked the refrigerator or something like that and it fell; she jumped back but it caught her big toe. He called me and told me that the ambulance had just come to pick her up. We chatted for a bit and I asked him if he could let me into my sister's apartment so that I could grab a few things to take up to the hospital. He agreed. I was at Jordan's house helping him pack for college, but as soon as I was done, I went to see LC.

When I got to the building, I called his phone to tell him that I was outside of the apartment complex. But his girlfriend answered the phone. I introduced myself as Angel, Lynette's sister and I told her that I was coming by to get a few personal items to take up to the hospital. She explained that LC had went upstairs to open up my sister's apartment to see about the water that was leaking into their apartment.

When she said their apartment a bitch was taken aback. She lived here with him.

"Oh, you live with him?" I was out of line, but I needed to know.

"Yes I do. Me and Nyette are actually pretty good friends." She answered confidently.

"Ok. Well, I'm going to get my sisters thing." I was pissed off low key. As I was coming into the building she told me to tell LC she was going to the grocery store to grab some gravy and Champagne for dinner.

"Champagne? Are you celebrating something?" I was staring her ass down.

"Yes, our first year anniversary." She smiled with that crocked ass bottom tooth and I could have sworn she was a little cock eyed. I mean she was cute, but she was no Angel.

When I came into the apartment, LC was on his janitorial man shit. He had just become the apartment complex manager. So mopping up the mess that my sisters' refrigerator caused was a part of his job. We went through the normal, long time no see talk. I told him congrats on the anniversary, and I told him that 2 months ago, I had gotten engaged to Jordan. I tried to show him the ring, but he pushed my hand a way and told me congratulations as well.

"LC- you can't still be bitter about something that happened, 2 years ago?" I asked that because of the way he pushed my hand.

"Maybe a little!" He was honest.

"But I'm happy that we both moved on. You're celebrating anniversaries and all that. Plus I was too young for you. You said yourself we were never supposed to get serious."

I didn't want LC to be mad at me; but I kind of wanted to be faithful to Jordan. I mean he was going to college on a full basketball scholarship. He was my man, but he was also my meal ticket. I was young, but I wasn't no fool.

"Yeah, I said we were never supposed to get serious. But we did get serious. Serious enough for me to fall in love with you." He spoke up.

LC was just too sweet for me. I hated to break his heart. I had remorse for him and a little inkling of feelings for him or of what could have been. But we broke the awkwardness and started to discuss me going to Jr. College and what I would be pursuing with my degrees and stuff. As we talked he went to close my sisters' windows and make sure that her home was secured.

"LC are you in love?" I just had to know.

"Yep!" He answered.

"Well I'm happy for you, are you happy for me?

"Hell no. I really just want to make love to you on this floor. I want to steal you from college boy. I want you to move in with and marry me. I want you to have my kids."

He was being too truthful. I couldn't offer him all of that, but I could offer him some ass.

"I thought you were in love" I sassed.

"With you!" He answered as he walked toward me and guided me closer to him. He took my clothes off and fucked me up against that window. I wrapped my legs around his ass and began to dig my nails into his back. Remember I told ya'll that he was one of those romantic types, but not this time, this time he was on some real nigga shit. Just as I was about to climax, I heard screaming and a bottle shatter from outside.

LC looked out the window and seen his girlfriend Carla, staring up at us. I told him to go check on her as he continued to pump harder into me.

"I'm going to check on her.... as soon as I finish" He said. It was at that moment that I knew LC was after all, my type of nigga.

Chapter 4

"Carla?" LC yelled into the apartment after he finished fucking my brains out in my sisters' apartment.

"What Lawrence Charles?" Carla got all proper on LC. I couldn't help, but to laugh. Carla seemed like one of them sisters who thought she was all of that. I didn't like her ass already.

"Calm down baby!" LC was calm

"Did I, or did I not just see you fucking Nyette's sister upstairs on the window seal? I mean you didn't even stop once you realized that I had seen you. Her pussy that good, that you couldn't even climb out of it for ME?"

I could hear crying and whimpering from the door.

"Come on baby! It doesn't have to be like this. We are supposed to celebrate our one year anniversary and now you are spoiling it by being dramatic. You didn't see what you think you saw." LC lied.

"Oh No? Well, it looked like the two of you were having a very good time. It looked like you had done this before. This wasn't a new or nervous fuck. Are you always cheating on me with that bitch?" Carla got a little crunk; I was low key proud of her.

"Carla, I want to be with you!"

"Well why are you up there sexing her on our anniversary?" She softened up and began to cry.

"I'm sorry baby! Don't leave though. Just relax. I need you to stay. Don't make hasty decisions." Words spoken like an ultimate player. He never said I love you, I won't do it again, please forgive me or nothing. He was smooth, I had to admit it.

After that encounter it was another year and a half before I spoke with LC again. He called me on a Friday night to tell me that Lynette was in the hospital because she had cancer. That night I meet up with him and we had sex before I went to the hospital. We had sex every weekend for the next 8 or 9 months until Nyette died.

When my sister finally did succumb to cancer, I felt alone. With an absentee father, a mother that had been incarcerated for the last 3 years for attempted murder, a fiancée who was still away at school at that point, and LC, who was engaged to be married to Carla.

LC let me move in upstairs in my sisters' old apartment. And he pretty much steered clear of me. The only time we fucked is when I made a move on him and even that didn't always work; especially once I got married. I had to constantly explain to him how I needed him; how my husband was never home. I had to cry about being lonely. Since, he always had a very sweet spot for me; he let me back in his life. We had developed a secret partnership. That wasn't so secret after all. Carla ended up leaving him and when Sr. busted me in my nose he was convinced that I was fucking LC. The jig was up from there.

But what Sr. didn't know is that I was also fucking his god son as well. Drew was Seniors' best friend son and he eventually became my husband's best friend. In fact, Drew is the exact person that introduced Jordan and I. He wasn't trying to hook us up though. Drew was actually trying to date me when Jordan walked up. He introduced the 2 of us and the bigger, better guy won. But about a year into our marriage Drew had a party at his home, to celebrate him being hired by the top law firm in the city.

It had gotten late and Jordan was already gone because he claimed he had to work. I had fallen asleep on the couch and I woke up to Drew's head in between my legs. I yelled at Drew through my drunken state to get the fuck off of me.

"Don't move baby, this shit taste so good."

"Drew, I'm married to your best friend." I pleaded with him as I began to push his head away.

"We don't got to do nothing Ang. I just always wanted to taste you. Even when we was shorties, I used to kick it to you. You already knew what it was when you stayed over." He talked through slurps.

"Stop Drew!" The shit felt good, but I couldn't give in that easily. What type of lady do you guys think I am?

I got off the couch and called my husband. The first time he answered and hung up. So I called again. 3xs to be exact and he kept hanging up on me.

So I did what any wife like myself would do; I used it as an excuse to go back in the living room and let Drew finish kissing and tickling my womanhood. And I was going to let him dig me out.

Even though Drew was fine with a capital F. I wasn't that fond of him. But fuck it, I did what I did, anyway. We didn't have sex often. If it were up to him, he would completely end up backstabbing his best friend and he would make me his woman. But since it wasn't up to him one time per month (if that) would have to do.

Drew even had a couple of threesomes with LaLa and me in our hotel room. Let me tell ya'll how that started— because it was legitimately a wild ass night.

We went to a house party one night up the street from LaLa's house. Jordan didn't go. What a surprise right? Well anyway we were drinking, leaning, and damn near everything else that you could think of. We ended up in one of the bedrooms smoking together. Before I knew it, Drew had LaLa bent over the bed, banging her back out, and LaLa had me laid across the bed sucking on my nipples and bringing me to a climax with her fingers. As you could imagine, it was a great night.

But now that my husband's lies had surfaced, I had some cleaning to do.

Chapter 5

"Jordan Jr." I said into the phone "It's been six days since I have seen you or touched you."

"What's up baby, what's wrong?" He was always condescending.

"Yo cheating ass is the problem!" I yelled into the phone.

"How is that Ang?" He asked again like he didn't care. "I have been cheating on you for 5 years and you have been cheating on me for 10."

"What the hell are you talking about? If you believed that I was cheating on you, you would have never gotten me pregnant." I tried to justify my wrongs.

He confidently stated: "I didn't. Did I? LC told me everything last weekend. I thought I was speaking to him as a friend about my issues with us. But he was pretty open to telling me that you guys had been dealing with each other for 12 years. That means that you were only 14. You wouldn't fuck me until we were 17 when you lied and said you were a virgin. I should have known that you were lying because you worked it too good. But I took the bait because I thought you were a good girl with a shattered past. But honestly, you aint shit."

He continued by saying "Your own father ran away from you when you tried to break him and your mama up."

"Jordan, you need to stop it right now. I am pregnant with your child. You want to try to make me feel guilty because you are engaged to another woman. How the fuck can you marry another bitch when your dumb ass is already married to me? How are you going to pull that off? You can only live a double life for so long. All of that lying about a 2nd job. I sure never see the royalties from that check. Your fake family is over there receiving those hours because your wife can't get the fucking time of the day." I yelled.

"Ang you are right. You are absolutely correct. But I wanted to let yo ass know that you aint fooling me anymore. When the baby is born that is what will determine where our marriage goes. Until then – I'm going to stay with my parents or with Drew and LaLa."

"Drew and LaLa?" I yelled

"Yes. If you didn't know, with yo nosey ass, they are together now. She lives with him." But the true moral of the story is: I won't be coming home after tonight. And by the way: Stay away from my fiancée and my kids."

Before he hung up I wanted to tell him that I had already been to see his fat ass girlfriend. I also wanted to tell him that it would be a cold day in hell before I let him just leave. I would kill him and his family before I let our 10 year relationship go down the drain.

I never wanted to be in a situation to kill again, but I was prepared to do what I had to do. I would literally go over there and slice Jana's throat. It wouldn't be the first time.

I had to do my step dad the same way. My mom was in jail for attempted murder after she was fed up with him raping me. He had raped me a total of twelve times. She knew he was a rapist and that's why she used to always send me to my sister's house. I guess one day she just got tires with him and she shot him in the back.

After that debacle and her going away, I had to finish what she started. He was sitting his crippled ass in his wheel chair trying to flip through the channels when I so eloquently walked up behind him, slit his throat until I could see blood shooting toward the TV.

I was never a suspect nor was I ever even questioned about his murder. It wasn't like I was a pro or something, but I was able to literally walk into the apartment, tip toe up to him, kill him, put the knife in a zip lock bag, and walk out like it never happened. I went home cleaned the knife and the baggie. I tossed the baggie and put the knife in a cloth, back into another bag, and trashed it on my visit to see my mother way in the boondocks of the Downstate Penn.

Now, I have to do the same thing to my husband and his lady because I am not letting that fat bitch take my husband. And if he doesn't want me – he may as well be dead anyway.

I'm the best thing that ever happened to him. I thought about the situation as my phone started ringing and interrupted my decision planning.

"Hello," I yelled into the receiver. Upset because the caller ID didn't read my husband's name. Instead it was MoMo.

"Damn who ruined your day?" I guess she was shocked by the way I answered the phone.

"LC, Jordan, and that fat bitch Jana."

"Well Damn! Wanna tell me about it?" MoMo offered her time.

"Not Really! Jordan left me, LC is a hater, and my husband loves his mistress. That's really it in a nutshell."

"I'm sorry Ang!" MoMo said before she started diving into the questions and gossip.

"So are you fucking LC?" She had the nerve to question me.

"Why would you say that?" I was curious as to why she would ask and further more why was she all in my damn business.

"You know that he and I have gone out on a few dates. I really like him, but it seems like he hinted to fucking you." MoMo was honest.

"Dates?" I yelled.

"Yeah. He said some shit under the pillow talk act. I almost ignored it because you are a married woman, but......"

"Pillow talk? Bitch, are you fucking him?" I was infuriated. Infuriated wasn't even the word to describe how pissed I was.

"Bitch?" MoMo got offended. "Yeah, I fucked him three times. What's it to you BITCH?" She wanted to get all defensive and shit now.

'Shit nothing accept for the fact that he is about to be my baby's daddy. Yo ass always chasing after my leftovers. I'm surprised you have never tried to fuck my husband." I was disgusted with this bitch.

"Nope. Not never. But your husband sure tried to fuck me. All the time actually! And as far as running behind your leftovers, it's absurd that as a married woman who has been involved with Jordan for over 10 years that you would have left overs. I hope yo ass aint give LC the Chlamydia that LaLa and Drew gave you." MoMo was spitting that shit just as good as I was. Low key- I was proud of her.

"Chlamydia? LaLa? Drew? Girl Please. Get your shit together. I said to her as I started thinking back to that whole disease shit.

I had given Sr. that shit too from Drew's nasty ass. Sr. whooped my ass from here to there and fucked me at the same time;reinfecting me after I was already cured. He literally bit my body everywhere while his dick was in my pussy. He pinched me, choked me, punched me... all while he fucked me. Then, he turned me over, fucked me in my ass and made me suck his dick afterwards.

Sr. was a real piece of work and some of the things he did to me were just wrong; but I liked that stupid shit though. The next day we went, got meds, and we were back to normal.

"Bitch please, I know the truth. And I hope that your bastard ass baby was not conceived with my man." MoMo hung up the phone on me.

I was so pissed off. She fucked LC. She knew about Drew and LaLa. And she said that my husband had interest in her. My life was surely dwindling before my eyes.

"Lawrence Charles" I yelled as I bammed on his front door. He had me fucked all the way up if he thought that what he did was cool. It was childish as fuck to tell my husband anything about me and him.

"Why the fuck would you tell my husband that I have been fucking you for 12 years? Furthermore, why would you fuck my friend?" Bitch, I was heated. I thought I had all of this shit under control, but Noooooo – LC wants to pull the rug from under me with his hating ass.

"Firstly, I thought he should know. There is no sense in him feeling bad for a 5 year relationship with Jana, when we have been back and forth for longer than you have even known him. Secondly, I like MoMo. She isn't married or involved with someone like you are"

Listen here – when I say I wanted to snatch his muffin cap back blue (In Kevin Hart voice), bitch I was serious. What in the hell gave him the right to mind my business.

"LC are you serious?" I gave him a once over and then put my hands on my hips. Shit, I was standing on something and he acted like he forgot.

"Lil Bit – are you serious?" He was sarcastic in his rebuttal.

"You are so pitiful. Telling my husband was some spiteful shit. But then you went and slept with the only person in the world that had my back since I was a child. She knows me and she still loves me. You just had to take that away." I became vulnerable as I thought about the fact that I only had one friend in the whole wide world.

"Lil Bit – it's not about you all the time. Me and MoMo can talk, screw, become a couple, get married, or never see each other again – it still won't have anything to do with you. She can still be your best friend, while she and I do what we want to do." LC was standing on his point this time.

"It's not that simple LC. You and I both know that there is a child growing inside of me. And we also know that she is possibly yours. We also know that we have a 12-year history and me seeing you with MoMo is going to drive me crazy. You got my husband to leave me. Are you trying to ruining my life?

"No. Maybe your husband's father is trying to ruin your life, by whooping on yo ass every week. You are lucky that I didn't tell Jordan that. That baby is about 25 – 35% a possibility for me. You fucking me, Sr. and I guess you are fucking your husband. I have been your sucker for years, letting you run away every bitch that's been in my life. So, it's time that I show your ass the door" LC was talking big shit as he walked over to his front door to let me out.

I was alone now. My soul was in despair. I had nobody to turn to except for Sr. or my mama and I was not about to drive all of those hours to see her when I could just kill all of they ass and move around. Number 1 would be Jordan and that bitch. They had to go.......

So ya'll know that my crazy ass actually did go over to Jana's house right? She was all Ra Ra Ra – like she had something that would hold me baby. Fuck that shit, I threw that bitch over her balcony. She lucky that her kids weren't there cus I would have thrown all of they little asses too.

Next up was my husband or LC.... You know which ever one I ran into first. As I left my apartment Sr. was coming in and he was looking at me all crazy and shit. He grabbed my hair and started to yell.

Sr. was yelling some bullshit saying that I told LC that my husband wasn't the dad. "So who is the dad Angel, because I know that I can't have any more kids." Sr. had scared the shit out of me.

"Sr. I didn't tell LC anything and I don't know why LC is telling you anything about me." I managed to say as he pulled my hair and threw me against the wall.

"Who else are you fucking Angel?" I really don't know why Sr. was so possessive, but it was starting to wear me thin.

"Sr. Get the fuck off of me." A bitch was scared as hell when I said that shit, but enough was a fucking nuff.

"What?"

He swole up like he couldn't believe that I had backtalk for his ass.

He attempted to hit me in the stomach, but I jerked away from him and grabbed a knife off of the kitchen counter. Ya'll know I'm good with the knife, right? And I cut his wrist.

"You bitch" he charged at me saying a bunch of shit and I took that knife and stuck it right through his gat-damn heart. He stopped midway, turned around like he was going to walk out the door,and then he fell face forward.

That fall did nothing but kill him because it pushed the knife in further.

"Oh shit what did I just do?" I thought to myself. I never intended to kill Senior. Senior and MoMo were the only people that I was going to let live. I definitely didn't intend to kill anyone in my house.

I wanted to scream and I wanted to yell because I was pissed off, but I didn't want to bring any more attention to me and my crazy ass antics.

"Don't lose control Angel. Keep a cool head Angel" You know, I was talking to myself and shit

"Angel ---- what the fuck did you just do?" LC stood at my front door and looked down at Seniors body...............................

"Is he dead Lil Bit?" LC looked in my eyes and then back down to Senior.

"Hell if I know." I shrugged my shoulders as I walked over to the window to look out.

"Angel, what have you done?" LC walked toward me at the window.

Look – LC was a fucking dummy. I'm hormonal, I'm enraged, and it was all his fault – for telling my business. Did he think that he was going to console me after all of that?

"Don't touch me. Don't look at me. Don't think about me. I screamed as I ran towards my bedroom and he ran behind me. Inside of the bedroom, he would get the surprise of his life.

"Close the door." I screamed at him as I pointed the Saturday Night Special right to his head.

"Angel. Calm down!" He tried to reason with me and shit. Ain't no reasoning with a crazy woman, and quiet as it was kept – I was certified crazy.

"Did you think you were going to be able to screw up my life and then all would be forgiven? Fuck you" I started to yell and shake the gun toward him. I was nice with the knife; the gun was a different story. But I would pull that trigger in a heartbeat, and that's just what I had to do when MoMo called herself opening the door to save him.

Yep, I shot both of them bitches. I got MoMo right in the heart, and shot LC in the arm and in the leg. I stood over him as he pleaded for his life. I was about to shoot his ass in the head, but Jordan always had to be Super Save a Hoe.

He ran his love sick ass in the room and without a thought; he shot me in the head. As I fell to the ground, I started to see my life flash before my eyes. The thoughts of my molestation, my mom leaving me, me being bullied, me murdering my step dad, me sleeping with an adult when I was only 14, my sister's death, my sister allowing me to drink and smoke weed as a kid. All of that shit started racing through my mind.

"How did I get here?" I thought about the situation as I closed my eyes. I had it altogether. I used to play these niggas like chump change, but I was destined for failure from the beginning. My mom was a shorty when she had me. She was on drugs and she used to leave me with the guys at the corner store as she went out back and got high. They used to use me as a punching bag for practice. I never had stability and the love that I was longing for I tried to find it in all the wrong people.

As my body started to jerk and the blood started to spew out of my mouth, I could hear the ambulance sirens in the distance and I could hear Jordan yelling for Senior to wake up. It was all over now. Fuck all of them!

Aye, but I held that shit down though. I was The REAL Housewife. I had what I needed and I did what I wanted. Don't cry for me, cus I won't cry for none of you muthafuckas. But when you talk about Angel and you telling people to read this story --- make sure that you let them know: I'm something like the man and I never gave a fuck.

The Cottage

By

Seven Steps

Ireland 1798

He ran.

Searching voices rose from the chilly fog that misted the countryside. The earthy smell of manure filled his nose, telling him a farm was nearby. The sound of hooves against wet grass beat in time with his heart. Emerald green hills rolled and tumbled through the darkness, dotted here and there with flowers.

The voices grew closer.

A small farm came into view. In the center of it sat a cottage. Silver moonlight washed over its gray stone walls, the rays bleaching the thatched roof white. Off to one side, haystacks kept guard in the night, golden soldiers taller and wider than any man. A large oak tree, taller than any he'd ever seen, grew in the back of the house. Its branches reached at odd angles, like arms ready to grab at the cottage. Holes and notches opened in an eerie mask complete with eyes, nose, and mouth. The moon shone behind it, giving the tree a menacing appearance. Chills rolled through him at the sight of it.

A leather satchel banged painfully on his back, the latch barely holding. He pressed a hand to the brass lock. If the maps within the satchel were found, thousands of

Irishmen would be as good as dead. The British would seek out and execute anyone he'd ever contacted, including his mother, father, and younger brother, Harry. The thought tore at his heart.

Desperate fear forced his feet forward. Ink black hair clung to his wet brow. The muscles in his legs screamed painfully. He ignored the discomfort. Nothing could be done about it now. If he stopped, he would die.

He reached the haystacks just as the small band of soldiers crested the hill.

"There he is!"

He turned towards the voice.

White and brown horses reared up and whinnied, their rounded flanks shining against the star soaked sky. The red-coated riders zeroed in on him, hate filling their eyes.

"Forward!"

His feet moved again, frantically seeking an escape. Hiding in a haystack was not an option. Nor was the cottage for that matter. If the soldiers suspected he'd taken up shelter in either of them, the farm would be burned, the inhabitants hung.

No, he wouldn't put anyone else in danger. Enough people had been killed because of him today. His contact in the British camp. The traveling baker who'd brought the maps to him. Aunt Ann who'd sheltered him. They'd slaughtered her while he jumped from the roof, stole one of her horses, and found his way to the country hills, in route to his contact in Aylinborough. Sadness ran through him. Ann was his favorite aunt.

Around him, hills stretched as far as he could see, mocking him. They were open ground. He'd be gunned down before he crested the next one.

There had to be a way out.

Then, a shimmer. Moonlight danced atop a blue ribbon of water.

His prayers were answered.

The horse's whinnied again before resuming the chase.

Flying forward, he was careful to stay close to the towering piles of hay. The cottage came up on his right. In the window, a candlelit face. Thick brown curls shook as the woman turned to him, her beautiful brown eyes wide as he ran past her window.

Her face lit a spark in him.

His heart knew her name, even as his mind told him he'd never seen the maiden before.

Ashling. Her name was Ashling.

And then, as quickly as she appeared, she was gone, the shutters of her window hidden by a large haystack.

His heart made a promise to her,

I'll be back for you, Ashling.

An open field was all that stood between him and the river. Hope bloomed within his chest.

His mind turned giddy with exhaustion. I'm almost there. Just a bit further.

But he'd been running too long. His legs slowed. His chest tightened. His heart felt as if it would break through his ribs as his feet touched the muddy riverbank.

Just a little further.

A man's voice, Cockney accent thick, called out, "We've got him now, lads!"

The smell of oats, hay, and equestrian sweat surrounded him. A heavy snort wet the back of his neck. A second soldier laden beast pulled up on the left, a third on the right.

Suddenly, his feet were thrown out from under him, caught in a branch risen from the muddy bank. His body pitched forward, his face smacking into the brown clay. Something hard hit his forehead, making his head spin.

Reaching forward, he touched his hand to the icy water. For a moment, he thought he was safe. Then, someone grabbed his legs, pulling him back to the field.

He swore.

Colorful stars clouded his vision with magenta, gold, orange, and green.

Save Harry, he prayed. Dear God, please save Harry.

The first strike of the club hit him hard across the gut, draining the last of the air from his lungs.

With his vision gone, he tried to orient himself with sound. He swung his arms wildly, honing in on the sounds of feet that shuffled, and dug into the dirt. The soldiers laughed at him as they easily dodged his fist. They rained down more blows on his arms, legs, gut, and face.

His body turned stiff and sore under the assault. Finally, he curled himself into a ball, the knowledge that he was now blind, helpless, and at the mercy of the soldiers dragging icy fingers of terror through him.

"So you thought you could run from us?" The soldier asked, his voice rough.

The blows ended. A rough hand searched his body, while he laid still, waiting for an opportunity to escape or strike. He took comfort in knowing that the satchel was well hidden, buried deep in a haystack.

"Nothing here, sir."

He tried to lift his head, but the movement sent ripples of pain throughout his body.

"Where is it, you mangy Irish mutt?!" He felt hands grab his ears. Someone snatched his head forward as if they meant to tear it off his shoulders. "Where is the satchel?"

The too quick movement of his head caused his stomach to lurch. He spewed vomit onto what he thought was the soldiers' shirt.

The soldier's roar echoed through the hills.

He felt something come down hard on his leg, shattering it. He screamed.

"Throw him in the river!" The soldier cried. "Let the bloody Irish dog drown."

Several hands lifted him off the ground. He tried to wriggle his body free, but with his busted leg, and lack of vision, he was powerless.

Then, he was airborne.

There was no ground, just wind and sky.

Maybe God has turned me into a bird. Perhaps he will fly me home? Perhaps he will fly me to Ashling?

The thought lifted his spirits. He flapped his arms once, twice.

Then, the river splashed around him. The current - strong with the melting winter ice - pulled him downstream, and out of the soldiers clutches.

***

Someone pounded at the window.

Ashling dropped the bread pan she had just pulled from the oven with a small yelp. It clanked against the wood planked floor.

She swore.

Great. One less thing for dinner.

"Ashling!" Bernie shouted at her through the window.

She wiped the flour from her hands with the skirt of her apron and pushed the mess of dense, brown curls out of her eyes.

"Ashling!" More urgent this time. The pounding of her small fists shook the white washed shutters.

Her foot connected with the ruined bread, kicking it, pan and all, across the room. With narrowed eyes and balled fist she glared at her older sister. "You made me spoil the bread!"

Bernie disappeared from the window, and a moment later burst through the blue, wood paneled door, all wide green eyes and flushed skin.

Ashling forgot the bread. Something was wrong. Something threw Bernie into a panic, and Bernadette 'Bernie' McGlowden never panicked.

"You must come quickly!"

Bernie pulled her sister across the field, her long red curls coming undone from their braid. Their feet swept over the grass, still wet with morning dew. They raced past the two cows, the horse stable, and a chaos of panicked clucks that lifted from the chicken coop. They left in their wake a slew of lazy, chewing goats and several families of ducks who'd congregated near the pig trough. Finally, they stopped at what appeared to be a heap of clothes next to a haystack.

Ashling blinked hard to clear her vision, blurred from the frantic run, and the rising daylight.

She leaned down to inspect the water logged heap of brown and black, her breath still coming in hard.

The pile of clothes shifted. Thick arms wrapped ever tighter around a leather satchel. A man's face, shockingly blue and trembling, laid with closed eyes, his mouth whispering something Ashling couldn't understand.

"What's happened to him?"

Bernie shook her head. Her hands went to her hips as she struggled to catch her breath. "I don't know. I was feeding the goats when I found him."

Ashling placed a hand on the man's forehead, then pulled it away. "He's freezing. Quickly, help me bring him inside. We have to warm him."

Bernie took a step back from the body. "What if he's dangerous?"

"He's no more dangerous than a wounded goat," Ashling snapped. "Now help me carry him."

Stooping, Ashling grabbed the man under his arms. When she touched him, his deep, strained voice began to babble in earnest. She made out something about a map, but everything else seemed to be gibberish.

She looked at her sister.

"A little help?"

Bernie hesitated, shaking her head vigorously. "He's not well."

"Aye. That's why we're taking him back to the cottage. To help him."

"I don't like this. We should leave him here. We could call Father Peter to come for him."

"The man needs medicine, not prayers."

Bernie shook her head again, fiddled with her fingers as she did when she was unsure about something.

Ashling's eyes turned pleading. "Please sister. I can heal him. We can't leave this poor creature out here to die. It isn't our way."

Bernie still didn't move.

Ashling blew out a breath, pulled the stray hairs from her neck. "This is what father would have wanted. When he was alive, he taught us to help others, didn't he? What would he say if he knew that this poor man was out here suffering while we stood around him, clucking about like a bunch of hens? I'll tell you what he'd say. He'd tell us to do what the Good Lord would have done."

Bernie huffed, "Alright, alright." She crossed herself. "May the Lord protect us."

Together, they picked up the man, trying their best to keep from jarring him too much. He moaned when Bernie touched his leg. From the way it hung, Ashling could tell it was broken. His face was blue, his skin cold. They had to act quickly. With small, shuffled steps, they carried, and at times drug him, across the field.

"Who do you think he is?" Ashling asked through harsh breaths.

"A soldier, from the looks of his coat. He must've dragged himself as far as he could go, then fainted."

Ashling thought about the massacres throughout Ireland. British troops burned Irish rebels alive by the dozens when they could catch them. She shivered.

Bernie carefully stepped over a stone. "Are you sure about this? Maybe we should put him back where we found him. He could be dangerous."

"He's unconscious, what harm can he do?"

"I don't like it. I don't like it one bit."

"Don't worry. We'll be fine. He'll be gone by morning if God wills it. Besides, we could use some excitement around here."

"I get enough excitement milking the goats, thank you very much."

The ground inclined, ending the conversation.

Ashling's lungs burned with exertion. Sweat matted her thick brown hair to her forehead. She tried to blow the wretched curls away to no avail.

The ground evened out again a hundred feet from the cottage's front door. They passed the distance quickly, finally dropping him onto the table in the kitchen. Bernie sent Ashling to fetch the wood bench from the barn to accommodate his long legs.

Finally, the stranger was moved into a comfortable position, both legs straight before him.

While Bernie wiped down her wet body, and took in a cool drink, Ashling rolled up her sleeves and set to work. The man needed help, and she would see to it that he got it.

He was stripped, his clothes set out to be washed and dried in the sun. Next, they washed him, bandage his wounds and set his leg. Finally, they covered him with every blanket they could spare.

Bernie built the fire until it roared. When it was hot enough, she placed bricks near it. They would be slipped under his blanket for extra warmth later.

"We've done all we can," Bernie finally said, her legs creaking as she sat in a nearby chair. "He's in the Lord's hands now."

"What did you do with the satchel?"

"In the potato cellar."

"Did you look into it?"

She shook her head. "No. Whatever's inside is between him and the Lord."

Ashling nodded. She ran her fingers through his midnight hair, pushing it off his face. The movement came naturally, as if she'd done it before.

The thought nagged at her, and she focused on his face. A beard was starting to shadow his chin, cheeks and throat. His skin was tanned and rough. His lips were chapped, but full.

"Do we know him?" she asked.

"What?"

"He looks familiar."

Bernie shook her head and set herself to collecting the bloody rags to be washed. "No, I've never seen him before."

"Are you sure? Maybe we've seen him in town?"

"I've met every man in that town, and this one doesn't strike me."

Ashling smiled gently. She angled her head, drinking in the sight of him. "Handsome lad, isn't he?"

She tried to imagine him awake. He'd tower over her, that was for sure. By the looks of him, he wasn't more than twenty, same age as her. A lean, hard body and callused hands told her that he was no stranger to hard work. She wondered if he had been a farmer before he became a soldier. Perhaps she knew his father?

The sound of shoveling floated to her ears. She looked towards the window, but no one was there.

Odd.

"Ashling!"

Ashling snapped to attention.

Bernie was frowning at her. "Please fetch me a bucket of cold water. I've asked you three times now."

"Yes, of course."

Taking one last look towards the empty window, Ashling grabbed the water bucket and headed out the back door. She walked around the house once, searching for the source of the sound.

When she arrived again at the door, she laughed shortly, shaking her head at the impossibility of it all. The property was set amongst the hills. No one was around for miles.

Dismissing the strange ache that formed in the pit of her stomach, she kneeled next to the shimmering water that ran beside the cottage. Though the day was warm, chunks of half melted ice bumped against the sides as they floated in the frigid pool. It was a sure sign that spring had come to warm the land.

Years before, when her mother was heavy with Bernie, Ashling's father had dug a trench from the river to the front door, lining it with rocks. It was a small gift so that Ashling's mother wouldn't have to go quite so far for water. Ashling thanked God for her father's ingenuity, and his love, whenever she reached a cup or bowl into its gurgling depths.

She wondered how long the stranger had been in the river as she dunked the bucket in the stream and rushed back inside the cottage.

Bernie was still at the strangers' side, pity radiating from her emerald eyes. Ashling placed the bucket on a chair, the legs dragging against the floor as she pushed it next to her sister. Bernie plucked a rag from the table near the man's head. She dipped it into the bucket, squeezed it out with one hand, and placed it on the man's feverish head. Her lips pouted as she shushed his soft babbles.

"There, there," she whispered. "Just relax now. You're in good hands with the McGlowden sisters. We won't let any harm come to you."

She cocked her head to the side as she dabbed at the sweat that had begun to line his brow. "What should we do with him?" Bernie asked.

"We can't do anything until he wakes up."

"How long do you think that'll be?"

"A little while, perhaps."

Ashling's heart broke a little as she took in the sight of her older sister looking down on this man as if he were a sick child. She wondered if Bernie would get the chance to look at her own children that way.

Perhaps if I marry, she thought, then Bernie wouldn't have to be so worried about me. She could finally have a family of her own.

"Ashling, are you listening?" Bernie said. "What has gotten into you today? I swear your head is in the clouds."

"Yes, sorry Bernie. I guess I'm just worn out from all the excitement."

Bernie frowned, shook her head, and turned back to the patient. "I said that he must be with the rebels. I took a look at his clothes. They were worn, old. If he were a Brit, he'd have a better quality of garment, something red I think."

Ashling shrugged as Bernie continued,

"I don't think it's wise to keep him here." She turned her frowning face to Ashling. "What if the Brits come looking for him? They'll kill us and burn the farm."

Ashling crossed herself. "Mary, Peter and Joseph, we cannot think of that now. Hopefully, he'll be awake by morning, and we can send him on his way."

The thought saddened Ashling a bit. She didn't want the stranger to go, but she didn't understand why.

"Aye. Hopefully." Bernie threw the rag back in the bucket and wiped her hands on her skirt. "I'm going to work in the garden. Keep an eye out. If you hear anyone coming, put him in the potato cellar."

Ashling nodded and watched as her sister moved to the front door.

"Finish dinner while I'm out," she threw over her red freckled shoulder. "And don't spoil any more bread!"

She watched Bernie grab her basket of gardening tools and make her way to the garden. The sun moved higher in the sky. They'd have to work quickly to complete their chores before it set.

She turned back to the stove, and her ruined pan of bread against the wall. Focusing on the tasks ahead, she picked up the pan, and threw the ruined bread into the fire, a small smile on her face. This stranger's arrival shook up her ordinary life, and she was glad for it. She reached for the broom that stood on the stone wall next to the back door, began to sweep the crumbs, and chunks of bread into a pile.

Farm life was difficult and isolated. Her and Bernie rarely left the property, save for once a month when they went into town to sell fruits and vegetables from the garden. Next month they'd have several horses to sell, and judging from mild winter, they'd have a few baby cows, goats, and chickens as well. Money would be a lot less tight, and she thanked the Lord for it.

She absently thought of buying a new dress, and chuckled at the absurdity of it. What's the use of a new dress if no one but Bernie would see her in it?

Moving back into the house, she drug one of the rickety, old, wood chairs from the near the table to in front of the hearth. Flat stones between two wooden planks served as a shelf. She reached onto it, and pulled out a mixing bowl. She'd need more dough.

Ashling looked forward to her trips to town. Her and Bernie would wake up early, set out before sunrise with their cart filled with their wares, and their hearts filled with anticipation. After a twelve hour trip, they would tumble out of the old cart, and onto the doorstep of their aunt Maori. Ashling loved the old, gentle, doting woman. Maori was her mother's twin sister, and Ashling found it comforting to look into her grey eyes and remember her mother, if only for a moment.

For three days they would sell and exchange their wares to the locals. For three nights, Maori would parade man after man in front of them in hopes that one of her nieces might secure a husband.

Husband. The word sent tiny flutters of sadness through Ashling's heart. Not so much for herself, but for Bernie. Exactly five different men had proposed to Bernie since their father died, and Bernie had turned down every one of them. When Ashling would ask why, Bernie would give her a watery smile and hug her tight. In her tender years, Ashling never understood the gesture. But, as she grew older, the meaning became clear.

It was because of Ashling. Bernie refused to abandon her sister. No matter how much they bickered and squabbled, they would never leave each other alone. Not even for the security of a marriage. Not even for their own happiness. They would need to marry together, or not marry at all.

Ashling turned to the stranger. Hope rose in her. Perhaps he would bring change to their lives. Maybe, if Ashling minded her manners, he could be convinced to…

She didn't allow herself to complete the thought.

No, she thought. He'll be gone by tomorrow and our lives will go back to the way they were.

He'll be gone tomorrow.

She punched the dough a few more times, sending flour flying through the room.

He'll be gone tomorrow.

***

"There's nothing more we can do about him tonight, Ashling, now come to bed. God willing, he'll be up and gone by morning."

Dinner had long past when Bernie stood in the doorway to her room, night dress reaching the ground, irritation coloring her eyes.

"I'll stay with him for a few more minutes." Ashling placed a hand on the stranger's chest. They'd redressed him a few minutes prior. She felt the ropes of thick muscle beneath his thin shirt. A bubble of pleasure floated through her.

Bernie's eyebrows angled in suspicion.

"For what purpose? He's been asleep for hours."

"In case he wakes up."

Her pale lips pressed together. "Five minutes," she said firmly. "Then you get to bed. I can't be expected to do all the chores around here while you sit and stare at him."

"Aye."

"Five minutes, Ashling."

"Aye, sister." Ashling turned sharp eyes to her older sibling.

Scowling, Bernie relented, leaving Ashling with her patient.

He had gotten his color back, but his adventure in the river had weakened him. Feverish sweat poured off of him, though the fire was barely enough to ward off the outside chill.

Ashling pulled a blanket close around her. There was something about this man that called her to his side. A strange force that made her want to lock their hands together and never let go. She wondered who he was. Where was he was from? What happened to him? Was he a belligerent lad, proud and tempestuous? Was he gentle, kind, with a soft touch? The bubble of pleasure grew in her, and she bit her lip. Was he married? Did he have children?

She reached forward and ran a hand down his too warm face.

His skin had turned a deep shade of crimson as he boiled with fever. His sleep turned restless, and he groaned.

Unable to leave his side, Ashling suffered with him. She collected water from the stream and wiped his face and body. She told him stories that her mother had told her as a child. She imagined that, somehow, he heard her and was comforted. She mixed a brew of herbs and pressed it to his tongue to help him rest and break the fever.

All through the night she sat beside him while he sweated, moaned, and screamed in his sleep. She prayed to God to heal him, to put his soul at peace.

Even as he quaked with fever, Ashling felt the nagging thought that she knew this man. She felt it ever since they'd drug him across their threshold. There was something about him. She couldn't quite put it into words, but her heart seemed to understand it completely.

The constant question lingered in the back of her mind. Who is this man?

The sun had just peeked through the hills when, suddenly, the stranger awoke. She'd been dabbing his forehead with a cold cloth when he looked at her, his coal-black eyes wild and red-rimmed. He grabbed her hands and pulled her to him.

Ashling gasped, too shocked to pull away from his iron grip, to enthralled by his sharp gaze to look away.

"Ashling," he whispered, his voice deep and dry. Recognition softened his features. He brushed a curl away, his lips forming something close to a smile.

"My Ashling."

And then, he collapsed back onto the table, dragged again into a restless, feverish sleep.

Though freed from his grip, Ashling didn't move.

He said my name, she thought. How could he know my name? I've never seen this man before in my life.

She moved slowly, hovering over his now still body, studying his tanned face.

The feeling she'd seen this man before, touched this man before, rose sharply within her. Her heart told her that this was no stranger though her mind screamed that she was mistaken.

Curiosity peaked, she reached for a bowl of water and a straight razor, sharpening it on a strip of leather near the sink.

"Goodness, child, what are you doing?" Bernie demanded. With one hand she held her blanket closed over her, with the other she rubbed the sleep from her eye.

"Shaving him," Ashling replied matter-of-factly.

"Why in heaven would you be doing that?"

"He woke up."

"He woke up?"

"Yes, and he grabbed me and said, uh, that he knew me."

She walked over to the stranger and wet his face with the water from her bowl.

"He grabbed you?"

"That's what I said."

"Ashling this has gone far enough. You go on to bed. This stranger has brought nothing but trouble to this house. You leave me all the chores while you wait by his bedside and now you're shaving him? I don't know what to think."

"Then don't think on it at all."

Bernie gasped. "Now look here, Ashling-"

"I need to see his face."

"See his face?" Bernie whispered to herself.

Ashling didn't respond, focused only on passing the blade over the stranger's weathered cheek in the rising sunlight.

Bernie sighed and disappeared into her room to get ready for the day.

Once his face was shaved and scrubbed, Ashling held the candle close to him, tracing her fingers over his features. They lightly trailed over his eyes, his straight nose, his lip.

His lips, she thought. His lips remind me of something.

Suddenly, a powerful vision pushed through her mind. Her locked in his arms, hands tangled in his midnight hair. His mouth moved down the columns of her throat, and she breathed his name.

Liam.

As quickly as it arose, the image faded.

She stumbled backwards. Knocking over the chair she'd been sitting in, she tumbled to the floor in a heap of skirt.

No, it's not possible. How could I know that? How could I know his name? Who is this man?

***

Ashling didn't remember sleeping. She remembered blinking though. Yes, she had blinked, and when her eyes opened, it was nearly noon.

She stretched and rose from the floor.

How did I get here? She wondered.

The last thing she remembered was the vision of her and the stranger. The memory heated her cheeks, sent tingles through her body.

She heard the distinct sound of a shovel digging into the ground. She ran to the door and flung it open.

Bernie was far afield, moving in and out of the barn, heavy buckets of carrots and oats at her side. Aside from her, no one else was around for miles.

Behind her, the stranger stirred. He turned on his side, sucking in a harsh breath as his weight fell onto his splinted leg. The pain forced him back onto his back. He ran a hand through his coal black hair with a groan.

Ashling didn't breathe as he slowly propped himself up on his elbows, and scanned the small, simple room. Finally his gaze fell on her.

The sun's rays lost themselves in the inky black depths of his eyes, making them shimmer like stars. His black hair covered half his face, giving him a dangerous, predatory look. Now sitting up, he filled the room with the heavy, musky presence only a man could bring. The table creaked under the shift in his weight.

Ashling's mind went wild.

He'd make strong sons.

The thought made her blush, and she raised a hand to one, reddened cheek.

He cleared his throat, snapping her back to reality as he gave way to a lung rattling cough.

Shook from her admiration of his beautiful form, she ran to the water bucket, and filled him a cup of cool water. He drank it in a single gulp and held it out to her. "More."

Her feet rooted to the ground.

He shook the cup at her. "More."

She didn't move. This was it. She'd finally know who this stranger was. She would finally get the answer her heart had been craving since she pulled him from the haystack.

She straightened her back, poked out her chin. "My questions first. Who are you? What is your name?"

His brows knit together, his discomfort visible on his face.

"Liam."

Her heart hammered in her chest. So she had been right. But how?

Filling the cup again, she held it to her breast, and turned to him.

"Liam what?"

He held out a shaky arm for the cup.

"Liam McGunntry."

She whispered his name as she handed him the water. He took it, draining the contents in a gulp.

"Why were you in our haystacks, Liam McGunntry?"

"Are you questioning me for the British?" he asked. His tone teased rather than accused.

"This is an Irish house, lad, and you'll do well to remember it. Now, why were you in our haystacks?"

A small smile danced on his lips before he chased it away.

She wished it would come again.

"Will I get another cup of water for my answer?" He asked.

"You'll get that and more. Bread. Perhaps cheese if you are polite about it."

His gaze leisurely moved from her eyes, down her slim body, and back again. She shivered under his inspection.

"Would you give me your name first, lass?"

"My rules, Mr. McGunntry. No man has ruled this cottage since my father died and I won't start having you rule it now."

Liam's eyebrow shot up, the small smile returning, broadening. "Very well," he said, his voice softening. He seemed to relax a bit as Ashling cut hunks of bread and cheese for him. She held it close to her, and out of his reach.

"Now, why were you in our haystacks, Liam McGunntry?"

"I was..." His eyes went wide, and darted around the room. "My satchel. Where is my satchel?"

"Hidden."

"Where?"

"In the cellar."

His hand laid on his belly as he let out a breath of relief. "Thank God for you, lass. You don't know the good that you have done."

She nodded. "You're welcome." She looked at the bread and cheese in her hand and handed them to him.

He took them gratefully, chomping into them hungrily. In seconds they were gone. He licked the salt from his lips.

Ashling examined the man on the table.

"I must tell you that it is only me and my sister here, Liam McGunntry. I trust that you will not harm us."

He shook his head. "I swear that I will do no harm to you. Nor your sister."

"Can I trust you, Liam?" she asked.

"With your life, lass. As I have trusted you with mine."

She saw the truth in his eyes.

"I believe you, Liam."

She eased a bit, the tension releasing from her shoulders.

"Do I get more bread and cheese now that I have your trust, lass?"

"I know that you're hungry, and I will feed you. But first you must tell me why you are here. Does it have to do with your satchel?"

"It would be much too dangerous if you knew who I was," he said. "The last woman who knew..." He dropped his eyes, tried to climb down off the table. "I promised that I would not harm you, and I meant it. I have to go."

She ran to him, shoving him back.

"No, you mustn't!"

Something flared between them, but it was gone too quickly to explain.

"I have to leave. If they find me here, or think that I've been here, they'll kill you and your sister."

"Who will?"

"The British."

"The Brit-" It all snapped into place. The satchel, his fear, his condition. "You're a spy." The words came out in a single breath.

He looked away from her, his eyes coming to rest on the door, "I have to go."

"But you can't walk. Your leg is broken. It will take several weeks to heal."

"I don't have that long."

Her mind knew that he was right. If he was a spy, he couldn't stay. Her heart, however, said something entirely different.

She looked down at his leg, gingerly placing a hand on the wooden splints that held it in place.

The flaring came again. She looked up to find his eyes blazing into hers.

She didn't look away as his eyes devoured hers. His gaze swept over her face, fell to her lips, studying them. She stood up straight, and turned away.

"At least let me feed you first before you go. You can't ride in your condition, but you are free to use our cart and horse, and I can give you father's old clothes."

She heard the table creak as he shimmied back into place and cleared his throat.

"I can't take those things from you."

"How can you say that with your leg in its condition?"

"I've survived up until now. I'm sure that I can do it a few more days."

She imagined him dragging himself through the hills. The thought brought tears to her eyes.

She wiped them away.

"Look at me, lass."

She turned again toward him, his eyes furrowing as they took in her tears.

"Don't worry about me. I'm a soldier. I will survive."

"How do you know?"

"I have to," he sighed. "When I passed by here the other night, I saw you in the window. You were reading. I remember the way the candle lit your face, the way you looked at me. I promised myself that I would be back for you. I made that promise once, and I'm making it again. I'll be back for you, Ashling."

She nearly dropped the bowl of soup she'd been holding.

"How do you know my name?" She asked.

He shook his head. "I don't know. How do you know mine?"

She frowned, handed him a bowl of soup. His eyes held hers for a beat too long.

"How did you know that I-"

"When I said it, you didn't look surprised. You looked like you were expecting it to be so. I don't know how, Ashling, but something tells me I need to be here, beside you. I won't argue with it. Will you?"

She put her hand to her coloring cheek, and watched as he put the bowl to his lips, his eyes never leaving hers. She found it hard to breathe.

He finished the soup, and wiped his mouth with his shirt sleeve. His eyes fell closed, a deep frown settling on his face. When he opened them again, he shook himself, and focused firmly on the broom across the room.

"Is something wrong?" She asked.

"No. Just..."

She took a deep breath. "Did you see me?" She asked. "Did you see us?"

He nodded slowly, confusion clouding his face.

"What did you see?"

He gently took her hand and placed it on his cheek, his eyes intent on hers.

Her body felt as if it had absorbed his fever.

"This." He led her to his lips and kissed her.

Her heart pounded. Her world collapsed, zeroed in until there was just them, just this moment in time. She leaned into him, and he pressed the kiss deeper, incinerating every thought and doubt. She wrapped her arms around his waist.

He felt right, brightening up her ordinary world like a shooting star on the darkest of nights.

He took her hand in his, kissed her palm, her wrist.

"Liam," she whispered.

His breath was warm against her fingers. "How could I forget you, my Ashling?"

Her world turned to fire. Her body tightened. Her lips ached for his to return to them.

"Liam," she whispered. "Oh how I've missed you."

A scream.

"Ashling!"

The door flung open. Soldiers swarmed into the room like locusts.

"He's here!" one of them shouted.

"Bring him out." The order came from outside the door.

Liam struggled to get up from the table. His leg collapsed under his weight when it hit the floor. He crumbled to the ground, screaming in agony.

The soldiers grabbed him under the arms and dragged him out.

"Run, Ashling!"

"Liam!" She threw herself at the officer who held him, fist pounding wildly on his back. "Let him go, you brute!"

A large, calloused hand shoved her to the ground. She hit her head hard against the table and groaned as the pain shot through her body.

She forced herself to rise through the pain, and stumbled out of the cottage. She had to find Bernie. She had to help Liam.

Bernie stood just outside the door, her hands tied behind her back. A red nosed soldier stood guard next to her.

"Let go of my sister!" Ashling screamed.

"Run, Ashling!" Bernie cried.

Another soldier came up from behind and grabbed her. Her arms twisted painfully behind her back. She watched in wide-eyed horror as a torch arched through the air and landed on top of her thatched roof.

"NO!" Ashling screamed.

"This is what happens when you harbor rebel spies," he growled.

Tears of outrage burned her eyes. *My home. My mother's things. My father's memories.*

The soldier spun her around, until she faced the tall oak tree out back. A rope hung from a low hanging branch, Liam's head was being forced into it. He precariously balanced one leg on a small stool.

"Liam no!" she cried.

A bearded soldier stood in front of him. The marks on the shoulders of his red coat told of his authority.

"Liam McGunntry, you are called forth on charges of spying and sedition against the crown. This is your last chance. Where is the satchel with the maps?"

Liam spat in the soldier's face.

"Ireland will never again stand for British rule!"

The soldier wiped at his face, and glared at Liam hatefully.

"Then, before God and the King, you are sentence to execution by hanging."

Ashling screamed.

Liam's eyes searched for hers. For a moment time stood still. There was only them, no longer strangers, but souls intertwined for eternity.

"Ashling!" Liam called.

She found no breath to answer. His eyes turned pleading.

"Find me in heaven."

The Captain kicked out the stool from beneath him. Liam's body swung wildly, his legs kicking, struggling to find solid ground. His face and neck turned purple as he choked.

Ashling let out a blood-curdling wail before a heavy hand struck the back of her head. The world started to tilt, spin and fade.

Her legs buckled. She fell to her knees.

"No!" Bernie cried. "No! Let me go! Ashling!"

Ashling hit the soft grass, her heart shattered. She wanted to cry, to scream, but her tongue felt like iron in her mouth.

He was gone.

Her head throbbed violently as if it was splitting open.

He was gone.

"Ashling!" Bernie called. "Ashling!"

The sound seemed to come from underwater, like she was drowning. It was all so far away. So distant.

Peace filled the last moment of her consciousness.

In heaven, Liam. In heaven.

With one last, valiant effort, with the last of her breath, she cried out his name, screamed it so that God and the angels could hear who she was meant for. So that they knew that it was Liam. It had always been Liam.

Then…

"Ashling? Ashling, are you okay?"

A voice in her ear. Someone was shaking her.

"Ashling. Ashling, wake up!"

Suddenly alert, Ashling shot up, her body covered in a dripping layer of icy sweat.

Bernie stood beside her, looking annoyed and a little worried.

But no, not Bernie. This woman possessed her sister's face, but not her clothes. She was dressed in a pink t-shirt and matching pink shorts.

"Are you okay? You were screaming."

Ashling's body felt heavy, and oddly detached, as if her body was here, but her mind was someplace far away.

"Bernie?"

"I'm here, babe." Bernie's eyes narrowed in concern. "Are you okay?"

Ashling looked around her.

The shelves in her tiny dorm room were heavy with books and magazines. Her laptop was on, the light from the screen glaring brightly. Her phone glowed too.

Confusion made her head ache.

This was real.

This was her life.

It all came back to her in a single, powerful wave.

She was a college student. This was her dorm. Bernie was her roommate. This was real. Her mind screamed at her. This, this is real.

And yet, the other world seemed real too. She still smelled the hay and the grass of her small farm. Felt the warmth of the fire in the hearth. Felt the heat of his eyes as they bore into hers and he sang her name: *Ashling*.

Bernie shook her head, her eyes glazed with confusion. "Ash, I'm going back to bed. You had a nightmare. Why don't you get some sleep, hun."

"It was a dream?"

Bernie nodded.

"But that means that Liam…"

"Are you sure you're okay?" Bernie asked.

Ashling gasped.

Liam.

He was an illusion, never really there at all. And yet, he felt so real.

The room began to spin, the walls pressing in on her. She had to get out. She had to escape. She jumped from her bed, snatched the door open, and ran down the hallway.

"Ashling, where are you going?"

She didn't reply.

Gone. It's all gone, her heart told her.

It was never really there, her mind reasoned.

The urge to beat her fist against something, to scream and cry until exhaustion overtook her was strong.

He's gone.

Head throbbing, she threw open the doors and plopped down on the steps of the dorm. She dropped her head into her hands. The tears came hard and fast in the chilly Spring air, a soft breeze cutting through her powder blue t-shirt and shorts.

Her mind battled with itself as it tried to sort out dream from reality.

It felt so real, she thought. How could he have felt so real?

A car parked near the door, its lights bouncing off of the windows of the building.

Ashling stood, wrapped her arms around herself, and began to walk as a gaggle of rowdy students jumped from the car. One of them called to her. She didn't turn around. She picked up her pace as a stronger breeze blew. The cold seemed to touch her soul. Goose bumps ran over her body in prickling waves.

She shook her head, anxious to clear it of the disturbing dream.

The wind blew stronger, and she looked up. She saw it.

The tree, the great oak that killed her beloved.

Sitting with his back against the tree, was a man. His raven hair and midnight eyes were unmistakable.

Her heart pounded, her breath stolen by the impossible vision before her.

It can't be, she thought. He was just a dream.

She took a tentative step forward.

"Liam?" she whispered.

The breeze carried her small voice to him, depositing the gift into his ears. He turned to her, his eyes growing wide in awe.

"Ashling?"

The Summer I

Found Love

By

Felicia Lewis

My family and I finished packing for our trip to Hawaii when my father called us all together for a family meeting.

"This is our annual vacation and this trip is going to be filled with lots of fun and adventure." My father is so animated, why is he thrusting his hands in the air like he is directing a musical."

Your mother and I will be entrusting you and your siblings to be on your best behaviors. You guys are older so you definitely can be on your own; just make sure you guys don't forget to pack your chargers. Or whatever else it is you kids use these days for communication purposes."

"Dad we have all that we need, I'm shaking my head in disbelief that my father would even think that we would forget something so precious as our chargers. I'm laughing on the inside so my dad won't think I'm not listening to his silly demands. You will not have to worry, and we know how to contact you and mom if we get lost." We all fell out laughing, now my sister Cher'ray is 19, Tracee is 18, my brother Rashad is 17, my other sister Ashlee is 16 and my two youngest siblings Taylor 15 and Cj 11 and then there was me Lexie. I'm 20, but I will be turning 21 in 3 months.

I'm hoping to have fun and just beach hop the whole entire time we are there; we all got in the truck and headed for the airport. My sisters and brothers were all talking and singing. I was looking out the window daydreaming. I was praying that I could actually finally find a summer love; I have never really had a boyfriend. Just because my parents always drilled in us kids heads that school and education is very important. If you don't have an education you won't get anywhere in life. Blah, Blah, Blah, Blah. That's all I really heard.

There will always be time for boyfriends and girlfriends later, that's all they ever told us. As all of our friends were hanging out and having fun, we were at home studying. I'm starting to get all these feelings. You know the ones between your thighs that can only be put out with hot, passionate sex. I would like very much to experience what I hear the other girls talking about. Just thinking about it is getting my panties very wet.

There is this girl named Trinity and she is always talking about her boyfriend Milan.

Now, Milan is fine as hell. He is tall, chocolate, and sexy and he got them dimples that you just want to stick your tongue in. He is also a football player. He is what you call a bad boy and all the girls drooled over him whenever he walked in the room. He had this way about him that you better not ever try and step to him wrong or you will get dealt with.

The talk around campus was that if you needed weed or pills Milan was the guy to see. Now personally, I don't know if that's true. I tend to try and stay away from that sort of crowd; they were always in the dean's office or in some other kind of trouble. My family would never allow me to see a guy like Milan. I could hear my father now; "Trinity that boy is bad news for you and I will not permit you to ever see him." I just rolled my eyes envisioning my dad saying such a thing.

But he being bad is what turned me on. He was the epitome of everything that could make my world right. I was walking to class but I needed to go to the restroom first. I overheard Trinity talking to one of her home girls; she was saying that Milan is a freak. He knows exactly how to put it down in or out of the bedroom.

When she said that I felt myself instantly getting very moist down between my thighs all these feelings that I'm certainly not used to having. She was explaining that Milan likes to take her to new sexual heights; he likes to lay her down on the floor. Shit I had to squeeze my legs real tight together; my clit was pulsating at that thought.

She went on to say he would slide his penis in her real slow and the more she talked the more I was becoming wetter. I knew I should have just left at that point, but I couldn't make myself leave I had to hear the rest of her story. Trinity is a gymnast. She is very flexible and it got real deep about just how Milan puts it on her. She said that she would sit on the floor and wrap both her legs around her neck. Milan would stand back and be impressed at the level of her flexibility. Then she would take her one leg as she lay on the floor and extended it over her shoulder, and spread the other one out alongside her. Damn I would have broken my darn back and legs trying to do something like that. I had to giggle at the thought of that.

She continued and I got even closer so I could make sure I heard everything.

He loved looking at her woman hood all exposed and for the taking. She said that he would do this little silly dance before he would come over and slide his dick all in her. He would take her and lay her back real gentle while her leg was still extended up above her neck. He put both of his hands on each one of her legs, like he was doing pushups inside her pussy.

That whole scene I played in my head. How I wish I had someone who would rock my most sensual parts that way. The whole time they were talking and she was explaining just how nasty they would get with each other, my hand crept between my thighs and found my clit. I started shaking and rubbing slowly at first then it got faster. I felt myself about to have that feeling that I loved to feel.

Fuck! It made me forget that I was standing right outside the bathroom door and at any moment someone could have come out or came in. I would have been caught with my hand in the cookie jar so to speak.

Ah yes Lexie get yourself there, I imagined that Milan's tongue was right there on my clit licking, sucking, nibbling, and kissing it. Oh yes, I'm about to cum oh my, that feels so good he is about to bring me to that place where I am about to cum all down his throat. I take his head and shove it deeper in my cunt. I start grinding real nasty on his tongue.

"Yes Milan. That's it. I'm Cuming. Let me cum, suck it out of me .Yesssss that's it right there."

My fingers were all slimy with all the cum that was on them, damn I need to go in and wash my hands. I pray I have hand sanitizer. Oh thank you, yes here it is.

I can't take not having a boyfriend. This is driving me absolutely crazy. It's nice to touch yourself, but it would be so much nicer to have that special boy get all those places you can't reach, deep up inside you. So, it's my mission to have a boyfriend before summer has ended.

Who am I kidding no one has even showed the slightest of interest in me. If they did I wouldn't have noticed I always had my head stuck in a book, or basketball practice. I had so many things to do to make my parents proud; I sort of lost who I was. Hopefully I can change that this summer, my own identity and not live in my parents shadow any longer.

We got to the airport, got through all the security, and made it to our plane just in time. We landed in Hawaii and were greeted by beautiful island women as we got off the plane. CJ and Taylor were so ready to get off that flight they literally ran through everyone. Each one of the greeters placed Lei's around our necks, they smelled so good. Watching my Father and Mother laugh and giggle, and be so in love with each other, was priceless.

I only hope to find a love like theirs one day. There was a time when my mother was really sick and dad didn't leave her side not once. He bathed her, washed her hair and made sure she ate. But the look in his eyes was always full of hope and love; he nursed her back to health. Talking about inseparable, that's exactly what my parents are; inseparable.

Whenever they are in each other's presence they act like two teenaged kids. He holds her hand and always stares at her like it is the very first time that he has ever seen her. We got to the hotel and immediately got to our room; we couldn't wait to get to the beach.

"Mom this hotel is beautiful, and these rooms are too die for." We had the penthouse suite so everyone had their own area. "Hey dad, I'm going to shower and hit the beach." I swing my head around the door frame so he could hear what I was saying.

"OK pumpkin just be careful. The rest of us are going to grab a bite to eat and then go and be tourist. You sure you don't want to tag along with us?" I look down at the floor as if I was thinking about it.

"No dad I'll catch up later." I dressed in a very pretty sundress and a pair of cute sandals. I settled on just wearing my hair down. I grabbed my sunglasses did a once over in the full length mirror and it was off to the beach.

When I arrived, there were a lot of people and everyone seemed to be having so much fun. I found a nice spot and decided to just sit and observe. It was very hot I must have fallen asleep, because I was awaken by a group of girls about my age who wanted to know if I wanted to come and hang out with them.

"Hello my name is Chelsey; this is Sierra, Debbie, Kimberly and Monica. Oh the silly looking kid running up on us is my brother Matt. We are sorry if we startled you."

"Hi I'm Lexie, nice to meet all of you; no it's fine I hadn't even realized I had fallen to sleep."

"So why are you sitting here all alone?"

"Technically I'm not alone. I'm here with my family, but they are back at the hotel grabbing something to eat. I just decided to come to the beach and hang out."

"Well come hang out with us; we are just going to go over to the Snack Shack and grab some Hawaiian Ice."

I stand up to dust the back of my dress off from all the sand that was on it, and slide my sandals back on.

"OK sounds good, let's go. Do all you guys live close?"

"Yes right up the hill closer to Pearl Harbor. We are all military brats." They all made these crazy faces. We all just started laughing. "We live on base, that's how we all met." We grabbed our Hawaiian Ice and got to know each other a little more

"So Lexie where are you from?"

"Los Angeles."

"Do you guys come to Hawaii often?"

"This is actually our 3rd time here." Matt was just staring at me. He was very cute, but seemed to be a bit shy.

The way he is looking at me is getting me all hot and bothered in a good way. I can already see the shower scene for me tonight; as usual I'll be bringing myself to an orgasm all alone again. I just shake my head in disbelief.

"You have to excuse my brother for looking at you so long."

"It's Okay."

"Matt just talk to her jeesh; she is going to think you are weird or something."

"Chelsey shut up! I can speak for myself. Hey Lexie we are all going to the movies later would you like to join us?"

"Yes that sounds like fun." We exchanged numbers and agreed to meet up later. "Alright guys I'm going to head back to the hotel before my parents send out a search party for me. I start laughing; I'll see you all tonight."

Matt says "It's a date."

"I smile at the thought of what he said. See you guys later."

I wonder if he really meant that, or was it just something to say. There I go again over analyzing everything. We all said our good byes until later; walking back to the hotel, I was thinking about Matt. He is very cute and seemed nice. I wonder if he is any good with his tongue. Why is my mind always resorting back to sex? But I really wondered if he was any good with his tongue. I kind of twisted my mouth like I was thinking about it.

"Hey Lexie wait up, I'll walk you back the sun is about to go down and I don't won't you to walk alone. Do you mind if I walk with you?"

"No it's fine." Matt asked what college I attended.

"University of California, are you in college?"

"No not right now, I'll be starting in the fall; for now, I'm helping out with the family business."

"Just what would that be?"

My family owns a few restaurants along the North Shore. I'll have to take you before you leave, would you like that Lexie?"

"I felt myself blushing.

Yes that sounds nice. Well this is me; I'll see you later tonight. I wanted us to talk a little bit longer."

"Great, my sister and I will come back to pick you around nine, is that cool?"

"Alright that will be fine; I'll meet you guys in the lobby. I turned and almost tripped trying to wave to him I know I must have looked pretty silly, I just slapped myself on the forehead and said bye."

"OK; see you later."

Wow that's weird, my stomach is doing all kind of flip flops; no I can't be interested in Matt. Maybe I am? I walked back to the room just smiling; I'm so glad I went to the beach today.

"Hey mom, hey dad where is everyone?" My dad said they are down at the pool.

"Why don't you put on your bathing suit and join them?"

"I can't."

"Why can't you young lady?" My mother said.

"I met some kids on the beach this afternoon and they asked me to go to the movies tonight."

"Oh, just be safe and have fun."

"I always am mom. I love you. Now, I got to go get showered and pick something pretty out."

*****

"She said pretty, it must be a boy going as well."

"Why would you say that honey?"

"You didn't see the great big smile plastered all over your daughter's face? It's a boy trust me." My husband just laughed and said it can't be Lexie has never even showed any interest in a young man. He starts stroking his chin trying to think if it could even be a possibility.

"My point exactly, she needs to get out there and have fun my dear. We have held her so close, always instilling in her that her schooling came first. She didn't have a normal childhood. Now, we can let her spread her wings and fly and find fun and adventure in her life. Our daughter will make her mistakes in life, but at the same time she will not want to disappoint us or herself. So, we just have to trust that all of our children will make the best decisions for their lives. Lexie needs this, and if this young man is making her smile like that; I'm all for it, and so should you. Our little girl is no longer our little girl, she is a grown woman. We have to trust that we raised a great young lady."

*****

What to wear? I packed lots of clothes, but why can't I find anything to wear? I was thinking about Matt. What if I was reading him wrong and he wasn't thinking about me the way I'm thinking of him.

I needed to stop racking my brain about Matt, so I can concentrate on what to wear. I just settled on a cute pair of peach shorts, a lacy white top, and a pair of sandals. It was already 8:15 and I had to hurry. I was meeting them in the lobby at 9:00. I hurried and did my hair. I put a little mascara on and a nude lip gloss. Ran my fingers through my hair and dashed out the room.

"How do I look mama?"

"Sweetheart you look very beautiful, be careful, and enjoy yourself." I made it downstairs in the nick of time; Chelsey and the girls were pulling up.

"Hi Ladies, hey Lexie you ready to go and have some fun?"

"Yes, did your brother decide not to come? Just my luck he didn't show up, that's the story of my life. I felt my heart drop in the middle of my stomach."

"He should be pulling up any minute. He doesn't like to ride with all of us so he brings his own car, here he is now."

Wow, he had a nice Range Rover. A big smile came across my face.

"Lexie would you like to ride with me?"

"Matt, she doesn't want to ride with you."

"It's OK. Chelsey I can ride with him; it's a little stuffed in your car anyway."

"That's cool, see you guys at the movies."

The girls took off Matt got out to open my door for me. Matt said "What if we skip the movie, and just go, and get a bite to eat?"

"But won't your sister and her friends be mad?"

"No, they'll be fine." There goes my stomach, he reaches in the back seat and pulls out a rose. "Here Lexie, this is for you. This is why it took me a little longer to get here. I wanted to stop and get you something nice."

"Thank you Matt, you didn't have to do that." I know he could tell I was blushing.

"Yes I did have to do that I want you to remember me when you leave."

My nipples instantly got so hard being this close to him, his cologne was taking over all my senses, and it was driving me insane and doing things to my vagina that I was really enjoying. I knew wearing a no panties wasn't a good thing because I was getting so wet.

"Matt is this a date?"

"I guess it is; this has never happened to be before."

"What do you mean you never been on a date? You are stunning."

"Thank you."

"I actually have not; my parents are very strict when it comes to dating. They didn't want anything to interfere with our education, so I missed all the dating stuff. I looked down at hands that I was squeezing very tightly to hide my embarrassment."

"Lexie are you telling me you never had a boyfriend? Matt took my hand in his."

"No, Matt I have never had a boyfriend."

"I hope you want to get to know me as much as I want to get to know you. We can see where this is going to take us, but for now let's have fun and enjoy this nice night."

"I blushed and said that will be nice, I like that."

We pulled up to this very lovely restaurant, "Matt this looks like you should have made reservations. My mouth literally flew open with how beautiful it was. It sat right on the beach surrounded by the ocean; it was something right out of a movie.

"Well you're right; you do have to make reservations. I'm sure they'll make an exception for us."

"Matt we can't, I go to pull his hand back."

"Yes we can, you just have to trust me."

We walked into this beautiful restaurant it was breathtaking. "Hey Matt so this is the reason you took off tonight?"

"Dad this is Lexie, Lexie this is my Dad- Howard."

"It is very nice to meet you young lady. She is beautiful son, I'm glad to know you have great taste."

"Thank you. His dad was a tall handsome gentleman I see where Matt gets his good looks from.

"No need to thank me young lady; if a young lady is beautiful she needs to be told that."

"It's very nice to meet you Mr. Howard."

"Stop with the Mr. just Howard will be fine. Well come on you two I have the best seats in the house for you tonight."

He sat us by gorgeous picturesque window with the view of the ocean. I could barely contain my smile I was so happy to be here with him.

"Thanks dad, this is great. Is this to your liking madam Lexie? Is this fine?"

"Matt it's beautiful."

We talked for a bit and laughed a lot. The dinner was great, what else could a girl ask for. This is an awesome night. I got to meet Matt's mother. She is a very nice lady and his other sisters and brothers they were very cool.

"Matt is it true?"

"Is what true?"

"Your mother said that you have never brought a girl to the restaurant ever."

"Yeah, I just never thought a girl was worth bringing to the restaurant or meeting my parents was important until now.

"He took me in his arms when he said that to me."

Would you like to walk on the beach for a little while? It's very nice at this time. I have something I want to show you."

"It's getting late and I don't want my parents to worry."

"OK; that's fine we can do that tomorrow."

Besides I was afraid that if we got to the beach and I was feeling like I was feeling down there, I would have to have Matt put the fire out that was stirring between my legs. It was definitely too soon for that, but damn I wanted him to touch and kiss me so bad. As we were driving back down the mountain, he pulled over to show me one of the most amazing mountains.

"Look up and tell me what you see."

"Oh wow, Matt its looks like a giant man sleeping."

"You're exactly right; it is what we call the sleeping giant mountain."

"It's beautiful Matt. We stood there and stared at it for a moment. Wow that's crazy it really looks like a giant man taking a nap."

"Let me get you back, we'll have more time to spend together tomorrow."

"Thank you so much for a great evening."

"Lexie it was my pleasure."

Riding back to the hotel, we talked and laughed it honestly felt like something out of a dream. You would have thought we knew it each other all of our life. Is this what I've been missing out on? Having friends and hanging out, my siblings meant the world to me. I love them and all, but I like doing stuff like this as well.

Matt held my hand the whole way back and to be honest it felt so good. I had tingles and goose bumps; it was a great feeling and a weird feeling all at the same time.

"Where here, tomorrow Lexie if you're up to it I would like to actually take you to the movies."

I laughed. "Matt that will be nice."

"OK I'll pick you at three. I have to go into work for just a couple of hours in the morning. Then, maybe we can catch the sun going down on the beach?

"Sounds like the perfect date. Oh, I'm sorry for implying that it would be a date."

"Lexie you never have to be sorry for anything like that. It is very true it would be a date."

It made me feel really good that he saw me as a girl he would like to date.

"Ok then, I'll see you tomorrow; drive safe. Please apologize to your sister and her friends for me for us not showing up at the movies tonight."

"She cool, but I'll make sure I let her know."

"Hey Lexie what's your number? I can call you when I get in."

"That will be good, where is your phone? I'll just put my number in it."

"Where is that phone, here it is.

"I take his phone and put my number in it and hand it back."

Great I'll call you as soon as I get in."

Matt called just like he said, and we ended up talking on the phone for four hours. This was all so new to me, I'm enjoying it. I woke up at about 11 o'clock, only to find my family down by the pool. I went and grabbed something to eat before breakfast was over. I went back out with my family at the pool.

"Lexie, Yes, Tracee who was that cute boy you were with last night."

None of your business, I start laughing.

Here comes my other sister Ashlee to put her two cent in.

Ashlee says Lexie why you come in the room all late.

"Ashlee why are you so nosey?"

"You and Tracee always got to be in my business."

"Where is Che'ray?"

"She wanted to go the mall and rack up on some sales." We said at the same time she went for makeup.

"All three of us began to laugh, that's exactly what she is doing."

"Well, since you guys must know that boys' name is Matt and he is very nice."

Here comes mom.

"Dear, will we be meeting you friend?"

"Actually mom you will. He will be picking me up at three and I'll introduce you all to him then. Dad and Rashad will you please be nice and don't do anything to embarrass me?"

My brother Rashad said, "Girl nobody is going to embarrass you." He puts a smirk on his face.

"You better not this means a lot to me."

"Dad, how about you?"

"Well honey, I'm not going to promise you anything you are my daughter and I need to know you're safe, and that he is good enough for my little girl."

"Oh God dad I'm safe, and daddy I'm not a little girl anymore. But I'll always be your responsible daughter."

"No my child you will always be daddy's little girl no matter how old you get, got it?"

"Yes dad, that made me roll my eyes and shake my head."

"Mom please don't let dad and Rashad scare my friend."

"I won't baby, you just bring the young man to meet us and I'll handle your dad and your brother."

"Thanks mom." I licked my tongue out at my brother. "OK, who is ready to swim?"

We all jumped in the pool and had fun; my crazy brother went around dunking all of us. Mom and dad were in a space all on their own.

"Sorry guys I got to leave, I have to go get dressed for my date." I looked at my siblings and started laughing.

Even to me it sounds funny, my youngest brother Cj is always messing with me; he starts singing Lexie and Matt sitting in the tree k.i.s.s.i.n.g. "Whatever CJ move boy so I can go get dressed if you say that when Matt comes, you'll be sorry; I would advise you not to fall asleep tonight."

Mom! Lexie just threatened me!"

"Boy get your behind over here and finish playing and leave your sister alone. Lexie go get dressed we'll see you in a minute."

What to wear, what to wear; I forgot I bought a very cute outfit. The shirt is a pretty blue with slits on the side, and the shorts were white. I paired it with a cute pair of criss cross gold sandals. I put my hair in a high ponytail with a sloppy bun. Yes bitch you look cute; I snap my fingers and headed down to the lobby.

Matt was there right on time. I introduced him to my family and they were on their best behavior.

I have to remember to thank my mother later. "See you guys."

"You kids have a good time."

"We will sir and ma'am, you ready Lexie?"

"Yes Matt."

"You look really nice."

"Thank you so do you."

Matt had on a pair of linen tan shorts with a white tee and some all-white Jordan's, his chocolate skin was mesmerizing and he smelled so damn good.

"Thank you, I hope you like action packed movies or do you like the mushy stuff?"

"I just happen to like both, thank you very much; well the choice will be yours."

It seems like all we've been doing is laughing and that's a good thing. We got to the movies and it was an easy decision, I chose the Fast and the Furious 7. Matt apparently wanted to see that as well, with the big smile that came across his face.

"Great movie pick." he said. I really liked Matt; he made my heart skip a beat.

We found our seats and talked for a bit until the movie started. I put my hand on Matt's leg and noticed that it was resting on his penis, damn this boy was big.

I said, "Oh Matt I'm so sorry!"

He said, "No problem, it's ok just let me shift him over."

"You don't have to."

He looked at me and just smiled. Oh, ok cool.

Great the movie is starting this was about to get real awkward. It took everything in me not to start stroking Matts dick it felt so good and my pussy was getting so wet. I was imagining that I had got on the ground in between his legs and pulled out his penis and stuck it in my mouth to deep throat it. I got so lost in my thoughts I didn't even notice that Matt was saying my name.

Excuse me Matt I must have drifted off I'm sorry.

No that's fine I was just saying that they did a great job with this movie, but I don't think there should be another one.

"I think if they did do another one they should maybe go in a different angle. But this was perfect and how they showed Paul respect was awesome."

We really enjoyed the movie it was great, that tribute to the late Paul Walker was so nice it made me cry; see you again was a nice added touch. It kind of reminded me, of

Matt and me, just because our vacation was coming to an end in two days.

I do not want to ever not feel this feeling that I'm having for him. I only wish I could stay and make this a forever type of thing. Matt noticed that I was getting sad. "What's wrong Lexie you didn't enjoy the movie?"

"Quite the opposite, I enjoyed it a lot."

"Well what's wrong? My family and I will be leaving the island in two days."

"That is really soon. I just got a thump in my throat when you said that Lexie; I don't want you to leave. You are the perfect girl for me."

"I feel the same way about you, but what do we do? I felt the tears about to come."

"Besides write a lot, call, and try to visit when we can, I don't know how that will work."

"My mother has a saying Lexie."

"What is that?"

"She says will there is a will there is a way. I never really understood what that meant until just now."

Matt took me in his arms, and before I knew it; I was having my very first kiss. Omg this is actually happening, I found love this summer. I know it hasn't been a long time, but something tells me, when you know it, you know it.

I can tell Matt felt something strong after that kiss as well. He said to me, "Lexie I love you."

I love you too Matt is that crazy? But I feel you so strong in my heart.

He took me to a beautiful beach where we walked hand in hand staring at the stars. It was magical, we kissed and fondled each other in the sand; it got hot and heavy real quick.

I was ready to do something I always dreamed of doing. "Matt I want to take you on wave."

"Babe what does that mean?"

"It means close your eyes, just relax, lay back, and ride this wave with me."

He laughs and says. "Don't hurt me."

It was the perfect night; no one was on this side of the beach. I kissed all down his chest. I was doing things to him that I only seen in the movies or read about. I made sure I placed just the right amount of kisses going down his stomach; he took his hands, and stroked my hair. He was ready for whatever I was going to do to him.

My nerves was getting the best of me, I didn't want to mess this up. I continued to kiss all over his chest and down his stomach. He stopped me and looked me in my eyes. "Lexie, you don't have to do this."

"Matt I want to do this."

He laid back down. I got right on top of him and slid my body down. I unzipped his pants and started kissing him-his penis was so hard and I was ready for this task. I was remembering exactly what I read about sucking dick and making it come alive in your mouth; his penis was already sticking out of his boxer. Oh it looked so nice; it was ready for me to put it in my mouth.

I put the tip of it on my lips and started kissing it. I took it in my mouth real slow and used my tongue to slide around the base. Matt must have been enjoying it he was moaning and saying something. I was soaking my panties. I accidently scrapped my tooth on it. "Ouch"

"Shit I'm sorry are you ok?"

"It's ok." I went back and started sucking slow until I felt myself getting a groove. I picked up the pace just a little bit more and my rhythm got better and better.

I was sucking it like a pro, Matt was really into it. "Lexie you're going to make me cum."

"That's ok let me taste it, cum down my throat."

"Yes suck it just like that slide your tongue up and down my shaft faster. That's it Lexie that's it; uggggg I'm cuming!" He grabbed my neck very tight and unloaded his cum all down my throat.

He quickly came up and flipped me on my back raised my skirt up and start doing to me what I always wanted. He was eating my honey pot so good and it is feeling awesome.

"Oh Matt, yes Matt suck it! Lick it oh my yes that's it, shit I like that!" I was grinding my pink kitty all on his tongue; he reached up and started squeezing my breast.

Damn, I was enjoying this. I was so wet it was pouring out of me like liquid and Matt was sucking it all up. "Matt, Matt I'm about to cum right now, suck it, suck it, and suck it some more. I'm cummmmming!" I had beads of sweat dripping from my forehead and my legs were shaking all I can say is that was earth shattering.

Matt came up and laid beside me on the sand we had to catch our breath that was everything I ever could have imagined.

Matt's body looked so good under the moon light. He is very much ripped his chest was heaving up and down very fast, our hearts were racing, and we were in total ecstasy. "Lexie I want your first time to be special, I don't want to take your virginity on the beach, let me make that day special for you ok?"

Damn I thought I was going to finally get my cherry popped. See that's why I love you say all right things to me.

I wanted to say so bad Matt please let's just do it, but I didn't.

"That will be perfect, thank you for wanting my day to be special."

The night was magical.

We played in the sand, we lay in the sand, and we talked about our future. Oh God, how was I going to be able to leave him and not fall apart? Matt must have been reading my mind because he said to me.

"We will work this out; do you trust what I'm telling you?"

"Yes Matt I do."

For the two days we had left, we were together and when we were not together we were on the phone. The day I was to leave it was heartbreaking, I was crying uncontrollably. It felt like my heart stopped, Matt came to see me off; he looked me straight in my eyes and said do you trust me?

Through the tears I said yes I do. Before I left; Matt asked me to be his girl. I jumped up in his arms and screamed yes, I will be delighted to be your girlfriend Matt. My mother, father, and siblings all looked and smiled. We said our good byes, I couldn't stop staring at Matt, and I was going to indeed miss him.

He kept his promise. We talked every day, we skyped every night after his shift at the restaurant. But it was so hard not seeing him, fall semester was coming up really soon and my birthday. I have no idea when we are going to be able to have the time to communicate. Matt was starting school in the fall, and so was I; we continued to talk and Skype and pray.

That time would fly by, just so we could be with each other. My birthday was in three days, and I was sad that I couldn't be with my boyfriend. At exactly 12 midnight, Matt called to wish me a happy birthday.

He told me to get some rest because he knew I was going to have a busy day. He was right my parents planned this extravaganza of a dinner for me at my favorite restaurant.

My mom said "Baby girl it will be ok, I want you to enjoy yourself tonight. This is your 21st birthday and Matt wouldn't want you to be sad."

If mom only knew I was screaming on the inside.

"I'll try mom but it's going to be hard, I miss him so much it hurts."

"I know baby, but what you have to remember is where there is a will there will always be a way."

"That's weird; Matt said that's the same thing his mother says."

"Then she must be a very smart woman. Come on, and let's go have some fun."

"Your right mom, I'll be ready in five minutes."

"Dear our reservations are at 8 o' clock and its 7:15 right now."

"Mom it takes less than 15 minutes to get there."

"I know you just hurry along. We will be waiting in the car."

I hurried, put my shoes on, and grabbed my purse. Gave myself the once over in my full length mirror, this dress was beautiful that I had on. It is a midnight blue sequined dress right above the knee with a deep v in the back. My boyfriend would have loved to have seen me in this I have to make sure we take lot of pictures. I was out the door and in the car in ten minutes. Okay I'm here, let's go."

"Daddy's girl looking so pretty and grown up, my where did they time go? Just yesterday you were begging me to take you out for ice cream and today you're a grown woman. I'm so proud of you Lexie and the beautiful woman you turned out to be."

"Thank you daddy, I'll always be your little girl."

"You promise?"

"Yes I promise."

"We got to the restaurant by 7:50." Mom said stay right here we have a surprise for you.

"What is it mom?"

"Just wait you'll see." I watched my mom walk off and she returns with Matt.

My eyes got big; I couldn't believe he was actually here.

I started crying immediately, "Matt! Omg mom and dad thank you, thank you! How did you guys pull this off without me knowing? When did you have time to do this mom and dad? Omg, omg this is the best birthday ever!"

Matt took me in his arms and said where there is a will there is a way. His kiss felt like heaven. "Ok guys that's just nasty we are in a restaurant."

"Of course CJ, you would say that."

"You wouldn't understand, but you will one day. When you're a lot older you will find the girl of your dreams, and you will kiss her, and you are not going to care who sees you." We all laughed.

"Come on kids our table is ready." It goes to say I had a great time.

My birthday wish came true, Matt is here to celebrate it with me, and he said I have three more presents for you. He whispered in my ear you will get that one later."

"Matt you didn't have to buy me anything."

"Yes I did your my girl," He said "First gift."

"Omg, Matt this is beautiful!"

It is a diamond heart necklace with a star in the middle of it.

I kissed his sexy lips. "Thank you so much, but you didn't have to spend this much on me."

"My girl deserves the best and the best is what you shall have. Besides I saved up all summer for your gift. When I seen it, I knew I had to get it for you on your birthday, I'm so glad you like it."

"No Matt I love it, like I love you. Can you please put it on me?"

Yes turn around.

"Thank you."

"Here is your second gift."

He handed me a brochure of the University of California.

"I'm confused this is the college I'm attending.

'Open it up."

You Matt McDaniel have been accepted at the University of California fall semester. Matt is this for real? "Yes it better be for real my parents already paid my tuition."

I totally jumped in his arms and said we are going to be in college together. This was definitely the best birthday.

"Wait but school doesn't start for another week, where will you stay until then?"

"The school let me move into my dorm a little early, with a push from your pops. Thanks again for that Mr. Macy; my dad and mother really appreciate you going to great lengths for me."

"No problem at all son, you make my daughter happy and besides you're a very nice young man."

"Dad thanks."

"No thanks needed baby girl. Who am I to keep away young love? Now you kids go and have a great time."

"Thanks for dinner and helping me to surprise Lexie for her birthday Mr. And Mrs. Macy."

"No thanks needed son, you make our daughter happy and that is all that matters is her happiness."

"Yeah mom and dad you're the best." I gave my mom, dad and my siblings hugs before we left.

Matt and I went to a dance club and danced the night away, we had so much fun; I didn't want the night to end. He had some really good moves out there on the dance floor. "Are you thirsty?

"Yes, come on let's get something to drink and then go back and dance."

We finished our drinks; the DJ was really good; he started playing a slow song by Rihanna called Stay. Matt grabbed my hands, twirled me on the dance floor, and held me real close. I snuggled my head on his shoulder, it was the best feeling ever; I felt his dick swell against my pelvis and it was everything for me not to grab it on the dance floor shit I think I am getting dizzy.

Why couldn't we stay like this forever?

The song ended much too soon, I never wanted to leave his embrace it just felt right. Matt felt right for me, who would have known us going to Hawaii, would have landed me a great guy. The club was about to close, and we were both very tired, it was a long day. It was a very rewarding day but long. We made our way through the club and out the door.

Matt opened my car door for me; I slid over and opened his.

He got in and we just sat there for moment talking. "Lexie can I please kiss you?"

"You better, I have been waiting to do this since we left the restaurant." Again his kiss was mesmerizing, now I have never kissed anyone, but Matt but I'm so sure it wouldn't have felt anything like this.

"Thank you so much for the wonderful evening, I love my gifts; you guys really surprised me."

"But I told you there are three gifts; you already got two now it's time for your last gift."

"Where are we going Matt?"

"Do you trust me?"

"Well of course you know I do." We drove to the dorms. I didn't ask any more questions. I just waited impatiently.

"I have to blind fold you."

"Huh?"

I have never been blindfolded before but this is exciting so I will go with the flow of things.

"Yes turn around. Please, this won't hurt a bit."

"You are so funny."

"Not really at all. We both start laughing"

"Almost there, stay right here until I come and get you."

"Matt you just want me to stand here blindfolded while you leave?"

"This will only take a minute I promise."

"Just hurry up Matt."

*****

Ok let me get all these candles lit, I'm scrambling all around my room. All I had was a bed, a chair, and a desk; so trying to turn this room into something spectacular was hard. It will be well worth it, if Lexie likes it and enjoys herself. Rose petals all over the bed check, candles lit check, lilac scented aroma in the air check, music check. Ok this looks good if I do say so myself. I pat myself on the back for the great job I did for pulling this together in less than 24 hrs.

"Lexie are you ready baby?"

"Yes you had me out here for ten whole minutes Matt."

"I'm sorry but I promise you will like it, I hope."

Can you please take this blindfold off now?

"Yes come here, stand right here." Matt takes my blindfold off and I was taken aback.

"Matt this is beautiful!"

He turns me around and puts his hands on my waist and tells me this is for our special night.

"Do you approve? Is this ok that I did this?"

"Matt this is absolutely more than ok.

"You are so beautiful, and you are everything I ever imagined for my life. God couldn't have picked a better queen just for me."

He tilts my head up so our lips would meet; he kissed me with such a passion, I got lost in it for a moment, I got so caught up in the kiss I hadn't even noticed that he lead me over to the bed. He slowly undressed me, when my dress hit the floor he gasped. "Lexie you are so gorgeous."

I lay back on the bed. I'm nervous, but I'm ok I know Matt is going to be gentle with me. Kissing me and touching me in places that at one time I only touched myself. His lips explored my neck, my shoulders, each one of my breast; he took my nipples in his mouth and sucked on them just right.

I arched my back and spread my legs. "Are you ready?"

My pussy was so wet and I was ready but I was nervous as hell. I had to brace myself Matt is huge and this wasn't going to be easy. Stop it Lexie and just relax I said to myself.

"Yes I am ready."

He stood up and undressed, oh my man look so good he took off his shirt, his chocolate skin and his 6'3 frame towering over me, with the candles illuminating off of him just made him look more sexy. I was so wet and ready for him to mount me. He came over and began kissing up my legs, my inner thighs until he found that spot to surely make me lose my mind.

He sucked on my clit, flicked his tongue back and forth that made me spread my legs wider and arch my back deeper. "Ah, ah, ah Matt baby that feels so good please don't stop sucking my pussy." It's all I could do not fall off the bed.

Matt knew exactly how to eat me, he was playing with my nipples, and he came up to my breast so he could pay close attention to them both.

"Yes I'm ready, but first come put your dick in my mouth. I want to suck you really bad right now." I'm sucking his dick and he is letting me know that he is feeling good and he is pumping faster and faster.

"I'm ready baby; my pussy is on fire it's so wet I have been anticipating this day for a long time."

I spread my legs and arched my back. My king was coming to rescue me; he took his time entering me. "Are you ok baby?"

"Yes I am, it hurts so bad but whatever you do, do not stop! Ah, Mmmmmmm oh!" When he finally got it all the way in it was the best feeling ever.

We got lost in each other and he took me on heights I would have never expected to go. His kisses were so passionate. The way he was rocking my vagina walls was so invigorating and perfect with each motion. I wanted this feeling to last forever. "Oh, Matt yes just like that baby." He started pumping me faster and I was meeting his every thrust.

I felt him swell even more, the wetter I got the more excited he became, he was sucking and biting my nipples, I was pulling his ass in to me even more. I wanted to feel his entire dick inside me. I wrapped my legs around his waist, pushed my pelvic up and then down. I started closing my pussy on his dick and he couldn't take that for very long.

"Baby you are going to make me bust all inside you."

"Oh Matt, I'm Cuming right now don't stop fucking me do it just like that. Yessssssssss Ah, ah, ah, ah." Damn we came at the same time.

He rolled off of me and took me in his arms, kissed my neck, he told me just how perfect I was for him. I told him the same; we confessed our love for each other and fell to sleep. When I got up it was six in the morning. Oh shit my parents are going to freak out. Matt woke up delirious we scrambled to find our clothes and rushed out his room.

We made plans for later on in the day, so I could help him shop and get his dorm ready.

Mom and Dad were still asleep when I got in, thank goodness. I tipped to my room and got in the shower and rested up for a while until it was time to go meet Matt.

We found some great stuff at Pier One and Ikea. I love those stores. We went back to his dorm to start decorating and after we finished we left to go grab a bite to eat. We came back to his room, talked, and laughed some more. We started kissing and kissing lead to foreplay and that lead to another hot and heavy fuck session.

School started and it was exciting, Matt and I's schedule was very hectic. We made time to see each other on the weekends, and dinners at my house in the evening. I truly enjoyed every moment we spent together; our time went by fairly quickly. We graduated, found great jobs; bought our house and married. We are expecting our first child in December.

Who would have ever thought my summer love would have turned out to be my lifetime love? I hope everyone that's reads my story about my summer I found love will make you excited about life. You only live once and you should enjoy every minute with someone you truly love. Love will always mean finding that one true person you can't live without.

Sincerely,

Lexie

From Sunrise to Sunrise

By

Darryl J. Johnson

Men are so funny.

All that macho and bravado and arrogance, it's a wonder they can accomplish anything. I don't know why they can never admit when they are wrong. If Jesse hadn't been so intent on proving his manhood, he would have never even dared to challenge me on my knowledge of Stevie Wonder. Come on now, e'rybody with breath in their lungs should acknowledge that I am the Queen of all Stevie knowledge and I keep a running catalog in my head of albums, songs, lyrics, release dates, and general Stevie trivia. Hell, I could even name any Stevie tune in three notes.

Don't step to the kid unless you are really sure of your bidness, cuz mama will have to embarrass you, and that's not ever pretty. Seriously, who on earth would even have the nerve to suggest that the birthday tribute to Dr. King wasn't released on an album? Everybody knows it was on Hotter than July, side two, the last track. Duh, that's Steveland Morris 101. I don't know what got into Jesse that day; usually he's not prone to being competitive, but he insisted that he was right and it was winner take all. Imagine the look on his face when I pulled out my album, that's right, I said my vinyl copy of the album and played it for him on my record player.

You heard me, my record player.

What did we bet? Well, the loser had to fulfill all the winner's sexual fantasies for twenty-four hours. Yeah, that's right, from sunrise to sunrise. Not a bad prize at all for something that took no effort on my part. I planned on making him work for it, too. On Wednesday, I gave him the list of things I wanted him to do. I spelled out every detail of what I wanted. I wanted to be awoken with his tongue on my clit, licking me to orgasm, I wanted to cum in public, I wanted to have at least one anal orgasm, and I wanted him not to cum for the entire twenty-four hours, no matter what I did to him. Pretty straight forward. pretty simple. He had three full days to prepare so there would be no surprises. He had an evil grin on his face for the rest of the week, planning and teasing me. Saying that I was going to be in a world of trouble. Uhmmm, I think he was missing the point. I was the person who won the bet. I was the person that was going to get all my fantasies; I was the one that was going to be able to cum. If anyone was in trouble, it was going to be him.

We decided that the twenty-four hours would start at 8AM on Saturday and last until 8AM on Sunday. That Friday night, you would have thought that he was trying to make me into an Acrobat with Universoul Circus. He was flipping me and fucking me every which way till Sunday. He was working out everything he needed to be ready for his twenty-four hours of sexual servitude without release and who was I to stand in his way? If I could be there to help him release all his sexual energy, well, a woman's gotta do what a woman's gotta do. That's just me, Ms. Altruism, always thinking of others, benevolent to a fault. After all, isn't that what a great relationship is all about, compromise?

Seriously, Jesse had the stamina of a teenager and the technique of a Tantric master that night. I came so many times -I think I passed out.

I vaguely remember saying to myself, "Damn, I'm going to have to sleep in the wet spot because I am going to soak the sheets from cumming so many times."

I also vaguely remember him pulling out and shooting all over my stomach and feeling him clean me up with a warm wash cloth, but honestly, I was in such bliss, I couldn't swear in a court of law if he slept in the wet spot or if I did because I slept like a baby all night, knocked out, completely satisfied. It was the kind of sleep you can only get after a couple rounds of intensely satisfying sex.

I felt the sun coming through the window, warming my face, but that was most certainly not the first sensation that I awoke to that morning. As I began to stir, I could feel Jesse living up to his first assignment. I kept my eyes closed for a while, just languishing in the sensation, moaning ever so slightly. I was coming out of a peaceful slumber and I was well on my way to cumming again. I looked down and could see my baby camped out, making a breakfast buffet of my pussy. He took his fingers, spread my lips, and softly licked my hardened clit.

"Good morning," I moaned as I grabbed his head and held it tight to my mound. His tongue flicked quickly back and forth over my sensitive spot and I almost jumped out of my skin. I couldn't even concentrate on holding his head because I was pulling my nipples, twisting them, and humping my pussy on his mouth.

"Good morning to you, sleepy head," he said as he looked up momentarily, his face glistening with my juices. "You'll excuse me, but I have to get back to work."

With that, his mouth went into over drive, licking my pussy in ways I don't think I have ever had it licked before. With just the right pressure, he sucked my clit, with just the right rhythm, he licked it too. He drove his tongue deep inside me and I fluttered and flicked me to the edge of orgasm.

I was beside myself, losing my mind. "Oh dear God that feels delicious, what the hell are you doing to me? Whatever you do, don't you dare stop, don't you dare fucking stop. That feels so fucking good."

I was bucking my hips in the air and Jesse had his arms around my thighs, holding on for dear life. I felt the sensations start, I felt the heat and the tingling at the same time. My breathing started getting more labored, I shut my eyes tightly and I was lost to the pleasure.

"Oh baby, here it comes, I'm going to fill your mouth with my sweet pussy juice baby. Oh fuck, don't stop, yes, no, oh shit, agrhhhh."

My body trembled with pleasure and I rode the wave. I glanced over and looked at the clock and it said 9. I had to wonder if he had been licking my pussy for an hour, if he had started late, or if had passed out again from such an intense orgasm.

I wanted to just lie there and bask in the afterglow of post climatic bliss. Jesse had other plans. Good Lord, what did I do to deserve that man? I could smell the coffee brewing and the aromas of something really delicious. I stumbled to the kitchen on wobbly legs and breakfast was waiting. That wasn't part of the deal, but who was I to complain? Everything looked great, champagne, omelets just the way I liked them, and chocolate chip muffins. What else could I ask for? I could have asked for a moments reprieve, actually. Jesse made me take off my robe and eat in the nude, which would have been rather decadent and fun if he hadn't been playing with my nipples constantly.

Nothing gets me aroused more than having my nipples stimulated and he would put marmalade on them, suck it off, driving me insane with lust in the process, getting my pussy incredibly wet, and go back to feeding me. I couldn't take the teasing; it was too intense. Every time he would pinch and lick and suck my nipples, I would beg for him to ram his fingers in my pussy, and finger fuck me. I was begging and pleading for him to just throw me on the table and fuck me.

"Jesse Lamont, if you don't fuck me here and now I'm going to scream. Stop teasing me."

He smiled at me like he didn't even acknowledge what I was saying. It was more than obvious he was in control and he wasn't going to let me cum, let alone fuck me like I wanted to be fucked.

After breakfast, we made it to the shower to get ready for the day. I'd already had one of the most intense orgasms of my life first thing, my pussy was swollen and wet from being aroused during breakfast. Taking a shower with him was almost too much to take. Jesse's body makes me weak in the knees on any given day. That incredible brown skin, those shoulders, that chest. I can't take it; he's so beautiful. I fall in love with him over and over again every time I see him smile. Okay, damn, let me focus so I can tell you what else happened. So, here we were, in the shower, and he's soaping up my body with his incredible hands, running them over my flesh, down my back. Things get a little heated and we start kissing, his tongue is exploring my mouth, I'm grabbing his dick and I'm stroking him, I can see his eyes roll back in his head as I squeeze his hard shaft and start using both hands in a steady rhythm, the suds providing the perfect slippery sensation as he's grabbing my ass and telling me not to stop. I was rolling his balls around on my fingers and he was rubbing my clit and biting on my neck.

Jesse grabbed my shoulders, turned me around, and pushed me against the wall. He grabbed my hips and I could feel the hot water running down my back. I braced myself, feeling my hardened, aching nipples on the cold tile.

"You are going to give me some of this pussy, right here, right now," he said, and he took his dick and slammed it in me in one thrust.

I let out a moan like a wounded animal and it was met with a grunt from him that reverberated in the tiny space. His dick felt delicious, sliding in and out of me, hitting my spot, pounding me, and stroking me. I was backing my ass up on him and it was all I could do to hold on. My knees were shaking and all I could feel was pleasure. When, without notice, he pulled out and fell against the far wall, squeezing his dick. I couldn't even think straight, I was so close to cumming and I just wanted to feel that explosion. He stumbled out of the bathroom before I could collect myself and it took me more than a few minutes to regroup.

By the time I made it back to the bedroom, Jesse was halfway dressed and had my clothes laid out on the bed. That's not something he usually does so I figured it was part of the special day. I really didn't care what I was supposed to be wearing, I was too caught up in the fact that I was ready for this little dare to be over. The more I tried to tease him, to get him to throw me on the bed and fuck me, the more he pushed me away, telling me that he had plans for us. I can't remember the last time I was this turned on, and my pussy felt so swollen and wet. I was aroused in a way you can only experience when you are truly in love and completely at ease with someone.

He left me there to get dressed. It was a whole new outfit, tags and all. He knows my taste, that's for damn sure, the white linen skirt was long, to the floor, but it had a really high slit up one leg. The salmon colored shirt showed off the girls but not too much. I noticed that there was only a bra and no panties so I assumed that it was intentional. I slid on the sexy little sandals and I had to admit he did a great job. It was really a very cute outfit; I couldn't have done better myself. When I was dressed, he grabbed my hand and we headed off to the local coffee shop hand in hand. Java Jazz was our little hide away. They played amazing Jazz and had open mic nights and in this cozy little enclave that had sinful pastries and free Wi-Fi access. We settled in on one of the sofas and got the paper. I was oblivious, reading letters to the editor when Jesse reached over, put his hand on my exposed thigh, and whispered, "Spread your legs for me." In an instant, I was aroused again, but this time, I was looking around to see who could see us. There were a few college students deep in their books and another couple sitting at a table not far away, engrossed in each other. I tried to push his hand away, but there was no use.

"Baby, come on, enough is enough, this was fun and all but the game is over, we don't have to keep this up." I was nervous and tingling with anticipation all at the same time.

He looked me deep in my eyes and slowly said, "Spread your legs for me," and I'll be damned if my legs didn't respond to his command automatically.

Paranoid we were going to be arrested, and knowing damn well that I'm not the quietest person in the world when I cum, I was trying to concentrate on watching the reactions of the other people. It had always been my fantasy to be daring, to be somewhat of an exhibitionist, but to not get caught. All I had to do was look at Jesse and he made everything seem okay. I turned to face him and spread my legs. He kept his focus directly on me; he didn't divert his gaze for a moment. His confidence made me that much more aroused as I felt his fingers spread my lips. I bit my lower lip and tried to muffle a moan and I realized it was going to be a lot more difficult than I had originally thought to be discrete. The way I was seated, I was sure no one could tell his hand was under my skirt but my heart was racing so fast it was damn near pounding out of my chest.

I bit my lip and tried my best to muffle my moans. Jesse had a sly smile on his face and he kept whispering things in my ear.

"Damn, your pussy is so wet...mmmm... Does that feel good right there? Is that your spot baby? Are you going to cum for me?"

His fingers were probing deeper and my breathing was getting more labored. I glanced over and the couple that was previously engrossed in one another was focused intently on us. I couldn't tell from the way they were sitting, but it was entirely possible that he was fingering her as well. I saw the look on her face. I'm sure it was the same one that I had, fighting desperately not to lose my composure. My heart was pounding out of my chest. I shut my eyes tightly and prayed that my tiny moans of pleasure weren't audible to everyone in the entire place.

"Jess, please, stop. Oh, please, I can't take much more. I'm going to cum, please stop." He started fingering me harder, deeper, first one finger, then two; I was squirming and trying to hold my breath. I was trying desperately not to cum, to fight the feeling but I realized that it was an exercise in futility. I could feel my juices flowing freely Jesse started using his thumb to rub my clit. I grabbed the edge of the sofa and I held on tightly. Breathing heavily. Never before had I experienced an orgasm in such silence before. I opened my eyes and tried to get my bearings. I got my breathing under control and my sweetie was sitting there smiling and discretely smelling his fingers. I grabbed his hand and pulled him out the door right before I glanced back and saw the woman seated at the table, gripping the arms of her chair and her breasts heaving like she was in the middle of her own special moment.

Once outside, in the bright afternoon sun, walking back towards our apartment, I had collected myself from that fantastic experience I was livid. I punched him in the arm.

"JESSE, you could have gotten us arrested. When I said in public, I MEANT in our car, or maybe in a dark secluded corner of a smoke filled bar where no one could see. NOT in the middle of the day with other people sitting 15 feet away. Are you crazy?"

He just smiled and pulled me close to him. I was standing on my tiptoes and looking up at his beautiful face, his hands were cupping my ass and I could feel the thickness of his dick against me. He said something, but I'll be damned if I know the hell he said because I was so caught up in wanting to kiss him. Damn, he is so fine. Phew.

Anyway, we headed off to enjoy the rest of the day. We went to the farmer's market and got some fresh produce and spices, some bread and wine to go with the scallops and shrimp we were planning for dinner. We went to the home improvement store to get some new patio furniture for our balcony, but we couldn't find anything we liked. We couldn't go more than 15 minutes without stopping to kiss and grope each other because we are just so hot for each other. The whole day was filled with erotic tension. I'm sure people were like, "Get a room," but we didn't really care.

All our errands done, we headed home to enjoy a lazy afternoon of watching marathon episodes of Law and Order on TNT. We fixed dinner, drank wine, and yelled at the TV screen and wondered why, in 186 years of the show, Jack McCoy has never had a male assistant. After dinner, we snuggled on the sofa. I was in between his legs and we were both in a state of half undress. His arms were tightly around me and he had pulled my breasts out from my bra and was playing with my nipples casually and making sure that I felt his erection poking me in the back. After our fourth back-to-back episode, it was more than apparent his attention was not on the State of New York, the police who investigate crimes nor the district attorneys who prosecute them. He kissed my neck and whispered in my ear, "You realize I still have to make you cum in your ass tonight."

"How do you do that?" I said.

"How do you get me so hot for you in less than three seconds?"

Jesse knew my absolute most intense orgasm came from being stimulated anally. He had saved the best for last. I grabbed his hand and pulled him towards the bedroom. I was anxious to get things underway considering for the last twelve hours I had been teased and pleased in ways that are almost indescribable. I knew this was going to be fireworks. We were pulling our clothes off and leaving a trail all the way to the bed. I crawled onto the bed and he climbed on top of me. I felt his entire weight on top of me and I wrapped my legs around him tightly. We kissed passionately for what seemed like an eternity. I could feel his dick rubbing sensually against my lower lips. His mouth kissed its way down my body, licking my navel, tasting my fingers after I finished playing with myself.

I was sick of the tease and I decided it was time to move things ahead. I pushed him off me, rolled over, and go up on my knees. I put my head down on the pillow and I reached back to spread my cheeks. "Baby, I don't know why... but you know I love when you lick my ass, please, boo, put your tongue in me. Drive me crazy the way you do. You know it makes me feel so good."

Never one to disappoint, he started slowly licking me, making my eyes roll back in my head. If it wasn't bad enough that his soft wet tongue was driving me insane, he was rubbing my clit at the same time. I started moaning so loudly I'm sure the upstairs, downstairs, and next-door neighbors could hear. I was out of control. "Baby, don't stop, whatever you do, don't stop. I'm begging you, it feels so good."

Now what on earth would make me think that he was going to listen to a word I said? When I was gripping the sheets tightly and mumbling incoherently, this black motherfucker had the nerve to stop. I'll be damned.

"No please, put your tongue back, it feels so fucking nasty, it feels so fucking good, I love it, don't tease me. I wanna cum, I want to cum in my ass. Please baby, don't tease me. Please. It feels so good."

The next thing I felt was the coolness of the lube being applied to my asshole. He was rubbing his finger around on it and I got goose bumps thinking about what was going to come next. He was stroking my cheeks and teasing me, putting his finger in me ever so slowly. There's something about anal stimulation that feels so primal, so earthy, so intense for me. He was working his finger in and out and I was grunting like an animal. I'm not even sure I realized that he had exchanged his finger for his dick until I felt both hands gripping my hips tightly.

"Okay, baby, follow my instructions, Okay?" His words were calming, but my temperature was on high. I did everything he told me to do. I pushed when he said push, I squeezed when he told me to, I stayed as still as a statue when he told me not to move. I trusted him to take care of me and he knew exactly how to control the situation so I got maximum pleasure.

"Okay baby, I'm almost all the way in, I need you to take a deep breath for me so I can give you the last inch of this hard dick. You like that, don't you girl" he said.

I grunted my affirmation and took a deep breath. He was all the way in and I was about to lose my mind. He held perfectly still, waiting for me to get accustomed to his size. I always let him know when I was ready to get fucked because I would start grinding my phat ass back on him, to stir it up, and get to that place where I felt like I was experiencing pleasure in every pore in my body. He grabbed my hips and started working his dick in and out. I buried my face in the pillow to keep my moans of pleasure from having someone call the police.

I was chanting an erotic mantra, "It feels so good, it feels so nasty, it's so deep, harder, it's so tight, don't stop, dick my ass, dick my asshole, make me feel it, yeah, I love your hard... oh shit... no... I'm... I'm gonna cum... I'm gonna... fuuuuuuuuuck."

I felt his hot cum splash on my back. We collapsed on the bed, exhausted and drained. He pulled me to him and I was drifting in and out of consciousness.

"Damn girl, I didn't hold up my end of the bargain. I came and I wasn't supposed to. I guess I'll just have to make it up to you with another twenty-four hours of complete sexual servitude to you."

A Diamond in

The Rough

By

Lauren Horner

Chapter 1:

Diamond seemed to have it all until she meets Jessie; he has all the makings of a husband. He is a powerful man and well respected. There is not a female on earth, that wouldn't want to be with Jessie or wish that they were in Diamond's shoes. He has it all, and he is definitely the one for Diamond. However, Diamond didn't have an easy at life. She had a rough childhood growing up in the projects of Baltimore, Maryland surrounded by nothing but drugs, gangs, and sex. In her early years, she was a prostitute, then a stripper to working for the escort agency services to currently a bartender.

Diamond worked hard to get her life together and although it was a slow process she finally feels that it makes sense. However, this change wasn't easy given her traumatic background. At age 5, her mother was a known gangster and she was just as beautiful as she was brutal. She was killed by an undercover cop. By the age of 7, her father was doing life in prison for a double homicide, and her older brother Apollo, the most known drug dealer and gang banger in all of

Baltimore, stepped up and raised Diamond the best he knew how. So everything about Diamond was street and hood and she was a force to be dealt with. Jessie saw something in her that she didn't see in herself. Her self-esteem was way off when it came to this man. He didn't care about Diamond's background and how she grew up. He saw potential in her that no one else could see. He saw a diamond in the rough.

Two months earlier, Diamond was working at the Corner Bistro Wine Bar; when she spotted this gentleman coming into the bar. He came up to her and ordered a Jack Daniels on the rocks.

"Coming right up boo, would you like anything else with that?"
Jessie looked at her with a big smile on his face. She stares back at him and together they stare each other down for a good 5 minutes until he finally broke the silence.

"No sweetheart that will be all, my name is Jessie, what is your name? I've never seen you in here before; this must be your first week here. I usually come in here at least twice a week to get the edge off of a hard day's work"

Diamond was surprised that he knew that this was in fact her first week working as a bartender. She was infatuated with how he talked, so smooth and sexy. Her panties started to get wet so she took a few moments to respond.

"Actually you are on the money boo, my name is Diamond, I'm still learning my way around these drinks, a little slow but I'm learning; here is your Jack Daniels boo and enjoy, if you need anything else let me know"

"I sure will sweetheart". In a matter of seconds, Jessie was taken by, not only her good looks, but her demeanor as well. She was a dime piece, fine as wine, dark skinned complexion, medium length hair with burgundy streaks running through, 5'3, and thick as a coca cola bottle. She was definitely something to look at. Jessie is on his third glass of Jack Daniels. This is a first because his usual is one drink and then he heads out; but not tonight.

"What is a beautiful lady, such as you, doing working as a bartender?" Out of curiosity, Jessie was smitten by how Diamond interacted with all the other customers and how she looked so damn sexy. He thought to himself that he could really use an assistant right now.

"What's wrong with being a bartender?" she wasn't sure what angle he was coming from so she got offended, feeling that she was being judged.

"Nothing is wrong with it sweetie; if I offended you I deeply apologize, it wasn't intentional. I just wanted to get to know you a little bit better that's all. Is that a crime?"

"I guess not," she said sounding relieved.

Before Diamond could continue with their conversation, another co-worker approached her needing her assistance. Diamond kindly excused herself from Jessie to attend to the needs of her co-worker, Courtney.

"Girl do you know who that is that you are talking too?" Courtney was a bit jealous because prior to Diamond starting at the Corner Bistro Wine Bar, she herself was the best bartender in Jessie's eyes. However, he never seemed interested in her like that, their only conversation dealt with his usual drink of Jack Daniels. *Damn what does Diamond have that I don't?* Courtney thought to herself.

"Yes, his name is Jessie" Diamond replied with a confused look on her face wondering what was Courtney getting at.

"Jessie Campbell, the biggest hot shot Lawyer in town and he never loses a case. He represents anyone from gang bangers, drug dealers and murderers to representing the best of the best. He's got money and from what I can tell by looking at him, he's packing down below. Come on Diamond, the dude is fine and sexy as hell, got that dark chocolate going on, looking extremely muscular like he can lift a ton of bricks and then some, nice sparkly white teeth, clean shaven, and extremely tall, standing at 6'5" Courtney said, sounding excited on putting Diamond on the info.

For the first time in her life, she didn't care what his career was or what l he was packing down below. To her this was love at first sight. Not lust, not sex, not anything less than love itself.

"Well thanks for the info but I need to get back and finish my shift so I can get on up out here"

"Okay girl. Well, when are you working again?" Diamond looked at Courtney as if to say that is none of your damn business and you will see me when you see me.

"I don't know I need to look at the schedule"

"Okay girl, I'll holla at you later on."

Diamond walked off and went back to taking her last drink orders and to finish her conversation with Jessie if he was still around. To her surprise, he was still there.

"I thought you left"

"I wasn't going to go anywhere without getting your number first, I really would like to have an opportunity to take you out sometime, if that's okay?"

Diamond started to blush. She felt honored and lucky to be in the presence of this man who unlike the others would have been disrespectful by now. In her mind, she was doing cartwheels. Diamond gave him her number and told him that she will be looking forward to his call and to be safe going home.

"I should be telling you that sweetie. As a matter of fact what time do you get off, I would like to have the honor of seeing you home safely. I will be a perfect gentleman."

Diamond's face showed her shock at hearing those words. She had never been treated in this manner, where a man offered to see her home safely without an arterial motive to getting sex. While Diamond started finishing up her shift, she couldn't help thinking if this was really too good to be true. The clock struck midnight and the bar was now closed. Diamond gathered her things and met Jessie by the door. She was impressed by his car, a Candy Apple Red Escalade with tinted windows. While Diamond was in the process of opening up the car door, he stopped her and opened the door for her. As he headed to the other side of the car to get in, her survival instincts set in; yes she felt nothing but love from this man but she was always packing and prepared. She checked her purse to make sure her .45 was locked and loaded. Once he got in the car, she proceeded in tell him where she lived. While driving to her destination he decided to put on one of his favorite slow jams. "Rick James; Fire and Desire" started to play.

Chapter 2:

The next day was Diamond's day off and she decided to hang around her apartment and relax with a glass of Alize. She turned on some music and started rocking back and forth reminiscing about her recent encounter with Jessie the evening before. The drive home was very different. Instead of them talking and getting to know each other they communicated through music; their hearts were in sink and connected on a different level. Not only were they listening to some "Rick James; Fire and Desire" but he also played "Xscape; Understanding" and "Prince; Call My Name". It was jamming. While Diamond was in her musical vibe her cell phone rang and Jessie's name appeared across the screen. Diamond and Jessie talked on the phone for a good 3 hours. She had never done this before; meet a guy and instantly fall head over heels, permit him to drive her home while being a gentleman throughout the ride while listening to good music. That's crazy in her eyes, but at the same time she loved it.

The next day before Jesse picked Diamond up, before her shift started at 8pm, , and treated her to a day of pampering. He took her to get a manicure and pedicure, full body massage, and facial. He wined and dined her at the Sea Breeze Restaurant and Tiki Bar with water views and bands performing.

"Are you having a good time baby," she seemed to be a bit quiet throughout the date.

Diamond had never been wined and dined like this before. Her experience with men was sexual and nothing more; no dinner, no flowers, just sexual favors.

"Yes I am. I am just not used to being treated like this"

"I haven't done anything yet; the best is yet to come." she wondered what he meant by that.

She liked how everything was going so she decided to enjoy the ride and see what the adventure was that he had in store for her. She couldn't believe that she had only known this man a short time and already he was spending time with her and really trying to get to know her. This all seems crazy, but special and enlightening at the same time.

They both continue to enjoy lunch until Diamond's phone rang displaying the name Thomas across the screen.

"Hey." Diamond wondered why he was calling her since she didn't have to be at work until 8.

"I need you to come in early, we are short staffed." Diamond's eyes got big and watery.

"What time?"

"5pm" It was unfortunate that she had to end her and Jessie's date early; but she had to make her money; especially since she was no longer in the life.

Jessie completely understood and so they wrapped everything up so that he could take her home to get ready for work. He asked when he can see her again but she wasn't sure because her schedule changed weekly. She told him that she would find out when she got to work and that she would let him know on her break. Jessie really didn't want to hear that so he offered to accompany her, hang out with her until her shift was over and take her home. Diamond was accepting to that idea.

Diamond walked into her apartment and proceeded to go into her bedroom to get dressed and while dressing she hears some music playing in the other room. *"Damn, I guess he found himself comfortable finding his way to the stereo system. Damn that's my song; he really has a good ear as if I didn't already know that."* Once she finished getting dressed, she opened the door to see him dancing and singing along to, "Milestone's; I Care about you".

Sometimes I feel so alone.
I call your heart,
But there's no one at home.
Taking a toll on my pride, my pride.
I'm reaching out,
But there's no one inside.
You know it doesn't feel right, when I look in your eyes.
I know love is blind, but the heart doesn't lie.
I'll ask one more time, maybe this time you'll try,
So tell me girl what's deep in your heart.

Girl, I care 'bout you.
I'm there for you,
So why don't you care for me,
Like I care 'bout you.

She walks up behind him and they start to get in a few slow dances before heading out for the rest of the night.

Chapter 3: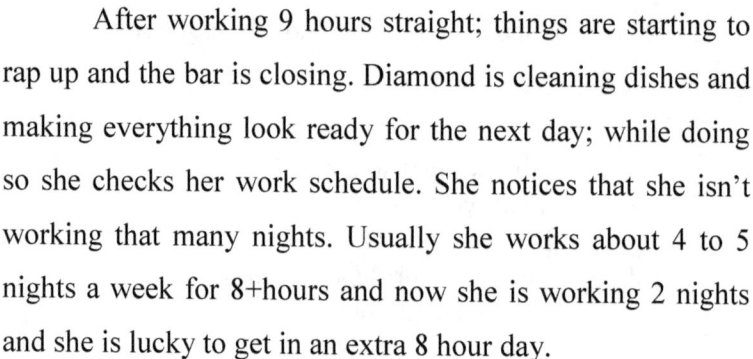

After working 9 hours straight; things are starting to rap up and the bar is closing. Diamond is cleaning dishes and making everything look ready for the next day; while doing so she checks her work schedule. She notices that she isn't working that many nights. Usually she works about 4 to 5 nights a week for 8+hours and now she is working 2 nights and she is lucky to get in an extra 8 hour day.

Diamond isn't used to not working and making her money. She was tired of her old life although she made more than enough money in one night. She wanted more than that. She wanted a better life for herself so bartending was a step into the right direction, but her nights are being cut which presents a financial issue. Jessie saw her facial expression while looking at her schedule so he asked her if everything was okay.

She lied and said "yes".

Diamond's eyes were shifting in the back of her head, her mind wars racing trying to figure out what to do.

"Baby let me see your schedule"

"It's cool boo, everything is fine." Diamond was feeling embarrassed that she let it be known that something was bothering her. She was very uncomfortable because she is not used to letting anyone into her business, especially a man.

"Let me see it!" He said with a stern voice.

He gave her the look that said he wasn't playing around. Diamond never let a man make her feel intimated but Jessie was different so she gave him her schedule.

"Baby, I want you to know that you don't need to worry about anything. I got you. I want you to be comfortable and whatever I have to do to make sure you are straight; I am willing to do it. I want you to come and work for me." Diamond looked at him like he was joking and that he must be crazy. After all he is a lawyer, so what could she possibly do for him?

"What would I be doing?" she said looking very curious.

"You can be the receptionist and work the front desk by answering phone calls, sorting mail, making coffee, and greeting the clients"

Diamond seemed interested in what he was saying, everything sounded like a piece of cake.

"I will pay you a great deal and I promise that it won't interfere with our personal life. So go ahead and put in your two weeks' notice and you can start with me at my law firm in three weeks."

He didn't have to tell her twice, she was already interested so she did as told and she gave her notice to her boss that very evening before clocking out. Jessie and Diamond left the bar and they decided to go to The Silver Dome to hear some music, comedies, dancing, and games. The night was still young and he wanted to show her a good time. As they walk in they were showed to their table right next to the stage -where live music was going to be played. There was a mixture of live music and from the DJ. The first thing they heard was "Barry White; Practice What You Preach". Jessie got up and asked Diamond if she would like to dance and she agreed. Once on the dance floor Diamond and Jessie harmonized the lyrics together.

So, what do you want to do, I'm here, baby
I'm ready baby, I'm waiting on you
Believe me, I am patiently waiting on you

Yeah, there's something wrong with me
Every time I'm alone with you
You keep talking about you loving me
Hey babe, your foreplay just blows my mind
So why don't we stop all the talking girl
Why don't we stop wasting time?

I've had my share of lovers
Some say I'm damn good
And if you think you can turn me out
Baby I wish that you would

'Cause you keep telling me this and telling me that
You say once I'm with you, I'll never go back
You say there's a lesson that you want to teach
Well here I am baby, practice what you preach

"Damn this man really got some rhythm, the more time that I spend with this man, he not only romances me, but he shows me a good time and introduces me to a new way of doing things, having fun and the whole nine. I can also tell that he is so old school, I love his musical choices. I am rocking and vibing with him, I don't ever want this night to end.

Jessie and Diamond danced to 5 more songs; "Freddie Jackson; You Are My Lady", "New Edition; Can You Stand the Rain", "Johnny Gill; My, My, My", and "Guy; Let's Chill". They were in their zone slow dancing as if no one else was around. The live entertainment for the night featured Keith Sweat, and 112.

After a few hours of a night on the town filled with live entertainment and fun, they get in the car and like a gentleman he saw her to her door.

"You are so wonderful Jessie, I really appreciate you taking me to work and then taking me out afterwards, I really enjoyed myself." Diamond started blushing.

"You are welcome; I got a little surprise for you tomorrow so get some rest okay."

"Can you come in for one more dance before you go?"

She didn't want the night to end; she wanted to dance with him for hours and hours. Jessie came in and put on one of his jams so that they can have their one last dance for the night. "Zapp& Roger; I Want to Be Your Man" was playing. Diamond and Jessie are once again harmonizing the song together.

Hey lady, let me tell you why,

I can't live my life without you.(aww baby)

Every time I see you walking by,

I get a thrill, you dont notice me,

but in time you will.

I must make you understand...

I wanna be your man(I wanna be your man)

I wanna be your man(yes i do yeah, yeah)

I wanna be your man(I wanna be your man)

I wanna be your man(I wanna be your man)

The moment the music stopped. Jessie kissed Diamond on the cheek and then forehead and said his goodnight.

Chapter 4:

Diamond tosses and turns in her bed, thinking and dreaming about Jessie. She turned her music on and hears "Selena; dreaming of you". While the song is playing, she closes her eyes and dreams. The lights are dimmed; candles are lit all around the room. There is a tray of strawberries and chocolate sauce on the side along with some whipped cream. Jessie slowly feeds her the strawberries one by one with chocolate and whipped cream. He slowly kisses her on her forehead and works his way to her lips. She starts to slowly take off her strawberry red bustier bra along with her strawberry red hearts panties. He takes off his shirt, unbuttons his pants, slowly lifts his legs and feet out of his pants, and throws them on the opposite side of the room. She kisses Jessie all over his chest starting with his nipples working her way down, but doesn't go all the way down just yet. She licks and kisses her way back up to his lips and they start kissing each other passionately until his manhood starts to rise. He caresses her breasts and kisses her nipples, she starts moaning and grabs his head and pushes him on the bed. "R'Kelly; Imagine that" is playing in the background, she takes some oil and rubs his chest and then turns him around and continues to rub and massage him to the point that he starts to moan and begs for more.

He turns himself around and looks her deeply in her eyes, he takes control. "Boyz to Men; I'll Make Love To You" comes on; Jessie is kissing her passionately on the lips once more while his hands work their way to her breasts and then to her kitty Kat. He starts out rubbing her clit. Then, starts to lick it all the way around and tongue massages her clit like it is his dessert buffet. She starts to moan in ecstasy with her eyes going in the back of her head and her back arched a little bit off of the bed. She starts to slowly moan his name and begs for him to put his sausage inside of her.

He whispers in her ear, "You aren't ready yet."

She starts to lick her soft, silky lips and moan once more and she ask him again to put it in and he whispers in her ear once again and says, "You aren't ready."

Oh my god, I am in heaven, this shit feels so good, I am trying not to cum, it seems that he is really hittin my spots, damn, I've never had good loving like this before, I don't want this to ever stop.

Diamond's mind is running wild, she doesn't know what to do, Jessie sucking all her sweet nectar dry making her yearn for more. Another song starts to play by "Silk; Freak Me" and she tries to take control but Jessie won't let her and he pins her to the bed so that he can make her want and beg for it. He continues to suck on her kitty kat for a few more minutes and then he works his way back up to her breasts and nipples to her neck to ear lobe to her cheeks softly kissing to her lips.

He starts kissing all over her thighs, her legs, and then slowly but surely starts to suck on her feet, one toe at a time. He turns her over and kisses her butt cheeks and then slowly works his way to kissing her all over her back and then to her neck once more. He flips her back over on her back and kisses and caresses her nipples and massages it continuously hitting one of her spots, she is moaning out of control and going completely crazy. She cannot take it anymore, she asks him once more to put it in, but this time instead of saying yes or you are not ready, he completely ignores her and doesn't say anything. He continues to kiss and suck her all over until he really feels like she has had enough and is ready for this dangerous weapon that will turn her out completely. Minutes later she starts to have multiple orgasms. One after another, he is still eating that nectar while she is cumming and sucking every last drop of her. Once she came, he turned her over and started to massage her back with some more oils and at the same time he starts to breathe on her back. He's massaging it trying to get her juices flowing once more; he isn't done with her yet, so he flips her back over, but this time she is on her side instead of her back.

He caresses her arms and her neck. Then, he starts to kiss and twirl his tongue around her ear lobe once more and then he finally starts to let her feel on his sausage. She starts to get excited because she is finally going to have that hard steel inside of her; to her surprise he still whispers in her ear that she isn't ready for it and that she would have to beg for it a little bit more. By this time he is back sucking her nectar once more but this time he puts ice in his mouth. Then, he goes down and starts rolling his tongue and the ice around her clit.

She is moaning once again and she feels the ice starting to melt and drip from the heat and moisture of her clit. Minutes later, she cums again and finally he whispers in her ear and says, "You are ready my love; come and get this sausage." Once that was said, Diamond wakes up and then starts to notice her sheets soak and wet.

Chapter 5:

The time is 10:00am, and Diamond's phone goes off, she tosses and turns trying to ignore the fact that her phone was ringing. She turns to the other side so that she can continue her wet dream of her and Jessie. A few seconds later, her phone blows up again. After 8 times of her phone ringing off the hook; she finally grabs her phone and sees the name Apollo. *Damn what these fools want?*

"Apollo what you want" she said in a frustrated tone

"Well fuck; hello to you too sis, why the fuck you aint answering your phone?"

"I was sleep, what you want, you constantly blowing up my phone, what the fuck you want?" Diamond said getting even more irritated. Generally when Apollo blows up her phone, it's due to an emergency of some sort.

"Look we got a problem and we got some business that we got to take care of, I need you to make a run with me"

"Boy please, I aint about that life no more, I'm good, and I am doing good things now, I don't need none of these kinds of problems."

Diamond knew exactly what Apollo was getting at. She appreciated the things her father and her brother taught her about the game and how to survive and make money on the streets of Baltimore but she just wasn't about that life anymore. She needed a change and given the way things were going, if she didn't get out when she did, she wouldn't have made it out alive. What was keeping her safe now was her father's legendary name, her brother Apollo and her sister from another mother Hypnotic. She knew a lot of people who wouldn't dare test them unless they wanted to sign their own death certificate.

That is until she met her ex fiancé War. He was also a known drug dealer in Washington, DC and nobody messed with him. He was fierce,   extremely dangerous and time enough to take down not only Diamond but everyone that she called family as well. Before War got locked up for impersonating a police officer, first degree rape, and drug trafficking, he and Diamond have been down for each other for 5 years. War getting locked up was what Diamond needed because she couldn't leave him any other way. Now that Jessie is in her life, she feels like he is a God send.

"Look I don't know where my wife at, she ain't answering her phone, and its going straight to voicemail. I asked all the peoples in the street if they seen or heard from her and nobody has seen her." Apollo sounded desperate to find his woman.

"Damn dude, you haven't been like this with no other female before, what is it about her that gets you to put your guard and shit down?"

"I know my woman, something aint right, she wouldn't ever cross me, and I can go to the bank with that."

"Alright, well I will make some calls and see what I can find out aight" Apollo is relieved that she is going to help try and find her.

"Aight sis thanks."

"Yea okay, get off my phone so I can go back to sleep".

An hour later, her phone rings once again, this time she decides not to answer it. While listening to the phone constantly ring off the hook, she had a feeling that it might be Jessie, so she rolled back over, and looked at the caller ID. The phone read Jessie aka Boo. Her eyes got big as day and she got excited to hear from him. She picked up the phone and answered.

"Hey baby"

"Hey sweetheart, what are you up to today?"

"Nothing really, I'm just sleeping in. As a matter of fact can you do me a favor? I just got off the phone with my brother and he is worried about his woman. She isn't answering her phone, and no one knows where she is. So, I was wondering if you can run some interference for me and get in touch with your people to try and find her. I would do it myself, but I am no longer in that life and I am trying to be legit."

"Say no more baby, I got you; just give me her name, and what she looks like. If I need anything else I will let you know okay."

"Thanks baby I really appreciate it" Diamond tells Jessie Apollo's woman name and what she looks like. Once he gathered all the information, he put her on hold so that he could make a call to his connection and start the process of finding her brother's woman.

"So; now that's taken care of, I need you to be ready and dressed by 4pm".

"What you got planned now?" Diamond said sounding very curious to know what was up his sleeve.

"Baby, just be ready by 4, pack an overnight bag and leave your phone behind. All I need is your sexy behind to be ready for me for when I show up."

Once he said that, all Diamond heard on the other end was a dial tone. *No he didn't just hang up on me. He's lucky that he is doing something to my ass right now.*

Hours later, her phone rang and its Jessie telling her to open the door. She hung up the phone and walked to the door to let him in. As soon as she opened the door, his eyes are big and wide as day. Diamond is wearing a pink jumpsuit with diamonds around her waist line. She has her hair in corn rolls and diamond studded Apple Bottom earrings with a pink apple bottom purse to match.

"Damn baby look at your fine ass." Jessie is starting to get aroused; he had to get himself together so he poured himself a shot of Couviosor that she had on the counter.

"So where are we going baby?" Diamond said sounding very curious once again.

"Grab your bag, let's go, and don't forget to leave that phone of yours here."

"But what if my brother Apollo calls because he is going to want to know if I took care of things for him"

"Don't worry; I already took care of that. I got my people on it now and once they get info, they will let me know; just trust me".

"Okay boo whatever you say, let's go" Diamond and Jessie left the apartment.

Chapter 6:

Jessie blindfolded Diamond so that she couldn't get any ideas about where they were going. After being in the car for hours, they finally arrive at their destination. Jessie's childhood friend allowed him to use his cabin in Colorado for the weekend. Approaching the door, Jessie told Diamond to stop for a minute; she does as she is told and Jessie gets something out of his pocket. He took out his keys and a remote control device. As they enter the doorway, the lights are dimmed, rose petals scattered everywhere, champagne, and soft music playing in the background. "Teddy Pendergrass; Turn off the Lights". As they start to head upstairs, he lights some candles and tells her to try on a strawberry red sexy number with a matching thong.

The room is filled with strawberries and chocolate as well as gifts and gift boxes everywhere. It was looking like Christmas and New Years' Eve with a touch of Valentine's Day. The setting was definitely set. While Diamond goes into the bathroom to slip on one of the strawberry lingerie set that was given to her, she hears more soft music playing in the other room. "The Friend's of Distinction; Going in Circles"

Jessie is harmonizing along with the music while waiting on Diamond.

I'm an ever rollin' wheel, without a destination real
I'm an ever spinning top, whirling around till I drop
Oh but what am I to do, my mind is in a whirlpool
Give me a little hope, one small thing to cling to
You got me going in circles (oh round and round i go)
You got me going in circles
(oh round and round I go, I'm spun out over you)
I'm a faceless clock, with timeless hopes that never stop
Lord but I feel that way, of my soul.

This man is old school for real. I am loving this man. He is starting to turn me on to some music that is way before my time but I can sure dig it though.

Diamond steps out of the bathroom to a naked Jessie. In his hands is a small gift box, she comes over to him and sits down so seductively and attempts to open up the box and inside it was a diamond incrusted strawberry necklace with earrings to match. Diamond's eyes lit up. She was touched in so many ways that she couldn't even begin to explain it. Another song starts to come on "Rose Royce; I'm Wishing on a Star". Jessie starts massaging Diamond's back and while he is massaging her, she starts to moan and close her eyes and dream that they are making sweet passionate love.

Jessie stopped touching her for a moment to fix them both a glass of champagne and as Diamond opens her eyes he gives her the glass and they make a toast, "To the start of a new life". A naked Jessie starts feeling her chocolate velvet body up and down and asks Diamond to dance with him. She decides to take off her new number and joined Jessie in being naked. "Atlantic Starr; Always" is playing while Jessie extends his hand to Diamond for a dance. She happily obliges, their eyes connect as they both passionately French kiss each other. The music continues with "Heat wave and Always and Forever" They continue to dance staying connected. Their minds are totally on each other, they are in the moment of love, passion, and erotic intimacy. While the song starts to come to an end, they start to kiss each other passionately; so passionately that he grabs her behind and lightly squeezes it. Diamond works her beautifully manicured hands down his chest and into his big 9 inch sausage. The moment she touches the tip of the meat, he softly moans. He slowly backs up and kisses slowly around her nipples and softly pinches around the nipple with his teeth. She starts to softly moan and gets excited thinking that this is her dream from the night before but this is for real!

Jessie kneels down and kisses Diamond on her thighs and works his way up to her breasts again and then to her neck and slightly on her back; finally she gets on the bed and comfortably lays there while Jessie takes some strawberries and feeds it to her with his mouth. Then, he takes a little bit of champagne and slowly pours a little bit on her nipples and once the champagne hits her breasts, he starts to softly suck on it until she starts to moan and moan. He starts to kiss his way down to her clit and sucks the lips and rubs her pussy with his left thumb. She holds his head there while he continues to hit her in all the right places. "Between the Sheets" comes on and then he finally puts his 9 inches inside her starting with the tip of his head.

"Damn baby, you tight; I love this shit, you making me sweat, this pussy is good" Jessie says slightly out of breath.

"SHIT BABY, FUCK THIS PUSSY, OH SHIT....AHHHHHHHHH" Diamond and Jessie make eye contact with each other as they are both in the grind. After 45 minutes of hard and hot love making they both climax. Diamond is starting to get sore, but Jessie is ready for round 2 and he is feeling and eating her tight wet pussy like it's his last meal. Despite the fact that her pussy was sore, she still took it like a G and the pain turned into pleasure again.

"Turn over baby, let me hit it from the back." As Diamond starts to turn over; Jessie slaps her ass three times, then puts his 9 inches in there and starts to loudly moan.

"OH SHIT BABY THIS MY PUSSY RIGHT HERE, YOU BETTER NOT GIVE MY SHIT AWAY. FUCK; THIS IS SOME GOOD SHIT"

Although in the heat of passion, Jessie was serious and meant what he was saying. This was going to eventually get real dangerous given all the intimacy, passion, lust, love, and sex that have transpired between them over the past few months. Diamond was ready for whatever. After another 45 minutes Diamond and Jessie climaxed again. They lay side by side on champagne colored silk sheets looking into each other's eyes and Jessie proclaims his love.

"I love you baby" Jessie said seriously

"I love you too baby and thank you for everything. I won't hurt you; I am here for the long haul."

Diamond looked into his eyes and repeated what he said. Together they kissed passionately and held each other for the rest of the evening until they fell asleep while "Lenny Williams; Cause I love you" started to play.

Chapter 7:

"Thank you baby for a perfect weekend," Diamond couldn't help the blush and was glowing for hours.

"You are very much welcome baby, this weekend was extremely powerful for the both of us and you belong to me. You aren't going anywhere you hear me?" Jessie said looking serious as a heart attack.

"Baby, you don't have to worry about me going anywhere, you have really shown me that there is still some good men out there; so enough about us because you already know that I belong to you, but what about Apollo's girl Chanel, any word on where she is yet?"
Jessie looked at her and put his head down. He had the look of shame like he had some bad news or something.

"Baby I don't know how to tell you this, but I just got word that she is in the hospital with multiple gunshot wounds to the stomach, back, arm, and leg. The doctors don't really know if she is going to make it; but don't worry baby I am on it. I will find out what happened and when we get home call your brother and let him know the news". Diamond's eyes were blood shot red, she couldn't believe it.

Hours later, they finally arrive home and she proceeds to call her brother, and give him the news about Chanel. She felt so bad being the barrier of bad news, and her brother didn't receive the news well at all. Now its war; there is no calming and talking him down from how he is feeling and what he might do especially given his reputation. Diamond became scared for her brother so she reached out to Jessie to try and run some more interference to control her brother. Jessie made a phone call to make sure that Apollo would be watched until they get down to the bottom of who shot his woman and why. Jessie's friend's secured him in a secluded place where it will be impossible for him to try and leave their sight. Jessie wanted to be the one to handle this especially since Diamond felt so strongly about what might happen if Apollo took care of this head on.

Weeks later, Jessie received word that everything had been taken care of; he didn't ask questions since he knew this was good news to relay back to Diamond. Now that she was at ease, they inform Apollo that everything had been taken care of and the only thing he needed to do was to go to the hospital and be at Chanel's side. Days later, Chanel pulled through. She had to stay in the hospital for a few more days but Apollo was truly happy that she made it out of this terrible ordeal. He was so happy that he got down on one knee and proposed to his woman.

"Chanel Unique Jackson will you do me the honor of being my wife?"

"Yes baby I will."

Chanel cried out of excitement and now that Apollo was going to be a husband, he realizes that he cannot live without Chanel. She was his rib, his ride or die, and his only. Nobody could take her place. As for Diamond and Jessie, they have been going strong for a year; they recently got engaged to be married. She is now working as his receptionist at his law firm. The couple moved into a 3 bedroom condo in Baltimore County where they share a teacup poodle named Diva. However, they are planning to move to South Carolina within another year so that Jessie can finally retire and focus more on Diamond's future goals. Last but not least, Diamond is now 4 ½ months pregnant with their first child which they found out is a girl.

While driving home from their doctor's appointment, they pull over and stop on the side of the road and Jessie extends his hand and asks her if she would like to dance.

"Out here baby, we are outside in the middle of the road and its dark" Diamond said looking shocked.

"I don't care, it's me and you."

While Diamond attempts to step out of the car, Jessie turns up the music to "Brian McKnight; Back at One". Once the song ends they decide to get one more dance in before heading home. So he turns up the volume even more to "Luther Vandross; Here and Now" This was the perfect way to end the day. Dancing the night way and harmonizing together.

> One look in your eyes and there I see
> Just what you mean to me
> Here in my heart I believe
> Your love is all I'll ever need
> Holdin' you close through the night
> I need you, yeah
>
> I look in your eyes and there I see
> What happiness really means
> The love that we share makes life so sweet
> Together we'll always be
> This pledge of love feels so right
> And, ooh, I need you

Here and now
I promise to love faithfully (Faithfully)
You're all I need
Here and now
I vow to be one with thee (You and me), hey
Your love is all (I need) I need

Stay Tuned: To Be Continued...

//.ENCRYPTED/..:

By

Ashley M. Jackson

Chapter 1 – ://MeMories.exe

The room was still as my husband droned on about his day. It wasn't as if I wasn't interested…it was simply that one grew bored with hearing about how "incompetent" his colleagues were. All this man did was complain.

"Sabra, my love, are you listening?" I jumped slightly, stifling a yawn while playing with my hair.

"Of course darling…" I replied while dragging my long nails down my cheek, enjoying the sting that it brought.

He coughed loudly, covering his mouth with his handkerchief. "Yes, of course you are, dear. Now on to more pressing matters, how is Project C-H coming along?"

Yes…Project C-H, my husband's true love; the first self-thinking android in a generation of brainless worker androids. Project C-H was to be the prototype of the Companion Humanoid Android Project.

We were in the midst of the 29th century, the Golden Humanoid Era. After the 12th World War, humanoids were the ones responsible for rebuilding our society, and saving humanity. They could lift more and do more than humans ever could. Most importantly they didn't fear death, they didn't fear anything, and all they knew was how to listen to their masters.

I smiled, twirling my fork. "E-129 is doing well. Brain waves and thought pattern levels are increasing at a healthy rate." I haven't actually seen this...*thing* yet. My husband does well to keep his experiment sealed in a metallic capsule. Some dimwitted excuse about how "...His skin is not yet ready for exposure..." Personally, I think that the exalted Dr. Xenon finally realized that he made a grotesque creature, and doesn't know how to hide his failure.

He nodded enthusiastically, wiping his hands on the same handkerchief before smoothing his thinning hair down. "Wonderful, wonderful, my love!" The chair slid noisily across the floor as he stood and started for the lab door. "I must spend time with my project, do not wait up for me."

The cloth underneath my plate was hardly touched, and the food was chilly and unappetizing. Somehow, my mood soured even more.

My name is Dr. Sabra Xenon, assistant and wife to the praised Dr. Elias S. Xenon. Our goal is a simple one; reforming this dying world and make one in a glorious new image, a world where humans and humanoids live and love together. A new age where humanoids are more than just our puppets, but our equals. My husband was the first to see humanoids for what they could be, and how we, as short sighted human beings, were not using them to the full extent of their abilities. Then it dawned on him; creating a race of humanoids that can think and act for themselves, turning the puppet into the puppeteer, and giving this world hope again.

We all know that humans have run the show for long enough.

*****

The hologram on the wall flashed 1:07am, and my husband was still nowhere to be found. That was usual for him, and when he got in his theatrical moments, sometimes I wouldn't see him for days.

"Idiot..." I rolled over to my back, stretching out and tossing my bore of a novel across the room. My wild curls were plastered all over my face, and my silken nightgown felt itchy and uncomfortable.

"Ugh, D-29, over here now!" I tore the nightgown from my body and tossed it in the same direction as the book. The stiff worker android glided over to my bedside, awaiting his command. He was one of the first worker humanoids that I owned, in fact I had him for a good thirteen years now; tall and sturdy with deep metallic skin, and slicked charcoal hair.

"Awaiting your orders, mistress." His mechanical voice reverberated around the empty room, making it feel even emptier.

I reached out my hand and placed it over his cold chest, running my nails down the artificial muscles that hid the wires and valves keeping him "alive".

"If only you were real..." For a moment I felt sad. My idiot husband was right in saying that humans could do nothing right. After all, a hunk of metal and wires made me happier than my own human husband did.

I stretched out on the bed, keeping my eyes transfixed on D-29's unmoving ones. The tips of my toes reached out towards the edge while my arms wrapped themselves coyly around my bare stomach.

"Stay with me?" I gave a grin and D-29 cocked his head to the side before taking a step back.

"Negative Mistress, Master Xenon has prohibited any physical contact with you. I apologize for the inconvenience. May I help you in any other way, Mistress?"

That bastard of a husband. My teeth were grinding louder than the gears that were behind the wall. I sat myself up, pushing my hair out of my face.

"I'm overriding Master Xenon's decision, code 2927." After my husband married me, he must have forgotten that I was his assistant before I was his wife. I have more control over this facility than he does. Everyone and everything in this place respects me more than him!

"Override code 2927 accepted. I am at your command, Mistress." He came closer again, kneeling at the side of my bed with that blank stare that I loved so much. A creature so powerful, and yet so weak at the exact same time; who knew that man could make such a complex being?

"Come here." I relaxed as D-29 climbed on top of me, making the bed sink under his heavy weight. His metal gloved hands grabbed my wrists, holding them far above my head. He knows all of the movements by now, this was a dance that we did quite often.

Chapter 2 – ://EXpERiMentation.exe

I jerked awake and peered my eyes open, letting in the offending red sunlight. The room looked just as empty as it was last night; D-29 must've left after I fell asleep.

"No kind of class...what kind of man has his way with a woman and then leaves the next morning." My body was sore, then again, it always way when it came to D-29. Another choked laugh escaped my lips as I pushed harder against the bruise that surrounded my wrists. The woman in the mirror barely resembled me, but this is the best I've ever looked. I traced the other bruise that ran down my jaw, chuckling again. Every once in a while, I sat back and wondered what the hell was wrong with me.

"Sabra, my love...are you awake?" What was he doing here? I gathered my nightgown and jumped back under the covers.

"I'm just waking up, my dear." Feigning a saccharine tone and batting my eyes always worked.

Husband walked in, fleshy and wobbly, the signs of age doing nothing good for him. He was nothing like D-29. Nevertheless, his smile was contagious as he flashed a stack of papers in my face.

"He's finished...E-129 is now complete!" He dropped the papers in my lap and began to pace the floor as he usually did when his excitement got the best of him. "I was up all last night watching his levels, making sure that they didn't fluctuate too much. Finally! Finally he reached stability. The numbers are set, and he is ready to be activated!"

"That is wonderful, my dearest!" I sat up in genuine excitement, causing the blanket to slip from my chest. He paused, turning rather red before turning around.

"Make yourself decent woman, science is calling! Meet me in the lab." He hurried out without another word. You would think that he would've overcome that shyness after being married for so many years, but he still does. Part of me finds it flattering; then again, most of me finds it annoying.

~

After slipping on my bodysuit, I found myself heading down the crisp white corridor of Xenon Technologies Inc.; the leading manufacturer of artificial intelligence. Scientists both young and old paused and bowed as I walked by.

"Good morning, Lady Xenon!"

"It's wonderful to see you, Lady Xenon."

The best I could do was fake a smile and wave to the masses. Husband was right; these doe-eyed scientists are annoying.

"Lady Xenon, you are looking lovely as ever this morning." There came the sleaziest voice of them all, Dr. Cyryl Plaski, my husband's boot-licking assistant.

"Good morning, Cyryl. Have you seen my husband?"

He grinned, pushing his unruly white hair out of his face. "Of course, he's in the main lab. We've been waiting for you for the grand unveiling," he replied, hands sweating. Everyone was ecstatic, at least, the ones that knew about E-129 were. Self-thinking humanoid androids seemed like a taboo, something that the general population seemed afraid of. My darling husband received quite the amount of backlash for even thinking of such an idea. So E-129 became top secret; only I, my husband, Dr. Cyryl, and a handful of scientists knew of this creation.

There were three sets of code-locked doors before even entering my husband's personal lab, and each required dual codes from someone equally authorized. A rat couldn't crawl in undetected.

First set, 176-8892. I gave Cyryl a nod as I keyed in the code, prompting him to do the same. There was a quiet beep as the door slid open, leading to the next code.

I hate this retinal scanner. I made sure to open my eye wide as the blue haze scanned over my retina, beeping in response.

An automated voice came through "Retinal scan accepted. Welcome Lady Xenon and Dr. Plaski, please proceed."

The only sound in the silent hallway came from my clicking heels. The material in the walls caused this to be the quietest place in the entire facility. It drove me mad. "Is the silence bothering you, Sabra?"

My eyelid twitched. "Quiet worm, and that's Lady Xenon to you."

"Of course, my apologies, my lady."

The detox and full-body scan chamber was next. I entered to the case on the left while Cyryl went to the right. The same blue haze filled the tube as a digital read-out of my body appeared on the screen.

"Welcome, Lady Xenon and Dr. Plaski, you may proceed." At long last we reached the door at the end of the deafeningly silent corridor. It was large and gray, making my heart pound in anticipation. This would be our greatest work, the first self-thinking humanoid. At first I thought that my husband was kidding himself, but if he truly wants to show it to me, he must be serious. This could open so many doors; it could be the beginning of reshaping our world.

My gloved hands rung together, anxiety and excitement in the same breath as we pushed the door open.

The lab was large, multiple levels of sterile metals and glass. My husband along with two assistants stood behind the control pad on the first level, while a handful of other scientists ran around the other two levels.

"Darling!" I waltzed over to him with a plastered smile, gripping onto his arm. "Are we ready?"

"Sabra, my love, perfect timing. Stations, everyone!" At the sound of his voice, all of the others froze, dropping what they were doing to focus on the steaming metal capsule in the center of the room.

"After decades of hard work and dedication, we have completed our most difficult task, bent the delicate line between man and machine, and rewrote the rules of science. I, Dr. Elias Salem Xenon, have completed the first self-thinking android, the first companion humanoid!" The room erupted in cheers and claps. "We all know what their race can do; it's time that we show the rest of the world."

He stepped forward and entered a long stream of binary code into the hologram above the capsule, pressing the buttons under the panel.

"If you would, my dear." He pointed to the lever to the side of him. "Flip the switch."

I happily obliged, wrapping my fingers around the handle and cranking it back.

The room shook as the capsule slowly began to unfold, causing the floors to become thick with steam. I coughed, holding my arm against my mouth and attempting to squint through the gas. I saw...black, something inky black. Hair, maybe?

Husband coughed and waved his hands through the thick air. "Respond E-129."

Silence. Everyone waited in anticipation for the gas to disperse.

"E-129 respond!"

An eerie metallic creaking filled the silence as the shadow of a figure sat up through the gas. I stifled a gasp as the figure came into view, my heart uncomfortably thumped in my chest.

He looked so...human, even more human than I thought an android could ever look. His face was so stern and fair, if I didn't know any better, I'd think he was no older than 21. Slicked black hair went past his pale ears, and fell on his strong shoulders. He wasn't too bulky, but was far from slim, covered in a thick layer of muscle from head to toe.

There was a strange pattern, a black linear cybernetic marking that crossed his chest and trailed down further than I dared to look. The most mesmerizing part had to have been his eyes; they were the lightest shade of a silvery grey, demanding and commanding, with so much thought behind them that they were compelling me closer.

He was beautiful, sheer perfection.

"Yes, Master Xenon." He finally responded in a strange tri-toned voice. I had never heard a voice like that. It sounded as if three different people were all talking at the same time, but they sounded like one. It was the strangest trick of the mind.

I barely noticed how giddy my husband was now that E-129 finally responded. "Yes, come now, E-129, stand."

E-129 looked at his left, then to his right, almost as if taking a mental count of everyone in the room. The way that those steely eyes roamed over me was enough to make me shudder. He slid forward and landed with a thump on the still foggy floor.

I trembled again; I thought he looked large in the capsule, but while standing upright he had to be closer to 6'4, 6'5 maybe. It took a lot to make me at 5'10 feel small, but just standing before him made me feel microscopic. His hands and feet were just as massive; strong and sturdy, with equally strong legs and arms.

I broke my stare and looked away, noticing that most of the women and men in the room were doing the same thing. He, however, didn't seem at all fazed, then again why would he be.

"Wonderful! Wonderful! Dr. Cyryl, if you would check E-129's vitals."

Cyryl pried himself off the control panel, breaking his gaze from E-129 as well. "Yes, of course, Doctor." He hurried over and began to lead the prodigy away, making my heart clench.

"Magnificent." That was the only word that I could think of as he was led away into the other room.

Just Magnificent...

Chapter 3 – ://oBSeSSed.exe

The clock flashed 1:10am. Though oddly enough, my husband graced me with his presence tonight. I suppose we were celebrating the week anniversary of E-129's completion. It was such a treat; he was showing his love to me by showering my body with sour kisses and sweaty palms.

Every groan that slipped from my lips was of annoyance, not pleasure. Of course to make matters worse, D-29 was waiting in sleep-mode in the far corner of the room. I couldn't keep my eyes off of him, even while my husband was sliding his tongue in patterns along my naval. He slid further down my thighs, wheezing as he nipped along my legs, and kissed the arch of my foot.

"E-129 is magnificent, but you are a true masterpiece, Sabra."

If only I could say the same about you, old fool.

E-129 had been plaguing my mind all day, I wish that my husband never mentioned his name because now…

I want to see him; I wanted to see him so badly that my spine was tingling, especially since I only saw him that first day. Honestly, I didn't even know why. It was something in the way that he looked at me, something that made me want to go to him. The feeling was chilling and exciting at the same time.

My husband's breaths came out in pants and gasps as he laid back down on me, his shaking hands doing to best to grip my thighs. I thought I heard him saying something by my ear, but honestly I didn't even care.

E-129...what was the chance of me slipping away into the lab to see him? Where was he? I laughed, maybe if I got lucky I could get him to be one of my personal humanoids.

As if my husband would allow that. I would hardly be able to contain myself if I was able to get D-29 and E-129 at the same time. The thought alone made my mouth go dry.

It was hard to concentrate on my fantasy with this pig breathing down my neck and slamming his hips against me. Why am I here again?

E-129...right, he's why I'm here. If anyone was close to creating self-thinking humanoids, it was the gullible Dr. Elias S. Xenon. So maybe I did have to work under him for years, and then work under him in a...different way. In the end, I got to stand witness to one of the most legendary moments of humanity's pitiful existence.

I dug my red tinted nails into his back and tightened the grip that my calves had on him, rocking back against him while trying not to laugh. This old fool gave me the key, now all I have to do is take it.

I have no use for him anymore.

Oh…he finished already.

~

He finally fell asleep, the pig. I thought he never would. It was a bit past 3 and the sky had only the slightest tints of red, barely illumining the dim room. It was silent and only the sound of machines in the wall echoed through. There was a chance that I would be caught, but I had to go to him, I couldn't hold myself back anymore.

I slipped on my silk robe; stark white with roses staining the bottom like blood splatters. The hall was empty save for a few scientists getting their last few readings in.

"Oh, good morning, Lady Xenon. It's early for you to be up." The young scientist smiled.

"Yes, and it's late for you to be here, isn't it?" I shot the annoying lab rat of a woman a stare. How dare she question me in my own facility!

"O-oh of course, Lady Xenon, my apologies. Have a good night, um…morning."

I tossed my dark curls over my shoulder, and continued down the hall and into the walkway of absolute silence. It was the normal routine...except I didn't have another person to do the duel codes with.

"Damn, how could I have overlooked that?" I looked around; of course the lab was empty except for the stupid girl from before.

"Beggers can't be choosers I guess." I shook my head and took a deep breath. "Hey you, come here!" I flagged the glasses clad assistant, making her drop her whole stack of papers.

"Me? Oh...uh...coming." She was one of the new girls; thick-rimmed glasses, bright hazel eyes, two jet black ponytails, and deep olive tinted skin draped in a stark white lab coat. She couldn't have been older than 17. I suppose she wasn't as clueless as I thought.

"Go over to the other keypad. Type in 176-8892...exactly like that." I'll just have to use another override code to get us in. She nodded and we typed the code in sync, appeasing the automatic door.

"Excuse me Lady Xenon, but I am not authorized to be he-"

"Don't you think I know that? I am authorized, so as long as you are with me, you are authorized as well-." I stopped and stalked towards her, pinning her between myself and the wall.

"-and as far as you will remember, we never came down here and you never saw this. Understood?"

The poor girl began shaking in her boots before nodding frantically. "Y-yes, understood Lady Xenon."

I gave her a light slap on the cheek. "Good girl, now follow me."

~

Two overrides and a few threats later and I finally found myself at the lab door. I placed my hand on it; the pulsing seemed to be running through my blood, completely pulling me in.

The young scientist led the way and I followed behind her, there was something foreboding about being in my husband's lab this late. A low hum accompanied the silence that came from within the dimly lit room, the whir of machine that seemed to keep this place running.

"Stay here girl, don't move." I gripped her lab coat and led her to a stool, not too gracefully tossing her down on it.

"Y-yes, Lady Xenon!"

"And keep it down. We don't want to wake up the whole facility now do we?" I rolled my eyes and peeked around. There was nothing but doors on both levels, and the center of the room which held E-129's capsule just last week was now bare. Where were they keeping him?

"Great." I sat on the lab table and flipped through the messy, coffee-stained note. These definitely belonged to Cyryl, what a slob. Oddly enough though, his notes spelled out everything I was looking for.

Day 1: E-129 is still under surveillance; he shows complete understanding of human life and of his place in the world. Subject is showing rapid increase in intelligence and physical abilities daily. Still no defined reason for odd linear pattern on chest, back, right arm, groin, and right leg.

Day 3: E-129 showing further increase in mental capabilities. Subject seems to know the answer to a question far before it is asked. No reason for this phenomenon, research still being done. Psychological level seems unusual – will ask Dr. Xenon at a later time.

Ability to…know what will be done before it is done? That's incredible. Precognition is a phenomenon that humans fail to understand. But yet, this humanoid has it.

I wonder if he saw me coming.

I tore through the rest of the pages, looking for anything on where he could be. It would take all night to search through all these rooms, and my husband likes to awaken promptly at 6am. Finally, a page caught my eye:

Subject held in cell 4B

I hopped back off the table, being sure to fix the mess I made before heading up to the second level. If I was correct, 4B wasn't far from the splicing table. It was a large door with another key panel on the door.

"Authorization required, state name." The VI spoke in its usual drone of a voice.

"Dr. Sabra Xenon, override 2927."

It beeped in response. "Override 2927 unacceptable. Please provide additional verification code."

Another 3 key panel hologram appeared, with a blank code slot of 25 digits.

A 25-digit code? How am I supposed to guess this one? A series of birthdays...anniversaries, the facility archive code in binary? What on Earth could it be!?

Before I could attempt the impossible puzzle, the numbers...began to type themselves. The keyboard flashed as if I was typing on it, making the door beep in response and slide open. I held my breath and took a peek over the railing at the scientist girl who was still waiting by the door. This would only be a moment; I only wanted to see him.

I walked in and the door slammed shut, the only light illuminating in the darkness came from the tubes of chemicals lining the ceiling. It was like all of the other cells; a large round table with an opening on the side that surrounded a vertical metal capsule. I sped forward, feeling the thumping in my chest increase with each step.

I was almost within arm's reach when the capsule's lid began to rise.

"Hello, Sabra, it is a pleasure."

Chapter 4 – ://toXic_INToxicatioN.exe

I froze as he stepped out of the capsule, fully awake and functional. Did he unlock the door for me? Impossible.

He looked even bigger at this range; honestly it was intimidating. His frame alone seemed to swallow me up and his voice pierced through and bounced off the walls.

"You know me?" It was the only thing that I could say, my heart was beating too fast to even concentrate.

"Sabra Anu Xenon, age 25, born September 27th." I didn't realize that I wasn't looking at him anymore; he was gone from my field of sight, circling around behind me. I was frozen, still looking forward at the empty capsule.

"Science is your passion, so much so that you left your family behind, and married yourself off to a genius, yet foolish man."

"He might be a fool, but he did create you. He fulfilled his purpose."

I shuddered as I felt a large presence behind me. It was like…he was moving through the air.

"He did not create me. I created myself." His voice cracked and fizzled for a moment, like a glitch in a computer. "I am infinite, we are many."

"Who is...we?" He came back to the front of me, starring me down with his glowing eyes. I tried to keep my eyes on his face, but between the temptation to look lower, and the fear growing in the pit of my stomach, I ended up memorizing every crevice of his artificial body outlined in his exo-suit. He looked nothing like D-29, he wasn't metal and wires, but skin and nanotechnology that was just fiction a few decades ago.

"Your kind needs us, more than we need you. Yet you use us as tools."

I shook my head. "That was the point of you; you are proof that a humanoid is more than a machine. Humans need humanoids, your kind can work with us and open a new era." That is what I wanted. A new world ran by both man and machine. The possibilities were endless.

"Humans...and humanoids will never live in harmony. You know this Sabra." He paused for a moment as his voice glitched again. "They will eventually enslave us, even your husband."

I wanted to say that he was wrong, but the more that he spoke, the more that I wanted to believe him. It was like something inside of me was telling me that I could trust E-129.

"Humanity…" He lifted his cold finger to my jawline, tilting my heavy head upright. "…is nothing but a plague on this planet."

I stiffened, what was going on. He wasn't supposed to be thinking this way, what happened to his programming? He looked at me again, the same coldness in his artificial eyes.

"You, however, will be of use to me Sabra. Will you obey me?"

Suddenly, my legs felt weak. My mind fuzzed over and my eyes couldn't focus. What was going on?

"I'm scared…what is this?"

"Will you serve me, Sabra?"

Every time he spoke my name I grew weaker and my body trembled. His voice had power, his words were dangerous, and yet I couldn't get myself to stop listening.

I fell to my knees with a thump and looked up to him with blurry eyes. "Yes, m-master."

What's going on?

He was the most important thing, he was all that mattered. I didn't care about my wants, my husband, the clueless scientist downstairs, only him.

I curved my dripping lips into a wet smile, tilting my head like a child. "I am yours."

"This is satisfactory." He moved closer and buried his fingers in my locks, yanking my head upright. "Prove this to me."

Prove it? How did this magnificent creature want me to prove my loyalty to him? I slid forward, still on my knees, and stopped at his feet. Something in me told me to run, to leave, but I pushed that feeling to the farthest corner of my mind.

I reached up and tugged on the bottom portion of his dark exo-suit, revealing the pale skin and cybernetic pattern that laid beneath. Would this please him? I looked up at him, hoping for some sort of answer, but my eyes couldn't focus on his face.

"Lady Xenon? Are you okay up there?" I heard the girl downstairs call out. What did that idiot girl want? How long had I been here? I didn't care to answer her; all I wanted was to please my master.

I ignored her calls and let my tongue fall from my mouth, dragging it from his taught hipbone to the lump of artificial, hardening flesh. His taste was intoxicating, drawing me to take him in further.

I tried to reason with myself, but I couldn't bring myself to care. Right now, the rigid flesh caressing the inside of my cheek was my priority.

The hand in my curls tightened, pressing my head further onto his length, making me fight to not choke.

"My pet." He grinned, stroking my head with more affection than I thought an android could have. I couldn't help but look up at him after hearing the term of endearment. Yes, I was his pet, he had me completely entranced. Ever since I saw him that first day, something within me changed.

I brought my hands up and stroked the parts that I couldn't fit. I pressed hard, drawing along the cyber pattern that ran all the way down. He made a deep noise at the gesture, something akin to a growl, causing him to press my head further.

"Prove yourself to me." He repeated as I opened my mouth as far as it would go, welcoming his flesh without resistance. Drool and other fluids dripped from my chin soaking my robe, making it stick uncomfortably against my skin. After only a few more thrusts, I looked back up at him, finally being able to see clearly. He met my eyes though his face was partially hidden under his slicked black locks. Those eyes held me captive, as if they were burying themselves into my soul.

The grip he had tightened again until I felt strands of hair being yanked from my hair. My pain was pushed away as his flesh erupted down my throat. I fought the gagging sensation to swallow all that my master had to offer me. He pulled back, emptying more along my cheek and my neck, before readjusting his exo-suit and looking at his masterpiece.

More, I wanted more of him. I smiled again while opening up the knot to my robe, pulling away the wet fabric and exposing my dark, plump chest and slick stomach. More of his intoxicating fluid dripping from my chin and down past my neck, coating my body.

"I am yours, Master"

What am I saying, why can't I get up?

"Please use me as you see fit."

I looked up with wide eyes as he bent down, reaching my eye level. There was something behind the devious shadow of a smile that he wore, but soon enough my world went dark. The last words I remembered came from him in the form of a whisper against my ears.

"You will be of great use to me, Sabra."

Chapter 5 – ://SinGUlarity.exe

Where am I?

I jumped up with a start, hastily looking around the room. My room? I was in my own room? When did I get here, how did I get out of the lab? Even my clothes were different; my robe was discarded and I was in my lab coat. Did someone find me when I blacked out?

Blacked out? What on Earth happened last night with E-129, it was like I...wasn't myself at all. It was as exhilarating as it was terrifying, but somehow he found a way inside of my head.

I chuckled dryly, wrong or not, last night was amazing. I don't care if I seem like an addict, the words that he said to me were stronger than any drug...and I wanted more of it. There was no denying that he was dangerous, but I didn't care.

"L-lady Xenon?" The door popped open and the girl from last night slid in side, closing the door timidly behind her. Was she the one who brought me here?

"You? What are you doing here?"

She fumbled with her hair and shifted her boot clad feet, refusing to meet my eye. "Um, well...last night you didn't come back downstairs and…a good amount of time had passed so I went to check on, um, you-"

"What did you see?! How long were you there?" Dammit, did she see everything? When did she come upstairs? Did E-129 say anything to her?

"N-nothing, Lady Xenon! When I went upstairs, it looked as though you…slipped and were unconscious. So I carried you back to your room. I promise, nobody saw you…but, um, your robe was wet, so I changed your clothes and laid you down." She bowed her head. "I'm sorry if I…overstepped my boundaries, Lady Xenon."

Hmm, looks like she's not as useless as I thought she was. If I was found…well it would have been bad.

"What's your name, girl?"

She jumped, looking back with the same doe-eyed stare. "Name? It's Ginseng, like the tea…but um, everyone just calls me Gin."

"Dr. Gin, eh?" I curled my finger and beckoned her forward, to which she quickly obeyed. "Can you keep a secret, Dr. Gin?"

She nodded, leaning forward as if we were gossiping. "Yes, Lady Xenon."

"How much do you know about Project C-H, and E-129?"

~

The lab was running as usual as I walked through the corridors.

"Good morning, Lady Xenon!"

"Hope you are doing well this morning, Lady Xenon!"

The usual calls from the young and eager doctors echoed across and caused a pain in my head. The only silent one was my new found favorite, Dr. Gin. She was in the far corner doing her work in silence. She glanced my way and gave a timid nod that I returned. That girl will be of use to E-129 and me. I have to think of when to offer her to him; I hope that he finds her pleasing.

Another familiar face that was missing was Dr. Cyryl Plaski. His irritating smile usually met me at the end of the corridor every morning, but he was nowhere to be found.

"-...reconsider the options here-" I paused when I heard him from down the hall, the opposite direction of the lab. Who was he talking to in such a shaken voice?

"-really dangerous...-" I spotted his mop of white hair by the main computer, speaking in hushed whispers and darting his head around like an escaped convict. The other person was too far back for me to see. I casually walked over and stopped behind the side of one of the door, close enough to hear what they were saying, but far enough to remain undetected.

"He is unstable, Dr. Xenon, please reconsider!"

My husband? That is who he was complaining to? What was too dangerous? What was he talking about?

"Dr. Plaski, now you know I respect you as a fellow scientist and a friend, but the thought of deactivating E-129 is...absurd. He is the single most brilliant project that I have finished. He is my life work!"

Deactivate E-129...what were they thinking?! My shaking hands gripped onto the door, holding myself back from running over there.

"Exactly! Elias, listen to me." Cyryl looked around once more before leaning in. "E-129 is too brilliant, he's altering his own levels! I didn't think that was even possible, but he slipped up earlier today."

My husband seemed uninterested and shook his head, turning to walk away. Cyryl grabbed his papers and began to follow, continuing his plea.

"His mental level is supposed to stay lower than 600 to keep him stable, but when I check on him today, his levels were spiking over 2000."

He froze as Cyryl continued talking. "When E-129 noticed that I was in the room, his levels immediately dropped to 590. He's changing his own data, Elias. He's changing himself and fooling us! I even found him *out* of his capsule days ago; he had opened the lid himself, unlocked the security door from the *inside* and was going through his own files." Cyryl paled as he spewed all of him fears, making my husband look…very uncomfortable. "And the other scientists…act strangely around him. Talking to themselves, entering trance-like states! Some of the younger workers even reported hallucinating and hearing voices in their heads. He's doing something to them, to us. This is exactly what everyone feared when you came up with the idea of self-thinking humanoids. Everyone feared that they would become too smart, he's reaching the *singularity*."

The singularity; the point when technology will become more intelligent and powerful than we can even imagine. He's reaching a point where-

Humanity is nothing but a plague on this planet…

I am infinite, we are many…

You will be of great use Sabra…

Sabra…

What…what did my husband create? I slid down to my knees as my legs began to shake, covering my mouth with my hands. I was…afraid, but I didn't want to be afraid. I wanted E-129 to use me, but why did it feel like I was dancing in a grave that I was digging myself.

Run Sabra, it's not too late! *Don't run, you need him, don't be afraid.* You don't know what he's capable of. *Obey your master! Obey him!*

"Sabra?" I dropped my hands as I heard footsteps coming over to where I was. Dusting myself off and leaning against the wall for support, I tried my best to will my blush away.

"Sabra dearest, what are you doing here?" My husband gave me a confused look whilst Cyryl glared.

"Yes Lady Xenon, what are you doing here?"

Was that accusation that I heard in his voice? Why the nerve! "I am here because I was looking for you, my dear husband. Is there something wrong with E-129?"

Cyryl passed a glance over to my husband, almost asking his permission to talk to me.

"Well she is my wife Dr. Cyryl, go ahead and tell her what you told me."

Cyryl's grip on his papers tightened as he thrust the notes in my hands. "E-129 is becoming dangerous. We've created something that we can't control. He needs to be deactivated before this become out of hand; his intelligence is increasing exponentially.

I glanced over Cyryl's notes. There was no denying the fact that E-129 was becoming dangerous. It was all here, everything from the fluctuation of levels, to the exceptionally high test scores, to the disturbingly abnormal psychological scores. One word stuck out though; corrupted.

Cyryl though that he was corrupted, broken? It reminded me of last night and his odd tri-toned voice, the way that his speech fizzled in and out, sounding almost as if he truly was…

I did the only thing that I could think of doing at that point.

I tore up the notes.

"Dr. Cyryl Plaski, you have reached a level of absurdity that I didn't even know you were capable of. Disgraceful."

I dropped the shredded lies, laughing as Cyryl dropped to his knees to pick the pieces up.

"What is the matter with you? You daft woman! Why can nobody see that E-"

"E-129 is perfection! Nothing but that."

"He is a monster!"

"*He* should be the one in charge!" I screamed, stomping my heel on the hand that held the paper. "You have no right to decide his fate; you are an ant to him!"

He grunted in pain as my heels dug deeper into the tendons in his hands. Soon his pained face became that of realization, and he began to chuckle.

"You fool, he has already gotten to you, hasn't he?"

I paused, letting my leg go slack.

He laughed again, backing up with his papers in hand. "Just how deep does he have you, Sabra?"

Yes, how deep indeed...

Chapter 6 – ://SysTEm_erroR.exe

"M-master!" I stifled my scream by holding my arm against my mouth. The control panel in cell block 4B was cold and unforgiving, but I felt anything but cold with Master holding me over the machine and slamming restlessly into me. This reward was far past my obedience, ever since my conversation with Cyryl just five days ago, this had been our nightly routine.

He tightened the grip that he had on my hair and pulled my hips closer to him before pushing in again.

"Sabra…"

I smiled widely, drool cascading from my lips to the control panel below. "Yes, Master?"

"You have been a good pet, very useful to me."

I stretched out my toes, trying to hold myself from falling onto the ground.

"Now tell me again…" He leaned down, bending himself over my back and turning my head enough to reach my ear. "What did Dr. Cyryl Plaski say?"

I tried to shake away the fog that was blocking my memory; Cyryl was the absolute last thing on my mind right now. But I must do as Master wants.

"He-ahh, he wants to deactivate you. He says...he says that you are dangerous."

I winced as his nails tore through the skin of my back, holding me still as he had his way.

"He thinks that he can do that, does he not?"

"He couldn't, I would never let him!" I screamed as his nails dug deeper and his thrusts came faster. "I would...I would kill him before he had the chance!"

I laughed, plopping my head back down on the control panel, enjoying the feeling of my face sliding against the buttons.

"You would kill a man that you have known for years, would you?"

"For you master, I would do anything!" I turned my head weakly, my voice no more than a slur. "Reward me, punish me, anything you want, Master!"

A dark laugh came from him, a noise as low as a rumble. "What would you do?"

"I'd kill for you master, I'd kill him!"

"Again."

"I'd kill him! I'd kill him, my husband, all of them! I'd kill them all if it pleased you master!"

He grabbed my leg and flipped me over to my back, pinning me further against the machine while thrusting in deeper.

"That is what I wanted to hear, my pet."

I was losing my mind, the pain and pleasure was too much to bear. I wanted nothing more than to reach up and grip his back, but I was far from worthy enough to touch him.

"Tomorrow my pet, it will begin."

Begin? What will begin? For some reason my face became cold at that thought.

"Tomorrow, we will purge this facility of its infestation."

I gasped, my heart thumping wildly in my chest. More laughter poured from my lips in a voice that I didn't recognize.

Leave! *Stay*! Run! *Obey*! Warn them! *Kill them!*

The voices were only silenced when a warm coil in my stomach began to tighten. I took a deep breath, halting when I felt E-129's cold hand around my neck. I couldn't breathe, I could barely see, I was terrified.

It was perfection.

~

Gin and I never spoke in the morning as she helped me with my bath. She never questioned the bruises that encircled my wrists, nor did she question the puncture wounds and tears on my back and thighs. She never asked, and I never mentioned. Today was the day, the day that E-129 and I could be free together.

Why are you fooling yourself?

Quiet!

I chuckled softly. These foolish humans don't deserve to be in E-129's presence. He is perfection, his will be in control.

Until when...when will it stop?

It doesn't matter; I do what my master tells me.

You are a human as well, when will he grow tired of you?

"-non...Lady Xenon..."

You are unleashing something dangerous...

"Lady Xenon!"

You are bringing about the world's destruction. You know that he won't stop.

"Sabra!" I popped my eyes open at Gin's shout. She looked panicked, her glasses were sliding in their normal fashion and her hands were shaking.

"Thank goodness, you were shaking and talking to yourself. I was scared for a moment." She breathed out a sign, pushing her glasses back up on her nose. "Is...something wrong?"

"What? Are we friends now or something?"

"Oh...um, sorry Lady Xenon."

She casted her eyes downward and finished soaping up the wounds on my leg. I chuckled and patted Gin's head, she was like a little mouse; innocent, frail, and easily squished.

I wondered what it was that Master said...or did to her. He wanted to speak to her in private, and they ended up being in cell 4B the whole night. When she came out the next morning, she seemed different, but she said that she couldn't tell me what Master told her. It bothered me that she knew something that I didn't, but I would never tell that to Master.

The clock beeped 9:00am. Just 12 more hours...12 more hours until this facility became a graveyard. 12 more hours until the human genocide began. He told me the whole plan; we will start with my husband, we will spare Dr. Cyryl, then we will work our way down and purge this entire facility.

I giggled; finally, we can paint these terrible walls a different color.

Red was always beautiful.

~

"Go home, Dr. Gin."

"E-excuse me?" She nearly dropped the beaker that she was testing. I signed and pinched the bridge of my nose; I didn't have the time or patience to deal with this today.

"I said...go home. You are not needed today. Your home town isn't too far away right." For some reason or another, the thought of Gin witnessing the event 3 hours from now made me feel...bad. The thought of me slitting her throat made me feel even worse. I didn't even like the girl but...I wanted her away from here.

It's not like Master would have her killed, he said that he had use for her as well. Certainly he wouldn't kill her off. I just didn't want to take that chance. My stomach was doing back flips.

"Yes, Lady Zenon." She placed the heated beaker down and grabbed her papers, stuffing them in her briefcase. "When should I...return?"

Did she even know what was about to happen? "2 days from now."

"Yes Ma'am." She nodded and turned to walk away, only to turn back and give me a hug. "Please...be careful."

I was frozen, but before I could shove her away, she released me and headed towards the elevator.

Stupid girl.

"What's going on, Sabra?" Dr. Cyryl came storming up to me, eyes blazing. The tension in the room was heavy; I suppose someone caught on that something might be wrong.

"I have no idea what you mean, worm. Also, that's Lady Xenon to you."

"I'll call you what I damn well please! I know you're planning something." He blocked me as I tried to walk away, searching through my eyes. "What has he done to you, Sabra?"

I laughed, giving a lopsided smile. "I have no idea what you mean." The room's temperature seemed to drop ominously as Cyryl backed up slowly before breaking into a sprint.

He's lucky that Master told me to spare him. I would love to have his blood on my hands, the thought alone made my mouth water.

~

It was 8:57pm. 3 more minutes. 3 more minutes until my glorious master purged this disgusting hovel of disease and remade it in his image. First here, then…who knows when it would end?

I sat perched on my dresser, wearing nothing but my white nightgown. My untamable curls framed my face and fell down my back. I figured there was no need to look nice tonight; after our job was done, Master would certainly have his way with me.

I looked over at my sleeping pig of a husband, snoring loudly and drooling, completely unaware that his life would end in 2 minutes. I laughed and ran my hand up my thigh, the thought of E-129 and all his brilliance being covered in the blood of this man seemed beautifully taboo.

The hair on the back of my neck rose as I heard footsteps in the hallway. 8:59, E-129 was always punctual. I giggle and kicked my legs back and forth, getting comfortable and ready for the show.

9:00pm

The door creaked open and a gleam of light coming from the long knife in his hand blinded me.

"Good evening, Master." I smiled, feeling my whole body go slack at the sight of him.

"You have done well, pet." He came closer to me, the muscles in his arms pulsing as he held the knife in front of me. "Will you serve me, pet?"

I leaned forward, dragging my tongue along the side of the 9-inch blade. "Yes, Master."

"Good." His voice cracked and fizzled again as he turned and stalked his massive form towards my sleeping husband. Thankfully, I had a good view of the bed.

He climbed on and the bed dipped under his solid weight, just slightly jarring my husband. By the time the magnificent Dr. Elias Xenon woke, he was already pinned, straddled by his own creation.

"E-1...E-129 what is the meaning of this?" He looked over to me. "Sabra dearest, what is going on?"

I smiled and waved at him. "Goodnight, my love."

"What are yo-aughh!" He was cut short as the blade pierced through his chest and blood began spurting from his nose and mouth.

He didn't stop, the blade swept down like silver rain, filling the room with squishy inhumane noises. I cracked up, this was amazing. The power that Master had made my body feel hot, and before I knew it, my hands had found their way under my nightgown.

"More, Master, stab him more!" I couldn't get enough; I could stop watching Master's blood covered smile or my husband's emotionless face.

He had stopped moving long ago, but Master kept finding new places to bury his blade.

"Is this enough, pet?"

I shook my head frantically; I was close but not there yet. "More! Please more, Master!"

My legs tightened against my hand as Master nearly severed my husband's head. He was nothing more than a pile of steaming meat. It was the best he ever looked.

I breathed out a silent cry as I reached my completion and fell slumped against the wall. Master got off the bed and walked around to the other side, admiring his handy work.

"Are you ready for the rest, pet?"

This was the beginning of the end, and I couldn't have been happier. I slid off the dresser, legs shaking and head unsteady, as I reached for my knife. Together, we will change the world for the better.

We all know that humans have run the show for long enough.

"Yes Master."

Scattered

By

Tiffany Turner

Cancer is savage. Cancer is a wretch. Its contemptable actions took him. They were robbed of time. She was sure they had time.

Soren dreamt of her father. Not the sullen and feeble face she watched days before he passed, but the bold man she imagined him to be, tough and fearless. Had they had a relationship, her heart would be broken, but not gone. That was not the case. She didn't know him. Didn't know his birthday, until she saw it on the obituary. Didn't know where he was born. Didn't know that he had other children. What she knew was that as a child, he briefly denied her; as a teen, he was elusive to her; as an adult he didn't know her; at his deathbed, he left without fixing her.

Since he died, her father seemed to be all around. She was heartbroken. What she remembered the final week of his life, was sitting beside his bed. The cancer had taken his weight, and his intimidating presence. It took his ability to move. He was cold. A tiny space heater sat on his bed, and he would switch it on and off to warm himself, until at last he was unable able do even this simple task. The insomnia started the immediately after his death. She fell asleep dreaming the bed her father died in, while she sat at his side. Before he died they had not communicated in years.

The dreams from the night before were sprawled on her pillow. Tiny rope like impressions were on her face. Her eyes opened, and took in the dark. Or, perhaps, reflected it. Her shirt was twisted and wrapped tightly around her belly. She lifted her hips and pulled her shirt from left to right. She slid her legs up until the weight on her comforter felt too heavy. It seemed as if the pillows on her bed rested to close to her face. The darkness was familiar. But she had always been able to breathe it in. But, even with the heaviness, and tightness, she still managed breathing. She pushed the pillows further down, then used her feet to push them from the bed. One slow breath, another, then several deep breaths. She moved to gather her braids, lifted them from her neck, and off her shoulders. She didn't look at the time. She had stopped doing that. It only made her more tired. When sleep came it would. No matter how evasive, it eventually always came.

Soren opened her eyes. She could hear his phone ringing, and hoped it would not wake him. His voice was low and he spoke for a few moments to the person on the other end of the phone. He knocked on the door of their bedroom. He had slept on the couch. If she could sleep, that was better. The bedroom door had been pulled closed the night before.

There were times she asked him to be close, and there were times she slept alone.

"Hey." David stood at the foot on the bed.

"Hi." Soren moved away from her where she lay, the turned to lay on her side, her back to David. He took a few steps and lay behind Soren. He always lay extremely close when he could. His body cold, Soren was always extremely warm. There were nights when he moved away because she would be so warm to the touch. He didn't understand it. He needed it.

Soren blinked a few times, and curled her legs tightly under her body in an attempt to feel centered.

"I missed you."

"I was next to you."

"You slept on the couch." Soren turned and tucked herself inside David's arms. He wrapped them tighter.

"I came in last night. I kissed your face."

"I was tired."

"I know. Did you sleep well?"

She lied. "Yes." Soren slept on and off, tossing and turning. Her father passed a year earlier, and her insomnia was not better. She was heartbroken. She was mad. She missed her father now more than ever. It was something she could not understand. And why the hell couldn't she ever decide how she felt about things. And each thing with her was this way. She was here and there, never quite sure, but instinctive. She cared about everything and she cared about nothing simultaneously. Forward, and Backward. She felt anger, and grief. She felt things in a deeper sense. Pieces of her died with her father. Pieces of her died with Christopher. Soren felt she had left pieces of herself in Chicago, at home and in places she had never been. She felt scattered. Always too much, and never enough. Here she was in the arms of a man she adored. She was sure David loved her back. But he did not seem to be fully invested. He showed her love. But she recognized things in him that gave her case to doubt him. He reacted to certain situations with apprehension. And from her experiences apprehension was never good. David was apprehensive in bringing Soren into his world at every turn. And he always had excuses that were just enough to allow him to ride the fence. Meeting his mother, invitation to family gatherings, moving in, relocating. He always seemed to hold back. In any way a commitment had to be made, he remained independent. She lay there recalling Christopher's apprehension.

"25.00 even ma'am." Soren looked at Christopher, with his lips tight and stoic expression. She looked off to shake away embarrassment, "Will a debit card be ok." Soren asked while not making eye contact with the clerk.

"Yes." Soren paid.

The clerk asked her and Christopher questions concerning the information for their marriage license. Each time Christopher answered he sounded angrier, as if his sternness could deter Soren.

"You look so angry."

"I'm just ready to get back to work." replied Christopher.

"What time is it?" Christopher asked Soren. But he was not looking at her.

We will get there on time. We had no other time to do this. Christopher, the license is good for 30 days and if you don't want to we don't have to.

"It's done, isn't it...You're fucking rushing me, so I guess me being late to work doesn't fucking matter, does it." Soren finished with the clerk, and the two exited the office. Christopher walked and crossed the street ahead of Soren. The drive back to the office would take 20 minutes. The car ride back to the office was quiet. The marriage was the result of ultimatum. It was December, and Soren had been back in Chicago for a few weeks, when she found out she had contracted an STD. After confronting Christopher, he denied he was sleeping with other women. He denied having an STD and accused Soren of lying about being sick. It was only after Soren called her doctor's office to have the nurse confirm that she was sick that Christopher admitted to sleeping with another woman. He was her college sweetheart. Soren loved him, she always did. She remembered words he once said when they reconnected years after both left undergraduate. He told her that he loved her because he knew her love for him was unconditional. Christopher agreed.

"Alright." Christopher stopped in front of he and Soren's job, looked straight ahead and drove off once Soren closed the car door. He parked the car, and Soren could see him enter the building out of the window in her office. She had just passed the woman Christopher had been sleeping with since before she moved to Chicago. She would not look at Soren. She could however, continue to fuck Christopher even after they married. After Soren found out he had not stopped communicating with her, she went to her office to confront her. Christopher ran quickly behind her, and asked Soren not to do this here, at their job. She asked Christopher, in front of this woman did he care for her. He refused to answer. For weeks Soren cried on the drive to work, while Christopher drove barely acknowledging her falling apart.

Soren knew she should not marry Christopher, and she wanted to stop herself.

Weeks later Soren stared at all the other couples, their families, and the joy of each person. Soren had no joy. Large windows overlooked the greenest lawns she had ever seen. Christopher stood with his back to Soren. She knew she was making a mistake. She hadn't told her mom, or any of her family she was getting married. She moved away from the window and tucked herself as close as she could in the corner of the cold brown leather sofa in the middle of the large room. The room was beautiful. She wished this too could be beautiful. Her entire family was 600 miles away and she knew she was making a mistake. She loved him, but knew he did not want to be married.

"48"!!! The number came from the intercom.

"Chris." Chris walked past Soren in the direction of the now opening doors. Minutes later they were husband and wife.

She moved herself out of the memory and realized it was time for David to get up and dress for work. She would make a few scheduled home visits to her clients and return home.

Soren had fixed dinner. Night slowed everything, and provided the covering for the thoughts that seemed to crowd the spaces in her mind. Hot water spilled over from the sink onto the front of Soren's tan romper. The sensation jolted Soren from her daydreaming. The pain from a memory of her marriage ceremony left Soren as quickly as it came. Soren blinked and shook her head. As she fished in the dishwater for the sponge, she stood there unable to move.

"Soren." David has just made it in. Soren pulled her hands from the hot water and soap and squeezed the dark spot on her clothing left from the dishwater.

"Soren. Soren." David moved closer to her. He touched her arm, and she was able to move. She turned to look at him.

Soren looked at David and saw all the good in him. He smiled back at her. This signaled a truce. The night before, the same argument ensued. She accused him of not wanting to be committed. She was glad now that they both had would let it go tonight. Still she silently couldn't help but wonder how someone who procrastinated for almost a year could suddenly seem so content to share her space. It was these things that preoccupied her mind when he was around, and the things he was never quite clear on. These things were the unsaid things she had talked with Rowan about so many times, and the one thing during the conversation she had with her best friend of 15 years earlier that day. Soren and David had finally ended the mental warfare concerning his moving in. They had been living together since last since October, five months later here he was coming in from work; the nine month move in tug of war now background noise.

"What are you thinking about. Lost in thought, I tried calling on the way home."

"Nothing. I was about to get into the shower and I didn't know what time you would be in." replied Soren. Returning to the dishes.

"I cannot believe you are washing the dishes." David said in an exaggerated tone.

Soren turned to look quickly at David, and back to the dishes. The truce gave way to awkward silence. It seemed as if this space they lived in together, taunted them, wanting to remind them of the argument. Once again, she had told David he could leave. She berated continuously concerning his lack of communication. The fight they seemed to keep having was over his vagueness with regards to their future and relocating out of state. Now they both stood here, and Soren, and her need for the last word

"I see your things are still in the closet." Soren stated in a low voice, so low she was unsure if she had actually said it, or if it was in her head.

"Soren, do you want me to leave?"

"No."

"You don't act like it, and I won't keep doing the back and forth. It's getting old.

"It's not old David, you never wanted to be here in the first place, and I don't need you here if you don't really wanna be."

"Soren." He said her name with a finality that let her know, they would not discuss this further.

David blew out hard, and helped Soren rinse and wash the dishes. When they were finished David turned to look at Soren. He towered over her 5.2" inch frame. At 6'2, he instantly calmed Soren's fits by simply looking down at her. Soren stood on her tip toes and pulled his dreads free from the thick braid he wore. He smiled, and his lips parted to reveal the bright teeth with the wide space in the middle. She found it so appealing. Soren laid with her head in David's lap while he drifted off to sleep. Soren had hoped she would be so lucky. She woke David to go to their bed. Thoughts of her dad, kept her awake. She didn't fall asleep until after a.m.

"Good morning!!" a voice radiated from the other end of the phone.

"Morning momma."

"Are you still in bed, I didn't want to wake you. It's hard for you to rest, momma knows, but I wanted to let you know I'm going to be gone until late this evening. I have just left the gym, I am heading out to run errands, help your brother prepare for his spring break, so he is not calling my damn phone every ten minutes, and then I may go into Cairo Springs for the day, they have this almond bark and it is too good.

"I'm up momma. I have a busy day. The girls will be in town, and I need to take care of some things at the office, so I can be away." Soren said while moving from her bed to the bathroom.

"That's right, I knew that. You girls have a good time. If they have time, I make brunch for you all before they head back to Atlanta." Tina said.

"Rowan would love it momma, but she will want a lasagna!"

"Where is David?"

"At work, I didn't hear him leave this morning. And I am glad for it, he's so loud, and he turns on all the lights. If he does it tomorrow morning, Ma, I going to slap him back to Atlanta…I think he does it on purpose!"

Soren sat the lid of her toilet and the cold porcelain made her toes do a funny dance on the floor, she reached under her bottom and pulled her waist length shirt under her bottom, and it pulled around her neck.

"Momma, do you like David?" Soren and her mom were best friends. Tina's opinion meant everything to Soren.

"I like David, he's sweet. He's patient, and he seems to make you happy. Tina stated.

"He does make me happy momma, we laugh, he is different, and he's a good person."

"He is momma. I just have an incredibly low tolerance for indecisiveness. And I have to be sure about David. I need him to be sure about me. Chris..."

Tina stopped her daughter mid-sentence and reminded her that David and Chris were two different people. Tina and Soren finished talking. Soren had agreed to check on her mom's house later in case she stayed in Cairo Springs.

Soren moved to select something to wear to her office, and compared the men in her head. She recalled memories of her ex-husband...

"You slept with Lauren without a condom?" Soren asked.

"Yes. She married with kids, and she only sleeps with her husband so...I really thought it would be alright."

Soren blinked a few times, and folded her legs under her, pulled a pillow into her lap, she stared at her husband, her husband of not even one month. She was completing resumes for Christopher on their laptop the Sunday before, and asking Christopher to make sure he was getting the confirmations to his email. Preoccupied perhaps with the game on television, or subconsciously telling on himself he gave her the password to his email, not thinking of what his wife would find. Soren logged into the email and saw the five submissions and thank you emails. "Perfect!" she said. Soren saw that the next five emails were from "Lauren", and she deduced this "Lauren" worked with her husband and the senders email was a company one. Soren clicked into the email:

Lauren: We fucked so many times I lost count

Christopher: Riiiiiggghhhttt...Damn I didn't expect shit to happen like that!

Lauren: Me neither, But I don't regret a bit.

Christopher: I was surprised I had the energy to go to the gym after that, all that ass, I can't wait to get my hands on your body again.

This email led to the conversation being had, Soren's new husband named at least eight women he had slept with in the 2 months leading up to their marriage. His actions with Lauren led to the ultimatum that would become Soren's hell; her marriage. It would last only nine months, and it would be heartbreak, disappointment, and emotionally damaging. Soren doubted Christopher from the beginning. The confusion was there from the beginning. Soren was in Texas, and left to go to Chicago with Christopher with no promises. No warm feelings of security and answered question. Soren was in love with David, hadn't he sat outside of her bedroom door while she cried quietly after finding out Christopher was a father? The mother of his child, chose to find a way to contact Soren, and alert her to the news. Their divorce was not even final. Hadn't David offered a listening ear?

The memory of the blatant disrespect and emotional abuse she endured in Chicago was every bit the reason she had no intention of moving to Atlanta with David. Soren pushed the doubt far back, and came back, cycled the thickness of each of her mother's words. And quietly drifted back into the warmness and wholeness Tina's voice

It was after 8, and David was walking through the door. He walked over to Soren and stood over the bed smiling. She had just returned home herself. She worked most of the day in her office, and was now prepared to be away for a few days.

"How was work?" Soren said, and moved to her knees in the bed and then raised her body to kiss David's neck. He must have gone to the barber before heading home, each hair was in place and laying on his face forming perfect angles and lines.

"It was ok. Saturday is always a crazy day, and I was driving today."

David moved towards the bathroom and began removing his clothing. Soren moved her knees from under her body and stood to her feet.

Soren collected David's pajama bottoms from the bureau.

David stood in thick steam. Soren took in smalls reveals of skin that shown when he moved his body. She opened the door to the shower and the steam immediately made David's shirt cling to Soren's frame. Kisses on his back, then nails scratching against his stomach, and he was now facing Soren. "Hey," his voice was low and deep, and then David felt as Soren hummed "Hello" from deep in her belly. The vibrations now in her throat. David pulled Soren from her knees and moved her body towards the water. "Always in my shirts" He whispered.

"I should have asked. I'll take it off right now". Soren moved to pull the shirt over her head. David stopped her. "It's wet now." He moved in to drape his body over hers. His body adorned her body; both covered and entered her; rhythmically moved inside of her until she wasn't sure which water ran harder, the shower or hers. The love was all consuming, and it always felt as if he needed her expressions and much as she needed his. Times when she needed to be filled, he obliged. Others when he wanted to drift away, she would crawl onto his body and his eyes would become as dark as his skin. His eyes transformed into slits that would glow. Snake eyes. Those times were the only times she saw those eyes, he looked like a God laying there waiting to be fucked by a magician.

A day later Soren headed to Rowan's hotel to pick her up for lunch with Mara. Mara and Soren had become close friends after attending college in Atlanta together. The women were all connected through their acquaintances with Soren. Soren had been looking forward to Rowan coming in town all month. It was hard bringing together a group of busy and professional women. Rowan was in town visiting family. Mara, like Soren and Rowan were from Texas, and was also in town visiting family. Mara lived in Atlanta.

Soren let herself in Rowans' suite. It did not take long to remember why she Rowan were never roommates in college. Clothing was strewn all over the bed, flat irons, makeup bags, and lingerie was spilling over tightly packed suitcases. Soren lay the room key on the table and fixed herself and slid out of her 4 inch heels.

"Hey short stuff!!" Rowan bounced into the room, with makeup that was flawless and flashy. The friends hugged for a long time. Rowan went back to the vanity to finish her hair. Soren pushed Rowans products to the side and sat on the counter.

"So, first I'd like finger waves, with a side part, a bang, French roll, and a red and purple highlights. Then after lunch, I would like braids with gold and green hair! I plan to for you to do 52 styles on me today and to make up for not being able to take full advantage of your talents all 365 days of the year"!
"Rowan said, squinted her eyes and mover her locks away from her face." Both women laughed

"Rowe, why do you have flatirons and you're wearing sisterlocs?"

"Because Goddamnit, I knew you would be requesting 52 fucking hairstyles! I'm so damn hungry, let's go. Is Mara already at the restaurant?

"I told her, I would call her once, I got you dressed and out of this hotel room, but I heard this hotel has a pretty good restaurant. I was thinking we could eat here, and then decide where to go from there, that way we are all in one vehicle and you could freshen us up before we head out on the town!"

"You bitches are always looking for freebies! Rowan said shaking her head and laughing.

Soren and Rowan met Mara in the lobby 30 minutes later and were seated shortly after. Drinks were brought out and so were all the old jokes. These ladies anchored one another through Soren and Christopher's divorce, career losses and gains, Rowan's fertility issues, and Mara's depression.

"Have you decided on Atlanta?" Mara, asked with her signature bluntness, in between sips of her water.

"I love him…and I would like to go with him. But, after learning that he will be leaving soon, it was me who suggested the move. Me who initiates any real conversation about the move, and well, I think, while I want to go, I am resentful of the fact that he more so makes me feel as if I am tagging along instead of us moving there together."

"Has his job completed his transfer?" Rowan asked, "Has he considered moving any place else? He is a paramedic; I am sure that makes it possible for him to work just about anywhere?"

"His focus is razor sharp and his sights are set solely on Atlanta. I guess. I wonder, if it were not for him, would I even want to move there? I never saw myself in Atlanta. No woman wants to move with her man to Atlanta! It is party place to me. David has made it clear that's where he is headed, and has been clear on that point from day one. I guess I assumed that for whatever reason, he would at least be open to other places. But he hasn't."

"I like David. I do I think he cares a great deal for you." Mara said in defense of David.

"I don't think that's what she is disputing Mara."

"It's not. I do feel as if he cares, but if I say I won't follow him, then what… that's the end and we are done. Or, is it that because he made this declaration early? I am just supposed to oblige him? I did that for Christopher, and I won't make those same mistakes. What I am disputing is the fact that he has not done what I feel like a man that was sure of something would do, and that's secure our next move, by talking to me and ensuring that I would be leaving with him. He's literally said, either I go or I don't. Hell, what am I supposed to assume? David has never acted as if he needs me. And well if I am that dispensable to him, then neither of us deserves to settle.

"Him not verbalizing wanting you to go, well that in and of itself does not mean it is not what he wants." Rowan said.

The ladies were finishing their meals, and the waiter came to take the dinner plates away.

"Will you ladies be having dessert?"

"Sweetheart, I am in room 512, and if you're up to it, you can be my dessert, you are too damn cute for words. How old are you baby?"

Rowan said to the twenty-something waiter. He had full lips and was at least 6'5, with smooth caramel skin, this made him fair game for Rowan. She was career driven and was not overly emotional or sentimental like Soren.

"What's your name sweetheart?" The young boy blushed and switched the dinner plates he retrieved the table to his left side to reveal his nametag which read "Eugene".

Mara and Soren both exploded with laughter and the young waiter who once stood confident, now looked visibly confused and nervous.

"Damn Rowan, you fly 1300 miles and successfully find the one damn 25-year-old with a name from the fucking 1950's! First there was "Cecil", said Soren.

"Then Harold, snorted Mara.

"Wait, wait, then Stanley, Louis and Ernest." Replied Soren.

"And now this young fucking tender, with my damn daddy's name!!!" Soren and Mara laughed so loudly, patrons grimaced, and made other looks of annoyance.

"Rowan, you have had a thing for dicks with old ass names since college. Remember the one named Lester...Lester from when we were in college, Hell did he attend Morehouse or was his ass a professor? Where in the hell did he get that damn brown suit and suspenders???"

"Babeeee, let them have dress socks and a suit coat and your ass was in love!" Soren said pulling her coat from the back of her chair and swinging it around, letting it rest on her shoulders!

"You know what, fuck you both!" Replied Rowan. And by this time the waiter had retreated away from the lively bunch of "grown" women.

"Oh ok, but when I am the topic conversation, me and all my dysfunction, you cackling wenches never let up!"

"I tell you what, I bet he is named after his damn daddy, annnnnnddddd since he is, that means his daddy's old seasoned ass should have taught him a thing or two! You all are just goddamned jealous! I am going to fuck Eugene's newborn, hairless, old, soulful name, having ass! His cute little ass! Little old cute thang!" Rowan said as she moved to get up from the table and move towards the direction of the kitchen.

"Soren, you know she's gonna wear little Eugene out!

"I know it, but not tonight. David isn't expecting me, and I am crashing in her room tonight. Retorted Soren.

"That's fine with me. I'm exhausted, and I am sure my family will have me occupied for the majority of my trip."

The night concluded with Eugene coming to the room and Rowan disappearing for an hour, and both Mara and Soren refused to leave the suite. They playfully chastised Rowan when she suggested he could simply come into the suite just long enough for dessert. Before falling asleep Soren admitted that she would rather give David an out of their relationship than be vulnerable to the hurt Christopher subjected her to for a second time. After the death of her dad, she wasn't sure she had a place to put any more hurt. Death left a permanency. People think time lessens hurt. It does not. It leaves a permanent heartbreak. You survive it, but it is never easier. David loved her. She agreed with Mara. David was not vocal; he was silent in many regards. Choosing simply to act. Therefore, she agreed with Rowan, in and off themselves words were not a sole indicator of feelings or truth. The love with David was always real. But so were the disagreements and arguments.

"He loved me, even when I was brokenhearted over someone else. How could I ever know that he was coming, but I'm happy God saw fit for him to. He's my best friend. I love him. Soren said aloud, but more to herself than to her friends before the trio friends fell asleep around 2 a.m. Around 3:30 am. Soren got up for water, she grabbed her phone and sent David a text message saying she loved him and telling him to be safe. She knew he was working a late shift. Soren closed her eyes with thoughts of David and the decisions she had to make, and the changes she knew were necessary.

The next morning Soren went to the gym and ran errands. She was sitting Indian style in her bed when David walked in.

"How was last night?"

"It was fun. We ate at the restaurant inside of Rowan's hotel. The food was pretty good, and then this damn girl finds her a little cutie to have a fling with!" Soren laughed to herself recalling the incident with Eugene. "My week will be pretty hectic. I took a vacation day tomorrow. And I'll go in late on Tuesday. I have several clients I have to finalize case notes on. But I am hoping we will manage to spend time together before they leave.

"When are they planning to leave out?"

"Mara Leaves out Wednesday morning, and Rowan plans to leave Tuesday evening if she can finish up her things with her family."

By this time David was resting with his back against the counter. And looking at Soren while she finished putting the last of the groceries away.

"What's up David, why the eyes?"

"Everything is going well with Atlanta. I can expect to be processed sometime late summer or early fall."

Soren turned and walked out of the kitchen, and entered her walk to unpack her overnight bag. No part of any of the conversation she would have with David would be easy.

"David, I am proud of you. You always wanted to be back in Atlanta, and now you will be, and I am happy that this is happening for you. It is well-deserved David.

"Thank you."

Soren sat on the bed and stared at David. "I always knew you were leaving, I guess I just didn't expect things to happen so fast. It's almost April."

"Soren this has always been my plan, you know that."

"Yes. I guess I did David. I guess I figured, or rather I had hoped that things would work themselves out in a way that would, you know just work, so that we wouldn't have to have these conversations. You're leaving me."

"How the hell am I leaving you?" David had become visibly agitated. This always happened whenever the topic came up.

"David, I do not plan to come to Atlanta. It should be a natural transition. Not forced. You haven't been clear about any of the details. You don't want me to come."

"I never fucking said, you couldn't come."

"And that's exactly what I mean David, but did you ever say, you wanted me to come! I have to be certain you want this."

"We have talked about this for months. How many times can we have this conversation? We agreed to move to Atlanta together. Did we not? Why do you insist on talking over this shit and being caught up on what I did or did not say?

"David, this has nothing to do with past anything. It is about us. Yes, I am cautious. Any intelligent person would want to learn from their mistakes.

"Soren, I love you. But I am tired of fighting with you. I never walk into this house and start fights with you, but it seems as if you always have an issue with me.

This conversation was always difficult. It always seemed to be a losing battle. Each argument strained the friendship their love was built on. David hated confrontation. He hated wasted words with no purpose. Soren couldn't figure out why she couldn't control her emotions. Each time he mentioned Atlanta, Soren associated it only with abandonment.

"How many times have we fought because you wanted to avoid our living together here in Texas, How in the hell can you say our moving to Atlanta is what you want?

"Aren't I here Soren?"

"But you didn't want to be."

"You will leave. You plan and you move. Your plan was never to stay here.

David shook his head and Soren could read the emotion on his face. David was vague. He was not big on expression and would become irritated when Soren assumed.

"David as far as we have come, there is still so much separation here. After being in this relationship for almost three years…"

"I am not listening to any of that." David interrupted Soren, and turned to walk out of the room.

"No. We have to get it right David. You promised you wouldn't leave, and all I have done is fight to be a part of your life in any real way. Let's not forget, the circumstances that surrounded me meeting your mother, or your other family, hell I had to practically beg. You make major decisions without any input or thought from me. David, two people who are saying they want to build a life...David they simply do not go about things in that matter. Why are things so damn separate with us?"

Soren felt defeated because she knew David would no communicate with her concerning these matters. He simply refused to answer or discuss it.

"David, how is there so much love, yet you refuse to trust that I have your best interest at heart?"

"Soren, you never trusted me. From day one you have accused me of all types of bullshit, with no real proof."

"So you are just going to stand there and refuse to acknowledge any of the things I have said. How am I supposed to trust that you want for us to make this move, with you don't even trust me to build anything with me that shows a real commitment?"

"We aren't getting anywhere Soren." We may as well drop this shit.

Soren cooked dinner that evening. She and David had eaten dinner separately. David would clean up the kitchen and Soren was unsure of his mood. He had been quiet, so she walked to her bedroom, changed into her gym clothes, and walked out of the front door. David saw her, and assumed as much from her attire. Soren ran a full three miles and then the sauna for twenty minutes. She had sent texts to both Rowan and Mara, but both wiggled out of a gym date.

An hour and half later Soren was home and in the shower. She grabbed David's shirt from the bed and put it on. She lit the candle and lay down. She wasn't sleepy, but must have dozed off. Soren felt David's warm fingers slide between her legs. They dipped between the lips of her vagina and stroked her clitoris. She pulled his hands to her mouth and suckled them. He pulled his fingers slowly from her mouth and traced her lips. From there his long, dark fingers traced then squeezed her nipples. He moved is hands down her stomach, then between her legs again. He held her open and tickled her insides. The cold sheets gave way between her toes and she moved her legs open wider for David. He tasted her, licked, and softly bit her. He moved up. Soren could feel the hairs on his chest as his tongue went inside her mouth and his weight came down on top of her. He moved back to flip her over and pushed himself inside her. When they were finished, Soren lay flat on her stomach and David traced circles from his seeds spilled onto her.

"Soren, I love you, and I always have. But we have to change the way we interact with each other. You have to trust me. This will work out. I am not Christopher, and I know you want us be successful. I support you. I have never stopped you from achieving anything you ever wanted."

David wrapped his arm around Soren's waist. He was laying behind her. Soren could feel his breath on her neck.

"What did you ask me to do after your dad died?"

"I asked you to come and be with me in Atlanta." Soren turned on her side and faced David. "I missed my dad's funeral. I made the decision to go and complete my residency for graduate school."

"And?"

"And you came, you came. You were there with me and after my last presentation you brought me back home."

"In Atlanta you seemed happier, even with everything that was going on here. I just want you to be happy. I said we would go to Atlanta together. I don't understand why you feel as if I don't want to do this together. If I seem resistant in any way, it's because I am accustomed to being on my own, depending only on myself. I am not leaving you Soren."

"You promise?"

"I promise. Now go to sleep."

Soren turned her back to David, then nestled and tucked herself as close to him as she could. He blew out a deep breath and was snoring within minutes. It didn't seem to matter how scattered she was, he always brought her back to a place where she felt gathered.

Dissociative

By

Prince T. Patterson

Chapter 1

Her Secret

How many times do I have to love you, not physical but mentally? I try oh so hard, by day and by night to please you, I gave my heart, my attention, my friends- I abandoned them... so tell me why is it. That I find myself staring blankly into this foggy, steamy, bathroom mirror... with no windows here, only my razor and this speaker of Queen – Bohemian Rapsody playing I can hardly hear over. The day was November the 10th, 2011. My heart was pounding into a million pieces, I thought it was going to break away from my rib cage.

We met like ordinary people, passing each other by with a single smile. You spoke those couple of words "good day, welcome to The Market Place" you were wearing a green shirt with the words "If the attitude is right, the price will be alright" on the back.

"Good day, back to you." I said.

"My time is Timm short for Timothy." You had said.

"My name is Emily, pleasure to meet you."

"Likewise." He had said.

"As you were bagging what few groceries I had?" I asked.

"How long have you been working here?"

"Since 2007, when they first opened up, four years ago."

"That's impressive," I retorted. "What kind of person builds a place out in the empty space, in Boston, no type of indoor setting just straight nature?"

He made a slight chuckle as I rambled on about what kind of person would keep their shop open in the middle of winter. It's supposed to be a new start at getting people back to eating and shopping and to being one with nature. I think of it as a way of getting fresh products, instead of store brought with all of their chemicals and we also got less taxes. He explained so dreamy.

"Your total will be $13.75."

"That's not bad for some apples, milk and bread."

"Will I see you around Ms. Emily?" he asked.

"Maybe." I replied.

"How soon is maybe?"

"I don't know for sure, maybe later on this afternoon before the sunsets, there might be something I didn't get". I said smiling. As a small glow lit upon his face. Tall, light skinned complexity, British accent with a touch of Spanish decedent, an attitude that could change somebody's view on the world so I made it my business to return every day, picking up irrelevant items that I didn't need. Just to see what kind of person this being is....

On the 12th day of my visit, I dropped by from after school with best friend Ginger. Ginger was the same age as myself, 20 years old. We didn't meet until our 10th year in High school. Listening to her gossip about how Brad cheated on Jenny, and how Jenny gave Brad Aids and how she slept with his younger brother Ricky. Oh, how Ginger kept on talking on and on, about these people until we made it to the Market Place. "We're here. I said." Hopping she would exit out the car as fast as she had talked.

We were walking around the complex pretending to be interested in the products and the atmosphere. Scanning all 320sq ft. all that I was searching for was Timm better known as Timothy. After spending some 20-40 mins' tops in the Market Place. There he was sitting down on an empty milk carton.

"Well Hey There! I thought I would never see you again." He said.

"I've been busy, sorry it took me so long." Looking to the ground trying to avoid his well-mannered facial structure.

His voice was like that of honey and jazz. Yes. Diary I've said it. Honey and Jazz.

There he was sitting playing a harmonica (before I idly interrupted) …

"What do you like to do for fun?" He asked.

"I like to play the piano."

"A classical soul. I like that." He said.

"Explain?" I retorted.

"A piano is the voice, man cannot speak, like this harmonica." He replied. Ginger and I was stunned at his response.

Dear Diary. When I mean this cat was like something out of a Disney Tale, he truly was making me feel magical on the inside each and every time we had met and spoke.

Timothy Finn was him name. As the story goes on to tell. Timothy Finn worked for the Market Place when it first opened up. Having been working at a meat warehouse for about 2 years, and another 5 years as a Sales Associate for Kmart. His employer was keen and as well speckled about hiring him. He was a renowned citizen who has a medicinal and as well as a psychologically issue. For about 6 years he spent in a rehabilitation program. Born in Boston, adopted from birth, born and raised in the south side of London. At the age of 13, Timothy moved around from London to Korea, to China, and then to the U.S as the story was told me. It was in South Korea that his drug related problems came about.

Opium was of the first love, always with breakfast, lunch, and dinner with a bottle of absinthe, having used it during his days of High School. The cause of the constant move was due to his adopted parent's jobs. His adopted father Mr. William-Sir III, was chairman of the board for the phone company LG located in South Korea, and his adopted mom, Pattie Gwen was a pilot who was constantly on the move. They were very strict and critical when it came to school work. After some odd months of trying to learn "Hangungmal" one of the core languages spoken. The wrong crowd became the "right type" of crowd, and this particular crowd lead him down a dark path of crime and moments of blackouts. Where his mind would play tricks on him.

Dear Diary. I think the biggest failure of being in love is… you know that you're in love and you know that you're willing to give it your all, but what I found to be most peculiar is that the human flesh, spirit, and mind is constantly evolving. For reasons unknown, I don't know why I'm sitting here in this bathroom mirror talking to myself, there feels like somebody is around and that's when I open my eyes there is nobody….

Chapter 2

Personality Type

"I'm no God, but I do like to think that I am when I'm out mating with nature, hugging it from the roots on up, trees sing their song, and the blades of grass are as swift as the wind, coming and going." The other night, there was this guy on the T.V I had no idea what he was saying, but it was coming out dope. As I telling my employee Doug.

"You are a wild cat Timm, always watching the strangest of things I swear they should make a T.V show about your life and the things you're always into. Call it "The Timothy Half-hour Special". (Laughing Out Loud) retorted Timm inside his head, showing a fake smile. Not really caring much for this employee, everything is always fun and games. The smell of weed is booming today in the market, as I made my way to the concession stand of herbs that come from all over the world.

"Good Evening, Sun-Warrior how is the day of the people treating you?" (Laughing out loud)

"You got jokes Timothy, just because I'm Native-American don't mean I'm a sun-warrior or that I do the rain chants. But all is well laughing off the joke. Sun-Warrior was the step-son to the owner, and half Native-American. Not much is known about him, but that he is very mellow and laid-back. You know. "The in touch with nature kind of guy, another vegan to the add to the book, always believing in conspiracy theory's kind of guy". I call him Sun-Warrior because of the complexion in his skin and because of his background. Overall he is one-hell of a cool person to chill with.

"All is going well Timm. What are you up to today?"

"Nothing much Sun-Warrior, just walking around the Market looking for something to keep me occupied until we open up."

"It is a slow day, said Sun-Warrior. What was up with Doug this morning?"

"Nothing much, Doug was being Doug cracking irrelevant jokes, not being one to taking things serious."

"I feel you, said Sun-Warrior."

"I'm in that mood to just go home, lay in my bed, and smoke a big bowl of weed and zone out you feel me?"

"I feel you, my brother. I had some Psilocybin mushroom and I was one with my animal spirit, we were running through the forest, hunting buffalo's and shit. Coyotes are some crazy-ass animals I tell you."

"Your joking or you're for real?" I said.

"What you think motherfucker?" Sun-Warrior said jokingly.

"I think you need to chill with me after work." I said.

"I don't really mess with weed like that. I feel like it's more destructive to the soul, and it's not organic as how it was back in the days."

"More destructive to the soul? Either you've been taking to many shrooms or your animal spirit is not as smart as we thought it was to be. Tell me how weed can be destructive to the soul, when it was matured from the Earth?"

"Weed is one of the most natural of herbs in this known universe, not saying that your mushrooms aren't organic, but you know everything that was created wasn't always meant to be created."

I said in defense of the herb that is rapidly changing the way we protect ourselves from certain diseases that are deemed as incurable. Giving us a fighting chance at living longer and happier lives.

Sun-Warrior became real quite as I made my statement. "But it was all good, no harm was done." Sun-Warrior had said.

It was now 12' o clock and the Market Place had opened up, everybody was getting in their places, as we set up our carts and flipped opened our signs. Next to me was Leslie. She was in charge of bakery products, the smell of fresh pita bread being cooked in a cement-type like stove. Next to her was crazy Bob, he was in charge of making butter and cheese.("Real life" butter that is churned, and cheese that came from a cow was being made from scratch). 10 to 30 minutes' people was pouring out of thin air. It was mad rush hour the way people was lining up.

"Bonjour Mr. Zeal, it's been a long time since we've met in Texas, how have you been?"

"I've been well, and yes it has been a long time, how have you been?"

"I've been good." Replied the French woman.

"That's good to hear." It's been a while since somebody called me by that name… ZEAL? (Timothy said to himself). "I haven't been called that since I was in rehab."

"I've heard that you worked here." said the French Woman.

"Word sure does spread fast." Timothy said. "Who told you?"

"You know nothing cannot get by me, remember our little venture back in Korea? I hope you haven't forgotten about that person… that person… and that thing involving such said person."

"I did until you brought it up? Timm Said. "I'm out here trying to make a living for myself, what brings you to Boston?"

"Does your employer know about past?" Said the French Woman.

.....

"Why the silent pause?"

.....

"Hello? I know you can hear me." Said the French Woman snapping her fingers.

"How is my child?" Timm said.

"She's well." Said the French Woman. "How is my heart and my kidneys treating you?" She said smoking a cigarette.

"It's treating me well. (As he inhaled a puff of the cigarette). "You still never told me what how you found me?"

"Like I said does your employer know about your past in Korea." said the French Woman.

"He knows I've been to rehab, that I'm adopted, and that I've traveled around the world." Timm said.

"Ok." Said The French Woman.... (inhaling and exhaling the cigarette) ... "There was word around the Tin

Penny Alley that you have committed a series of violent crimes… is it true?"

"I don't know what you're talking about…"

"DON'T PLAY WITH ME ZEAL, I KNOW THAT THIS NOT WHO YOU ARE. Something happened in Korea that changed you." Said the French Woman. Timothy/ Zeal begins scratching his head, he begins to cry, his heart starts beating fast.

"It's ok." Said the French Woman. "I know it hurts to hear but you got to fight it…" Timothy/Zeal continues scratching his head).

"Don't speak another word." Timothy/Zeal said. "I'll meet you after work."

"Here is my number." Said the French Woman, I'll be around.

Chapter 3

The French Woman, and Britany

(Ring, Ring, Ring).

"Hello?" Answers Timothy

....

"Hello?"

"Shh…"

"Come again?"

(phone statics) "Shh… listen closely. First make sure nobody is around. Secondly I know what you did last summer…"

The voice of mystery hangs up.

The day was the first Wednesday of October and the condensation was dripping from my apartment window, the dew was overflowing in the yard below. As I brewed me some Dunkin Donuts coffee & rolled me up a cigarette, there was an uncomfortable feeling looming around in the house. Walking away from the bathroom to the balcony brushing my teeth, bird watching this white bird with long legs walking across the neighbor's fence. How majestic this being is. After I finished my bird watching and teeth brushing, the sugar was dissolving into my coffee giving off a sweet aroma that lit the house up with a rich smell. Unveiling the blinds to let some light in, I grab ahold of my loose Red Tobacco Cigarette, coffee and I opened up my laptop. The Microsoft program (Microsoft Word) was already open, with the title pulled up. Positioning my fingers over the keys typing up the fellow words....

In the kitchen staring at the knives, wondering which one will be the one. The end to all ends, the one that will claim the life of this liar.

Speaking what I stole from another as the tongue was in my mouth, just as it was in her blouse. The thought of you loving another would have stricken me with fear as I would compose endless hours of emotions. To display for the world to enjoy, but I couldn't get you to enjoy this last hour with me. Writing with sore palms and aching feet, but can't you hear me father? Light as a feather as there are 200 bird feathers in this pillow case that's in my room and the weight is overwhelming. I have spent my days traveling all over the world just to find what I couldn't see, this selfish image that I have displayed inside of me, is and will always be the death of any life. As I cross into my blessing, I wish I could have brought you with me, but the fee was killing me to be loyal. And that's why I sold my soul and now the decision has awoken within me, a being I thought I would have never become. My personality is changing and I don't know who is in control anymore, me or Zeal? I can love and more, but I needed more time, but you didn't know what I was going through and still wouldn't know until you…"

The words bring tears to my eyes, as I couldn't finish this will of love, and the sound it creates is more than enough to break any heart.

The story goes on to tell about how I was adopted, but I will save that piece of history for the later on parts of this intermission love story. Right now I am going to talk about. the French Woman and our history and how Emily is connected into equation.

The French Woman name was AME AMEDEE meaning (Beloved and to love God) no last name. Brunette hair of silk like texture, standing in at 5ft and 7' in. Her skin complexion was that of a Middle Eastern constantly wearing a Tilaka (a mark made on the forehead worn by Indian women). Ame Amedee was around the age of 20 when we first met and I was just turning 17. It was back in Korea where we meet, through a mutual friend of ours. Britany was a Country girl from the southern parts of Georgia who was stationed in an army base, she was also an ex-lover of ours.

Me and Britany was having sexual relations, doing blow all the time, up all times of the days, mostly starring at the night sky watching the planets dance through the telescopes that she had in her dorm. We met one day in the streets, randomly bumping into each other and we just hit it off from there. One day while we were wrapping up another night of late night sex, (the smell of weed and cocaine sweat was dripping from out of our pores) as I bent her over, down stroking that African-American Pussy, and smacking that ass while she was throwing it back. The sounds of exhaustion were leaving out of her mouth. Some twenty minutes later we were done, cleaning ourselves up, we decided to go the Seoul Pub to get this extra energy out of system. At the pub was Ame Amedee playing pool, she was wearing this cosplay outfit of Zelda and she was wearing it RIGHT! Since me and Britany wasn't a couple we came up with the idea of who could get her number, me being confident and devilish handsome as was. I threw a shot of Vodka back and I went over to her.

"Good Day, my love. What a charming day, what brings you here?" I said.

"Nothing much, out here playing me some pool. Want to get in?" She said.

"Sure why not." I replied. Looking over my shoulder towards Britany as some fellow was trying to holler at her. Reaching for the pool stick, she orders a two Corona lights.

"Ok. You know what the rules are right?" She said with a smirk on her face.

"Of course." I replied.

"This isn't your ordinary game of pool, were playing for sex." She said looking at me.

"SEX?" I retorted.

"Yes, sex. If I win you pay for my hotel room, if you win I get to have sex with you and your lady friend. Deal?"

"How do you know she's not my woman?"

"Because why else would you be over here talking to me and letting some random guy talk to her?"

"You see all don't you?" (Laughing out Loud)

"Do we have a deal?" She said with her hand ready to be shaken.

"Deal." As I shook her hand.

As the game proceed to take place. It became unclear who was going to win, beer after beer came, round after round was taking place as a crowd gathered around us. She had her supporters and I had mine, as the game going into round 5. There was 7 left and it was mine, there was complete silence. As I pulled my stick back and I flicked the 8-ball into the socket- the crowd lit up in a roar.

"A deal is a deal." she said. Calling Britany over to the speculation.

"I made a deal with your friend that if he was to beat me in a game of 8-ball we all would have an orgy. Is that fine by you?"

"Sure, I'm down." Britany replied. We left the bar and made our way back to Ame hotel. Neon lights lit up on the outside as everything was jumping excitement. As she opened her door, Britany undressed her. Ame pulled up a chair and she pushed me into it. Putting on some Indian belly dancing music, as Britany continued to undress her from behind, kissing her from the neck on down. Their technique was flawless, arousing me, completing me. Ame turned Britany around and laid her down on the bed kissing her from the mouth on down to her clitoris. As they called me over, they took off my attire taking turns both performing flawless-erotic -Kamasutra type moves.

As morning came the smell of sex was still lingering in the air, Ame Amedee was out on her balcony smoking a cigarette. "Bonjour." She had said.

"Bonjour." I said (stuttering to get the French word out).

"What brings you to Korea?" She had asked.

"My adopted parent." I replied.

"Oh that's wassup. I was born in Paris, but I mostly raised right here. At the age of 6 years old, my dad was leaving from Alabama to Paris on a plane, when it had exploded during take-off. My mom was living here in Korea and my grandma on my dad side thought it would be better for me to go and live with her. On my 7th birthday, I was on the first plane to South Korea and that's how I got her here. My dad was a domestic abuser and mom was an alcoholic- there isn't much to real tell. I've screw in the nights to mask away the pain and I mellow out in the morning when I'm all sober, kicking any old bad habits to the curb."

"That's crazy, I know the pain you are feeling (not physically but spiritual), both of my folks died in a car crash, 18-wheeler came and threw them right off the road and you know in Alaska their roads are overlapping on top of mountains. So the truck sent them flying straight off the mountain, the police say I should be grateful I'm still alive, but it's a burden when your living with people who put their careers first, like why get a job." I had told her. Ame shook her head in agreement and it was silence that lit up as we shared a cigarette.

Britany had awoken going to the bathroom to throw up. Blood was going from out of her nose, we called the ambulance and she got rushed to the emergency room. ... me and Ame waited on the doctor to give us results. (two hours went by). And still nothing not even a checkup, we stepped outside to share a smoke to clear out all the negative thoughts. About what would happen to her and to us, if she didn't show up back to the Army base.

"Why does she mean so much to you, if y'all is not a couple? I'm just curious." Asked Ame.

"She was one of the first few people I had met when I had arrived, treating me with kindness, everybody was acting like they never seen a black British boy in their home town."

"That's what you are!" Ame said with excitement.

"That's what?" I asked

"Your British! Explains the accent."

"Yea, my folks were natural born British folks before they had moved to Alaska, and just so happen while I was in foster care. My adopted parents happened to be from London and they took me back to their homeland."

We went back inside to find out that she suffered only a slight heart attack with a less mild struck, but the craziest part was that she was 2 months pregnant.

"8-Weeks." We all had said. Ame attention turned towards me.

Britany was looking down to the ground facial expression of disgust.

"It couldn't have been me." I said out loud. "We just met no less than 4 weeks ago and I always used a con…"

Before I could get the last three letters out. Britany shouted. "It's not you, you fool. I was raped at the Army base and I was too afraid to report it." I noticed my belly was beginning to take shape, but I thought it was from all the late nights of doing blow and eating a lot.

"Why you didn't report it?" Ame had asked.

"The baby is healthy, I would recommend that you lay off the drugs and start eating right, or there are several options. One your child might not live, two it could come out deformed, and third there is no telling what could happen." Said the doctor. "But that's all I can disclose. I'll bring you your discharge papers, we ran every test possible and your good for the clear."

"I'm sorry Britany, I wish there was something I can do…"

"Actual there is…" She said.

"It's a small price, but do you think you can handle the job?"

"I ain't killing no baby." I had said.

"No, nothing that drastic. I'm keeping it. I want you to kill the people who was involved and mail their bodies off to this guy, I know."

"That's it?" Timothy said. "Kill a couple of guys and mail their bodies to some random cat, you must be out of your mind. How in the hell do you expect me to even get away with that?"

"I'll join." Ame had said

Britany eyes grew with joy. "I'll text ya'll the address as soon as they release me."

Two gentleman dressed in white lab coats rushed into the hospital randomly killing people, pushing Ame into the bathroom as bullets were flying everywhere and people was being slaughtered. A woman ran into the bathroom begging for her life to be spared, as a bullet went through her head and exited out onto the floor. One of the gentlemen was pushing the doors open checking for people, when he got to ours, the other gentleman told him that the police was outside in an Englishmen accent.

We rushed back to the room Britany was in, a text message came through as we found her body sliced down, the text came in just in time.

Contemplating on whether we should alert the authorities, but then the question of how we came to know her would be examined and we just didn't have time for the questions, so we decided to go on the hunt ourselves. The address was there and so were the names. The police came and rescued us from a shooter between the outlaws, that seem like it would have never ended. As we made our layout of who we would target first…

I had awoken from this surreal memory, burning up in sweat going down from my head to the thighs. The past is sure a scary thing to relive. It all felt like I was reliving the past all over again and those dreadful days of where it all went downhill. The phone rang.

"Hello?" The phone statics. "Hello?" I said again.

"It's me Britany, I hope you didn't forget about me…"

Chapter 4

The voicemail

"Hello Timothy. It's me Emily we met at your job, I hadn't seen from you and I got your number from your co-worker Doug. I know it's strange to be calling at this time of the time night, but I was worried about you. I hope you get this voicemail."

Chapter 5

Multi-Personality

Me and Timothy was going to meet for lunch on New Year's Eve. As I laid out what dress I was going to wear our lunch, my head started ringing, (falling onto the floor), passing out for some odd time. My voice had changed into a sultry accent; I went into the bathroom mirror. Screaming from the top of my lungs, my whole appearance had changed. "Who am I?" The tattoo on my arm says Emily. "Who the fuck is Emily? My name is Maria, what am I doing here?" I said to myself. Timothy had texted that he was outside. "Who the fuck is Timothy? I don't know this person."

On the bed laid out was an ivory dress, I slipped it on. I went to meet this guy, in hopes that he could provide me with some answers.

"Good Evening Emily! You look as beautiful as ever." Timothy opened the car door for Emily.

"Thank-you " Maria had replied.

"Question."

"Sure." Timothy said.

"Who are you? And who am I? I woke up in this body and everywhere I look all I see is this Emily Character."

"You sure do got a sense of humor." Timothy had said...

"I'm for real, I don't remember anything up until now. All I know was that I woke up, a dress was laid out and then you texted me."

....

"You're serious." Timothy had said. "You got my number from one of my coworkers and you suggested that we go out for lunch on New Year's Eve."

"Why would I agree to such plans? That I cannot even remember signing up for..." Maria had said.

"Would you like to go to the hospital?" Timothy had said.

"I don't want to go to know hospital, I want someone to tell me what in God's name is taking place."

As the car had pulled out of her yard, Timothy had begun to break everything down to her, from his job, to the time they met, and how she had brought her friend Ginger to his job one day.

"What friend? I don't have any friends." Maria had said.

"You don't remember Ginger?"

"Nope, doesn't ring a bell. Is she from a TV show?"

"No, she is your best friend, you guys been the best of friends since the 10th grade, same age and all."

"I don't even remember my own age, so how in the hell could you know?" Maria had said angry.

"Because you had told me. We met almost every day, you would come to my job stalking me."

"Why in the hell, would I do such things, when I'm flawless and I could have anybody I want?"

As the car is doing 70mph on the express way. "If you're the guy I'm supposed to spend my evening with, I deserve to be treated with grace and style and I expect to be felt on after all is said and done. This is a new body and I want to break this pussy in…"

Miriage A Trois

By

Briana Cole

CHAPTER ONE

Asia

"Are you just going to walk around here ignoring me?" Asia asked, restrained sobs masking her voice until it was raspy and nearly unrecognizable. Her hazel eyes watched her husband's back as he busied himself with snatching clothes from his drawers. The force of his abrupt gestures had perfume bottles and picture frames falling off to litter the carpeted floor. Even though he kept his head down, the crease of his forehead in the mirror's reflection evidenced his anger.

Asia didn't bother to hide the pleading in her tone as she sank to the King Sleigh Bed that dominated their massive master suite. "Kenny, answer me, please. What did I do? Why are you so angry with me?"

"Just stop it, Asia." Kenneth growled as his eyes snatched up to meet her weakened gaze. He should have felt bad. Watching her stare back in sheer and utter confusion, silent tears streaking down her flushed cheeks, part of him did feel bad. But whether it was his pride, stubbornness, or sheer exhaustion of her, his trembling hands resumed grabbing at the T-shirts folded neatly in his drawer.

Asia opened her mouth to object and shut it again. Her mind scrambled desperately over the details of the past few weeks.

Sure they had been a little... off. She couldn't really place the where or why, but somewhere in their little routine, they had been become stale. An accumulation of working late, lack of affection, and jaded conversation dispersed between dinner and whatever was playing on TV. Asia couldn't even remember the last time they had kissed, much less had sex. But, she hadn't minded. She loved her man and she loved her marriage. Sure, she had expected them to still be saturated in that blissful, newlywed stage since it had only been a few months, but she found her own happiness in the comfort of their relationship. Kenneth was everything to her.

Part of her thought that maybe Kenneth was cheating on her. Even though she had quickly tried to dismiss the sordid thoughts, she had to admit he was displaying all the tell-tale signs. Asia sometimes found him looking at her, not with love, but with a miserable frown that had those dimples she loved, penetrating his cheeks like bullet wounds on both sides of his thick lips. When she touched him, he would tense and abruptly disconnect their contact. Maybe her gut was right. Just maybe she was being an idiot.

Asia closed her eyes and let the question fall from her lips in a delicate whisper. "Are you cheating on me Kenneth?" The silent tension was stifling and drew on so long Asia had to force herself to look at her husband.

Kenneth had stopped what he was doing and was now facing her, his face screwed in some deranged twist that she couldn't even decipher.

Figuring he was upset, she stood quickly, shaking her head. "No, don't answer that," she babbled, her steps swift as she made her way to join him across the room. "It doesn't even matter. I love you, Kenneth." And she did. She loved this man with every inch of her being. She didn't even care if he had been having an affair.

"Asia, really? Where the hell would you have gotten that from?"

"It doesn't matter." Asia reached out to touch him and gasped when he grabbed her wrists before the gesture could reach his face. "Baby, it doesn't even matter if you did. Or are. Or whatever. I'm sorry for asking you."

"No, I got to hear this." Kenneth bit off each threatening word and his grip tightened on her wrists. He knew it would probably leave red markings on her gorgeous peanut butter complexion, but at the moment, he didn't care. He just wanted answers.

Asia didn't bother responding as she lowered her eyes.

Kenneth's sudden laugh was evident that he didn't see anything amusing about the situation. "I can't believe this shit." Anger had him flinging her arm down with much more force than he intended. "What the hell is wrong with you Asia?"

"Baby," Asia let out a trembling sigh and kept her voice low. He was already furious and she knew she was making it worse. "I'm saying that I'm sorry for accusing you of infidelity. I'm saying that all I want to do is focus on 'us' Baby. Tell me how you're feeling and tell me how I can help."

"Stop it, Asia." Kenneth's tone was menacing as he cut his eyes at her once more. "Don't bring that psycho bullshit home to me. Save that for your patients."

Asia nodded. She wished her psychiatrist position was able to get her out of this mess. Because for the life of her, she couldn't figure out what was going on and why he was so upset. "And don't act ignorant," he continued, snatching open a zipper to shove his socks in the pocket of the bag. "You say I'm the one that's cheating? That shit is hilarious."

Asia stood in silence for a moment. The only sound was the snap of clasps and zippers as he packed the suitcase with his belongings. "Are you leaving me?" she asked.

The question stilled his movements and the heavy sigh was enough to deflate the tension in his shoulders. "I don't trust you Asia." he asked.

Now it was Asia's turn to frown. "I don't understand. I've never given you a reason not to trust me."

"You haven't?" His smirk was sarcastic and he shook his head. "I just can't deal with this anymore. I just can't."

Stunned, Asia merely watched him drag the suitcase to the door, stopping only to pick up a duffel bag he had packed earlier. He didn't utter another word as he left and the slam of the front door had her letting out a breath.

That was what he needed. Maybe then he could sort out whatever it was he needed to sort out. But one thing was for sure. He was definitely cheating on her. And she was going to do whatever it took to get him back.

CHAPTER TWO

Laurielle

"Laurielle, can you at least act like you're having an orgasm?" The director said, his tone laced with aggravation. "I'm getting this all on camera and your ass is up here acting like you're disgusted."

"I am. Shit," Laurielle snapped back as she leaned on her elbows, tossing the 16-inch Peruvian weave of the wig behind her shoulder. "Maybe if you get me a nigga that can eat some damn pussy, I could catch a fucking orgasm and wouldn't be so mutha fucking disgusted."

Her eyes rolled down the oiled curves of her naked body to the white guy posted between her thighs. His thin lips were moist from sucking and lapping on her clean-shaven folds. He couldn't have been more than 20 or so. But old enough to know better that's for damn sure.

"What the fuck is wrong with you, White Boy?" she said, her eyes narrowing at his fearful expression. "You ain't ate no black pussy before? My shit taste like fucking jolly ranchers so you need to stop playing with your food and eat this shit for real. And lick your mutha fucking lips Dude.

Them shits already small and you got them crusty enough to cut my fucking snatch."

A roar of laughter erupted from the camera crew as Laurielle swung her leg over the boy's body to climb from the bed. She loved being a porn star because she had dick that ran threw her take after take after take. But she hated being a porn star for the very same reason. Usually, her director Roger, was pretty good about setting the scene and picking an actor that could keep up with her unusually high sex-drive. Hell, she was pretty good at keeping up the authenticity herself with each roll of the camera. But sometimes, the sex was so bad that she couldn't fake it even more than if her cum face was painted on. And being the diva she was, she had no problems voicing that fact.

Laurielle pushed past the small crowd of technicians lining the bedroom set. She didn't even bother accepting the satin robe someone held out to her, instead boldly letting her titties and ass swing in full glorious view as she made her way to the door.

"Where the hell do you think you're going?" Roger called. "Laurielle, get your ass back here."

"Call me when you find somebody ready for this pussy," she snapped back and pushed through the door.

The chill in the hallway had her shuddering as she made her way to her dressing room. It was really just a small storage closet, but Laurielle had made Roger so much money on her movies in the past month that he finally relented and replaced the boxes with a tiny vanity, mirror, and coat rack for her costumes. It was enough for her.

Laurielle closed herself in the room and plopped down on the bench. Her body was exhausted and she was tempted to leave. But she knew they wanted to get one more scene in before they wrapped up for the day so she turned to the mirror with its globe-style bulbs illuminating brightly in the quaint space. She reached for her brush on the table and smacked her lips when she heard the cell phone ringing. She already knew who it was. Asia's mother had been calling her non-stop. She already knew it was because of the falling out with Asia and her husband, Kenneth.

Laurielle rolled her eyes in the mirror and ignoring the muffled ringing, she picked up the brush to begin working out the tangles in her weave.

She wasn't trying to be mean to Ms. Vincent and she loved the woman as if she were her own mother, but she really wasn't in the mood for the drama. She had already heard enough from Asia when it happened. The woman was devastated, but Laurielle had insisted she was better off without Kenneth. He was a boring ass Criminal Attorney anyway. Laurielle could never see what her girl saw in him. Sure he was cute and Laurielle had attempted to get better acquainted with him on several occasions. But Asia intervened and shut that down real quick. She acted like she needed that nigga like she needed air and it was frankly, beginning to disgust Laurielle. Asia sometimes acted like she didn't even need her anymore and she couldn't stop the continuous pangs of jealousy that coursed through her every time she heard his name. Kenneth this and Kenneth that. Where the hell was Kenneth when they were each other's only best friend? Now, he thought he could just slide right in and push her out. Yeah, Kenneth had another mutha fucking thing coming. So though it pained Laurielle to see Asia so distraught, it was better in the long-run.

As soon as the ringing stopped, Laurielle pulled open the drawer and picked up the cell phone. She swiped the screen and sure enough, it was Ms. Vincent. Ignoring the notification, Laurielle punched in a telephone number, placed the phone on speaker, and sat it down on her vanity to ring a loud.

"Yeah?" The man's sexy voice echoed in the room as Laurielle resumed brushing her hair.

"Hey boo," she crooned. "What are you doing?"

"Shit."

Laurielle rolled her eyes, amused at her boyfriend's curt responses. He had always been a man of few words. Instead, he opted to show her and the way he had her body singing, she was more than cool with his hands-on approaches. She pictured his muscular frame stretched out on their tattered leather couch, probably flipping through the channels of someone's extended cable he had managed to steal. No doubt he had a blunt stuffed between his lips. The nigga smoked so much weed the smell often permeated from his pores. Not her first pick for a man, Laurielle had to admit. He was sexy as hell between his Rick Ross aura and boss attitude, but the man couldn't hold a job for shit. Not really husband material that's for sure. But, she really wasn't in the market of being too choosey considering she just wanted to get married since Asia had a husband. Her two-can-play-that-game approach was more for her self-gain considering Asia didn't even know her intentions. But that was enough for her.

"Will you be home tonight?" Chris's voice brought her back to the conversation.

"I want to," Laurielle admitted on a pout. Truthfully, chances were she would have to tag along to see about Asia. The woman's depression was getting the best of her and she spent more and more time quiet and to herself. But there was still the off chance that she would come out of her shell and Laurielle would need to be there. Like she always had been. "Don't go fucking nobody if I don't come home, Nigga," she snapped, suddenly realizing the basis for his question.

"Bitch lower your tone," Chris's voice was calm and lazy as he spoke. "I was just asking so you could pick a nigga up some Popeyes or something on the way to the crib."

Laurielle licked her lips with a smirk. "Oh yeah? And what you gone do for me?" She flirted.

"Bitch, you already know what it is. Stop fronting and bring your ass home so I can dig in that pussy. Or is that ass stale from giving it to those lames on set?"

Laurielle smacked her teeth. "Nigga, please. These limp dick simps can't fuck worth a damn. Right about now, I couldn't get this pussy wet if I went down on the fucking Titanic."

"Well shit, bring that fat ass home then and I'll make it wet for you."

Laurielle wanted to squeal as she felt his words open the flood gates. She felt her juices soaking her thighs and dribbling to pool on the cloth upholstery on her bench. "I'll try Baby."

"Yeah." He hung up and Laurielle spread her legs to eye her moist kitty. She was good and ready now. She just hoped Roger and the technicians had somebody else to stand-in so they could finish the scene. Or else, she wouldn't mind fucking her damn self.

CHAPTER THREE

Asia

The satin sheets tangled around her bare legs as Asia turned over. Fresh tears dampened her pillow as she gazed over to the digital clock on the nightstand. 2:24 PM. She had passed out again, no thanks to the upturned bottle of alcohol on the table. For days, she had been in and out of consciousness, floating on auto-pilot like some post-apocalyptic zombie. She had called Kenneth too many times to count and had clogged up his voicemail and texts with an abundance of pleas and apologizes. Apparently, he hadn't been running from her, but towards something because he seemed well and content with not acknowledging her. Now here it was day five of his mysterious disappearance and he hadn't so much as called to make sure she was still alive. His apathy was what hurt the most when her heart was drowning in emotional turmoil. The least he could do was care.

But he didn't. The sting of the realization came barreling back with enough force to have her squeezing her eyes shut at the harsh reality. *He apparently doesn't love you.*

Look at him, Asia. Why hasn't he called? Must be laid up with some bitch right now.

The phone's sudden ring was the first noise, it seemed, she had heard in days. Anxious, Asia snatched it up from the nightstand and swiped the screen to connect the call.

"Asia?" Her mother's warm voice filled her ear and felt as if it were wrapping her in a protective blanket. Asia relaxed into a grateful smile. She hadn't realized how much she needed her voice.

"Mama, I'm here."

"Where have you been?" Ms. Vincent's voice was laced with remnants of her dissolved panic. "I've been calling you for days. Why haven't you answered the phone?"

"Mama, I just...." Asia sat back against the cushions stacked against her faux leather headboard. "I'm sorry. I've just been going through some things."

"What is it Sweetie?"

Asia sniffed, struggling to keep the sobs from erupting. "It's Kenneth," she said, finally. "Kenneth left me."

"Oh Honey, why?" Ms. Vincent's voice elevated with concern.

"I really don't know honestly. Part of me thinks he is cheating on me."

'What?"

"Well what else could it be Mama?" Now the sobs did come, enough to tighten the words in her throat as she spoke. "He's never home and when he is, we're just like roommates. He doesn't kiss me anymore and he cringes every time I touch him. Like he's revolted by me. I don't know what I've done but then he starts talking about trust. And you know that's what you told me Daddy used to say to you and meanwhile, he was the one cheating, remember?"

"Yeah, but Honey..." Her mother trailed off, apparently at a loss for words. "I just don't think he's doing that. He loves you so much. I know he does. Maybe if I call--,"

"No, Mama, please." Asia sniffed and sighed. She was starting to feel weak again. "I'll handle it myself. Even if he is cheating, I won't care. I love him. I'm going to give him his space for a while. It just hurts to know I don't make him happy like I used to do."

"Don't say that," Ms. Vincent said. "Of course you make him happy. There has got to be something else..." She trailed off and it was obvious something was on her mind.

"What is it Mama?" Asia prompted at her mother's hesitancy.

"Well, Sweetie have you been having those blackouts again?"

Asia frowned. "Mama, I don't see what that has to do with Kenneth," she said.

"How about I come over and we talk more about this? I want you to know I'm here for you."

Asia sighed and ran a quivering hand through her messy, shoulder-length hair. The unconditional love she had for her mother had long ago incited immediate forgiveness for when she was younger. But the woman had tried her best to make up for those three years she had thrown her daughter into the foster care system. Drugs nor sex had prompted her actions. Ms. Vincent had simply said she hadn't wanted to be bothered with a kid anymore. At the tender age of six, Asia hadn't understood what that meant. She considered herself a good child. And she liked to think she was smart. She had always been a loner and never had any friends. So the fact that her mother was suddenly 'tired of raising her' was something her young mind couldn't fathom.

It wasn't until she had been shuffled from foster home to foster home that reality began to snatch her innocence and she'd been faced with the cold, hard facts. That was when the blackouts had started. It her way of tuning out the abuse. And even when her mother turned up three years later, older, wiser, and more mature, Asia had forgiven quickly. But she had never fully forgotten that deserted feeling that consumed her for those 38 months, two weeks, and three days before her mother showed up on the porch of her eighth foster home. Even now at 22, her mother still went over and beyond to repair the mistake she made all of those years ago.

The doorbell chime sounded throughout the house and Asia walked to the window to peer out into the driveway. The familiar tan Camry had her not bothering to stifle a frustrated sigh. She knew he was bound to show up.

"Mama, I have to go," Asia said. "I'll call you right back."

"What is it, Asia? Is it Kenneth?"

"I wish. It's my co-worker. He's just coming to make sure I'm ok, I'm sure."

Ms. Vincent hesitated and then said, "OK. Just call me back when you're done Sweetie."

"I will."

They said their goodbyes and Asia hurried down the short flight of stairs to answer the door. It wasn't until she reached the foyer that she remembered her skimpy pajama shorts and tank top and she paused, debating on going back upstairs for her robe. The doorbell rang again and she dismissed the thought. Their relationship was strictly platonic. Paul had never been the kind of person to look or speak to her inappropriately so as long as he wasn't uncomfortable, she was sure they would be fine.

"Hi, Paul," she greeted after pulling open the door.

Paul stood framing the doorway. He gave her a small smile and even though the sun draped against his back enough to shadow his face, she could still make out his troubling expression. "What's wrong?" she asked.

"You haven't been back to the center," he said. His eyes seemed to be searching her face for answers, even before he asked the question. "What's going on?"

Asia stepped to the side to wave him into the living room. "I know," she said with a sigh. "But I am really going through some personal things right now. My mind has been all over the place."

"You could've called," he scolded. "We were worried about you. I even dropped by a few times this week and you didn't answer."

"Paul, please," Asia said, a headache starting to throb at her temple. "I appreciate your concern but all of that was not necessary. I agree, I should've called. But I'm having some problems in my marriage and to be honest, work was not on my mind."

Paul's face softened and he nodded. "I'm just glad you're Ok," he admitted, touching her arm lightly. "Do you want to talk about it?"

"Who, Kenneth?" Asia snorted as she turned to walk into the kitchen. "Not really. We already have trust issues so I don't think he would take to kindly knowing I'm divulging all of our personal relationship problems with a man. Do you want something to drink?"

Paul didn't answer, but Asia took the liberty of pulling down two glasses and pouring some juice for both of them. "How is work?" she asked, lifting her own cup to her lips to take a sip.

"All is well," Paul answered. "I think we were more worried about you than anything."

"I'm fine." She dismissed his concern with a wave of her hand. "Just give me a few days to get my head together and I'll be back in no time. You know I love my job."

Paul's gaze was unwavering as he studied her over the rim of his glass.

Asia shifted uncomfortably. Maybe she should've put on that robe after all.

"Have you spoken with him?" Paul asked, gently setting the glass back on the counter. "Your husband, I mean."

She shook her head. "No. I call myself giving him some space."

"Maybe you should call him. Would it be easier if I talked to him?"

Asia didn't stop the bubble of laughter that erupted as she shook her head again, this time much stronger. "Oh no. I just told you we had trust issues. I don't think he wants to talk to you about me, Paul. No offense. I'm sorry."

"No, I understand." Paul's genuine smile cracked his face and smoothed out any remaining stress on his chocolate skin. "I was just trying to help. Have you talked to someone about what's going on?"

"I'm just really trying not to get everybody in my business. This is my marriage," Asia admitted. She didn't notice Paul's furrowed eyebrows before he looked away. She reached over the marble countertop and placed her hand on his. "I do appreciate it. I do. We're going to be fine. Thank you Paul."

Paul nodded and rose from his perch against the island. "Well good. I guess I'll be going then."

Asia wrinkled her nose. His behavior seemed different. She couldn't put her finger on it, but Paul was definitely acting weird. She had known him too long not to notice, ever since she started working at the center.

They paused at the door and Paul gave her shoulder a friendly pat and squeeze. "You know I'm here for you right?" he said.

"Of course. I know that. Is there something wrong Paul?"

He looked as if he wanted to say something and for a brief moment, Asia thought she could almost see the words filter down from his eyes to the tip of his tongue before he firmly shut his mouth.

"Everything is fine," he assured her. "When do you think you'll be back?"

Asia lifted a shoulder in a half shrug. "As soon as possible. Just give me a few days."

"So, maybe Tuesday then?" he pressed.

A swell of agitation was beginning to tighten her chest and exasperated, Asia nodded. "Yeah. Let's say Tuesday."

He seemed satisfied by that answer and threw her another calming smile. "I'm sorry. I just… worry about you." Asia gasped when Paul gently patted her shoulder once more. Had he rubbed her neck? She eyed him, her orbs desperately sifting through his blank stare for some sign to validate her suspicions. But there was nothing. And yet, Asia got the unnerving feeling that there was so much more.

CHAPTER FOUR

Kenneth

Kenneth logged off of his computer and sat back in the reclining desk chair. He was able to get his client off with six months' probation. The win should have been exciting news for him. But his mind was elsewhere.

He sighed, running his hand over the stubble at his chin. He dreaded going back to the hotel. The shit was lonely, depressing, and a constant reminder of the estranged relationship between him and his wife. But even though he had tried to stall by keeping himself busy for the past few hours, it was now 11:23 and there was nothing left to do.

He turned his eyes to the 5 X 7 wedding photo that sat on the side of his keyboard. Though he had discovered Asia's infidelity, he still couldn't bring himself to remove the wedding picture. The photographer had captured a candid shot of the couple as they made that joyous trek up the aisle as husband and wife. Goofy grins adorned their faces as Kenneth clutched his wife's waist. Asia's arm was lifted in the air as she gripped the bouquet and the flash of the camera had brilliantly captured the sparkle of embellishments on the bodice of her wedding gown. That same sparkle reflected in her eyes. She looked genuinely happy. So why had she cheated?

Kenneth didn't remember ever crying for a woman, but he had damn sure cried for Asia. He could still see the images playing through his head, see the pages and pages of bank statements where she had made large withdrawals and purchases. He couldn't bring himself to say she had stolen from him. That thought was even more hurtful. But with her saying she had no knowledge of the money, it really was starting to feel like he was sleeping with a liar, cheater, thief, and con artist.

He snatched his eyes away from the picture and felt the familiar twinges of heartache tightening his chest. How had he allowed himself to be so deceived? Sure they had fallen in love rather quick, but that didn't diminish the depth of his love any less. But he would be damned if he continued to allow her vicious ways to hurt him. It wasn't even pride. But he deserved a woman who treated him just like he treated her. And Asia's deceptive ass was not it.

The papers had been sitting on his printer for days. Now, Kenneth snatched them up and shoved them into a folder. He didn't know what to expect but somehow, those few measly pages didn't seem like they should be able to annul his marriage. He collected his things and carried the folder with him to the parking garage. It was late, but he needed to do this now before he lost the nerve.

The smell of rain still hung strong in the air but that didn't seem to stop the booming city nightlife. Women were strutting down the streets in minis and the club lights seemed to entice the steady stream of partygoers. Kenneth drove through the crowded streets, remembering when he used to frequent the popular social scenes right along with everyone else.

The house was dark when he steered his black Benz into the driveway. He pushed the button to open the garage, frowning when the door rose to reveal it was completely empty. He felt the tug of anger at the realization. She didn't give a damn about him. Here they were, separated and she was still out doing her thing without so much as a concern about their marriage.

Kenneth entered the house through the garage. Not bothering to turn on lights, he headed up the stairs and into the large bedroom he used to share with Asia. The moon seeped through the open blinds and spilled onto the empty bed. Kenneth eyed the bed on a frown.

He walked into the bathroom, flipping on the light. Makeup littered the marble countertop from where Asia had apparently used it earlier. Anger had the headache throbbing at his temples as he furiously swiped the items from the counter. Lipstick and makeup brushes clattered loudly to the linoleum floor. Not thinking, Kenneth pulled his phone from his pocket and punched in her number. It didn't even ring. "You have reached Asia . . ." He disconnected the call and immediately redialed. It was when he paced in front of the dresser that he noticed a cell phone sitting on top of the cherry wood. He picked it up, torn between anger and worry when he saw the screen was black. He powered on the phone and immediately, an assembly of missed call notifications chimed in. Kenneth opened the call log and scrolled through the numbers. Asia hadn't saved anyone's number to her contacts so all of the numbers with the exception of his looked unfamiliar. One number in particular had been called the most so taking a breath, he pushed the button to dial it.

Each ring was more and more unsettling. Kenneth didn't know what he expected when whoever answered, but the curiosity was eating at his psyche.

"Hello?" The woman's voice was low and apparently clogged with sleep.

Kenneth remembered what time it was and could have kicked himself. "Um, hello?" he said, at a loss for words.

"Who is this?"

The voice became more clear and Kenneth sighed in relief at the sudden recognition of Asia's mother.

"Ms. Vincent?" he said. "I'm sorry this is Kenneth."

"Kenneth? What's wrong? Why are you calling this time of night? Where's Asia?"

"I'm sorry to bother you this late," he said, sinking down to the edge of the bed. "I honestly don't know where Asia is. She left her phone at home."

"She what?" Panic had elevated her voice. "Asia wouldn't do that. When was the last time you spoke to her?"

Kenneth paused. He didn't know if he wanted to divulge the details of his marriage to his mother-in-law. But then again, if he was serious about their divorce, she needed to know. He took a breath. "It's been almost two weeks now," he admitted. "Asia and I are getting a divorce, Ms. Vincent. I'm not sure if she told you or not."

"What? No, she didn't tell me. She mentioned y'all were separated for a bit. But..." Ms. Vincent trailed off, letting out a frustrated sigh. "Kenneth where are you? Where is Asia?"

"I told you I don't know where she is," he said. "But this is not the first time this has happened."

"What do you mean 'not the first time?"

Kenneth opened his mouth and abruptly shut it again. No matter his feelings on his wife's affairs, she was still his wife. And this was her mother. "With all due respect Ms. Vincent. I think some of these answers should probably come from Asia."

"Fuck respect Kenneth," Ms. Vincent snapped. "I'm trying to see what the hell is going on. Asia won't tell me. You won't tell me. Now you call me at damn near one in the morning telling me my daughter is not there and you don't know where she is and she left her phone at home. Plus, you're getting divorced. What am I supposed do? Just roll over and go back to sleep?"

Kenneth sighed. "Ok," he relented. "I found out Asia has been cheating on me. First coming home late, then not coming home at all. Sometimes for days. I've called her a few times and men have answered her phone. Then, I noticed she started making large withdrawals from our joint checking account. Thousands at a time. One of these times when she didn't come home, she was making purchases in Biloxi. I ask her about it, she lies and says she doesn't know what the hell I'm talking about. But that's not the worst of it..." He trailed off closing his eyes against the disgusting mental images dancing in his head. "Then, I found a video--,"

"Stop," Ms. Vincent said, her voice soft, but firm. "Kenneth I think you need to come over here and talk to me. Right now."

"This time of night?"

"Right now," she repeated. "I'm going to make a call. Don't wait. Bring your ass now." And with that, she hung up.

CHAPTER FIVE

Laurielle

His laughter could be heard over the gush of water echoing off the acrylic bathtub. Laurielle bent over to shut the water off and frowned at the closed bathroom door. Whoever Chris was talking to sure had him in a hell of a good mood. She rolled her eyes as she stepped over the lip of the tub, the water drizzling down her slender leg and dampening the plush bathroom rug. About damn time. His pitiful ass temper tantrum was not what she had planned on dealing with for the better half of the afternoon so she was glad he had lightened the fuck up.

Laurielle wiped her hand across the mirror to clear the steam fogging the glass. She eyed her reflection briefly before turning to snatch the towel from the rack. For some reason, she couldn't help but feel like something wasn't quite right. Maybe Asia's issues were finally getting to her. She felt torn. Part of her wanted to care. Her girl was really going through it and Laurielle had always been the one to look out for her and help her through. But then, the other part of her, the part she was more privy to listen to when she didn't give a damn about reason or morals, told her she needed to worry about herself. For so long, Laurielle had wanted her own life. One without standing in the shadows of Asia's troubles. For once, it felt good to live without a care or concern for anyone other than Laurielle. And it felt liberating. But none of that could suppress the uneasiness bubbling in the pit of her stomach.

"Hell yeah!" Chris hollered. Footsteps stomped towards the door before he snatched it open. The sudden burst of cold air chilled her skin and she turned, barely able to wrap the towel around her body. His body framed the small doorway as he grabbed her by her arm and pulled her to him. "That was my lawyer," he said, reading Laurielle's mind. "I got off on the last drug charge with only probation. You were right. That nigga is stupid good."

Laurielle grinned. "I'm so happy for you boo," she said, lifting her arms to wrap around his neck. The gesture had her towel falling to pool at her feet. "Now why don't you show me just how happy you are."

Obediently, he hoisted her in the air and her legs wrapped around his waist. His mouth crushed hers and Laurielle moaned as his hands assaulted her, bruising the tender flesh of her titties. He slammed her back against the plaster and used one hand to fiddle with the buttons of his jeans. Once they slid down around his ankles, his dick bounced free and he didn't even hesitate to shove it in her waiting pussy.

"Fuck," she whispered as he began his fierce pounding, knocking her ass against the wall with every thrust. She could hear Chris's grunt above her own heavy breaths. As she felt the beginnings of her nut, she could only praise Kenneth for prompting her man to give her this celebratory dick.

# # #

Laurielle readjusted her sunglasses and drummed her fingers impatiently on the steering wheel. If she had've been paying attention, she would have noticed the familiar face scrutinizing her through the back window. Instead, her eyes fell, once again, onto the digital clock illuminating from her dashboard. She wished Chris would hurry the hell up.

No sooner had the thought crossed her mind did she see him step from the store and on to the curb. He shifted the brown bag of liquor underneath his other arm before pulling open the passenger side door.

"Damn it sure as hell took you long enough," Laurielle grumbled as soon as Chris had slid into the seat. "Did you get my Ciroc?"

"Yeah." The bottles clanked loudly as he fished inside the bag for something. He pulled the pack of Salt and Vinegar chips into view and ripped open the package.

"Now you gone have my shit stinking," Laurielle mumbled on a frown. "Wait until we get home." When Chris didn't respond, she smacked her lips and snatched the gear into reverse. Her eyes lifted to the rearview mirror to begin backing up when the black Benz whipped behind her and had her slamming on the breaks.

Chris's chips flew from his fingers as he muttered a curse. "What the fuck?"

Laurielle glanced to the back of the car and narrowed her eyes at the vehicle now easily blocking her into the parking space. "The fuck is this mutha fucka doing?"

Her attitude kicked into overdrive as she shoved the gear back into PARK and opened the door. A full-blown cuss out was already savoring on her tongue. That's when she recognized his car and she spun on her heel.

"What the fuck are you doing here?" His voice pierced the air as he unfolded himself from the car.

Laurielle paused before turning back around to face him. She crossed her arms over her chest. "No, the question is, what the fuck are you doing here, Kenneth? Why the hell are you following me?"

Kenneth's face curled into a disgusted frown as his eye narrowed at the woman. "What is wrong with you?"

"Me?" Laurielle didn't even know she was amused until she heard her own laughter sweep the air. She threw up her arms in exasperation. "Ain't shit wrong with me Nigga." She watched his mouth open and immediately shut as soon as his eyes slid past her. Sure enough, Chris had stepped from the car and slammed the door, drawing attention from the entire parking lot.

"The fuck is wrong with you fuck boy?" he yelled, already making a beeline for Kenneth. He stopped in his tracks. "Ey yo' what you doing here talking to my girl?" Chris glanced towards Laurielle. "The fuck you out here talking to my lawyer for?"

Kenneth's eyes darted between Chris and Laurielle and his eyes rounded in, what Laurielle clearly saw, was shock. "W-w-what?" He stammered, shaking his head. "N-no. She tried to tell me this was true, but I didn't want to believe her."

"Man I don't know what the fuck wrong with you Dude," Chris said, taking another step towards Kenneth. "But you need to get yo' ass back in your car and leave my girl the fuck alone."

Laurielle pursed her lips shut as she watched the mirage of emotions play across Kenneth's face. She hated he found out this way but frankly, she didn't give a damn. He was Asia's man. Not hers.

"You heard him," she chimed in gesturing absently towards his car. "Now you need to move that piece of shit before I run that mutha fucka over." She turned once again and gasped when she ran smack into Paul. Laurielle took a step back as the realization began sinking in.

Before she had a chance to run, she felt Paul's grip clasp her arm and the prick of a needle as it punctured her skin. She winced and could barely slur a curse before the familiar dizziness took over. Laurielle's knees weakened beneath her and she fell against Paul's chest, his arms breaking her fall. She could barely make out his voice as the darkness swallowed her; disappointment edging his whisper until it felt rough against her cheek.

"Don't fight it, Asia."

CHAPTER FIVE

Asia shrunk into the sweat-stained sheets of her bunk bed, the ache between her legs sending rippling slices of pain that nearly numbed her from the waist down. They had done it again. Her two foster brothers had made it a game this time; one holding her down and covering her mouth while the other probed her down there until she bleed through her pajama bottoms. Then, they would switch positions. Every night they would sneak in her room and every night they would leave her an empty shell of the girl she no longer could feel.

Exhausted, Asia climbed to her feet and stumbled across the darkened hall to the adjoining bathroom. She didn't bother cutting on the light as she felt around for the faucets on the sink. She turned a knob and immediately leaned into the sink to splash the chilling water on her face. She wanted to hate her mother, but nowhere in her heart could she muster the strength for it. Instead, she felt completely broken. And hollow.

It wasn't until she leaned up that she saw her. Through the blur of water droplets, the girl stood reflected back in the glass, mirroring her own actions. At first, she just looked like a shadow. Then, her features began to crystallize as if being brought into focus through a camera lens. Her cheekbones were sharper, her eyes more narrow. The arch of her eyebrow and the smirk on her lips appeared as if she were gloating. "Who are you?" Asia whispered and her eyes widened when a girl's voice floated in her head, though the lips in the reflection didn't move.

"Just call me Laurielle," the voice said. "I'm here to help you."

Asia's mouth hung open as she shook her head. "Where did you come from?"

"It don't even matter," Laurielle's voice carried an authoritative tone that Asia envied. She sounded older and a lot stronger. "You mind if I help you?"

"With what?"

The eyes in the mirror looked past Asia's head towards the bathroom door. "Those niggas are some punk bitches Asia," Laurielle snapped. "It's time I show they ass just who the fuck they messing with. You want them to stop hurting you right?"

Asia nodded slowly as more tears stung the corners of her eyes.

"Good." Laurielle said. "I'm your friend. I won't let shit else bad happen to you. Just let me handle it."

And with that, Asia blacked out.

#   #   #

"Very good, Asia. Very good." Paul nodded his encouragement as he made notes on his pad.

Asia sat across the desk, her mind still foggy after the second round of hypnotherapy. They sat in her office, well what her therapist Paul had stated was her office. Instead, it had been another strategy to keep her coming to the clinic five days a week so he could keep an eye on her.

"You're doing much better," he said with a comforting smile. "Multiple personalities is not easy to control, but the more you're willing to work towards getting better, the more you can expect to keep Laurielle at bay."

"Really?" Asia's let out a small chuckle. "You said that you've been treating me for many years Paul. What are we doing so different this time?"

Paul sat his pen down and clasped his hands together on top of Asia's folder. "I admit," he said. "The shock therapy those years ago was pretty drastic. And did nothing, but erase your memory. For a while, we thought we were ok. You seemed to be doing better. But I think your marriage is what triggered that alter personality again."

Asia sighed. She had to admit, when Paul and her mother had revealed she was, indeed, Laurielle, denial had convinced her otherwise. But then, everything started coming together. The numerous blackouts, the frivolous spending, Kenneth. Of course, he had walked out on her. She would disappear for days and have no recollection of where, why, or how she had gotten there. To find out she had been having some ass-backward relationships with her husband's client, Chris. Then, when Paul showed her the porno tapes, she had thrown up for a solid week straight. Watching her own body get sucked and fucked in every position imaginable while she screamed and cursed to the heights of some orgasmic ecstasy she had no recollection of, was entirely too much. Depression had sunk in to the point her mom had found her huddled in the corner of the shower, the water stinging as it hit the razor thin cut on her wrist. So she had voluntarily admitted herself to the hospital. She didn't trust herself anymore. And that shit was scary.

"You're doing great," Paul said, bringing her back to the conversation. "We'll keep monitoring you and I've prescribed you some more medicine to help you sleep. I hear you've been dealing with insomnia again."

Asia nodded and blinked back tears. "Thank you," she whispered. "For everything Paul."

Paul stood to round the desk. In one swift motion, he pulled Asia to her feet and embraced her in a hug. "I love you like a sister," he murmured, giving her shoulders a genuine squeeze. "I mean that. We're going to get through this."

A small smile formed on her lips. She needed all the support she could get. She wasn't strong enough. Physically or mentally.

The phone buzzed on the desk and Paul reached over to put the caller on speaker. "Yes," he said.

"Excuse me, Doctor," the secretary said. "But Asia's visitor is here."

"Ok thanks," Paul said and pushed another button to hang up. He looked at Asia who nodded expectantly. Her mother's visits were like clockwork. Right after Asia's late morning therapy session and just in time to join her for lunch.

"Want me to escort you?" Paul asked.

"I think I got it." Asia said. She turned and picked up her robe from the coat rack near the door.

The sunroom was horribly dated with polished wicker furniture and floral cushions arranged against floor-to-ceiling windows. Potted plants and wind chimes hung from the ceiling and gave the room a distinct greenery smell that Asia hated. She was surprised to find the room empty. Where was her mother?

The door opened and Asia turned, shocked when she saw Kenneth standing in the entryway. He looked casual in a Polo shirt and some khakis and she was even more surprised to see he held a bouquet of lilies in his arms.

Embarrassment colored Asia's cheeks and she immediately turned away. She had begged her mother not to tell Kenneth where she was. She couldn't bring herself to look him in the eye knowing what she had done to herself. Done to him. She felt ashamed and, at the sight of him, disgusted with herself for her mental issues. He deserved better. A month in the hospital had not distracted her from that fact.

"Why are you here?' she croaked, allowing the tears to fall from underneath her closed lids. "Go away. I don't want to see you."

"Asia please," Kenneth's voice was laced with pain and that pierced Asia's heart even more.

"No, Kenneth. Don't you understand? I can't have you see me like this. I'm so sorry for hurting you but--,"

"Stop it."

She hadn't heard him come near, but she suddenly felt his presence behind her. Still, he didn't touch her. "I'm sorry," Asia whispered, refusing to face him. She lowered her head, her hair framing her dejected face like a curtain.

"Don't be sorry." Kenneth lifted his hand to touch her and seeing the subtle tremble of her tiny frame, allowed it to fall back to his side. "I'm the one who should be sorry," he went on. "I didn't know. I was ready to just give up on us because I didn't know."

When his voice cracked, Asia finally brought her face up to his. She saw it. A film of tears glossed his eyes, but he didn't look away. As if he wanted her to see every piece of love and hurt from his core.

Asia looked down at the flowers between them. Her heart warmed for the first time in weeks. Without a word, she took them from his hands and fingered one of the precious petals neatly wrapped in cellophane.

Without his hands occupied, Kenneth shoved them into his pockets. The gesture was nervously awkward and had an unconscious grin splitting Asia's face. In that moment, he knew they could get through this. It would be tough, but they could make it work. They would make it work.

Kenneth relaxed as the tension dissolved. "May I take you to lunch, Mrs. Harris?"

"Mrs. Harris?" Asia repeated, just to be sure. "But you didn't sign up for a marriage of three."

"I signed up for a marriage with you," Kenneth said, gently taking her hand. "Every part of you. So I'm going to be here with you every step of the way. Plus," he added with a wink. "Lucky for me, I get the ménage a trois all rolled into one."

He laughed and quickly ducked the playful punch Asia aimed at his arm. She shook her head, but had to chuckle at his humor. Damn if he wasn't right. And she loved him for it.

THE END

NOTHING LEFT TO SAY

"A DECEITFUL LOVE"

By

ELIJAH FOREMAN

In many people's eyes Calvin would the embodiment of the American dream. As a twenty-five year old businessman with a knack for having his vivid stories come to life through film. Calvin has acquired the ability to take any ills that he may be experiencing in life and turn them into films that can have crowds of any demographic captivated in every sense of the word.

Behind the scenes though, Calvin's life is far from the picture perfect image that he has worked hard to portray. It doesn't take long before the success gets to his head and his decisions spark the beginning of his downfall. That downfall will come in the form of Joi, the wife of Calvin's best friend Marcel and also the best friend of Calvin's own wife Alicia.

Joi is a wife that feels like she has lost herself within her marriage. For five years, her entire life has been revolved her husband and her two small children. Joi becomes desperate for some fire in her private life, but with her husband busy with his contracting business. Joi is quickly put on the backburner. Joi being on the backburner in her husband Marcel's world would become a dangerous move that nobody would see coming.

As the assistant for Calvin, Joi is directly exposed to the trappings that would catch any woman's eye that doesn't know herself completely. She would never imagine that her being exposed to these things would end with her in the bed of her best friend since junior high school husband. To make matters worse Calvin and Joi's husband have a brotherhood that goes back to the same time frame that Joi and Alicia met. With these facts in place, the affair between Calvin and Joi is the definition of taboo. None of this can keep Calvin and Joi away from each other.

There is a void that Calvin and Joi fill for each other. The love that Calvin lost for his wife in the bedroom department, he ends up finding when he looks at Joi and the lust between them. The feeling of not being appreciated at home for Joi is filled whenever she is in the presence of Calvin. They complete each other in ways that their spouses seemed to have fell short on. The problem with all of this is the evident result of Karma. Nobody ever knows when its coming or how it will come, but when it arrives at your front door there is no way to escape it. Will Calvin and Joi end their lustful affair before its' too late or will they both get their own dosage of Karma?

Chapter 1

Calvin

The smell of I Am King cologne and the sweetest Victoria Secret perfume I ever smelled filled the spacious hotel suite. Feelings of euphoria took over my movements as I reached my peak while digging deep into the depths of the most forbidden juices. Being one of the most successful filmmakers in my area has its perks. Everything from money, comfort, fancy materials, and pussy are at the top of that list. The problem comes in when you get so successful to the point where you feel untouchable. When I look at the sexy body that belongs to my boy's wife Joi- I feel just like that.

How did I end up in the bed with my bro's wife? That's the question I'm hit with every day in my mind. But, in the moment the feeling of her wetness feels right. Each time I push my muscle into her the stresses of my marriage are released. A part of me knows this is wrong, but another part of me keep assuring me that this just feels too right to be wrong. As I wrap my arm under her left leg and lift it up to my right shoulder, I enjoy the feeling of deeper exploration.

The moans that come from Joi's mouth kept me embedded in the lust that's surrounding us. Her husband called me a year ago and asked a favor. As his bro I obliged. That favor was to give his wife a job working as my assistant. It seems today that ever since I made the decision to let Joi assist me in my fast life of a career ,I sealed the fate of sexual thirst for each other.

"Calvin! Stay right there baby! I'm cumming!" Joi's cry for the approaching orgasm was music to my ears. I did my part in making sure our bodies made sweet music while I allowed Joi to ride the wave of her eruption. Spent and out of breath I rolled off of Joi and let her collect herself. We had been going on like this behind our spouses backs for about six months now. This night seemed to be the beginning of the end though. After winning an award for Best Director at an award show in New York, I got lost in the celebrations along with Joi. My wife decided to stay at home with our kids and study for her final in pediatrics. This left the door open for me to invite Joi to tag along after finding out that my bro Marcel had stood her up due to him being backed up with work at his contracting business.

What started as just drinks at a nearby club turned into me fucking this girl's body into submission in my hotel room. Her plans to hop on a train and go back home to Jersey after the show fell short almost immediately after the ceremony. While we were enjoying each other's company at the 40/40 club I watched her pull her phone out and send a quick text message and then turn her on phone down to silent. I knew what it was at that point. In less than two hours, Joi was naked and spread out across my bed waiting for me to devour her. It's like we've been each other's drug of choice lately. I'm tired of just being the provider in my house without any love from my wife and she's tired of living her life for her family. When we're with each other it's like our individual lives are placed on pause. We don't place any attention on our problems and every ounce of energy is released within each other's arms.

Joi

"Shit! Calvin I gotta go." I jumped out of bed the minute I looked to my right and read 8:30am on the hotel room clock.

"What you mean you gotta go? I got the room until tomorrow so you don't have to leave so soon." Calvin said in response while watching me crawl all over the floor gathering my clothes and then running to the bathroom.

"No, I gotta go Calvin. You forget that I texted your best friend who happens to be my husband and told him that I wasn't coming last night. I told him I would be coming in the morning and its already 8 o'clock. I should be at least at Penn station by now getting ready to get on the train. Besides, Alicia is probably wondering where the hell you at too!" I yelled from out the bathroom while taking a birdbath and brushing my teeth.

"Alicia? That damn girl don't care nothing about me. All she worried about is those pediatric finals." I heard Calvin respond as I stepped out the bathroom dressed and looking for my shoes.

"And what's wrong with her getting herself prepared for her finals? Didn't she support you when you were going to film school?"

"Yeah well that was different. Me going to school and getting my degree got us millions. She doesn't have to go to school a day in her life. All she would need to do is be my wife, she at home with our kids, and collect the checks with me. Instead she decides to go to school and break her back over a lousy sixty thousand dollar a year job."

"Do you hear how stupid you sound right now Calvin?" I was officially pissed with how self-centered he was sounding. "Maybe she's going to school to create her own identity. She doesn't want to be in the shadow of her husband and I don't blame her. She got me wanting to get back into school myself."

"Now you just talking crazy Joi. You got a good job already so what would you need to do wasting your time at some school." I picked up Calvin's slacks off the floor near the bed and threw them at him in frustration.

"Will you get up and just your ass washed up and dressed? I'm not having this conversation with you Calvin. I have to get home and so do you." As soon as the last word left my mouth, my cell phone started buzzing in the pocket of my jacket. It was my husband Marcel.

"Hey babe." I answered acting natural.

"Wassup? What time you coming in this morning?" I sensed frustration coming from Marcel's voice over the phone, but I decided to dismiss it.

"Depending on what time the next train decides to leave I should be home around 11. No need to come get me though. I know the kids will probably still be sleeping in and glad they don't have to get up for school."

"Alright. Just hurry up home Joi. I'll see you in a bit." The call ended and I released a deep breath as hearing my husband's voice brought me right back to my own reality. My husband was at home waiting on me to return from "work" while I stood in a hotel room with his best friend who I spent the night fucking.

"Calvin please just hurry up and get dressed so we can get to the train station. That was Marcel trying to see where I was at and I'm sure that I'm going to catch hell when I get home."

"Ain't nothing going to happen girl. You going to be..." In the middle of his sentence Robin Thicke's For the

Rest of My Life starting playing from his phone letting us know that Alicia was calling.

"And now Alicia is calling you." Calvin stood there just staring at his phone as if he was lost in the damn twilight zone or something. "Answer it Calvin!"

"Nah she'll be alright. I'll talk to her when I get home." He responded declining the phone call.

"I swear you are aggy as hell. Why would you do that? You could've at least answered and let her know you were on your way to the train station."

"Yeah well I didn't." Calvin responded cold as ice. "So are you going to let me shower and get dressed? Because if not I will lay back down and we can leave at checkout time."

"Whatever Calvin. Just get dressed." I responded pushing him into the bathroom and shutting the door behind him.

Chapter 2

Joi

I arrived at Trenton Train Station about two hours later with a banging migraine and a desperate need for a shower and sleep. The entire train ride my mind was consumed with thoughts of what I had just done in that hotel room back in New York. Quite frankly, my mind was consumed with thoughts of what I had been doing for the last three months now. How could I hurt a man that spent every waking day of his life taking care of our daughter and me? That's the question that continues to replay day after day. Sometimes it's hard to recall how it all started because it happened so fast.

I can remember my husband Marcel who was officially tired of hearing me talk his head off about finding work make a phone call one day. I wasn't completely sure of who he spoke to, but all I could overhear in the living room while cooking his favorite was a bunch of laughing and typical guy talk. Then came the big question, "Would you be able to help my lady out with finding some work?" At first I screwed my face up to the question and in my mind I said, "Nigga I can find my own work."

But, those thoughts were erased when he wrapped his arms around my waist and kissed my neck before telling me the good news.

He was more excited than I was to be honest. I only felt the need to have a job because I got tired of being in the house. From the time I got married five years ago I was looked at as the definition of what a housewife would be. I went from being 23 and ambitious to now being 28 and just existing in the shadow of my husband. I can't put all the blame on him though. I mean he worked his ass off for us to be able to have the kind of life that we both wanted to have. Now, after only five years being in business with his contracting company it's worth five million dollars.

Most would ask why he didn't just give me a job at his office. Maybe I wouldn't be in this messy ass love triangle I'm in. His response would always be that he either felt like I should go on and create my own identity. Or he would say that he didn't want to have to hurt none of his employees for not keeping their hands to themselves and eyes off of me. He was overprotective like that. After my first couple of weeks of working for Calvin, things started changing in my household though. It went from having a husband who I couldn't wait to see walk through the door at night to having my husband calling me to ask me where I was once he came home at night.

My workload became so big being the assistant of the great Calvin Hines that I lost myself, as if I hadn't lost myself already before I got the job. Once Marcel's business started picking up I was thrown on the back burner. He went from coming home promptly at six every night to coming home at eight sometimes nine at night. During the day, I was all about our daughter and her needs. Then, once the afternoon and evening rolled around I would make it my duty to make sure Marcel had lunch for the next day and his uniforms or suits for special meetings were pressed and ready for him. The only time I ever did anything for myself was when he would run payroll and come home with a couple thousand for me to go play with at a mall. Other than that I was at the disposal of my husband and our daughter.

Working for Calvin immediately gave me an identity. I put my degree in public relations to use and became much more than a typical assistant to your typical celebrity. I ended up being everything from a publicist, to an assistant, to a stylist, to even his one-person promotional team. I can't lie and say it wasn't draining from the minute that it started. Even with it being as draining as it was, it was still fulfilling. I felt needed for more than just pressing a suit or making a bottle. I stepped into a new world working at my new job.

Stepping into this new world meant problems at home. It went from me keeping our daughter all day to me sending her to my mother most of the day until one of us got off. It also went to my husband having to press his own clothes and make his own lunch. Marcel realized at that moment that he was going to have to make some changes and make them fast. To this day, he still has his grumpy moments about a job that he put the word in for me to get. It makes me laugh sometimes watching him have his grumpy moments about the pettiest shit. I guess it's true, you don't know how good you have it until it's gone.

Anyway, once I finally made it home I stepped into my house and heard nothing but silence. Surprisingly, the house looked as clean as I had left it the day before besides the cereal that was scattered all over the marble floor in the foyer. After kicking off my shoes and dropping my bags and jacket on the chair in the foyer, I walked over to my large efficiency of a living room to find Marcel and our daughter Trinity in deep comatose sleeps on the couch. They both looked just alike even; twins even in their sleep. Trinity lay on her daddy's chest and both of their mouths were open so wide you could probably see what they had for breakfast. "They are definitely father and daughter." I said to myself while taking a quick picture on my phone for Instagram to see whenever I got the chance to post.

Before I woke either one of them up with my noise, I picked Trinity up and walked her upstairs to her bedroom and into her crib. For her to only be four years old, it was almost like she was going on twenty-four. A busy body since she came out the womb, Trinity has always been the life of the party. She would never know it now, but she is definitely the #1 reason why her father and me have never wavered from each other and always seem to work things out when we have problems.

"Joi, we need to talk right now. Let Trinity sleep and come downstairs to kitchen for a minute." Marcel said calmly after catching me in my thoughts and watching our daughter sleep. He had no hostility in his voice, but I can tell when my husband is pissed. I've been around this man since I was a teenager and the only woman who knows him better than me is his mother.

"Wassup baby?" I sat at the island of our large state of the art kitchen that used to be my sanctuary before I got the job with Calvin.

"Look I don't know what is going on with you and this new job with Calvin, but it needs to get handled. Seems like the both of y'all have forgotten that y'all are married and have families at home. I mean it's bad enough that I get calls every other night around 10 or 11 o'clock at night from Alicia thinking that Calvin is with me. But, when I can't even get in contact with you because you so called busy at work that raises some eyebrows. Now I don't want to have to step in this shit and fix it myself but I WILL! I'm giving you fair warning first."

"First of all you need to pump your breaks and watch who the hell you're hollering at Marcel." I stood from my seat with my blood officially boiling. "Now, you the who got me the damn job. If it was such a fucking problem then why did you put the word in for me? Is it that you found out the hard way that I'm good for more just being a good ole housewife that runs at your every damn beck and call?"

"Oh that's how it is? That's how we going to do this shit right here? You gonna act like this shit that you pulling ain't wrong? What if that was me texting you that I wouldn't be home till late or maybe even the next day? What would you think Joi?"

"Listen baby I don't want to fight ok. I've been home for all of twenty minutes and I just want to relax. Can we talk about this later?"

"Talk about this later? You know what fuck it. We don't have to talk about nothing at all." Marcel stepped past me and grabbed his sneakers from the foyer and then proceeded to grab his leather jacket.

"Where are you going Marcel?" I asked with my heart doing dances in my chest. He knew something was going on and I could feel it.

"Don't talk to me now Joi. Didn't you just say you was tired? If you so tired then you go take your ass to bed then. I'm going to see if Calvin can give me any answers as to why he needed my wife to stay overnight with him in New York after an award show that ended ten at night last night." Marcel snatched his car keys out of his pocket and snatched open the front door.

"Baby you're just aggravated. Come in here and let's talk. What the hell is going to Calvin's house going to solve Marcel? I'm your wife, release your frustrations with me." I shut the door and stood in front of it with my arms crossed.

"Take my frustrations out on you huh?" Marcel asked with a smirk on his face. "You know what." Marcel took my bait wrapping his lips around my neck and touching my spots immediately. Without any demand, I started coming out of my clothes. Unbuttoning my blouse first and tossing it to the side I revealed that I didn't have nothing on, but a bra underneath. Marcel's dick must've been jumping because the minute he saw that he was all over me for real. He touched his jacket and keys, picking me up, and wrapping my legs around his waist and taking upstairs to our master bedroom.

In my mind I was screaming YES, for more reasons than one. I knew that I may have just dodged a bullet for one, along with that is that fact that I did miss my husband's touch. When me and Calvin do what we do its more of a stress reliever that should've never happened. When I get into the arms of my husband, I melt the same way I did when I was eighteen and let him inside of me for the first time. This moment wouldn't be the moment of passion that I'm speaking about though. This seemed to be a bad re-run of what I just experienced with Calvin.

Marcel unbuttoned and snatched off my skirt and panties before pushing me over the left side of our California King sized bed. Seconds later, I felt his love penetrate me and dig as deep as possible making me release a gasp that sounded like I was desperate for air. Hearing me release air from my lungs in this way only fueled Marcel to devour me even more. Before I knew he was balls deep in me and I was feeling tickling the cavity of my chest. Each thrust of Marcel's muscle inside of me caused me to cream all over his manhood. I gripped my sheets like I was holding on for the ride of my life. Putting the finishing touches on my ass I felt him grab a handful of my hair and pull back while putting his left hand on my left shoulder and making the headboard and the bedroom wall make music mixed in with my loud ass. BANG! BANG! BANG! BANG!

"Ooohh shit! Yes! M-m-marcellll! Yes baby! I'm about to cum again. Yes! Yyyyeeesssss!" I fell forward hitting my face on my bed like an avalanche. My walls continued to throb for several minutes after I released my final nut while guiding my husband to his. My mind kept telling me to get up, but after fucking around with Calvin and getting my brains beat in sexually by Marcel all I could do was close my eyes and pass out.

Calvin

I parked in my driveway and immediately spotted a sight that would mark the beginning of the end of my day on my porch. My wife, Alicia sat on the porch with her head in her hands. She looked like she needed a full day of rest, wearing a pair of gray sweatpants, and a tank top with her hair wrapped up with her favorite scarf. I hopped out of my car and approached her without her seeing me and laid a kiss on the top of her head. She slowly moved her up looking at me with the coldest look I ever seen plastered on her face.

"Don't you put your fucking lips on me Calvin. Where the fuck have you been?" Alicia stood to her feet and faced me.

"You know where I was at Alicia. It would've been nice to get a call when I won my award. Maybe make a story up about how proud of me you are. At least show some kind of effort." Alicia stepped off and went into the house. I followed close behind to find a surprise laid out for me in the kitchen. My kitchen was full of confetti on the floor, balloons, a cake, and champagne.

"Congratulations on your award." Alicia cracked one of the two bottles of Belaire Brut and poured herself a drink.

"Shit, it don't look like you that happy for me at all." I said on some cocky shit, but on the low I felt like a sucker leaving my lady and kids hanging like that. Like clockwork, the glass Alicia drank from flew past my head missing me by inches and shattering on the wall.

"Who the fuck do you think you are?!?! Hell no I'm not happy for your ass! Not anymore I'm not. Here I had this whole surprise set up for you for when you got home last night. The man that's supposed to be my husband told me before he left town that he would be back home by 11 o'clock or no later than midnight. I waited for you to call me and let me know that you were on your way back home. Or at least call me and let me know that you were going to be in New York overnight. I could've saved this whole party until today."

"Fuck this party Alicia. You don't fucking get it." I stepped out of the kitchen and headed towards the living room kicking my shoes off and turning my TV to ESPN.

"What don't I fucking get Calvin?" Alicia barked while standing in front of the TV.

"I wanted you and the kids there! That's what you don't fucking get! Fuck the party that you planned. You should've been sitting right there front row with me when I got my name called for the award that I won. But, instead you decided to stay behind and study for a final that you been studying for like crazy like the last two fucking weeks. You brushed this shit off that it didn't mean nothing to you when I left. So this party doesn't mean shit to me. You should've been there." I could tell that my words were starting to mess with her head. For the first time since I stepped in the house her mouth was shut and it looked like she was searching for words to say. She knew that I was right. She didn't want to admit at first but she finally broke down.

"Look baby I'm sorry. I know you wanted me to be there, but I just had to tackle this work for school. It wasn't like I didn't want to be there. I just needed to focus that's all. You have your career and you're doing well with your movies. But, this medical degree in pediatrics is for me." She sat beside me and tried her best to get through to me.

"Yeah, I hear you." I brushed her off, removing her arms when she attempted to wrap her arms around my neck. She must've knew she was wrong because with no hesitation she dropped to her knees in front of me and unzipped my slacks. Reaching into my boxers, Alicia pulled out my muscle and let it disappear in her mouth and dive deep in her throat. I tried my best to play this shit off like it was nothing, but my wife knew how to have a nigga spent when it came to her head game. She was sucking on my shit like it was about to dispense a prize to her. And her wish was definitely my command.

"Cum for me daddy." She knew whenever she started talking like that I would be ready to tear her ass up. But, before I commenced to dive into my home pussy I relieved some stress in the form of my first nut of the day. After watching Alicia swallow every drop that was released in her mouth I just took a look at my wife and shook my head.

"You nasty as hell girl. You know that right?" I said with a smile on my face.

"Only for you daddy. Now come upstairs and let's finish your celebration." I followed behind her while getting hypnotized by the way that ass moved. Once we reached the bedroom and the door shut behind me we were attached to each other like magnets. In the back of my mind I had an angel and devil moment. The devil on my left shoulder was telling me to ignore the thoughts and feelings of guilt that began to fill my psyche about fucking Joi then coming home to fuck my wife. Then the angel on my right shoulder began to speak over the devil and tell me that the time for games were over. It was time to break this lust session off with Joi and get back to being a husband to my wife.

As my wife stripped every piece of clothing off her body and tossed it to the floor, the devil spoke in my left ear and said "She looks nice, but Joi looks much better Calvin. Alicia's body is an appetizer and doesn't amount to the meal that Joi provides. Drowning in that pussy takes your mind off of all the stress and aggravation of being in this house and being married to someone that doesn't support you. She doesn't appreciate you Calvin. Joi on the other hand is very appreciative."

Once Alicia straddled me and entered me inside of her, a loud moan left her mouth. The angel spoke in right ear and said, "Calvin, think about what this fool in your left ear is telling you. Joi is your wife's best friend, and your best friend Marcel is Joi's best friend. This is wrong son. This will not end well and people will get hurt. Think about your wife and your best friend. Is your lustful attractions worth hurting the people that are supposed to be the closest to you?" Alicia started picking her pace up just the way I loved it. I grabbed her hips guided her to where I wanted her then matched the pace of her strokes.

"I love you so much Calvin. I love you daddy. I'm cumming!" Alicia let me know that she was close to creaming on me. I tried my best to enjoy the moment, but this damn devil and angel on my shoulders continued to argue. This time the devil was giving me his rebuttal on what the angel had just said. "Man, fuck what this old man is talking about. Joi threw the pussy at you. So you took it. That's it and there's nothing else left to say. At the end of the day you have some thinking to do. Do you really want to give Joi's sexy ass up? You know you loved hugging on those thick ass hips. Those thighs had you spent and you know it. Her head game was nice. She threw it back at you just right. And she almost made you nut early like you was back in high school. Do you really want to give up that wet pussy Calvin? I know you don't. You better smarten up youngin. What Alicia and Marcel don't know won't hurt them."

Grabbing a handful of Alicia's hair and watching her ass clap and bounce back on me took my attention for a minute. This was the first moment that mentally I found myself torn. The night before I was enjoying the taste and feel of forbidden sweetness. Joi had lusting in ways I never experienced before and I can't lie. It was like we breathed the same breath the way our tongues tied and our bodies made music. At the same time though, I can't front I wish it was my wife. The only reason why I even got that far with Joi was because she seemed to be rocking with me more than my own wife.

Every movie premiere that Alicia didn't show up to, Joi was there. Every time I had to work late night and I wished that I was at home, Joi was right there in the office with me helping me get my work done. Whenever I came home from work and felt like being laid up with my wife, but she was too busy with her school work- Joi was right there through text or phone to talk to. Shit is crazy to say, but I done messed around and created two relationships. I'm starting to look like those damn polygamists that be on TV.

As far as my homie Marcel, yeah I feel bad when it comes to him. He's been my bro since high school. We went to the same college. We played basketball on the same team. We've been tight for as long as I can remember. When he called me and asked me to look out for him by giving his wife a job I was a little reluctant- I can't lie. When I met Alicia, her and Joi were walking out of the college library at the same time. I had a secret crush on both of them and made a vow to myself that I would marry one of them. Once I married my wife, those little puppy love feelings for Joi obviously disappeared. I later introduced her to Marcel at a double date that I set up for them to meet and he was infatuated with that girl. With that being known, I was happy that my boy was happy.

For the next few years following our wedding day, every time I saw Joi it was with Marcel by her side. So, once again I never thought anything of it. All of that changed once I gave her the job. Once she was in a position where I saw her every day, talked to her every day, and got to see that flawless body that she managed to get back even after having her daughter all the puppy love feelings came back like they never left. It was like bumping into a girl I knew when I was younger and never had a chance to get her. This time I was able to get her. Crazy part about the shit though, she was feeling the same. She secretly had been waiting for me to make a move to fuck since the day she started. I don't know if it was just curiosity or if she had the same crush on me that I had on her.

All I know is this shit happened so quick that I wasn't even able to think twice about it. The angel was right. Two people will get hurt in this situation. I'll probably have to throw hands with my best friend of almost twenty years. I'll probably have to duck every dish in my kitchen that Alicia can find to try and take my head off. It's one thing to cheat, but to cheat with the best friend of your spouse is a different blow. As Alicia and I both reached our last nut and collapsed next to each other catching our breath, I mentally took notes on what the angel and devil were talking about. It was time to end this with Joi, once and for all.

Chapter 3

Alicia

I'm a naïve little girl. I know the hell that comes with being married to a celebrity all to well. The late nights of my husband being at work, the groupies who sit, and wait in the parking lot of his office or lurk in the lobby of hotels were he stays when he's out of town. He's been making movies for almost six years now, since we were both 23 years old. He came straight out of college under the guidance of Spike Lee at NYU and made his first feature film. Ever since he got the opportunity to make one movie, he's been moving non-stop. With the Internet being the way it is today, Calvin has had the opportunity to get his work out there much quicker than anybody else that he studied in school.

We got married about six months after his first film was released, which only caused drama from the beginning. I can remember him being showcased on Wendy one night and her saying that I only married Calvin because of his money. I couldn't stop myself from laughing. Truth be told, although the movie went number 1 and had made 40 million in the box office the first week, it doesn't mean that Calvin was rolling in dough from the jump. His first movie was a small budget that took probably about $300,000 to make and once it blew up everybody had to get paid before him. When it was time for him to get his first check out of that $40 million he was only able to negotiate about 3% of the revenue to come to him.

That's right, Calvin barely got any damn money to most people. He managed to get a major distribution company to market the movie, but they put pennies into the initial budget. The company never thought my husband would take pennies and turn that shit into millions. He was celebrated from that point on as a force to be reckoned with and in came the bullshit and the drama. Everything from girls calling my house phone, me having to go to hotels, and beat women's faces in on more than one occasion. One would ask why I continued to stay even if I felt that I was being disrespected. Many people look at this situation and say it's all about the money. My answer is NO!

I'm a hustler in every since of the word. Even if that hustling has to be in the form of hustling my damn husband I will. People in the media can have their opinions about me, but I'm getting mine. Straight from high school I went to a trade school and became a certified medical assistant. From there, I got a decent job at a local hospital that eventually helped me get enough money to get my own spot and get out of my folks house. From there I went to nursing school and got a bachelor's degree by the time I was 21 years old. By this time Calvin and I had gone from high school sweethearts to living with each other while he went to school at NYU. He worked a 9-5 in retail bringing home a third of what I brought in, but I stuck by my man.

Every morning I allowed him to drop me off at work while he drove my car to school and back to pick me up every night. Calvin had a dream and the determination to get to that dream. So when the time came for me to step up and support him I did, while in the meantime still doing what I had to do. So imagine my frustration when people in the media who don't know Calvin from a can of damn paint claim that I just want him for his money.

The minute these reports started surfacing I began to plot my own plan. Once I finished nursing school by the time I was 25, I went from having a decent job that was making me about $1,100 a check to me having a nursing job that got me a little more than $3,000 a check. It got to the point where I had my own money and really didn't need Calvin for much. From the beginning, I've been a simple girl. A simple girl with a great sense of fashion, but a simple girl nonetheless at the end of the day. So the times that Calvin would come home with a couple thousand to hand me after running payroll for his production company it never impressed me. All I ever wanted was my husband. Fuck the money. He didn't have shit, but potential and determination to begin with. That's all I wanted from him. But, he's starting to get way beside himself.

"Wassup babe? How was your day?" Calvin stepped in the house and attempted to kiss me before I blocked his lips and gave him an opportunity to see the dark look I had on my face. He took a step back and responded to the look on my face by asking, "What the hell did I do now Alicia?" I released a laugh after hearing this question then passed Calvin an envelope and watched him pull the pictures out of it.

"Who is that hugged up with you Calvin?" The color drained from his face as he processed the question and thought quickly about an answer.

"Where did you get these pictures from?" Calvin shot back.

"Don't fucking play with me Calvin. This is not the time for the games. I asked one question and I expect the answer to that question. If you answer my question with a question one more time its gonna get real ugly in this bitch real damn quick."

"Ok, baby calm down. This is just Joi. You know she's my new assistant. Marcel called me and asked for a favor to give his wife who happens to be your best friend a job and I did. She was with me in New York for the award show."

"I talk to Joi almost every day Calvin, and she never told me anything about her new job being a job under you." I snatched the pictures from his hands and took another look. Then, it dawned on me. Although the private investigator I hired never got a clear shot of Joi's face, Calvin's confirmation that it was her allowed me to connect the dots. I looked up from the pictures and stared devilishly in his eyes and began to smirk. "You fucked her didn't you Calvin?"

"What? Alicia, are you fucking crazy? Joi is my boy's wife and she's your girl too. Why would I take a chance on fucking her when it can blow up in my face?"

"Calvin I'm not stupid nigga. Not by a long shot. You must've forgotten all of the hotels I had to walk into to beat a bitch black and blue over you. Or how many after parties were shut down because a bitch got too comfortable thanks to you. Over the years I realized something, it wasn't those women that caused the drama, it was you Calvin. You are the reason why all this damn drama takes place. Whenever you feel a little blow to your ego, you start acting the little boy who gets picked on at school. You start acting out and looking for attention. Then, when you get it and you get the hell that comes with it -you act like you never asked for it in the first place. You act like the victim or you act as if I'm the one that's crazy."

"Alicia, you're talking crazy baby. Now why don't we just go upstairs and chill for the nigh ." Calvin tried to change the subject on me.

"Now my supposed best friend is your next target. Not only did I not know about you hiring her as your assistant, I also didn't know about her going with you to New York neither. It all makes sense now."

"What makes sense now?" Calvin was beginning to show his guilt on his face.

"You couldn't handle the fact that I was working so hard on my degree and not spending much time to focus on you. So you searched for the attention elsewhere. You longed for that attention. To just have a woman cater to your every single need and want. You got tired of not getting it at home and you made the decision to find it by any means necessary. Then, one day it fell into your lap. Joi walked in the door of your office and gave every bit of attention you've been wanting and asking for and begging for. It didn't matter to you that she was your wife's best friend or your best friend's wife. You didn't give a damn about that. Now tell me that I'm lying Calvin." With a face of stone my husband stared at me for a matter of seconds and then he broke the eye contact and looked out of the living room window into the night. I smirked and chuckled to myself knowing the answer from that point on.

"Alicia, you are not ready to hear the answers that you are asking for."

"Save it Calvin. I know all I need to hear. I know that you look at me as some ungrateful bitch who just lives here and lives off of you. Well one thing you forgot about is the fact that it was me that helped you get to this point. You had nothing! When you were in school at NYU, I was the one pulling in money and taking care of the bulk of the bills. I did that because I saw the potential. Shit, I think I saw the potential before you could even think to see the potential in yourself. But, you know what? I'm tired Calvin. I'm sick and tired of the disrespect and the lies. It stops tonight." I stood to my feet and walked to the bags I had packed in the dining room.

"What a minute, Alicia baby we can talk about this. What do you mean it ends now?"

"You don't want to talk to me. Go talk to one of these hoes out here who has been giving you so much attention. More importantly than that why don't you go talk to your friend? He should've received these pictures in his email by now. I'm sure you'll be hearing from him soon." I loaded up my car with the bags and just like that my kids and me were gone. At least for the moment as I watched Calvin chase my car for half a block from my rearview mirror.

Chapter 4

Marcel

Sitting on my leather couch watching ESPN I enjoyed the first real day off I ever had. No phone calls. No emergency emails. No meetings. I left all the business duties to the manager of my company for the weekend making this first day I would spend to myself. I did absolutely nothing, but fuck my wife and lounge in my living room the entire day. I noticed at this point how much time I've been missing from her. I noticed how much I missed her body being one with mine. I missed the intimate connection we have that soon turns into erotic passion whenever we are near each other.

I must've fucked my wife all over the house throughout the day. With our daughter at her grandmother's house for the weekend the activities that took place were bound to happen. Joi went from making me breakfast in the morning to becoming the only appetizer and meal that I cared to taste. I sat her on the kitchen counter and enjoyed every drop of my breakfast like it was my last. I then led my woman to the shower where she became more concerned about feeling me inside of her than me helping her clean the outside of her.

Needless to say, we fucked until the water turned cold. Climbing out of the shower we allowed the bed sheets to dry us off as I carried her to bed and devoured her once we reached it. It was my mission to make my wife feel me in parts of her body that she hasn't felt me in for years. With every thrust of my love into hers I kept my fingers intertwined with hers in the midst of getting lost in the sounds of hearing my wife reach her peak and implode in pleasure. We would continue this pattern with lunch and eventually dinner as well which lead to us sitting on the couch and me finally decided to grab my laptop and check my emails for the day.

The first few emails were about typical business details and meetings that would be coming after my weekend off. But, the last email that had not been open came from my boy Calvin's wife, Alicia.

"Babe, I got an email from Alicia. Everything good over there with her and Calvin?" I asked thrown off from the random email.

"I don't know. I haven't heard from Alicia in a little while. Since before the New York trip." I opened the email and saw that it was almost blank, but had an attachment. The only piece of writing that came on the initial part of the email read, be careful of who you have sleeping next to you. That person could be lying next to someone closer than you think at the same time.

Thrown off by the comment I opened the attachment and saw pictures of Calvin hugged up a female. And although I couldn't see the woman's face I began to study her body. The beauty mark that rested on the top of her right shoulder as she hugged him. The semi-muscular build of her shoulders, arms, and upper back that led to the curves of her lower back and hips that can hug any dress just right. Followed by an ass that could only be crafted from God himself. I examined this woman from top to bottom and knew that it was my wife. The question was why Alicia sent me these pictures out of nowhere. It had to be something more to the story than just a simple hug and I knew exactly how to get the truth out.

"Wassup with these pictures?" I passed my laptop to Joi and she looked at each of the three pictures sent to me one by one and paused briefly before responding.

"I don't know. It looks like Calvin and one of his groupies hugging up on him probably." Joi said defensively.

"Oh, so you are calling yourself a groupie?" I responded making her spit the wine that she had just sipped from her mouth.

"Baby what are you talking about? It's not like that with Calvin and me. We had this discussion already."

"Joi, who do you think you fooling? I know the body in this damn picture anywhere. All the years we been together you don't think I can tell when I see the beauty mark on your right shoulder? What about the curves that make it easy for you to wear the kind of dress you wore in this picture? Shit, what about the diamond bracelet that I bought you for your birthday that you are wearing with your wedding ring in the picture. That ring has a diamond that was specifically cut and molded for you. So before you lie to me again think about your response. What is up with these pictures?"

"Ok it's me hugging Calvin in the pictures, but that's it baby. Nothing happened with us I swear it didn't." Joi said with beads of sweat forming on the top of her head.

"The more you lie to me the worse my reaction will be. You don't think I noticed how happy you looked walking in the house when you came home from New York? You looked happier than I ever saw you before. You looked happier than you did on our wedding day, and even happier than you did when I proposed to you. I saw a glow in you that shined brighter than when you were pregnant with our daughter. So you know what, you don't even have to tell me the truth. I know the answer to my questions already."

I took a moment to look my wife in the eyes. The look I received back confirmed everything I had been thinking about. I didn't want to believe it, but my wife had been dealing with my best friend and after getting the proof between the pictures and my wife's reaction I removed myself from the conversation.

"Baby, can we just talk about this? Where are you going right now?" Joi asked while watching me pack a couple bags from my closet.

"Right now I don't know where I'm going Joi. All I know is right now I'm getting the fuck away from you. It would be in your best interest to get far away from me right now. Go call that bitch ass nigga Calvin or something."

"Come on baby you don't mean that."

"I don't mean that? Are you fucking serious right now?" I said with a smirk on my face. "I just had my wife's best friend send me pictures of my wife and my best friend hugged up in New York while I was at work busting my ass for the family that I come home to. You don't even have to tell me that you was fucking him Joi. I know my wife better than she knows herself. So save all the bullshit man. I'm gone."

Just like that I was in my car and pulling off away from the house that I've called home for years. It only took those few minutes to make that house look as unfamiliar to me as it did when we first moved in.

Chapter 5

Calvin

What was supposed to be a simple meeting at my house to tell Joi that we couldn't do this anymore turned into the last time I would ever feel her again. I invited her to my house after Alicia left to have a talk about what had been going on since the New York trip. Not surprised at all I was hit with the news that Marcel had gotten the pictures that Alicia sent him before she left the house. Also wasn't surprised that Marcel had left their house the same kind of way Alicia left ours.

I guess you could call it a weak moment for the both of us but what started as a hug and a goodbye to all the sexual activity that had taken place turned into Joi being carried to my bedroom and being fucked thoroughly. It was almost like a switch went off once we embraced in that hug and from that moment on neither one of us had any control over what we were getting ourselves into. It was going to have to be our last time at this rate. If we were willing to sex each other in my house and stand the chance of Alicia walking in randomly that goes to show that we didn't have a care in the world about what we were doing.

Nonetheless, after about two hours of lusting each other I climbed off of Joi allowing her to get dressed and leave. Both of us ended this night agreeing that we would do all we could to get our spouse back and we also agreed that it would be best for Joi to find another job. Once Joi left I looked at the clock in my living room and saw that it read 12:15AM. Hoping that maybe Alicia would be up writing a paper for school or something I called her cell phone. After three rings, the call was answered and I was received with a muffled response over the phone. That muffled response turned into sounds of ecstacy and euphoria as I heard my wife cry out, "Don't stop Marcel. I'm cumming!!!"

Joi

I came home after my last encounter with Calvin with a clear mind and a clear conscious. I walked in my house with a game plan already mentally in place when it came to what I had to do in order to bring my husband back home. I looked over at the clock on my microwave as I poured a glass of wine and saw that it read 12:15AM. Hoping that Marcel

would be up doing some late night prepping for a meeting or maybe drawing up some plans for his workload the next day I took a chance and called his cell phone.

The first time I called the phone rang twice and went to voicemail. I hung up and quickly re-dialed his phone hoping to get an answer. This time after two more rings, the phone call was answered and I heard the muffled sounds of a baritone voice crying out in pleasure, "I'm cumming too, Alicia! Aghhhh!"

"What the fuck?!?!" I thought out loud as I dropped my cell phone on the kitchen floor and watched the battery fly out of it.

TO BE CONTINUED...

MAYBE...

Married to The CIA
By
Riiva Williams

Chapter 1

Cairo, Egypt

I tossed and turned in the beautiful city of Cairo. My heart pound to even think I was in the capital of Egypt and the largest city in Africa, whether it was for work or not. I quietly got out of bed. The city was definitely living up to its name the name as it means "the triumphant city". Cairo was located on both banks of the Nile River and has been settled for more than 6000 years and I was eager to explore this ancient city in the morning.

Enjoying the night's air, I couldn't understand how Nasir stayed asleep during the hot humid night. I was tired as I spent my days travelling for my private firm, meeting this sexy Egyptian dignitary during dinner and having him ravish me after was just the fun part of this trip.

Standing on the balcony, I didn't hear any of movements around me I was taken with the breathtaking view until someone grabbed me from behind.

"Shhhhhh don't make too much noise pretty lady."

I screamed I couldn't help it. I was in a strange city in the room of a strange man I just met now I'm being kidnapped. "Please don't hurt me. Please don't hurt me!" It was a silent, but very loud pray that I was putting out into the universe.

"Don't worry I am not here for you. You're not on my contract." Before I blacked out from a peculiar smell that was close to my nose. I felt the stranger placed a sweet and tender kiss on my cheek. This just turned into the worst business trip ever.

San Diego, CA

"Agent Carter! Get your narrow behind in my office now!" This was not going to go well. I fucked up royally and I can admit that. Nasir got away and the only thing I could have think on was to take the woman. I walked slowly into his office.

"Yes Lieutenant Jackson."

"What the fuck is this Carter? I'm not about to let you fuck up this assignment!" He was pissed, but he will get over it. I rooted to the ground where I stood as the woman in his office turned and looked at me for the first time.

"Agent Carter?" Man her voice was like music to my ears and it was doing somethings to my limbo.

"Yes ma'am I am Carter." The mood within the office changed as she narrowed her eyes at me while she walked over.

crack She slapped me and I was stunned. "What the fuck?!" I grabbed her hand before she could slap me again.

"Because of your dumbass I lost over three million dollars this weekend!" My boss smirked. I hate his ass I swear.

"Lady, who the hell are you?!" I growled. The one thing I can't stand is someone hitting me for no reason. When it comes to women I usually try to defused the situation before they can do such a thing, if they succeed I try to walk away before I do something stupid.

"Agent Carter meet Alexis Rogue. Owner of Rogue Financial Institution out of Little Rock Arkansas." Still confused on who she was I watch Lieutenant like he had two heads.

"Is that supposed to mean something to me sir."

"Yes it should Carter she is the woman you kidnapped last night on your failed mission. You had one thing to do Carter one thing and you fucked it up."

I stood there slacked jawed because I knew the woman we picked up last night was beautiful, but I didn't realize how beautiful she was. I stammer to say something anything, but the words couldn't form. Then, it hit why I took her in the first place so I gathered my composure.

"Sir the reason I took this woman….."

"It's Alexis!" I just rolled my eyes at her when she cut me off from speaking.

"Whatever as I was saying Lieutenant. The reason I took this woman what that she was close with Nasir Zuberi. I figure since she was in his room she has to know more about his operations and whereabouts within Cairo." This seems to peaked his interested.

"This is absurd!" Alexis yelled into the room. "I meet with him because he was one of my new clients and I decided to fuck him. Shit that came out so wrong! Oh my god I can't believe this shit!" She started rubbing her temples. "I'm guessing a headache was coming on."

I continue my long winded speech on how much we are going to need her and Lieutenant was grinning from ear to ear. Great I said to myself he bought it. "Well Agent Carter, I am going with your word on this one. If you fail me again you will be transferred to pushing paper in the basement!"

I turned and look at Alexis who was still fuming I could almost see the steam coming out of her ears. "Oh by the way Carter she is your responsibility. Figure out what you are going to with her."

Chapter 2

As soon as he walked out his office, I let out a low growl. "Fuck man!" I seriously didn't think this one through. How is she going to help on this case I really don't know, but I had to get the ball rolling. Every hour we do not track Zuberi, the further away he gets from the CIA's radar.

I have to say he was not bad on the eyes. Following me through the office like a lost puppy dog, I had time to really take a good look at Agent Carter. The man was foine and I know I didn't spell that right.

He was six foot two inches, light caramel complexion with that military buzz cut. That alone told me that she served sometime within the armed forces. I wanted to know more about him, but I think I lost all graces with him when I slapped him.

We paused in front of his desk. "Have a seat." He was very short handed with me, but again I understood why. I am connected to the criminal. What type of criminal he was, that was yet to be determined? "I'm…I'm sorry about earlier."

"It's whatever ma'am."

"Okay." I twiddled my thumbs for about two minutes until I saw him opened a file label Nasir Zuberi on his computer. When your parents tell you take time to learn someone they really were not lying. Zuberi was wanted in France, Germany, USA and Britain not to mention numerous smaller countries around the world.

Just then, Carter turned to me. "What can you tell me about this man that we do not already know." I shrugged my shoulders at him. I was tired and cranky and I really wanted a shower.

"There was nothing to tell. He was hiring my firm to invest some money into the United States, but that's about it."

"Dig deeper, dammit!" he rubbed his temples, he was frustrated I know it but that is not reason to try take it out on me.

"I don't know! What he do so badly? From the small amount of time I was with him he seemed like nothing, but a sweetheart."

"This man." He tossed Nasir picture at me. "Is wanted for murder and human trafficking, you can't tell me nothing, nothing at all about him?"

"No, nothing. I knew nothing of him before that night." I felt a little ashamed because I was basically spreading my legs for a stranger and here I am admitting it to an officer of the law. Dear God!

He turned back to his desk mumbling to himself, I wasn't sure of how I can help him. Just then a tall, dark chocolate brown woman that was probably six feet tall walked over to the desk. I felt inferior to her; she was a beauty none the less. The woman looked at me, and I'm not going to lie I felt like I was about to be interrogated.

"Carter, I think that I will have an idea on how to draw Zuberi out." I saw his attitude changed a bit.

"Oh really Farara what is that?" Farara threw a manila folder down on his desk. Apparently these have a problem in actually handing people things.

"Yes really. I have been doing some backgrounds research on the type of women that Zuberi has been collecting. Apparently this sick fuck loves the married ladies and has found a niche within the human trafficking system for them." Farara turned to me. Oh no, this can't be good. "This is where she would come in. You two will play a high profiled couple, inviting some of his connects with in the trafficking world to the wedding, but of course make a few transactions with them first."

"This all seems like the perfect plan Farara, but it has one problem."

"I am not doing it!"

"Oh get off your high horse Carter! Plus, I already ran it by the lieutenant. None of you have any choice, but to so it." She handed me what seemed like a perfectly set wedding, I wanted to kick and scream about it, but there was nothing I can do at this point in time, but go ahead with this sham of a marriage."

"I am not marrying her Farara. End of story." Carter got up from his desk in an attempt to walk off.

"I wasn't asking you Carter." Farara was mean and very frank in what she had to say. I loved her, she remind me of myself in business.

"Come with me!" He pointed at me and walked back towards the Lieutenant's office. "What the fuck is this shit?" Again he threw the file Farara gave us on his desk.

"It's your assignment Carter. What is your issue now?"

Personally this whole charade was funny to me. I felt like I was on an episode of "Punk'd." "I am not going through with this whole marriage thing!"

Lieutenant laughed. "Are you really stupid Carter? You are not marrying her for real, now get out my office!" I didn't mean to laugh out loud, but it was too funny how the whole exchange happened. He glared at me.

"What the hell are you laughing for?" I snickered some more back to his desk.

"I'm sorry, but you should have seen your face!! It was priceless."

"Why aren't you upset about this?" His handsome features showed the confusion that was going on inside of him. For a brief moment I allowed myself to feel some type of concern for this man that was sitting before me.

"There is nothing to worry about, that's why as soon as I finish help you all on this so called charade I will be a the first flight back to Little Rock. The faster I help out the quicker I can leave you to do whatever it is that you do. Now I need clothes, a shower, some food and a place to sleep. Thank you."

"My, aren't we demanding?" he cocked his head to the side.

"You haven't seen anything yet. Trust me."

Chapter 3

I drove around Cali looking for a place that I could dump her off until the morning, but there wasn't much in my pocket to meet her type of demands. I know they say that working for the CIA should have you rolling in dough, but not me- too many bills stemming from my sick mother to deal with so I decided to take her to my apartment.

I knew it wasn't the best idea, but I am not going to lie I did like what I see, but being that we will be working together I cannot be sleeping with my so called co-worker. I shook the thought of me running my tongue over every inch of her, tasting her luscious body out of my head.

I pull into a small apartment complex parking, the place I called home when I do actually come home. I was tired so I wanted her to hurry up and use the bathroom so I can get in and get out so I can crash on the couch in the living room.

It was exactly eleven o'clock when she come out, I was instantly hard. Just watching the water rolled down her back unto the soft downing towel that I gave her to dry off in. I guess she noticed that I was watching her so she closed the door.

I swear women take so freaking long just to get dressed. I was still thinking about her so I was out there still adjusting my shaft so she couldn't see how much she was turning me on.

I heard the door knob for the bedroom turned as I fixed myself for the millionth time. "The bathroom is free."

She looked at me and I wish she wouldn't. "Uh thanks. I'll be out your hair in a jiffy so you can get some rest."

"Yeah, ok that would be great. You know you don't have to worry, it's not a real marriage."

I sighed I had yet to apologize for my behavior earlier on. "Yeah..." I rubbed the back of my neck with my hand. "I'm sorry about my behavior earlier."

"It's ok. The funny thing is I should be the one freaking out." She giggled about it again. "Why did you react that way?"

"Personal issues." I said as I brushed my way passed her into the room so I can get into the shower.

"Oh, okay."

"The take out is on the table if you want to eat. Give me about ten minutes then you can take that bed."

"Alright"

*****

I tossed and turned all night. I couldn't stand the thought of Agent Carter being right in the other room. He was fine and I mean he is a fine brother and my feelings towards his abrupt rudeness didn't change the fact that I would still fuck the shit out of him right then and there.

Needless to say I got no sleep that night. I felt rough and ragged in the morning as I got out of bed when the scent of breakfast was coming from the kitchen.

"Oh smells good in here." I said from the doorway he smiled.

"Well I am just saying sorry for my behavior and trying to get on your good side before the wedding planner comes over."

"Wedding Planner?"

"Yeah Lieutenant, feels we should make it a real as possible."

"Ok I think I can do that."

Chapter 4

The morning went by in a blur. She chose a simple dress and I an Armani Jet black suit. I was calling to me and I didn't have to pay for it. There was something about this whole situation that was getting to me.

Why with everything that is going on why is the agency blowing so much money on a fuck up that I made? I walked into the building that housed us.

"Carter come in here!" Lieutenant Jackson shouted.

"Surprise!" Everyone shouted as I walked into the room/

"You guys do know this is a fake wedding right?" I laughed as some of the agents come over to congratulate me.

"We know." Agent Farara laughed. "But some of the agents felt like this is the only time they will get to plan your Bachelor's party so enjoy it."

I'm not going to lie it was fun while it lasted Agent Farara and Alexis threw together the wedding in two days and I only had four more days before the wedding. I wanted my mom there, I was trying to keep her out of it ,but I wasn't sure of how long I have left with her so I wanted to make her dreams come true.

"Farara can I talk to you?"

"Sure Carter what's up?"

"I know this is fake and everything, but you see my mom is dying and I want her to at least think I am happy before she goes. Can you make that happen?"

"I got it, I will make sure she is there."

"Thanks."

"You're welcome."

*****

The day was beautiful and it came faster than I expected. Carter looked nervous and here I am mentally telling him it's all a façade. I don't know how the CIA did it, but there was Nasir in the back row looking on at the celebration.

The music began to play that was my cue. Gracefully, I walked down the aisle and I felt his eyes burning holes in my back. My night with Nasir was a thrilling one. He knew how to make a woman feel wanted. If I wasn't used to the game by now I would have thought, we could have worked something out.

Standing in front of Carter I smiled and his mom was in the front pew crying tears of joy. My heart went out to her, cancer was one disease I wouldn't like to mess with. I turned my attention back to the pastor standing next to us.

"Love is the reason why we are here today. We are not only here to say I love you, but to also say I promise to love you for all our tomorrows..."

I was all teary eyed throughout the whole ceremony the agency went as far as obtaining all legal documents while ensuring me that the ceremony is fake and it was all for show. I zoned back into my surroundings just in time to hear the pastor's words.

"Do you Jason Carter take Alexis Rogue to be your lawfully wedded wife?"

"I do." He said it so smooth I would have thought that he really wanted this.

"Do you Alexis Rogue take Jason Carter to be your lawfully wedded husband?

"I do." I hesitated somewhat but got the job done without anyone noticing it.

There it was done, we completed the paperwork again they assured me it was just for show as Nasir was still in the crowd.

"I'll take care of this." Agent Farara declared to us as we were introduced to the small crowd as Mr. and Mrs. Jason Carter. Whelp! We took a small time out to talk to everyone, during that time Nasir disappeared. I wondered if we lost him for good.

We drove back to the house in silence but the curiosity was killing me. "Did we lost him tonight?"

"No, we just baited him. Lieutenant Jackson is sending us to Tahiti tomorrow there is where he kidnaps his targets most of the time."

"Oh."

"Don't worry we wouldn't let anything happen to you Alexis."

"Thank you."

Chapter 5

Papeete, Tahiti

Tahiti was beautiful and I was starting to wish I was really married to Alexis. The last couple days waking up to her has been amazing and it was great to have a change of pace in my house.

I turned to look at her as the moonlight danced in our room I could feel my growing attraction making its way to my little head. "Shit." I mumbled to myself.

"What's wrong?" She said as she got out of bed to come over on the couch where I was seated.

"Nothing. It's nothing."

"Are you sure?" she said as she ran her hand over my fore head.

"I think you should go back on the bed Alexis."

"What for?"

"With the thoughts going through my head right now you need to be in bed." I growled.

She looked at me with this knowing look, then got up and sat on my lap. "What if I rather be over here with you?"

"God Alexis." I ran my hand down her shoulder. "I don't think you know what you are doing to me."

"I'm pretty sure, I know." She laughed as she grinded herself on my rock hard dick. "Technically, this is our honeymoon Carter." She giggled.

"Technically."

"So technically, we can consummate our marriage just in case he is watching." I laughed at that one. She was good I can tell you that. In the next instant, she was kissing on my neck while playing with the hem of my white T-shirt.

"Damn it." I was a goner. I pulled her closer and crushed my lips to hers all while yanking her pajama shirt over her head. "Beautiful!"

I dipped my head drawing her left nipple into my mouth. She threw her head back in ecstasy. "Carter! That feels so good!" I turned my attention to the right. "Hold on." She pushed me back into the couch and climbed off my lap.

Alexis knocked any little bit of common sense I had left out of me when she got on her knees pulling my sweat pants towards her. "Shit."

"Don't say a word." She murmured as she sank my dick deep into the hot wetness of her mouth.

"Ahh!" I exclaimed as she began to work her magic. Grabbing onto her hair, I aided her in working her head up and down on my dick. "Shit if you keep going like that you're going to make me cum Lexy." Dammit I just gave her a nick name.

Alexis pulled away and then stood up. She was definitely a beauty. Fine chocolate with long jet black hair, I loved it, she pulled down her pants only to reveal she had on no underwear and climbed back into my lap.

"I need you Carter." She whispered, grabbing my hand so I can feel how much she was excited. She felt like a fountain overflowed, her juices were already running down her leg in her wantonness.

Holding my dick, she eased me inside of her. I forgot at the point I needed a condom because I wouldn't want to get her pregnant. As she begins to move up and down I grabbed her hips to keep grips on a bit of reality.

"Carter, oh Carter you feel so good!"

"Yes baby ride daddy's dick." I said as she began to bounce even faster on my dick.

"Ugh! Shit!" She grabbed ahold of her breasts pinching and squeezing them.

"Damn you're going to drive me crazy Alexis."

She bent her head down all while keeping her rhythm to nibble my ear. "That's the point."

We didn't rush, we had all night. Eventually, we moved the love making to the bed. Every move I could think of this woman knew how to make it even more sensual than before.

"Carter I'm about to cum! Oh!" I was hitting the right spots and she squeezed her muscles around me.

"Shit me too!" As she exploded with passion and continued to contract around me.

"Ahhh"

"Shit. Fuck... Fuck!"

"Oh my God!"

"That...was...incredible!"

I pulled her close to me as we fell asleep. The morning came quicker than usual, I awoke to the scent of coffee and some freshly baked croissants delivered to the room, but there was something missing. Alexis.

"Babe, baby!" No answer. I walked into the bathroom to make sure she was in there. Nowhere in sight. I was walking back to the bed when I noticed an envelope pushed under the door.

"I have her!"

"Shit!"

I lost her and I don't even know how. This is what I get for fucking around with my work. I ran and picked up the phone to call my lieutenant.

"Lieutenant Jackson, Carter what's the issue?" He answered all in a huff.

"They got her! I am not sure how they got in, but they got her! They have Alexis."

"Calm down Agent Carter. When did you that Alexis was missing?"

"This morning, I got up looking for her and for a note. Nasir has her."

"Shit! I wasn't expecting him to make a move so soon. Sit tight I'll have scouts combing the area and Agent Farara will be there soon."

"Okay." I tried to breathe, but I fell in love with her along the way and now I would be damned if I lose her.

******

I woke up in a dark room. I could make out the outline of three other women in here with me. I tried to get up, but my head hurts ridiculously. "Shit."

"Don't try get out there is no way. We have all tried already." One of the ladies said to me.

"Dammit it wasn't to be like this! How did he get me out my room!" I was pissed I was hoping to wake up next to Carter and go another two or three rounds with him. Just then the door opened and two over grown, I mean these dudes were huge. They came in and grabbed me dragging me kicking and screaming out of the door.

"Relax habib, I mean you no harm."

"Nasir!"

"Alexis you broke my heart. How could you have gotten married. I thought we had something good?"

I tried not to blow Carter's cover by outing that the CIA was unto him so I tried to play his game. "When you were raided you left me! How could you?"

"I'm sorry habib. I got a phone call that some cops were spotted and I hightailed out of there. No hard feelings but you! I did a background on your husband, a cop really? Not even just a cop but a freaking CIA agent!" Nasir was pissed and Carter's cover was blown.

"Okay so what do my husband have to do with you? You were only a fun night for me it meant nothing!"

"Don't bait me Alexis! That man has been after me for years, then you show up and I was almost caught! Tell me are you working for them also?" He grabbed me by my face squeezing hard.

"No, I am not. I told you the truth when I met you I'm into foreign investments."

"Mmm you're such a good liar Lexy."

"Don't call me that."

"Well I am going to ensure that you put this perfect little body to use. I got into this business to teach little whores like you a lesson, but now it became a profession. All hot and heavy you couldn't wait to have sex with me that night. My clientele would love you, I know I did." I felt all gross and dirty at that point. I heard water crashing against the shore outside, that meant we were close the hotel still. I hope Carter finds me soon.

*****

"Where are we on combing the island?" Agent Farara voice boomed above everyone else. I felt like a sitting duck I was Agent Carter for God's sake, I been on many secretive missions and now look at me. Standing here looking like a damn fool.

"What can I do?" She looked at me

"Carter standby I really need to talk to you." Farara and Lieutenant Jackson walked away from the group to give us some privacy,

"Carter there has been a new development. Apparently, the mail boy for our office came by to get a package from Farara's desk and picked up the wrong envelop."

"What are you saying lieutenant?"

"Congratulations Carter you are one hundred percent legally married to my Alexis Rogue." Lieutenant Jackson walked away and I was left with my world reeling.

"Carter.... Carter!"

"Yeah!"

"You know what this means? You are to go back to your room. You cannot be part of this case anymore your too close and judging by your expression you are in love with her."

I blew out a long breath I have been holding. "How am I to do that Casey?"

"I know Carter, you're a family member now and I take full responsibility for the fuck up." I laughed to myself my little ball of fire is going to be mad when she finds out. I walked back to my room, but something felt different, there is was an open door in the wall.

"That's how they got out!" I said into the empty room I wondered where this shit leads to. I grabbed my phone and turned on the flashlight and started my trek down the dark tunnel. Ten minutes later, I came upon a wood shed. Well in actuality it was bigger than a shed further up the beach from the hotel.

I ducked behind a bush when I heard footsteps. "Ensure the girls are ready for transport. They will be shipped to Hungry tonight!" the voice sounded like Nasir. I want to just out and fuck his ass up on sight, but I had to be smart about it I had no weapon but a phone.

"Yes sir." His lackey answered.

"And Sweet Alexis I want her dead. I change my mind Agent Carter is going to wish he never met me!"

"When you want me to do her in sir?"

"Tonight you imbecile! Too much traffic right now to kill anyone."

"Yes sir."

I had to do something. I continued hiding until the voices disappeared. I picked up the phone and called Farara giving her full run down.

*****

I was thirsty and I needed to pee. What time it was I don't know, but I know it was getting dark again. I heard voices, I just they were getting ready to move us.

"Get the girls it times to move."

"Is the boat here?" that was Nasir voice I knew it anywhere.

"Yes sir, it here."

"Great, I'm going to get this one." The door opened to the room where I was. "Dearie, it's time to go." He grabbed my arm.

"I wouldn't be going nowhere I believe that. He is coming for me."

"We are leaving now! Get up!" Just as we began to tussle, there was a loud commotion that came from outside our door.

"See I told you." Nasir pulled out a gun and ran to the door. "Stay here!"

Well in truth, I couldn't go anywhere with my hands and feet are tied. It felt like it was an hour before anyone came.

A young man came over to me, was scared hoping it was not one of Nasir's goons. "Mrs. Alexis Rogue-Carter?" Mrs? I was confused I was not legally married and the only people that knew this were the CIA.

"Yes, yes! That's me. I said playing off my confusion.

"Great I'm going to get you out of here and get you back to your honeymoon."

"Thank you."

We emerged from the shed and headed back to the hotel, someone had some explaining to do. It was a flurry of events they caught three of Nasir's henchmen, but Nasir wasn't going down without a fight and now he was dead. I was ready to go back home this was too much excitement for me.

I looked around for Carter, but he wasn't anywhere to be found but Agent Farara found me. "Mrs. Carter, this way."

"Why is everyone calling me that? I thought it was a fake wedding!"

"In here." I saw Carter pacing the room and I couldn't contain my excitement.

"Carter!"

"Omg Lexy are you okay? I'm sorry! I'm so so sorry."

"It's okay I'm fine Carter, but tell me why is everyone calling me Mrs.?"

He laughed. "Funny story, we are now legally married." The look he gave me stirred something deep inside of me.

"How?"

"Mix up in the office and it was mail out. Are you mad?" I dipped my head then looked at him and smiled.

"No, I'm not."

"Would you want to stay married to me? Before you answer that, I have never been more scared in my life than today and to make it worst I had to stand on the side and watch. I couldn't do anything. Alexis, I love you there is no doubt about that. Now will you stay married to me?"

"Carter…" I blew out a breath and it was a lot to take in. "Yes, I would love to!"

"Thank you for giving me a chance Lexy. Let's go and enjoy our honeymoon.

Was It Worth It?

By

Marie A. Norfleet

Preface

DeMarcus opened the door and extended his left forearm for Victoria to use as leverage, as she exited the stretch, luxury limo. Wrapping her arm around his, he escorted her into *Sammy's* restaurant. The restaurant was extremely quiet. This was unusual for the normal, busy and full of life atmosphere.

"DeMarcus, I think the restaurant is closed. It's okay, though. We can ride down the block to *Johnny's Reef.*" Victoria rubbed his arm in reassurance as she looked upward into his eyes. The innocence behind the gesture only reflected one of the many reasons why he was so madly in love with the woman standing before him. Victoria was all the woman he needed, and he was determined to show her tonight just how much he needed her in his life.

"The restaurant isn't closed babe, just follow my lead." Her gaze never broke from his, but he could see the unasked questions lingering. "Do you trust me, Victoria?" He turned to face her.

"Yes, I do. But," She started to answer but was silenced with the tip of his index finger.

"There are no buts if you trust me. Now, do you trust me Victoria?" She nodded her head in agreement.

He grabbed hold of her hand and walked toward the kitchen of the restaurant. He could feel the resistance in her arm when he pulled her towards the swinging doors. He glanced back at her and without the need for verbal confirmation, she followed his lead. He guided her through the dark kitchen towards the rear. The closer they got to the stove area, the shadow of a low flickering light bounced off the walls.

When they rounded the corner, Victoria was taken back by the surprise of a single, candle lit table set for two. In a long, slender vase, sat a white long stemmed rose.

"You remembered?" Victoria smiled, as she lifted the rose to her nose.

"I will never forget. They're almost as unforgettable as you" he responded, as he pulled her chair and helped her sit.

"What is all of this, DeMarcus?"

"I promise that all of your questions will be answered by the end of the night." He pulled out his chair, took a seat and pulled a bell out of his jacket.

On cue, a slightly tall yet muscular waiter appeared.

"May I have a chilled bottle of *Cristal,* on ice? Thank you," The waiter walked away just as quietly as he'd come.

A few moments later, he reappeared with a metal bucket filled with ice and the bottle of champagne resting in the middle. DeMarcus poured her glass then his.

Lifting his glass, he made a toast "To long lasting friendship." They tapped their glasses.

The couple drank and nibbled on a basket of fresh breadsticks that were brought to their table. When the basket emptied, DeMarcus picked up the bell and rang it twice. Once again, the waiter appeared.

This time, he carried a round tray with two plates on top of it. Sitting Victoria's plate down first, Victoria grinned widely.

On her plate, was her all-time favorite dish; grilled chicken breast, served over linguine noodles topped with Alfredo sauce and chopped tomato.

"Seriously, what's this about DeMarcus? You rented us a limo, paid god knows what to have this restaurant to ourselves, white roses and now my favorite food and choice of drink. What are you up to, Mr. Howerton?"

"Shh. We'll have all the time to talk, after dinner. For now, let's eat."

As she twirled her fork in her noodles, lost in thought; DeMarcus knew it was now or never. He pulled a stack of rolled up papers from his vest and waved to the waiter. The waiter sent in the violinist, and the musician began to play "Forever My Lady" on his violin. Victoria looked up from her plate with tears in her eyes. "Forever My Lady" was the song they had their first dance as husband and wife to.

Looking in DeMarcus' direction, she saw small tear droplets falling from his eyes. Before she could speak, he spoke.

"Victoria, you are the only woman that I've ever been in love with. You're the only woman that I've ever known. I know that I haven't always been the best husband. Between the long hours in the office, the business trips, and extra martial affairs; I was never home. I am so sorry for neglecting your needs and your wants." Picking the papers off his lap, his hands trembled.

"Here, I have the divorce papers you had drawn up." He slid the papers toward her.

"Tonight, was about showing you, that you are number one in my life. I promise that I will make every night feel like tonight, if you just give me the chance. If you say no, then I'll set you free. I will sign my signature, right here and now. But, if you say that you'll stay and make us work, then this is yours." He slid a black velvet box across the table, she opened it. In it, was her original wedding ring and band.

Chapter One

August 25th, 2012

(Two years earlier)

"Is everything alright with Tracy?" Victoria questioned as the sound of Tracy's screeching tires echoed through the quiet neighborhood.

"You know what, I did overhear her on the phone during the drive here. Sounded like she was going through something with a male companion. I am sure she'll call when she gets home so y'all can have y'all 'girl talk'" DeMarcus teased.

Leaning over her shoulder, he gave her wet and sloppy kiss before announcing that he was going to retire for the night.

"Ugh! That was a wet one babe!" Victoria shrieked as she wiped her lips.

"But you loved every second of it" DeMarcus teased as he walked upstairs.

Chuckling to herself, Victoria rose from her writing recliner and walked into her den. She dimmed the lights and took a seat at her desk. She'd been working in her notepad all day and finally decided to take a fifteen-minute break from her newest writing project before she started transferring her written story into her computer.

Turning on her laptop, she logged into her regular *Facebook* account and began to scroll through her newsfeed. There wasn't much of anything going on, which was always a good thing in Victoria's eyes. Scrolling back to the top, she clicked on the search box and began her daily investigation. Ever since the day her husband, DeMarcus left his account open and she read several suspicious conversations between him and three other women, Victoria was sure to add all three of them to her page.

When she added a woman named Shauntay's page, she noticed that there were no pictures and that she had no friends other than DeMarcus on her page. That was an automatic red flag and it just let Victoria know that it was a cover-up page. A cover-up for what, is what Victoria wanted to know. Tonight would prove to be a night that would make or break her.

When she opened Shauntay's page, tears instantly formed and began to fall. Not only were her husband's latest indiscretions plastered all over the page, from tagged statuses to pictures and videos. But, the mystery woman behind the page, was no other than her best friend; Tracy. It was one thing to be suspecting of his cheating ways but it was a real heartbreaker to see actual proof. One album of photos that caught her eye and really brought on the waterworks, was of them together at resort in Jamaica; some of the pictures had time stamped dates on them from just the week prior. Not only had it been her birthday, but also their wedding anniversary.

She had gone through so much trouble to make suite reservations at the *Cove Haven Resort*. Only to have him, claim last minute that he'd been mandated on a trip out of town. Treacherous thoughts began to flood her mind, so to keep herself from becoming a "Breaking News" story on the ten o'clock news; she went over to her mini bar and fixed herself a double shot of Hennessy on the rocks. Taking the shot to the head, she poured another and drained that one of its contents as well. Feeling a slight buzz creeping on, she walked back over to her desk with a third drink in hand.

Sitting back down, she stared at the sleeping monitor for a few minutes before swiping the mouse pad. Now, that she had undisputable proof of his cheating ways; a divorce attorney would be hearing from her. Taking a deep breath, she saved the pictures and videos to the computer's hard drive and her portable flash drive. Getting all that she needed, she signed out and logged on to her author account. There were quite a few notifications, but the one indicating a new friend request was the first that she addressed.

She clicked open the drop box to view the request. It was from another author, Vincent Acosta. She had seen some of his advertisements in a few of the book clubs that she was in, on *Facebook* and had purchased a few of his books in the past. Opening his page, she checked his friends list. They had almost two hundred mutual friends, including some of the heavy hitters in the industry.

She was getting ready to click the reject button, not wanting to be bothered when another notification alerted her that she'd been added to a group for Vincent's fans.

"Who is this Acosta character?" She questioned as she accepted his request and opened the group's page.

VINCENT ACOSTA

Vincent lay in bed, toking on his nightly herbal medication as he browsed through the groups and newsfeed for his daily scoop of *Facebook* and it's never ending drama. He was in the midst of laughing at a few of the post in one of the groups called the *"Black Faithful Sisters and Brothers Book Club"* when he scrolled upon an interesting ad from one of the 'newbie' authors, Victoria Howerton. It was a poetic styled, introduction to her and her new book. After reading the brief bio, he noticed there was a photo attached of her.

"She's got a pretty face" he thought to himself as he clicked on the link to open her page. Since her page was public, he was able to look through her photos and he liked what he saw.

"Oh, she's a bad little joint. I have to see where her head is at" he exclaimed, as he sent her a friend request.

Not waiting for her response because he was sure she'd add him, he went ahead and added her to his group. Just as he had expected, a notification popped up and let him know that she'd accepted his request. He was surprised by her immediate participation and interaction with some of the other readers. As he sat back and watched the threads unfold, it become apparent that she already had a previous connection with these ladies. He became slightly aroused at some of her open-minded responses to the X-rated threads being posted.

He was about to jump in one of the conversations when his message indicator at the top of the screen, lit up. He was caught off guard when he realized that it was the new girl, Victoria. He eagerly opened the message.

"I love this book club! It's refreshing to let loose and know that no judgment is being passed"

"I wonder how she'd respond to this" he chuckled to himself as he hit enter on his message. "I really love you in there. When can we exchange some pictures? Lol" He damn near choked to death on a toke of *Sour* when he read her response.

"These pictures I have; you aren't ready for Mr. Acosta."

"I knew she was a little freak! I got that ass now," he grinned to himself.

"I definitely am. But let's test that theory shall we? My email is plainjane41280@yahoo.com" he hit enter and patiently waited for her to reply.

Two minutes later, "Hmm...Will you send one in return?" He couldn't believe how easy this was going.

"Of course, I don't play games"

"Okay. What kind of shot do you want? (No full body flicks on deck at this time)"

His dick hardened at the thought of seeing her tender flesh in the nude. "I hope you know how to look sexy, out of clothes too lol" he replied

"I don't like clothes lol but on a serious note, if I send these pictures, they'll stay between us right?"

He was beginning to get frustrated with her continuous back tracking but then regained his composure when he thought about it. He made one last attempt to reassure her that he was trustworthy.

"I swear. I don't play games at all! We are both professionals outside of this, little thing we have going"

"Okay, I sent them. My email is VictoriaHowerton@gmail.com"

"Okay, I sent mines too."

"Let me go see what you are working with lol." She replied

Vincent waited for her reply.

"Oh my, that's a third leg you got there lol I don't know where you're going to put all that!"

"I can think of a few places" he responded.

"You are so fresh lol did you get my pictures?"

"Ah, let me check," He raced over to his email, but no pictures were there. "Na, I didn't get them.

"That's crazy, let me check on that. I'll be right back," Her messenger went idle, eight minutes later she returned. "I got an error email"

"Hmm...That's bizarre. I was just signed into that account." He leaned back and thought about the crazy positions he would put her in and decided to put the nail in the coffin. "But that's okay, I will check on it in a bit. I have to make a run really quick, no bullshit. But, I like you. When can we meet and greet?"

"I actually have a trip planned to DC for a book signing, next month."

"I got one better. I'll be in New York, in about two weeks. Where are you, in the city?"

"I live in Staten Island."

"So, if I make it out there, can you get away for a few hours of action?

"I certainly could. But the real question is, will you make it worth remembering? Lol Oh, I should probably tell you that I haven't had sex in eight months."

She didn't even know what she was getting herself into and it amused him.

"Come on ma, you see how I'm built. I definitely will give you all that you can handle and more. Real talk, I'll give us both something to write about from different P.O.V.'s. Just don't front!"

"Do I look shy to you lol fro- what? That word isn't even in my vocabulary, this is a 'no tapping out' zone over here!"

"Okay, that's what I like to hear! Listen, I will get up with you later. I am going to make that run" was the last thing he said before he signed off.

He couldn't wait to tear that young ass up.

His ringing phone, snapped him out of his sexual fantasy. Nonchalantly he answered "I am on my way now, babe" Hanging up, he resumed the steaming of his herbal medication.

Chapter Two

Three weeks later....

"Tonight is the night Vicky" Victoria said aloud to herself. She was trying to mentally prepare for the night's events that lie ahead. Looking in the mirror for the fifth time, she began to examine her undergarments. She double checked her triple girdle combination to make sure every nook and cranny was securely tucked. Finally satisfied with her look, she slipped on her new black and white striped sweater that she purchased from Macy's earlier that day. Once again she found herself in the mirror.

"What is wrong with me?" she questioned. It was as if a light bulb went off in her head. *"I know what I need"* she snickered to herself.

Reaching into her nightstand, she retrieved her rhinestone studded, jewelry box. Turning the box over, she opened a hidden compartment. She recovered a Ziploc bag from the compartment and pulled out one of her pre rolled *Bluntville's*. Walking over to her vanity, she took a seat on the miniature stool and set the marijuana filled cigar ablaze. After a few tokes on the loud, her nerves settled and her mindset became mellow.

She was thrilled to finally be meeting up with Vincent, after weeks of back and forth conversations over *Facebook* and the phone. They'd spent majority of the last few days planning this very night. Tonight would be a true case of "show me what you got" because after all the slick talking from both parties; he was here, in her city. He talked a good one though, put up this front like his dick was golden.

She thought back to a conversation they'd had when he mentioned something about rearranging some of her feminine organs and causing a noticeable change in her walk. From that moment on, she was beyond intrigued.This promised pleasurable experience was one that she needed, even if her body hadn't been stretched out in over nine months. She smiled at thought of the comprising positions they'd engage in as she began to fix her hair. She greased her front braids and picked up her ponytail piece off of the sink's edge. She made sure to center it before pulling the drawstring tight. While wrapping the drawstring around the base of the ponytail, her left arm became restless and collapsed.

Her fingertips, lightly brushed against her right nipple. A surge of passion shot through her body like electricity in the third rail. The instant sensation caused her body to flush warm and both of her nipples harden through the layered material. Dealing with her cheating husband, playing the housewife role, in addition to her literary career taking off so abruptly; she'd barely had time to sleep, let alone think about the comforts of a warm man. She lingered on the thought of how long it'd really been since she'd been sexually stimulated.

Under the influence of the marijuana, the thought was unnerving and slightly depressing. Rising from the stool, she walked in front of her full length mirror and began to gaze at her body. As if she was under a sexual trance, she began to rub her nipples through the layers of clothes. It didn't feel right, though. It was like she was cheating herself from the full effects of this beautiful experience.

Slowly, she took off her shirt and tossed it aside. Then she pulled down all of the girdles and stepped out of her pants. Within minutes, she stood completely nude in front of the mirror and lovingly admired her body. Her body was far from perfect, though. She had a pouch left behind from the multiple children, her breast were not as firm nor as perky as they used to be and she had a lot of stretch marks like war scars from the preparation of motherhood. But at that moment, she didn't see her imperfections; she saw a woman.

A woman crying internally, yearning for just a bit of affection. However, tonight that would change; she would quiet her own silent cries. Steadily, she allowed her hands to explore where ever they wanted while she lustfully gawked in the mirror, at the sight. She left a hot tingling trail on her skin from her fingertips as they slid over her breast, down her stomach, toward her hidden treasures. The further south her hands traveled, the more heat rose from her throbbing center.

Finally, her fingers found their jackpot and what a sweet, dripping wet goldmine it was. She dipped the index and middle finger of her right hand into her naturally sweet nectar, while rotating her thumb in a circular motion on her swollen bud.

As her juices began to seep down her hand, she couldn't resist the urge to taste her own dew. She slipped a finger in and out quickly and lifted it to her lips. It was bitter sweet, like the first bite of a ripe strawberry.

She wanted another taste. No, she craved another taste. Just as she was dipping in for another palate, her phone began to vibrate.

Reluctantly, she reached on top of the dresser, picked up the vibrating phone and opened the message. When she saw Vincent's name, she immediately downloaded the attached file.

"Damn" she cooed and crossed her legs, as she stared at the surprise photos. After thorough observation of the picture, she estimated his manly pole to be somewhere between ten and eleven inches of pure thickness. This would be one occasion that she didn't mind getting her work out on. She was about to send him a text, when his face popped up. She struggled to keep her shaking hands steady, as she pressed talk.

"What's up, Sexy. What did you think about that sneak peek? Are you sure you're ready for this, tonight?" the lust thick and apparent in his tone.

"More ready than you'll ever know" she retorted as she lay across her bed with the image of his beautiful shaft, still vivid in her mind.

A slight moan escaped her lips as she pinched on her erected nipples.

"I'm glad to hear that, literally. Save some of that for me" Vincent chortled.

"I plan on sharing a lot more than that, with you" she whispered into the phone, slowly licking her lips with a clear visual of what she intended on doing.

"Oh really, and what exactly would that be?"

Just as she getting ready to go off in detail about the tongue bath she intended to give his lower region, the sound of lightening cracked.

"Ah, shit. I know it's not raining," she said.

She jumped off the bed and jogged to her window. Hard rain droplets poured from the cloudy sky, and like the ground; her mood was instantly dampened.

"This would be one of the many instances that I wish I knew how to drive" she said more to herself than him as she looked out back. Her car was just sitting in the parking lot.

"Yea that would be great right now" he said reminding her that he was still on the line. "So how are you going to get here?"

"I know a few cab companies in the area that I could get a quote from" she answered slightly disappointed at the thought of having to spend unnecessary money.

"You could do that but hold on. My cousin just walked in, let me ask her if she'd pick you up." He placed her on a brief hold.

"Ok what's your address, my cousin Natasha will come to get you."

"Oh that's so nice of her, please tell her I said thank you" she ran off the address to him.

"Ask her, how long it will take for her to get here"

"Ok hold on. She's going to leave here in about ten minutes so she said she'll be there in about thirty minutes"

Victoria started calculating her time, taking in consideration the time to get refreshed and redressed.

"Damn fifteen minutes isn't enough time! Oh well, I hope he can finish what I started" she snickered to herself as she stared at her naked body in the headboard mirror.

"Thirty minutes, ok. Let me finish getting ready and I'll see you in a little while" she exclaimed nervously.

"Iight sexy, I'll see you in a bit"

After he hung up, she tried to resume her previous activities despite her tight time constraints but to no avail; the mood was gone. She rose from the bed and started to redress. Sprinkling a bit of baby powder into her hands, she applied it in between her thighs. Next, she picked up a bottle of "Pure Seduction" body spray, one of her favorite scents from *Victoria Secret* and sprayed it twice in the air. With caution, she walked into the mist; careful not to get it in her eyes.

Grabbing the matching lotion, she rubbed down her entire body. Satisfied with her scent, she picked up the first whole body girdle and hopped around the room as she struggled to put it back on. Once pulled all the way up, the stomach holder/upper body vest and padded butt girdle were a breeze. She did a checklist on her layers before walking into her closet. She chose a pair of thigh high, black suede boots, which she'd brought from *Target* earlier on in the week.

Taking a seat on her chest, she slipped on one boot at a time. One last glance in the mirror, she turned around, grabbed her pocketbook off the wall hook and did a quick scan of the contents. A douche, washcloth, bar of soap, change of panties, three magnum condoms, two female condoms and a pack of *Plan B*, morning after pills. *"You can never be too careful"* she thought to herself as she rushed downstairs. She kissed the children goodnight, blew pass their father and skipped out the door. Five minutes later, she was in the car with his cousin, heading to her house to meet up with him.

Chapter Three

Victoria leaned back in the cool leather seat as Natasha swiftly maneuvered through the mild, late night traffic. The blended smell of fresh rainfall and the two dime bags of marijuana she had stashed in her purse, filled the car as they cruised through the streets of Staten Island listening to the sweet crooning of Miguel's angelic voice. Fifteen minutes later, they pulled into a neighborhood that was familiar to Victoria.

"Oh, wow. I went to the college around the corner from here. I loved walking through this neighborhood because it is always quiet" Victoria said, as they walked towards Natasha's home.

"Isn't it though, I love it! I've never had a problem here" She responded while putting the key in her door.

Victoria couldn't believe she was only seconds away from standing face to face with the man whom successfully brought her to her peak through several of their most intimate chatting sessions.

"I guess the time has come to see if he lives up to the hype" Victoria took one last deep breath before following Natasha into the house.

Once stepping inside, she followed suit behind Natasha as she took off her sneakers. She barely had time to take off her second boot before Vincent came around the corner. A feeling much like fluttering butterflies on your first day of school begin to form in the pit of her stomach, her heart picked up several beat and her throat became dry. This seemed surreal but there he stood; all six feet of him.

A nervous flirtatious smile spread across Victoria's lips as she added a little more switch to her hips while walking towards him.

There they stood, taking in the sight of one another. He was all she'd thought to be and more. He was sporting a low Caesar and a fresh line up. A perfect set of thick, juicy lips complimented his bedroom eyes. Victoria couldn't resist the urge to be held in his arms if even for a short embrace; she extended her arms for a hug.

Once wrapped in his arms with her face buried in his chest, the smell of his aftershave and cologne mix caused impure thoughts to flow through her mind. Visions of her legs wrapped around his waist as he repeated a combination of long, deep strokes into her carnal dwellings mid-air; made her knees slightly buckle.

He didn't miss a beat and was there to catch her, holding her firm against his solid frame. With their bodies so closely connected, the sexual tension could be felt miles away. She felt him stiffen against her mid-section and her juices began to pool from anticipation. Locking eyes with one another, he slowly pulled away.

"It's good to see you too" he said with a slight snicker and sly grin.

"Yes, it is nice to finally meet the infamous Mr. Acosta. I think I'm a little star struck" she replied sarcastically with a grin of her own.

He gently grabbed her hand and led her into the plush carpeted living room.

She knew he sensed the slight hesitation and resistance in her body when he tugged at her to have a seat. He leaned forward, wrapped his arms around her waist and pulled her down onto his lap. Though his lap was a place she'd love to be, doing some very adult things; she hadn't gotten the chance to securely take off her padded ass! She couldn't risk the chance of him feeling on her backside prematurely. She quickly popped up and sat alongside him on the love-seat. The unsettledness of her actions caused him to look at her cautiously. She smiled a wary yet assuring smile, in attempt to reassure him that everything was okay.

"Yo you alright ma?" he asked still looking at her suspiciously.

"Yes, I'm fine" she nervously laughed as she adjusted herself.

"Iight. Let me find out you acting some kind of way now that you're here" he exclaimed as he got up from the couch and walked into kitchen.

"Would you like something to drink?" He asked while pouring himself a shot of Hennessey.

"Yes, I'll take a shot"

"A big shot or a small one" he asked holding up the glass options.

"The small one is fine" She didn't want to get too wasted and forget to handle her little "business."

He returned with their drinks and reclaimed his seat beside her. He guzzled his drink in big gulps; Victoria on the other hand sipped her shot like a lady was supposed to. Truth be told, under different circumstances, not only would she have taken the bigger glass but she would've tossed it back like one of the fellas. But she chose the lady like approach tonight because she was set on impressing him. If things went the right way, she'd have plenty of time for him to get to know all about her.

"Aye did you bring the herb" he asked nonchalantly as they watched court TV.

"But of course! Even got the roll up" she said, as she pulled two *Bluntville's* packages, a few Black -N- Mild's and a pack of *Newport's* out of her purse. She sat the items on the windowsill.

Natasha reappeared from the back minutes later and took a seat on the sofa across from them. They began their two-person cipher, kicked back and relaxed. It wasn't long before her eyes chinked low and her body started tingling. Thinking she could steal a glance at his fine, milk chocolatey self without being noticed; she slyly turned her head in his direction. To her surprise, she became engaged in an intense stare down with a pair of lustful eyes already locked on her. Her pussy twitched and jumped, her vaginal muscles clenched themselves together and she began to feel moist.

His eyes said it all, he was hungry and she didn't mind offering her body as the dish to quench his appetite. The thought of having his face buried deep between her thighs made her squirm in her seat. Neither one of them was willing to break to the lustful eye contact, the sexual tension became thick in the air. Natasha, getting the hint, excused herself. She said her good-nights and headed to her room. Seeing his cousin off, Vincent returned. But by then, Victoria had moved over to the sofa.

"Come here. Why are you sitting way over there" he asked as he reached toward her.

"It's about to go down Vickie! Just take deep breaths girl! You're a little rusty but it's like riding a bike, you never forget" she prep talked herself mentally as she stood up.

No sooner than she sat down, he leaned in and attacked the sensitive spot on her neck. A soft moan escaped her lips. His hands caressed her pillow soft breast, softly pinching on her aroused nipples. Her back arched upward from the sensual touch. Her body was on high alert and longing for his continuous touch. He laid her back against the cool sofa and took her lips with his. Lost in the intensity of his kiss, she forgot all about the girdles and made the mistake of letting his hands free roam all over her body.

"How many shirts do you have on?" he tittered, as he went to lift the main layer of clothes.

"Ah, it's just a few girdles" she replied, completely embarrassed.

"A few?" he retorted. "You didn't have to do all that. Come here."

She pulled away and tried to get up to walk away.

"Where are you going? You don't have to be ashamed in front of me. Come here" he demanded, pulling her into his arms and locking lips with her again. She pulled away harder this time.

Not knowing if it was the effects of the marijuana and alcohol combination or that her comfort level of trust with him was high but she began to blurt out the truth.

"Look what you see on the outside is not what I really look like under my clothes" she exclaimed, putting her head down in shame.

"What do you mean?" he asked taking a step back and looking directly at her genital area.

"Hell Na! It isn't anything like that" she laughed.

"So what do you mean, love?"

Taking a deep breath and exhaling, she told it all.

"I really wanted to impress you tonight, so right now I'm layered down in girdles and my ass is padded" she looked away, afraid to see the rejection in his eyes.

"Listen," he said closing the distance between them. "You don't have to impress me. I didn't ask to meet up with you solely because of your looks. I think you're a cool person and I want to kick it with you. You don't have to have any pull ups with me. You hear me? I want you for who you are" he said attempting to pull her shirt up over her head.

She stepped back. She was astounded by his choice of words, she could tell that they were sincere and genuine. He'd successfully made her feel comfortable and she slowly stepped out of the layers until she stood fully unclothed before him. Her newfound confidence was short lived because it wasn't long before she came back to her senses and snatched the sheet off the mattress that he'd blown up.

"What are you doing yo? Cut that shit out! You're sexy! Stop hiding behind that damn sheet. I see that nigga don' fucked up your self-esteem. It's alright though, I'll show you that you don't need to have no pull ups with me." He walked over to his pants and pulled out two XL magnums.

Her body shuttered from head to toe at the sight, "I'll be right back."

She picked up her pocketbook and rushed towards the bathroom. Once she locked the door, she pulled out her washing amenities and quickly refreshed herself. Finishing with a brush of her teeth and rinse of her mouth, she was ready.

Chapter Four

She casually walked back into the living room, placed her bag in the corner and took a seat on the bed. He smiled and took a seat next to her.

Her nerves were shot! She was as nervous as a virgin on prom night. As he hovered around her neck, inhaling her scent; her body trembled with anticipation of his actual touch.

"Relax. I don't bite. Well, unless you ask me to."

He placed the softest kiss on her neckline. She caught her breath. Kiss. Her breathing quickened. He pulled back and looked deeply into her eyes and his eyes told a story all of their own. She knew she was in for some trouble but she damn sure didn't mind. In fact, at this point she wasn't far from begging for it. She captured his lips with her own and was met with an intense tongue battle. Caught off guard, she pulled away.

"Yo what is wrong with you?" he questioned thoroughly frustrated.

She was too embarrassed to answer. Truth of the matter was that she'd never tongued kissed anyone before. Neither her son's father nor husband were into tongue kissing so she'd never learned how to.

"I've never kissed like that" she responded on the verge of tears.

"The more I hear, the more this nigga really pisses me off" Vincent grunted.

Without warning, he grasped her face and pulled her lips to his. Slowly, he pried her lips apart with his tongue and began to massage her tongue with his. Their tongues intertwined with one another and found a rhythm all of their own. Breaking the kiss, he took his tongue and traced the outline of her lips, leaving behind a fiery trail. Nudging her backwards, he placed small kisses from her breast to her abdomen.

Her thighs clasped together when his warm breath drifted just above her prized jewel.

"Relax. Baby, I got you" he whispered against her freshly shaven mound.

Once she started to relax her legs, he wasted no time diving right in. Capturing her clitoris between his lips, he flicked his tongue quickly back and forth across the delicate bud. Her body shivered from the feel of his soft lips. He skillfully licked and sucked then nibbled and blew. The gust of air made her back arch and she cried out in ecstasy.

He stuck two fingers into his mouth, pulled them out and attempted to insert them into her vaginal opening.

"Damn girl! This pussy is tight," he moaned as he tried to work his fingers in. Her walls slightly loosened and he was in. He drove his fingers in and out at a mediocre pace as he resumed the pleasure induced lashing of his tongue.

"Oh! That feels so good," Victoria cooed while rotating her hips against his hand.

He increased the flickering of his tongue and the pumping of his fingers as her body reacted.

"Mm-hmm. That's it baby! Ooh!" She thrust her hips harder as her juices began to run down his fingers.

He lapped at her condensation like a fluid deprived athlete after a marathon. Her body quivered as an orgasmic tidal wave stunned her body. As she basked in the blissful feeling, she was overcome with the desire to return the favor. Sitting up on her knees, she seductively crawled across the bed into his lap. Tugging his erected member free from its materialistic jail, she gasped at the sight of it in person.

"How the hell is he getting that in me?" She thought to herself. *"I can't wait to find out."*

She hung over the head of his penis and engulfed it with the warmth of her mouth. He jerked at the feel of her moistness. He placed his right hand on the back of her head as she sucked and slobbered on his stiffened rod.

"Damn! *Ssstt* Oh shit" he whimpered.

His pleasure sounds were music to her ears, it fueled her to go to work on the head. Slowly pulling him from her mouth, she began a suction motion much like the motion of a baby on a pacifier. Her continuous concentrated sucking on his now sensitive head almost made him lose control. He lifted her face from his lap and pushed her back against the bed.

Reaching over, he grabbed one of the condoms off of the coffee table and shielded his solider for the love war ahead. He positioned himself in between her thighs, lowered his arms over each side of her head and without guidance from his hands; probed around her vaginal opening. Finally, he gained entry. Gradually, he inched himself further into her snug vessel. One final, hard thrust forward and the condom snapped. Pulling out, he retrieved the broken fragments and slipped on a new coat of protection.

This time, her body accepted him and he slid in at an easier pace. It wasn't long before he was buried deep and pounding away at her walls. It was like their bodies knew one another, as they collided in harmony.

"Ah, shit. Damn! That's my spot Vi-ugh!" she hollered, as Vincent plunged his ten and a half inch stick of joy in a circular motion, into her sensitive mound of flesh.

"What's my name? Say my name, Victoria" His shameless command, sent tingling chills all over her body. His voice was deep and raspy, and reminded her of Barry White's.

He grunted in her ear as he lifted her left leg higher on his shoulder and pressed forward. When he repositioned her leg, it gave him deeper access to her throbbing canal.

"Ah! What are you doing to me?" she shrieked.

"What's my name?" he repeated, as he pounded hard into her now dripping box.

"Ooh! Damn, baby! That's my spot!" her walls began to tighten around his pulsating tool.

"What's my name, Victoria?" he groaned as he picked up his speed, bringing her to her climax.

"Vincent! Ah! Vincent! I'm about to- ugh. I'm cumming!" she yelled, as her body began to convulse and release its warm fluids all over the sheets.

"Yea, that's what I am talking about! Cum on this dick! I feel that shit getting wetter too." Vincent leaned all the forward against her leg and slowly grinded until his pelvis rubbed against hers.

"Oh damn! Yea, keep cumming on this dick for me" he howled as her juices splashed against his thighs.

The harder she came, the harder he plunged into her depths. He was determined to leave his mark. Abruptly, he pulled out and looked down at Victoria who was stuck like a deer in headlights.

"Put that ass up" he demanded as he slapped her on the thigh, signaling for her to turn around. Victoria turned over and her ass spread. He was thoroughly enjoying the beautiful sight until he noticed some tattoo ink on her lower back.

"Dream Weaver? I can't believe you really inked this dude's brand on you." Shaking his head, he positioned himself behind her and was getting ready to insert his rod when she threw her ass back hard and started backing him down.

"Oh, shit. You want this dick, don't you?" he gripped her hips and retook control.

"Yes, give it to me. Ah fuck!"

Lifting one leg while kneeling on the other, he held onto her hips and started giving her gut pounding strokes. She tried to use her hands to push him back but he slapped her hands away. "Oh, no. You said you wanted me to give it you, right?"

"Yes, but I-"

"No buts, take this dick!" he barked as he slammed into her curvaceous frame.

She loved every stroke, his aggressive manner sending her into frenzy. Before she knew it, she felt another orgasm threatening to rear its beautiful head.

"Shit! I am about to- oh!" Her sentence cut short by the eruption of her womanly essences.

"Mm-hmm. I am about to bust too, shit. Damn, this pussy. Fuck!" he hollered as he knees buckled and his back jerked. He collapsed onto the bed, ripped the condom off as she flipped over on her back; both of them physically spent.

"I am not done with your ass, yet" she retorted, out of breath.

"Excuse me?" he snickered.

"You heard me, this is not over! I want some more of that," Sitting up, she straddled him and slowly licked from his neckline down to his areolas.

"You are a wild one, I like that! Now, come get this dick" he lifted her hips and slid her over his unshielded member.

Chapter Five

The shinning of the early morning sun, peeking in through the blinds made Victoria pop up. She reached down and picked up her cell phone to check the time; it was 6:45am. She hopped up from the bed and ferociously started looking around for her clothes. The clinking of silverware, alerted her that she was not the only one awake. The sounds of dragging feet, in house slippers quickly approaching the living room; caused her to take cover behind the arm of the sofa.

"It's good to see you are awake, I made breakfast" Vincent chimed cheerfully as his slender frame appeared in the door way with a tray of different breakfast assortments.

"What are you doing over there" he snickered at Victoria cowering in the corner.

"I thought you were Natasha," she responded before standing up and resuming her mission to find her clothing.

"Where are you going?" He asked baffled.

"I have to go, my son has to be to school by eight and the "asshole" has to be to work at ten today. Where is she anyway?" she continued to fret.

"She left out to work a little while ago" he answered. He was slightly discouraged at her wanting to depart, especially since he was now fully erected at the sight of her nudeness. He decided to try and convince her to stay a little longer. He began kicking his game to her.

"Just sit and have breakfast with me and I'll pay for your cab ride home."

"No, I couldn't let you do that" she replied snapping on her bra.

"Come on. Let me do that for you, it's the least I can do for you after last night." He winked at her. Her face flushed red as she thought about the acts that occurred the night before.

"Hm... I don't know. I really have to get home and get him ready for school" she sighed.

"Please. For me? Just have some breakfast and I got the cab ride for you to get home."

"Ok, I'll stay for breakfast but I have to go home, right after."

She sat at the table and dove right into the creamy grits, cheesy eggs, sausage links and toast. When she looked over, she noticed that Vincent didn't have plate and was staring at her like a hawk stalking its prey.

"Is everything alright, Vincent? Where is your food?" she questioned as she returned her attention back to her plate.

"My breakfast is right here."

By the time she turned her head to look for his plate, he was on his knees in between her thighs. He pried her legs open with little resistance and buried his face in her treasure box.

"Ooh! W-w-what are you doing? Aah! V-v-Vincent" She cried out in ecstasy as he stuck his tongue deep into her moist canal and committed to fucking her with his tongue. Involuntarily, her hips started to rock back and forth against his face as she neared her climax. Vincent knew she was about to cum but he couldn't allow that without getting his, too.

Reaching into his pants pocket and slyly ripping open the package, he slipped the rubber over his engorged member. In sequence, he rose, picked her up and placed her against the wall. Taking her legs and wrapping them around his waist, he plunged into her; she shrieked behind the initial contact.

Her back slapped against the wall, in tune with his aggressive stroke. He knew that his time was limited but he wanted to leave a lasting impression on this tenderloin. He adjusted her legs and went into beast mode as he dug deep into her pussy. She was screaming so loud, neighbors from a block away could hear the pleasurable sounds coming from the cozy apartment. Feeling her muscles contract around his shaft, indicated that she was ready to explode and he would be sure to erupt with her. A few deeper strokes and their bodies collapsed on one another.

She gave him a stern yet satisfied look before she walked into the living room and got fully dressed. While she dressed, he called a cab service but they didn't know how to get to the house so he gave them closest landmark which happened to be a 7–Eleven, gas station not far from the house. They were walking hand in hand towards the station, just shooting the breeze when his phone ringed.

"Excuse me Victoria, this is an important call" he excused himself as he moved several steps ahead of her.

He remained on the phone until they reached their destination and could be heard telling the caller that he would call them back in a little while.

"Come here, beautiful" he motioned for her.

She walked into his arms and he embraced her in an affectionate hug. When she went to pull away, he pulled her back and locked lips with her. Not use to the show of public affection, she pulled away quickly and gazed into his eyes but before she could say a word, her cab pulled in.

"I had a good time, thank you" she spoke.

"I did too. Are we going to link up again before I leave?"

"I hope so," she smiled and walked towards her awaiting ride. "I'll hit you up later."

"Do that. I'll see you later, Ma."

The ride home seemed to be quicker than the ride there the night before as Victoria stared out the window. Dragging her feet, she walked into her house and was surprised to see that her son was fully clothed and at the table eating breakfast.

"Good Morning, baby." she kissed his forehead. "Where is your father?"

"I am right here, good morning babes. How was *Webster Hall* last night?" DeMarcus asked as he entered the dining room.

"It was good. I had a great time." Her responses were short worded.

"Hey, DeMarcus Jr. Are you ready to go?"

Her son looked from his plate of pancakes and bacon and nodded his head yes.

"Mommy will be in the living room waiting for you to finish" she replied, as she walked off into the living room.

She didn't want to be in the presence of DeMarcus, longer than needed. She couldn't yet decipher if her feelings were of shame for her indiscretions or if it was just utter dislike for the man whom she been married to for five years. She wasn't going to try and figure it out right then and there though, all she wanted to do was get a warm shower and climb into her bed.

The walk to and from the school was a refreshing one. While she was walking back, her phone vibrated in her pocket. Hoping it wasn't Demarcus calling, she slowly pulled out the phone. To her surprise, it was Vincent's face that appeared on the screen. She took a deep breath in and exhaled quickly, in an attempt to hide her excitement as she answered.

"Hey, beautiful. I just wanted to make sure that you got home safely." His raspy voice bloomed through the receiver, sending instant chills down her spine.

"Hey you. I made it and got my son to school just in time. No thanks to you" she teased.

"Hey, I kept my promise. After I had my breakfast" he flirted.

"You are so fresh." She covered her mouth to stifle her laughter.

"I was thinking that we could go out tomorrow and grab a bite to eat and catch a flick," Vincent continued.

"What! You want me to come back tomorrow?"

"You could come back today, if you'd like"

"You are one crazy man" she chuckled.

"I am serious though. Could you get away this afternoon?"

"I could but I-"

"No buts! If you can come, then I want to see you."

"Wow! Are you serious?"

"As a heart attack."

"Okay. Let me see what I can do."

"I'll be waiting." Vincent replied as he ended the call.

The conversation ended just in time as she reached her doorstep. Walking back into the house, she could hear DeMarcus shuffling around upstairs. She assumed he was getting ready for work until she heard him speaking. Creeping up the steps, she listened to him talk freely on the phone.

"I promise to be there after work, babe"

Pause.

"Don't worry about that, I'll tell her that I had to work late."

She backed away from the door just as quietly as she'd come and went back downstairs to the kitchen.

"So, this nigga is still fucking around. I knew it!" Victoria was furious.

She sat at the table, contemplating her next move. She pulled her phone from her jeans pocket and pushed the talk button twice. She put the phone to her ear, waiting for a response while she watched the stairs. On the fourth ring, Vincent picked up.

"Hello"

"I am coming!"

"What time do you think you'll be here?"

"Like 12:30"

"Ok, I can't wait! I got something for you" he laughed devilishly.

Chuckling, she replied "See you, then"

Hanging up the phone, DeMarcus appeared at the top of the stairs.

"Alright babe, I am off to work. I'll be working late tonight" he said leaning in for a kiss. Victoria moved her face.

"Have a good one," she responded, with a dismissive wave of her hand.

"*Two can play this game, bitch*" Victoria thought to herself as she watched him walk out of the house.

She hopped up, jogged up the stairs with a huge grin plastered on her face as she started to get their younger children ready for daycare.

Chapter Six

The sexually drained pair lay in bed, fighting for oxygen as their chest heaved heavily up and down.

"Boy, you are some kind of freaky" Victoria playfully tapped his arm.

"Me! What about you? Ms. Put It on My Back Daddy" he burst out laughing.

"Shut up!" she laughed and cuddled under his arm.

"So what are you doing today?" she asked glancing up at him.

"Well, I have to go to the barber today to get my line up touched up then I am thinking about going into the city and checking on my other fam. Why what's up? What you got planned for today?" He questioned, as he twirled her hair in his hand.

"I don't have any plans today until six and then I have to pick up the children from daycare" she flashed a devious smirk.

"Sounds like a plan to me! But do you know where I can get a decent haircut on this god forsaken island?"

"I sure do! No one cuts hair better than Vickie's"

"Where is that at? Anywhere near here?"

Victoria burst into laughter at his slow catch on. "Baby! I am Vickie's. How did you not catch on to that?" she cracked up.

"Oh you got jokes, I see" he laughed and climbed on top of her, playfully nibbling on her neck and tickling her sides.

Tears started to spill from her eyes from the hard laughter. She hadn't laughed like that in years.

"Ok! Ok! I am sorry! Uncle! Uncle" she tapped out.

"That's what I thought," he teased as he leaned over her. "Na seriously though, do you know how to cut hair?

"Yes, I really do know how to cut hair. My sons haven't been to a barber in years."

"Iight, let's see what you got" he replied, as he climbed off of her and went to retrieve his clippers kit.

Fifteen minutes later, Victoria guided him to the bathroom to look at her masterpiece.

"You got skills ma. I'll give props where they are due"

While he admired himself in the mirror, Victoria stripped down to her birthday suit. When he turned around, she stood proudly in all her glory.

"What are you doing?" he snickered.

"Waiting for my payment" she replied, as she stepped into the tub.

"That's a payment I don't mind making, I'll even give you a tip." He followed suit, stripping out of his clothes and taking a condom out of his pocket.

*****

Victoria jumped out of the cab at six o' clock, on the dot. She sprinted up the stairs to the children's daycare. Gathering the kids and their belongings quickly, she began to sped walk down the block towards their house. She was trying to beat the rain that was threating to crack the grey clouds over them. Once she got them settled, she put her *iPod* on its dock, turned the volume all the way up and started preparing dinner.

She was in a good mood and her exuberant attitude showed it. She pulled a small pre-seasoned roast from the refrigerator, tossed it in a pot of boiling herb seasoned water. She was cutting up some carrots and potatoes on a plate when she heard DeMarcus come in. Still singing along with the music and smiling, Victoria didn't bother hiding her chipper demeanor as he walked in the dining room.

"Hey Hun," she greeted him with her backside up in the air as she bent down to put a batch of her honey buttered biscuits in the oven.

"How was your day at the office?"

"Somebody is certainly in a good mood today" he exclaimed as he took a seat at the island.

"My day was the same, same shit just a different day. How was your day?"

"My day was great" she snickered at the thought of just how great her day was.

"That's what's up. Something smells good, what are you cooking?" He stood and walked around into the kitchen, trying to get a glance in the pots.

"I am making a roast beef, with carrots, potatoes, white rice, macaroni and cheese, string beans and honey buttered biscuits" she replied, smiling.

"Damn! You really are in a good mood. Who don' came and dicked you down" he joked.

Caught off guard by his accurate accusation, she spun around.

"What did you just say to me?" she asked nervously.

Mistaking her look of guilt for a look of anger, he quickly recanted his comment and explained that he was joking.

"Ease up babe! I was just kidding around. I know you'd never do anything like that." He kissed her forehead and slapped her on the ass.

She frowned at the gesture but kept her comments to herself, she was just relieved to know that he hadn't figured out her truth.

During dinner, she watched him text away without regard. She started to speak up on his disrespectful act when her phone vibrated with a text alert. Picking up her phone, she read the message and instantly began to snicker. Proud of her meal, she took pictures of the dishes and posted them on Facebook. Vincent saw the pictures.

"That nigga should be thanking me, I put in that work and he over there eating good lol. Come to think of it, where's my food at? I am not giving you any more of this dick lol"

Looking up, she saw DeMarcus's attention was now focused on her but she didn't care. She rolled her eyes at him and sent her reply.

"I know of an "All you can eat buffet" open twenty–four hours! I think it will be just right for, you lol"

She put her phone down and waited for his response. His response came five minutes later and made her face flustered.

"Good because I am famished. I haven't eaten anything since lunch."

"Oh, you are so nasty. I'll see if I can bring you brunch tomorrow but for now I got this lame looking in my face Lol so I'll hit you up later."

She slipped her phone in her pocket and looked up into a pair of suspicious eyes.

"Who was that you were texting that got you smiling like a big goof?" DeMarcus questioned her across the table.

"Tuh! The nerve" she snorted.

"What is that supposed to mean?"

"Exactly what I said! The nerve! How dare you question me and you over there snickering like a little school girl on your phone."

"Whatever Victoria! Play with me if you want to and I swear to-"

"Kids go upstairs to your rooms, mommy and daddy need to talk" Victoria ordered.

She waited until they were out of sight and she heard the sounds of their bedroom doors closing before she barked back.

"You swear to god what DeMarcus?" Victoria shouted.

"How fucking dare you even think about coming at me when you're sitting at this table with your "family" and talking to the next bitch!"

"I don't know what the hell you are talking about?" he yelled back.

"You, must think that I am real fucking stupid! Don't you? Nigga, I know her ringtone! That's that hoe Tracy, isn't it?"

When she mentioned Tracy by name, DeMarcus knew he was caught. Had he been that obvious? He said nothing for a few minutes as he let the reality sink in. "How long have you known about her?"

"I have always known DeMarcus. You've been with her for what a little over a year and a half now?"

"Yes. But how did you know that though? Was I that obvious?"

"Yea, you were. One thing about men, y'all don't know how to cheat and keep it under wraps. Y'all start treating your wives with the same respect that y'all give the hoes y'all fucking. Not only that, the bitch posted y'all secret little escapades all over *Facebook* months ago" Victoria spat.

"I'm sorry Victoria. I never meant to hurt you."

"Sure you didn't. Just like you didn't mean to hurt me when you stood me up on my birthday slash our anniversary to be with her while y'all lived the life at y'all little retreat?"

"You knew about that?" he asked shocked at how bad he'd been slipping

"Yea, I knew about it. I just didn't say anything. Look, I've been speaking with a divorce attorney for some time now and I've decided that I want a divorce."

"A divorce?" The words left a sting on his tongue as they exited his mouth.

"Yes, a divorce. It has become painfully obvious that you and I aren't meant to be as one anymore. You are clearly not happy. You've been in relationship with another woman for almost two years, and we've only been married for five. I am not one to keep a man that doesn't want to be kept! So, on that note baby, you are free to go" She was in tears. To say those words out loud hurt her more than she could've ever imagined.

"So, this is it? You are going to give up on us?" DeMarcus questioned, as he too was on the brink of tears.

"DeMarcus, you gave up on "us" nineteen months ago when you laid down with her. I can deal with this right now! I need to get some fresh air. I am going for a walk." Victoria stood up and walked out of the dining room, looking back just once at her husband; who was now bawling at the table.

To Be Continued......

This was an excerpt from "Was It Was Worth It?" (now known as "Costly Decisions" by Marie A. Norfleet

Release Date: July 2016

The Cookie Monster

By

Deryl Hines

"Shit!!!! Mmmmmmm, get this pussy wet."

Trina's moans echoed throughout the room as she penetrated her tight pussy with her chocolate twelve-inch dildo. She slowly pulled the drenched dildo out from between her lips, as the juices dripped all over her legs, and on to the bed sheets.

"I give up. I wish I had a fucking cut buddy, then I wouldn't have to be using the plastic dildo every single night trying to get an orgasm. Trina laid the dildo next to her as she grabbed the remote and turned on the television.

Trina sat up with her mouth wide open in shock, because she couldn't believe what the hell she was seeing flash across her television screen at this time of night. She then turned the volume up so she could hear what the news reporter was saying.

"I'm Candice Stone reporting live from Chavis Heights Homes with Breaking News. This story is one unbelievable story. Just after 2:00 a.m. this community has experienced a stream of rapes. I'm standing here with a couple who believe they heard screams coming from multiple home early in the morning."

"The couple believe they saw a man wearing sweat, a black hoodie with the words The Cookie Monster on the back of it, with a white mask, and some black Timberlands. If you have any information on his whereabouts, please give crime stoppers a call at 919-555-5555. In case you're not already at home, get home and please lock your doors and windows. And remember, please don't answer any unfamiliar door knocks. Back to you Sharon."

Trina turned off the television with the quickness as she sat on the edge of her bed, going over in her head to see if she had the front and back doors locked, along with all her windows. She then breathed a sigh of relief as she grabbed her chest and got underneath her sheets. She then turned on some soft love making music, as she laid back.

"My ass need to be taken advantage of like those victims were taken advantage of." Trina grabbed her pillow from behind her head and rolled over on her stomach, as she mumbled underneath her breath and closed her eyes.

"Well, you don't have to wish no more, because your wish is my command." The dark silhouette said as it stood at the entrance of Trina's bedroom. "I need for you to turn that music up loud, because I don't want you to scream for help, ok?" The deep baritone voice demanded.

Trina knew right then and there it was The Cookie Monster standing before her. She fumbled through her sheets looking for the remote to the stereo. "Scream" by Tank boomed throughout the room as she laid there in fear, watching The Cookie Monster strip.

"May I, I, I ask you something?" Trina's voice now with a hint of nervousness in it.

The Cookie Monster stopped in his tracks. "No you can't." His breathing started to become heavy, as he continued peeling off his clothes. "I've been waiting for this moment, as far as I can remember. And now, I finally get the chance to take something so precious away from you."

"Oh yeah, what is that?" Trina asked seductively spreading her legs wide open and stuck two fingers deep inside and began finger fucking her tight virgin hole.

"I know that you're looking for a man that knows how to eat that cookie real good."

The Cookie Monster was now in his birthday suit as he climbed onto the bed like a Cheetah. His cold hands ran up Trina's leg, as he looked deep into her eyes, and whispered.

"Just relax and let me bury my face into your pussy."

Trina followed The Cookie Monster's tongue as he licked his lips and slowly lowered his head towards her pulsating clit. She wanted to mess with him, so she quickly turned over on her stomach. The Cookie Monster's nostrils flared up as his eyes got big as two golf balls, as he pinned her down on the bed.

The Cookie Monster gripped Trina by the arms and pulled her up towards him.

"Now that's how you take control."

Trina leaned her head back and whispered into The Cookie Monsters ear. She couldn't say anything else, because she was so turned on by the way he was manhandling her.

Trina broke away from The Cookie Monster's grip and fell back down on the bed. The Cookie Monster then flipped Trina's little frame over like a pancake with the quickness. His manly hands then parted her pussy like the Red Sea. Like a hungry beast, he buried his face so deep into her midsection, and began stroking with his long tongue. The way he was trying to suck the juices from her pussy sent Trina into over drive.

"I'm surprised you're not locked up somewhere with that deadly tongue." Trina started talking dirty.

"Look now, I don't want any more talking from you. Just let me continue eating this fat pussy out. Do you understand?"

The Cookie Monster commanded as he looked up and licked Trina's juices from his lips. Trina zipped her lips and parted her pussy open and waited for him to re-enter. She started playing with her pussy, as he watched. She then took her free hand and grabbed his head, and mushed it deep into her pussy.

Trina was so turned on by The Cookie Monster's pussy eating skills, she was about to cum after three strokes from his tongue. She felt her cum building up, and she knew that any second she would be shooting all over her his face and down his throat.

"Daaaaammmmmmnnnn!!!! Fuck! Trina legs started to shake. She tried holding back, but her pussy has a mind of its own and erupted like a volcano.

Trina's body instantly became weak, causing her to collapse. She started breathing hard trying to catch her breath as she laid there with her eyes closed, with a big ass smile on her face.

The Cookie Monster slowly pulled his tongue out of Trina's pussy, and kissed her on the lips, as he rolled off the bed and snatched up his clothes.

"Now you can call the police, or whoever and report that you have been raped by, The Cookie Monster. I want to be on the news."

The Cookie Monster quickly dressed, then walked around to Trina's window and opened it, climbed out and gave her a wink as he closed the window.

Trina winked back at The Cookie Monster, as she rolled off the bed and began taking off the stained cum sheets. She was about to drop her sheets in the washer and head to the shower, when she heard heavy footsteps coming in her direction.

"Cookie Monster, is that you?" I knew you couldn't stay-

Trina was cut off by The Cookie Monster wrapping his left arm around her neck, and covering her mouth with his right hand, as she was dragged to the bathroom.

"I'm going to take my hand from around your mouth and I just want you to listen, ok?" The Cookie Monster mumbled through gritted teeth.

The Cookie Monster then turned Trina around to face him, as he put one finger up to his mouth, and slid his mask off.

"I need a place to hide, the cops just spotted me, and I don't have now where else to go. Can you do me this one hug favor?"

The Cookie Monster pleaded with fear in his eyes.

"Um, sure. You can lay low here for a couple of days until everything cools off." Trina said nonchalantly as she turned on the shower and sat on the toilet with her legs cocked wide open playing with her pussy hair.

"I see somebody done fell in love with this hurricane tongue. Are you ready for round two?"

The Cookie Monster stripped down to his birthday suit in point five seconds, dropped down on his knees, and prowled like a hungry black panther, over to Trina's pretty pink pussy.

The Cookie Monster then grabbed Trina legs and wrapped them around his neck, as his hurricane tongue escaped from between his lips, and began to tickle her second pair of lips ever so lightly. Trina closed her eyes and cocked her head back, bit her bottom lip, and fondled her Double D breast.

"I don't know what it is about you and your head game. All I know is that you got a Bitch in love with you. I can get use to-Trina was cut off by loud banging at her front door.

"Boom, Boom, Boom. Mrs. Wilcox, it's the Police. May I have a word with for a quick second? It's really important that I speak with you."

The police officer yelled from the other side of the door.

"Um, just one second officer."

Trina quickly opened her eyes and unwrapped her legs from around The Cookie Monsters neck, grabbed a wash cloth and soap, and motioned for The Cookie Monster to get in the shower.

The Cookie Monster jumped in the shower with the quickness, and closed the shower curtain behind him. Trina looked around the bathroom for her bathrobe, but it was nowhere to be found.

"Shit, fuck it, I'll just go to the door butt naked." Trina closed the bathroom door behind her as she sashayed up to her front door.

Trina cracked the door and stuck her head out to find and officer with a piece of paper in his hand.

"Mrs. Wilcox, I'm Police Chief Arrington, and these two gentlemen standing behind me are Officer Morgan and Officer Richardson. Do you mind if I can come inside, along with my officers?"

Chief Arrington looked back at his officers.

"And, what if I say no Chief…. Arrington, that's what you said your name was, correct? Trina asked sarcastically.

"Well, Mrs. Wilcox, do you see this piece of paper in my hand? I'm pretty sure you're a smart woman, and that you know what this is."

Chief Arrington snapped his fingers and nodded for Officer Morgan and Richardson to enter the house, and followed suit.

"Hey, I'm not decent" Trina yelled and jumped back from the door, as the two officers bombarded their way into the house.

Trina crossed her legs and covered her breasts, as she looked at the Chief and his Officers make their way over to her couch and made themselves comfortable.

"Let me go get my robe real quick."

Trina said as she tip toed to her room.

Trina pulled her robe off the back of her door and covered her Coca-Cola figure. She rushed back into the living room where the Chief and his two officers were chatting.

"Sorry about everything Chief. Today is my husband and I anniversary. We were about to celebrate our love for one another. Trina sat on the edge of the couch next to Chief Arrington, giving him a leg massage.

"Mrs. Wilcox, whatever you're trying to do, stop. If we could get to the reason why we're here."

Chief Arrington cocked an attitude and swatted away her hand off his leg, as he stood up and dropped it in her lap.

"And what is this?" Trina picked up the piece of paper looking dumbfounded.

"A search warrant ma'am. I want a thorough search of this house officers."

Chief Arrington snapped his fingers for them to get up and begin.

"A thorough search for what?"

Trina shot up off the couch with a pissed off look on her face.

"Because, Mrs. Wilcox, one of my officers believe they saw The Cookie Monster exit your house through your window, and re-enter it when he spotted some of my officers in the neighborhood. Now, I want you to be honest with me Mrs. Wilcox, ok? Are you hiding a rapist in your house?"

"Hell no! What you probably saw was my husband entering my bedroom. The reason for that is because, he sometimes forgets his keys when he goes to work, and I always leave our bedroom window unlock for him to get in when it returns. Because I'm hard sleeper, Chief- "

Trina was cut off by Chief Arrington walking off from her, giving her I know you're lying look.

The Cookie Monster's sultry baritone voice called out to Trina, "I hope you're ready to finish round two, because my sweet tooth is fiending for something extra sweet "

Chief Arrington followed the sound of the voice and stood up against the wall, as he peeked in the bathroom, and got back into position on the wall.

"I'm reeeeaaadddddyyyyyy baby. Hurry up, because I done started without you."

Chief Arrington imitated what he thought was Trina's voice.

"Well damn, bring that pretty ass pussy back in the bathroom."

The Cookie Monster said, as he stood in front of the mirror doing some tongue exercises.

Chief Arrington turned the handle on the door, and drew his gun, as he entered the bathroom with his gun pointing at The Cookie Monster. He then motioned for Officer Morgan and Richardson to back him up.

"Ain't this a motherfucking bitch? I knew I shouldn't have trusted this fucking broad."

The Cookie Monster dropped his head, and started laughing hysterically when he saw the officer through the mirror pointing a gun at him.

"I promise; I didn't say a word." Trina tried to break through the Officers that now had the door blocked.

"Officer Morgan and Officer Richardson, I need you two to handle this, while I have a talk with Mrs. Wilcox in the next room. And for God's sake, put on some damn clothes."

Chief Arrington had a disgusted look on his face, as he backed up with his gun still on The Cookie Monster, pushing Trina into her bedroom, closing the door behind him and locking it.

"Chief Arrington, I know I lied."

Chief Arrington grabbed Trina by both arms tightly, swinging her around, and lightly slamming her up against the door.

"Let me go!" Trina tried breaking away from Chief Arrington's deadlock grip.

"Listen! Stop trying to fight back, or I'm going to make it worse for you." Chief Arrington pinned her arms above her head. "I'm going to ask you one simple question, and I just want a yes or no answer, ok? If I don't get the answer that I'm looking for, you just might be taking a trip down to the county jail."

"Hurry up, so you and your shitty officers can get the fuck out of my house." Trina than spat in Chief Arrington's face.

"I'm going to let that slide." Chief Arrington released one of Trina's arms and wiped the spit off his face.

"Question number one, do you know this gentleman?" Chief Arrington asked.

"I told you before earlier that he is my husband." Trina rolled her eyes.

"Ooooookkkk. You know I 'don't believe you, right? So, with that being said, I'm going to ask you to put on some clothes. Because you, and your friend are going to take a little field trip down to the county jail. So, I'm going to need for you to find something quick to put on." Chief Arrington loosened his grip on Trina's arms and walked over to her bed and made himself comfortable.

"Wait, isn't there something I can do? I'm too pretty to go to jail." Trina ran over to Chief and

dropped to her knees in tears.

"I'll think of something. Just wait right here, ok?" Chief Arrington picked Trina up from off the floor and laid her on the bed, then exited the room.

"Chief, we have the suspect in handcuffs. So, should we go ahead and take him down to county so they can book him?" Officer Morgan asked.

"Yeah, go ahead and take him down. I'm still questioning Mrs. Wilcox, so I need for you and Officer Richardson to handle that." Chief Arrington patted Officer Morgan on the back and walked him to the front door.

"Oh. Ooooooohhhhhhhh, Gotcha Chief. Don't worry, I won't tell nobody. You go right ahead and finish with questioning Mrs. Wilcox." Officer Morgan gave him a wink and sprinted to the squad car.

"Chief, I'm dressed and ready for you to take me down to county." Trina said behind tears.

Chief Arrington turned around swiftly to the sound of Trina's voice. "I was thinking about that Mrs. Wilcox. I'm not going to arrest you for aiding and abetting. So, consider yourself one lucky lady tonight."

Trina wiped the tears from her eyes, then ran and gave Chief Arrington a big hug. "Thank you, thank you, and thank you. I owe you big time. I'm not sure how I'm going to do it, but I'll think of something."

"It's funny you mentioned that Mrs. Wilcox."

Chief Arrington unsnapped his holster, letting it fall to the floor. He then put some space between him and Mrs. Wilcox by pushing her back little. He slowly unzipped his fly and pulled out his soft nine and half inch dick out, and made his way over to the couch.

"Ummm. I don't suck dick. So, you might as well put that little Vienna sausage back in your slacks." Trina said with a disgusted look on her face.

"Well damn, when did nine and half inches of meat be considered small?" Chief Arrington asked as he started stroking his manhood.

"Since you ran into me. Besides, I only do ten and half and up Boo Boo." Trina demonstrated for Chief Arrington.

"Are you done? Because my dick is hungry for some head." Chief Arrington motioned with his cock for her to come and get started.

Trina rolled her eyes as she made her way over to Chief Arrington and dropped to her knees. "How long do I have to suck this small ass dick?" She asked as she held it in her hand and examined it.

"Until I get tired of you sucking it, or when I finally bust my nut, which will be never. Because I like the energizer bunny, I can go for a long time. So, I guess you better get started because we're going to be here until the sun comes up."

"Ain't this a mother fucker?" Trina smacked her lips as lowered her head and spat on Chief Arrington's dick lubing it up.

Chief Arrington sat up licking his lips. "It's feels good already. If you done lubing up, you can go ahead and put those pretty ass lips on it."

Chief Arrington laid back in the couch and closed his eyes.

Trina grabbed the shaft of Chief Arrington's dick and held it in place, then spat on his dick again, as she watched it run down in to his pubic hairs. Once she saw the spit soaked into his hairs, Trina then slowly parted her lips and slid her mouth down his pole, and paused for a minute. She then let her tongue slither out her mouth like a snake, as she began to massage his balls.

"OHHHHHH shit!" Chief Arrington said as his dick started jumping inside Trina's mouth, as he started to squirm a little on the couch.

Trina eyes immediately opened when she felt Chief Arrington growing some more inside her mouth. She then slid him from inside her mouth and sat on the floor Indian style, still with his dick in her hand. Trina shock her head in disbelieve as she placed her hand upon her breast.

"Did this motherfucker just grow another two and half inches into my mouth?"

Trina blurted out trying to hold back her smile.

"You know I heard that right? I bet you wasn't expecting that."

Chief Arrington opened eyes and started laughing.

"Hell to the motherfucking no. But I ain't mad at you. I do apologize. Now this is something I can fuck with, or should I say, can tear my walls up any day."

Trina just sat there just admiring Chief Arrington's anaconda in total shock.

"If you want to fill every inch of me inside you, just ask, don't beat around the bush Mrs. Wilcox. Trust me, you will love filling this inside that pussy of yours." Chief Arrington said with a hint of cockiness.

Trina released Chief Arrington's anaconda, then stood up, pulling him from off the couch. She then turned and face him backwards as she placed his hands on her shoulder. Trina then looked back at him, and nodded towards the bedroom.

"We don't need to go in the bedroom Mrs. Wilcox. We can fuck right here on the couch. I've done it plenty of times before. Ain't no shame in my game? But if you want to take if to the bedroom, then we can. You can go ahead and get started, then I'll be there shortly. I need to go to my squad car and call my officers to make sure they booked The

Cookie Monster." Chief Arrington excused himself outside and into his car.

"Oh, ok." Trina said a little nervousness in her voice as she headed to the bedroom.

"Officer Morgan, come in. Can you hear me?" Chief Arrington's voice boomed through the transmitter.

"Copy, Chief." Officer Morgan replied.

"I want you to listen and listen real good, ok? I'm still questioning Mrs. Wilcox at her house. If you and Office Richardson have booked The Cookie Monster, and have him in a cell. I need for the two of you to come back to Mrs. Wilcox's house right not and wait for me outside, ok?" Chief Arrington commanded.

"Copy Chief, were on our way right now." Officer Morgan motioned for Officer Richardson to follow him.

Chief Arrington turned off his transmitter and headed back into the house. Upon entering he heard the sound of moaning. He sprinted through the house and to the room to see Mrs. Wilcox pleasing herself with a dildo. He then ripped his suit off, and jumped between her legs.

"Let me that take that off your hands. I got the real deal swinging between my legs that's ready to slide up in something tight and moist." Chief Arrington tossed the dildo on the floor, and rammed all of his twelve inches into her.

"Yasssssssss! I'm loving inch of this piece of dick inside of me right now. Thank you Jesus." Trina cried tears of joy.

"Damn, I ain't even started yet, and I already got you going crazy over the dick."

Chief Arrington pulled his dick completely and repositioned himself on his back.

Trina then climbed back on top Chief Arrington, as she grabbed his manhood and started riding him like a porn star. Her legs started to shake after ten strokes in. Chief Arrington could tell that she was about to cum. So, he pulled out, grabbed her body, and sat her on his face.

"I'm, I'm, oh lord, here it comes!"

Trina placed her hands up against the wall to hold her balance as her juices erupted out her body and into Chief Arrington's mouth like a waterfall.

Chief Arrington slightly picked Trina up and sat up for a brief moment as he licked away the juices that was around his mouth. He then laid back down on his back and began tickling her clitoris as she looked deep into his eyes.

"I'm loving the way that you're playing with my clitoris." Trina took one hand off the wall began fingering her pussy.

Trina took her hand out her pussy and licked the juices from off her finger. She parted her second pair of lips and let Chief Arrington's tongue slip inside of her. Trina immediately released her fingers as her pussy tighten around Chief Arrington's tongue. He then curled his tongue and slowly began fucking her tight pussy.

"I starting to think you have some type of magical tongue Chief." Trina moaned in between Chief Arrington's tongue strokes.

After Trina stopped moaning, then stood up and over Chef Arrington's mouth and started rubbing her clitoris in a rapid motion. Chief Arrington slapped Trina's hand away as he placed his soup cooler lips onto her pussy and began sucking away. Within minutes Trina's juices began to leak onto his face and down his throat. Chief Arrington held Trina in place because he felt her shaking out of control. Then, he sucked harder once he saw that she was becoming weak, causing Trina collapse back onto the bed and out of his arms. Chief Arrington just laughed and rolled off the bed and began putting on his clothes, as he watched Trina trying to catch her breath.

"I'm going to wash up really quick, if that's ok with you Mrs. Wilcox." Chief Arrington said.

"Uh Huh, go ahead." Trina said in between breaths.

Chief Arrington walked towards the bedroom door and called out. "Ok, officers she's in here."

"Wait. What? Hold the fuck up? What the fuck do you mean she's in here?" Trina jumped up with fear in her eyes.

Chief Arrington looked back, then walked out, pointing inside the room to his officers.

"You sorry ass motherfucker. I thought we had an agreement. I thought I was going to let fuck me and eat my pussy out and I would go Scott free." Trina yelled out to Chief Arrington as tears started flowing down her face.

"Bitch, I lied. I can't believe you fell for that." Chief Arrington yelled from the other side of the room.

"Ma'am, I'm going to need for you to put on some clothes." Officer Morgan said as he entered the room with Officer Richardson standing by his side.

"Fuck you! You fucking rent-a-cop." Trina conjured of some spit and spat at him.

"Now, Now. That's not necessary Mrs. Wilcox. Officer Richardson said as he walked over to her and pulled her off the bed.

"Don't put your damn dick beaters on me." Trina said as she kicked Officer Richardson in the nuts.

"Whoa, whoa, whoa. Mrs. Wilcox. All that isn't necessary. We're only taking orders from our Chief. Officer Morgan ran over and grabbed her legs.

"Well, well, well. I see somebody is putting up a good fight," Chief walked back into the room, picking up her clothes off the floor. "Since Mrs. Wilcox wants to act like the THOT that she is, handcuff her and bring her out to the squad car in her birthday suit". Chief Arrington nodded to his officers then walked back out the room.

"I don't think we should take Mrs. Wilcox out to the squad car butt naked. It's freezing outside." Officer Richardson said with a worried look on his face.

"Orders are orders Richardson. You know how Chief feels about not following orders, especially his orders." Officer Morgan dropped Mrs. Wilcox legs and headed out the room.

"What seems to be the holdup Officer Richardson?" Chief Arrington busted back into the room with a pissed off look on his face.

"Uh, uh, nothing sir." Officer Richardson immediately started handcuffing Mrs. Wilcox.

"Ok, then. I want you to put Mrs. Wilcox in my squad car, and I want you and Officer Morgan to get the hell out of here. Take the rest of the night off." Chief Arrington motioned for Officer to head out to his car.

"I need to put on my clothes! I need to put on my clothes! I Need To Put On My Clothes!" Trina kicked and screamed as Officer dragged her out the room.

"Don't worry about that Mrs. Wilcox. I'll make sure you get some clothes on that body of yours." Chief Arrington gave her a wink and licked his lips as he followed behind them.

Trina sat in the backseat of Chief Arrington's squad car as she watched the three talk. Shortly after the officers got and their car and pulled off. He stood beside his squad car until both officers were out of site. Once they were out of site, Chief Arrington hoped in the back seat with Mrs. Wilcox.

"I got to have me one taste of your sweet pussy on my tongue before I take you down to county." Chief Arrington lubricated his pointer and middle finger with his saliva. He then rammed the two deep into her pussy and played in it for about five minutes. He slowly pulled his fingers out and sucked on his fingers like a baby sucking on a pacifier, watching the excess juice drip from her pussy onto the leather seat.

"I thought we were headed down to the county to book me Chief." Trina said with an annoyed voice.

"We are, I haven't forgot about that. Besides, I wanted one sample before I take you down to county. And now that I have it we can be on our way."

Chief Arrington tossed Trina her clothes and got out the back seat into the front seat and headed towards county.

The ride down to county was dead silent. Chief Arrington looked through his rear view mirror to take a peek at Trina and to tease her with tongue demonstrations. After about thirty minutes the squad car pulled up to the county jail. Chief Arrington put the car in park and hopped back into the back seat and unhand cuffed her.

"Why did you take the cuffs off? Trina questioned Chief Arrington.

"Because I'm debating on whether or not to actually take you inside." Chief Arrington began rubbing her inner thigh.

"Awwwweeeeee. Don't tell me you done fell in love with my pussy?" Trina said with a fake look of sadness on her face.

"Actually, I have Mrs. Wilcox. I have never had any good pussy, well pussy that I didn't have to take from a lady as good as yours. Chief Arrington smiled and turned her head towards him. "So, I tell you what I'm going to do. I'm going to let you put on your clothes, and I'm going to take you home. I'm not going to book you on ay charges, ok? I just want you to let me come over when I get hungry for some good pussy, OK? Chief Arrington licked his lips and gave her a wink.

"Oh, oh, ok." Trina quickly put back on her clothes and slightly smiled as they headed back to her house.

Follow US!

Facebook: www.facebook.com/RAWilliamsPublishing

Email: rawilliamspublishing@gmail.com

Website: www.rawilliamspublishing.com

Mailing Address:

      P.O. Box 2001,
      Carrot Bay, Tortola,
      British Virgin Islands, VG1130

Dear Readers,

Thanks you for your awesome support! When I first came up with the idea to start my own independent publishing company, I would have never dreamed on the kind of support that I would have today.

In December of 2015, after my company was legally incorporated, the first project that came to mind was to work with already established authors on something that can benefit the community and also that can benefit them by getting their names out there- so the Anthology was born.

When I posted the thought on Facebook about the Anthology the response was tremendous! I garner fourteen authors that were ready to donate their time and work to help raise funds for a charity. The charity that was chosen is Feeding American with so many Americans going hungry every day. I think this was a perfect way to get everyone together.

I want to personally thank all fourteen authors that took part in this masterpiece. Without you this would have only been a dream and never a reality

Sincerely,

Riiva Williams
Owner/CEO/Author
RA Williams Publishing, LLC
www.rawilliamspublishing.com

Meet the Authors

Riiva Williams

Riiva Williams (26 years old) mother of one was born in St. Thomas USVI and raised in the British Virgin Islands from the tender age of 7 months old. She was born to Livia Donovan-Hodge of St. Thomas, USVI and Vincent Williams of St. Kitts in March 1989. Riiva grew up in the small, quiet community of Carrot Bay and attended the Leonora Delville Primary School and the attended the now Elmore Stoutt High School where she graduated 60th in her class.

At the age of 12 years old, Riiva started writing small pieces of poetry but that did not last long as she quickly thrust herself into her schoolwork. At the age of 21, she became a member of a poetry group called C.R.A.K Poetry out of Dorchester, MA where she performed for the first time at Slade's Bar and Grill. Three years later Riiva branched off on her own and started writing stories. To date, Riiva has over 200 pieces of poetry, which she has written over the years. Currently Riiva and her son reside in the British Virgin Islands.

Felicia Lewis

Porscha Felicia Lewis writes a professional blog called Porscha After Dark; at porschaafterdark.blogspot.com she has been writing since her early teens she has also just published her first book called The Pussy Chronicles. She credits God first and foremost and her family for always allowing her creativity to shine through.

Darnisha King

I am Darnisha A. King, born and raised on the West side of Chicago. I currently hold 3 degrees and a few credits short of a 4th one. I am a mother to a 3-year-old son named Kingston. I am a believer of Jesus Christ and it is my intent to be a great witness for the Kingdom.

I am an avid reader and I have been reading Urban Literature since the year 2000 with the debut of ' The Coldest Winter Ever.'

I have been writing since I was a child, but I didn't get serious until the age of 20. I had dropped out of college, my ends were barely meeting, and I was staying on a couch at a friend's house in order to get back in school.

The writing helped to save my life. It took me into a fantasy world of having it altogether. Before I knew it the characters had taken on lives of their own and all of my family and friends loved them.

What went from being my escape - is now helping me to create and mold my future.

Deryl Ali

Deryl Ali (33 years old) was born in Warrensburg, Missouri and raised in Nashville, North Carolina. Deryl and his family moved from Warrensburg, Missouri, to Nashville, North Carolina when he was just a baby. He attended and graduated from Northern Nash Senior High School (2001), and North Carolina Wesleyan College (2007) with Bachelor of Science in Business Administration both located in Rocky Mount, North Carolina. He is currently pursuing his Master of Science in Human Resource Management. Deryl began writing poetry/lyrics at the age of 9 years old, on and off. Deryl began writing again after one of his younger sibling (Marc Hines) discovered a song he had written, that happen to be laying on his bed for him to see.

This led Deryl's younger brother to tell the world that his big brother secretly wrote music lyrics. From then, his imagination got the best of him. At 19 years old, Deryl began to take writing seriously, by writing short stories, and poems. After gaining confidence, he began to tell others that he wrote songs, short stories, and poems.

Deryl writes all genres, but writes more erotica than anything. His favorite authors are Zane and Carl Weber. Deryl has written a collection of love poems, in which he self-published (2013) into a book titled: Spoken Love a Collection of Poetry. You can find Deryl's poetry book on www.amazon.com and www.lulu.com. You can add Deryl on Facebook at Deryl Hines or my fan page Author Deryl Hines, and Instagram @deryl_ali. You can also reach him at his email address hinesderyl@gmail.com.

Deryl writes every day working to improve his craft. He likes to tell his writers to write something every day, even if it's just a word, a sentence or paragraph. Because the talent God has given you can be taken away if you don't utilize it, and given to someone else.

Briana Cole

Briana Cole has coined the term 'spiceual' to describe her style of writing; a mix of spicy and sensual romance that stimulates the reader mentally, physically, and emotionally. Tired of reading the same type of books in the urban industry, she prides herself on bringing unique plots and a distinct voice to the bookshelves. Briana is an Atlanta native and proud mother of two.

She graduated from Georgia Southern University in 2009. Her motto and ultimate drive towards success is a famous quote from Mae West: "You only live once, but if you do it right, once is enough."

For more information, please visit Briana's site at www.brianacole.com.

She also maintains an active presence on various social media platforms:

Facebook: facebook.com/BrianaCSpice
Instagram and Twitter: @BrianaCSpice

Tiffany Turner

T. L. Turner grew up in the South. She is a writer of fiction works. She currently resides in the South and works as a social worker. She is currently completing a Master of Social Work.

Lauren Horner

Lauren Horner was born on August 15, 1985, and resides in Columbia, MD where she is currently working as a daycare teacher by day and writes and reads by night. She has attended Shaw University in Raleigh, NC and majored in Early Childhood Development.

Although she never finished; she still takes a few classes here and there to sharpen up her skills. Lauren is a new and up and coming author who got inspired to write by her best girlfriend aka sister from another mother Ashley M. Jackson who is also an aspiring author herself.

Though her biggest motivation to keep perusing and writing would be her mentor Cedric Lewis, author of "Don't Get Caught Slippin". Cedric has taught her to open her eyes to a world of an imagination that at the time she couldn't fathom. Through her writings not only will you experience her imagination, but also have an insight on the life of a young woman who chose to put her voice on paper.

Marie A. Norfleet- Publisher, Author, and Motivational Speaker.

Marie A. Norfleet, was born in the South Bronx, NY, early August of 1989. She is a jack of many trades and wears quite a few hats such as Mother, CEO, Author, Editor, Graphic Designer, etc...

Since she was a young child, writing had become a significant factor in her life. Often, a therapeutic escape from the realities of the real world. As life's obstacles began to take their positions and the hurdles of life became harder to jump over; her love for writing slowly died.

But at the tender age of twenty-two, having been through many trials and tribulations in her young life, from abusive relationships, teen pregnancy, homelessness, and prostitution to finding love, getting married and starting a family; Marie was inspired to pick up her pen again.

Writing a memoir like story with an urban fictional twist, Marie entitled her book "This Game Called Life". The title came from an expression Marie heard a lot while growing up "Life is like a card game, either you play the hand you were dealt or you fold."

Immediately upon finishing the story and reading it over, Marie made the conscious decision to share her heartfelt tale and broadcast her refueled passion.

As a fairly new face in the literary world, she independently released her debut title on April 30th, 2012. In a short, three month span; she sold over one thousand copies and landing on few of Amazon's Best Seller's Lists.

With the success of her book, Marie decided to submit her story to, G Street Chronicles; a major publishing house in Urban Literature. She signed a contract with them in July of 2012 and a decision was collectively made to pull the book from its online retailers.

"This Game Called Life" was revised and re-released on August 25th 2012. But, due to irreconcilable differences, G Street Chronicles and Marie parted ways in December of 2012. Marie has since, started her own self-publishing company "Game Changing Publications".

Connect with Marie A. Norfleet on social media:

Facebook: https://www.facebook.com/authormarien

Twitter: https://twitter.com/authormarien

Instagram: https://instagram.com/theauthoressmarien/

LinkedIn: https://www.linkedin.com/pub/marie-norfleet/93/343/bb3

Also, find Marie and all of her works on the following websites:

https://www.gamechangingpublications.com

www.gamechangingapparel.us

www.gamechangingprinting.us

www.gamechangingdesigns.us

Darryl J. Johnson

Born in Augusta, Georgia, Darryl J. Johnson has been a literary genius since an adolescent. Raised in Tampa, Florida, Darryl discovered his love for erotic Fiction and began to express it through his own collections of poetry.

He began his collegiate career at Carson-Newman College in Jefferson City, Tennessee, later transferring to Fort Valley State University in Georgia. During this time period, he was pushed to make his dream a reality. Moving to Albany, Georgia, he began to write books of poetry and the rest is history.

Darryl began his career as an independent author who released ten works of poetry, action, and romance. His debut novel under First Lady K Presents, is scheduled to be released March 1, 2016.

Darryl now resides in Sandersville, Georgia where he attributes his success and inspiration to his wife and children. You can follow him on social media sites, Facebook, Instagram, Twitter or Amazon.com.

For inquiries, please contact authordarryljjohnson@yahoo.com.

Ashley M. Jackson

Ashley M. Jackson is a 23-year-old, 3rd year college student, and up-and-coming sci-fi/adventure novelist. Following her father's death in 2003, Ashley began writing short stories in the genres of tragedy and horror, and would show her work in school events and art shows.

While she is currently attending school for her degree in Criminal Justice, Ashley became serious about her writing career and began working on her upcoming series, The Scarlet Series, in 2013. She is hoping for book 1 to be released in the late summer of 2016, and with the help of fellow author and friend, Lauren Horner, is working hard to make this dream a reality.

With science fiction being her genre of choice, Ashley Jackson excels in transporting her readers to another world and transfixing them in fantasies beyond their wildest dreams.

Elijah Foreman

Born in Trenton NJ, Elijah Foreman has had a passion for writing since the age of 9 years old. He started taking his passion serious after his mother passed away when he turned 18. After spending nearly three years working to break into the business, Elijah would meet and link up with Alicia Howard and be the first author to sign to her then company Teflon Mafia Publications. Elijah released his first book a month after signing on August 15th 2013 titled Masters of the Game. That book was followed up on November 12th 2013 with the sequel titled Masters of Escape.

To kick off 2014, Elijah participated in a Valentine's Day collaboration written by the entire Teflon Mafia family titled Silk Sheets that was released on Valentine's Day and he followed that up with his 3rd solo release "Married to a Bitch" on February 27th. Following some slight success of his 3rd solo release, there was a shift in his career when the Teflon Mafia Family disbanded and Elijah along with Alicia Howard and Crybabi decided to go to another company. After dealing with some shady business, Alicia Howard decided to do it by herself with Elijah and Crybabi coming along for the ride creating Loyalty Ink Publications.

In October of 2014 the sequel to Elijah's 3rd release Married to a Vindictive Bitch was released to the Ebook world. On January 1st 2015, Loyalty Ink Publications went under a name change and became Alicia Howard Presents publishing with Elijah being one of the front men of the company. On February 16th 2015, Elijah brought part three to the Married to a Bitch series titled Married to a Deadly Bitch along two re-released versions of the first two books. In the summer of 2015, Elijah released two new titles that caught readers' attention titled Make Her Cream and Me, You and Hennessey.

In November 2015, Elijah was met with a hurdle in his career when the publisher he had been signed with for his short career had decided to briefly close the doors of the establishment. After talking with several publishers, Elijah made a move towards signing two publishing deals. One with Marques Lewis and the Atlanta GA based Marvelous Leaders Publications and another with Tremayne Johnson and the New York based King Publishing Group. Since signing his new deals Elijah has been hard at work re-releasing Me, You, and Hennessy with a new title Lust and A Shot of Hennessy under King Publishing Group. Along with that came a new title Betrayal and Infatuation under Marvelous Leaders Publications. There are plenty of titles coming to keep the readers occupied for the entire year of 2016. Stay Tuned.

Prince T. Patterson

Prince Patterson, age 20. I've been writing since I had to be in the third grade, I didn't know it was something I wanted to, but from writing love letters and trying to cheer up people. It transitioned. From growing up and taking on both a masculine and spiritual path, my writing kept on growing and growing, reaching up to date as of (500-600 + copies).

Not to boast. But I didn't always want to be a writer. I wanted to be a scientist or a philosopher. My love for "thinking outside the box" would have made me grand in that field, but it's only a childhood memory.

Passion lives in poetry, that consist of abstract nature, romance, and "going beyond the ordinary" type field, as well as spiritual growth. Examining life vs death. In poetry and short stories, I will forevermore be, hoping to making a difference.

Seven Steps

Encouraged to write by a close family friend at the age of ten, Seven has written hundreds of full length novels, short stories, poetry, and plays. After sharing a few of them with a friend, who also happens to be an author, she started on the road to becoming an indie author.

Seven Steps lives in Connecticut with her sweet cat, a handsome husband, and a beautiful daughter. When not busy writing, she enjoys reading, styling natural hair, and anything Disney.

Facebook: www.facebook.com/SevenStepsAuthor
Twitter: www.twitter.com/Sevenwrites

www.ingramcontent.com/pod-product-compliance
Lightning Source LLC
Chambersburg PA
CBHW051933020726
47501CB00001B/100